Hurricane of the Heart

Goose Rocks Light

Farley Dunn

THREE SKILLET

GOOSE ROCKS LIGHT, Dunn, Farley L

First Edition

Hurricane of the Heart, Book 4

 THREE SKILLET

www.ThreeSkilletPublishing.com

Cover design by Farley L Dunn

This is a work of fiction.

Goose Rocks Light is a real lighthouse located in the Fox Islands Thorofare. It is privately owned. In this story, the proceedings surrounding the lighthouse are entirely fictional, including the owners, the events that occur, and any other references to Goose Rocks Light.

ISBN: 978-1-943189-37-3

Goose Rocks Light

Goose Rocks Light
Fox Islands Thorofare
North Haven - Vinalhaven, ME

Chapter 1

LISA BEVIER caught herself in the mirror over her fireplace and pushed her thick auburn hair aside to study her green eyes. She laughed sourly and reached for her remote, shutting off her television. It was the weather reports that twisted her inside. The approaching tropical storm was all the meteorologists had talked of for days, and it had her jittery. She wished they'd let it go. After all, this was September; at this time of year, tropical storms wandered back into the Atlantic in search of their tropical home, and that was certainly wasn't Boston.

Besides, she had enough on her mind. It had been three years, but the start of fall was still hard for her to take. Tomorrow, September 28th, especially. That was to have been her day. It was still hers after a sense. It no longer put her in a happy frame of mind, but it was still hers.

She had sewn nearly twelve hundred pearls on her dress that September, each one by hand. Her mother had wanted to help, but Lisa had been the one to shoulder the burden of the wedding preparations. Andrew had been worth it. They'd fallen in love on North Haven Island the summer before. He had charmed her during that magical month, unlike when she attended university with him years before. There she thought him a ladies' man. Andrew Archer-Jones was too polished and too glib with his words.

Lisa didn't abide gossip, and she'd ignored what she could. Her classes didn't align with his, and he'd been relegated to background status, put aside in her educational forays into bigger things. She lost track of him after graduation, and she never thought of him again.

Then, that summer, she was invited to North Haven.

It was a dream invitation, a whole month on one of the Fox Islands. One of the families at her place of employment, the Massachusetts Center for Children, was in need of a medical assistant for their son. The Reynolds wanted their boy, fourteen at the time, to travel with them on vacation to the family's summer home. He needed to be monitored medically, and only by having the school's nurse accompany them did they feel comfortable in such a remote situation.

The school had adjusted Lisa's contract, and soon the plans were in progress. Little Josh, actually not so little at fourteen, might have days, she was told, when he would be symptom free, and she was assured by the family that those days would be hers to do with as she pleased. She would be required to remain on the island, but they would provide walkie-talkies. She could wander as she wished and return if they needed her.

She had felt so lucky.

They'd traveled to a picturesque Maine town called Rockland to catch the ferry to the island. Lisa was charmed, but she saw one thing she didn't expect. There was a file in the school's records of notable ex-students who had gone on to lead very successful lives. She had seen one of those ex-students that day.

It was the name of the town that made the connection for her. They were in Rockland, and when she saw the red-haired man walking off the ferry, the name just popped into her head. Rockland Royster. He had matured from the picture in her files, but she could see the strong jaw line and the broad shoulders were the same. The darkly handsome eyes underneath brooding brows hadn't changed, either.

Her hosts had recognized him when she pointed him out.

"Rocky. Not Rockland. Rocky Royster, the prominent hand-crafted boat builder. You'll find his boats in the highest caliber of boathouses. However, he prefers to be left alone."

Lisa watched him walk away, but that small connection gave her a surge of pride. It was as if her school really did make a difference in students' lives, and she walked a little taller. Nevertheless, she'd been going, and he was returning. She would wander North Haven, and she would have the month of a lifetime. If Josh needed her, she would give him her time, and if not, then it would be all hers.

Now, she wished she'd never left the Reynolds' tree-shrouded house wedged in the interior of the island. It was near a rocky cove, and the first time she went exploring on her own, she ran into Andrew.

He charmed her, and that became her greatest downfall.

"ROCKY, COME give your grandmother a hug before you head out." Bette Royster waved her arm to get his attention. She adjusted her sweater around her shoulders. It was already crisp outside, and it was still September. The end of summer should bring the lingering aroma of grasses and flowers. Not this year, even if Bette was determined to push fall away until she had to give in to it.

When he stopped his old four-wheel-drive truck and rolled down the window, waiting without looking up at her, she stood on the front porch for a moment, shading her eyes against the afternoon light. Then she pressed her lips together and knew this would have to happen the hard way. That grandson of hers was trying to sneak out without listening to what she had to say, and she planned to speak her mind. He was a good grandson, and she appreciated the way he came up and worked on her bed-and-breakfast. The good Lord knew it'd fall down around her ears if she didn't have his help. There was one thing he wasn't doing, however, and his father would turn over in his grave if he knew.

She proceeded to grab the handrail and march down the series of steps that ran from the old Victorian's porch to the walk below. There was no uncertainty in her movements. There was no frailty, either. At seventy-five, she'd never brooked any of that doctor nonsense. Her knees might bother her a bit, and occasionally she might find it hard to get out of bed, but the good Lord in heaven had given her a good constitution, and the devil take her if she intended to let a few pains snatch away her fine gift of good health.

When she reached the truck, she slapped the bed and called, "Fish, boy! You sneaking little mutt. You get up here and get your ears under my hand. You're trying to do the same thing as that grandson of mine up in the cab."

The big black dog was indeed of indeterminate breed. He was of indeterminate origin, too. Rocky had been out seining one night with that scoundrel friend of his, Tramwick Haggard, and there the dog was when they pulled in the net.

When Bette first heard the story, it was more like they'd *tried* to pull in the net. It was a new moon, and they hadn't been able to see worth the whiskey in one of Tramwick's bottles. They'd tugged and tugged on that net, just knowing they'd hit a mother lode of fish. It wasn't until they heard a feeble bark that they suspected what they'd pulled up.

It was a hundred pounds of dog that was near drowned. To hear Rocky tell the story, Tramwick dropped down and put his mouth on that dog's, and he gave him resuscitation on the spot.

"Seven-Eleven," Tramwick cried. When Rocky replied that Seven-Eleven was a convenience store, Tramwick said it didn't matter. *"Get his heart to going. Seven breaths to eleven chest compressions."* Rocky tried to tell Tramwick the dog was already awake and breathing, just water logged. It didn't matter. That dog got the full treatment, anyway.

Now, Fish worshipped Tramwick, but he lived with Rocky. Bette found that to be a good arrangement. She liked the dog, and when her grandson brought the animal up, Fish had a good place to run on her property. To her way of thinking, Rocky having this mangy dog and her having her property was as good a cause as any for him to come up and see her as often as possible.

After she messed with Fish's ears for a moment, she opened the truck door. "Climb out of there, Rockland Royster. There's no boy that's grown too big to give this grandmother a hug."

When he clambered mournfully out and left the truck running—readied for a quick escape, she figured—she reached in and turned it off herself, slipping the key into her pocket. This boy needed a talking to, and she would make sure he got it.

LISA DIDN'T recognize Andrew when she first saw him. The morning sun was gentle, refusing to even burn the dew off the grass; so to avoid the damp paths that wound along the shore, she'd walked to a small dock where she could see out over the Thorofare, and she'd taken time to admire the big houses she could see on the Vinalhaven Island side.

She'd soaked in the weather that day. There was a light fog still floating over the water, just enough to make the landmass across the way seem like something out of a fairy tale. Her students at the school would love this, and she was memorizing the details for when she returned in the fall. With the autistic students she dealt with, sometimes a well-told story could get through when nothing else would. They might not seem to be listening, but there were times when she noticed eyes that followed her hands or repetitive noises that calmed at the most dramatic points in the storyline.

Andrew was rowing a small boat out on the Thorofare. Only later would she learn he'd seen her walking along the shore, and he'd "helped himself" to someone else's boat, hoping to catch her eye. It worked, and that was what irritated her when she later discovered his thievery. At the time, it seemed so romantic when he rowed up; in his casual island clothing, she'd thought him just a local boy who'd spent his entire life without leaving the isle. He invited her into the boat, and off he rowed, chattering away about his wonderful home far from the mainland, its rocky shoreline wrapped in the grip of the sea.

He told her he lived on the Vinalhaven side and was just over for the day. Would she like to visit his home? Oh, no, she told him. She had to remain on North Haven. She showed him the walkie-talkie. He laughed and rowed off to Vinalhaven, anyway. After a few minutes, he helped her step off at a small float, and holding her hand, they had run up the ramp to the semi-enclosed box at the end of the dock.

It was his parents' house, he said. He would inherit it as a gift when he married. He couldn't take her to it, or wouldn't, anyway, he'd laughed. They were having a party inside, and his parents' friends were very stuffy.

Just then, Lisa's walkie-talkie sounded. Josh was having a seizure, and could she come quickly? Panicked, she pleaded with Andrew. Hurry, she cried. She shouldn't have left the island. A little boy at her house needed her nursing skills. He rowed as fast as he could, and at the dock she clambered out, running at top speed to perform her nursing duties.

It was the part she learned later that told the real Andrew. He rowed the small craft back to the dock he'd borrowed it from, having seen the couple who lived there head over to Vinalhaven for the day. Then he walked to the old boathouse he and his mother lived in, all that was left from the estate his father had gambled away. When he walked in, his mother was busy folding other people's laundry, the only way she could make enough money to keep up the taxes on her ragged remnant of their earlier life of ease. Out the boathouse doors, the ground sloped to the water and a view of the big house where he'd taken Lisa.

BOTTLES clinked in the sack at Tramwick Haggard's feet. He throttled back his boat as he pulled up to the yard Rocky owned. Through the windows of the boat shed, he could see the outlines of the sleek new craft his friend was building. Idling to the dock, he cut his engine and looped his lines over the cleats, making sure his bumpers were in place to keep his boat from rubbing.

Grabbing the sack, he pulled his hat low on his head and jumped onto the float. Kicking the end of the lines off to one side, he let out a shriek of a whistle, looking for Fish to come running from around the house. He wouldn't come any farther than the dock, however. That animal would wet himself rather than get near the water.

When Fish didn't show, Tramwick clambered across the yard and up to the porch. With a fist, he pounded on the door. An old spar lodged in the joists overhead shifted and fell to hit the boards at his feet. He grinned when he looked up at the underside of the porch roof. Everywhere, and he meant every-where, Rocky kept anything he found that he thought just might make a better boat. There were multiple spars and fittings. Lines, stainless cable, and even an old sail from a boat that had been scrapped were up under his roof. If it had to do with boats, the man hung on to it. There was even a selection of specially grained wood he'd found. The whole mess was hung from brackets, piled on other items, or simply resting over the bare joists.

When there was no answer, Tramwick opened the front door and stepped into the kitchen. Rocky never locked his place, so there was no key. That was when he saw the calendar hanging over the table. He let out a sigh, hitting himself in the head with his free hand.

"Thursday," he groaned out loud. "Bette's. He said he was going up come Thursday." Whether he planned to return today was less clear. Sometimes Rocky drove back the same day. Other times his trips were overnighters.

Tramwick looked at the sack in his hand. If Rocky was on his way, it'd be late before he got back. His grandmother lived in New Hampshire, in the middle of the White Mountains. Tramwick had been up there with Rocky a few times. It was beautiful, but give him the ocean any day. He was happier here.

He glanced at the growing shadows stretching towards the shore. He wasn't piloting his boat home tonight, that was for dead certain, not after he opened the bottles in his sack, and he *would* open them. To be out on the water drunk was to risk damaging a good hull.

He *could* go check out the progress on Rocky's new boat. His friend was building it, although it was for someone else. This someone else—in Boston, he thought—had already paid, too. That was the only way Rocky would build. *"Keeps them from stiffing me,"* he once said. Tramwick knew his friend's excuse was only part of the reason. Rocky did all his numbers in his head. It was his dyslexia, and he *had* to keep all the numbers in his head.

He also had something else, and Bette had let it slip once that it was why Rocky had attended a special school in Boston. Despite that—or perhaps because of it—he was a whiz at keeping numbers in his head when he subtracted them.

Adding them? Tramwick was pretty certain Rocky was lost at that. That's why he *needed* the money up front. He *got* it because he built the best handcrafted wooden boats on the New England Coast.

Tramwick laughed. If attending that school could do that for someone, he could have done with a few years there, himself.

14

LISA SAW Andrew several more times that month. She insisted she stay on North Haven. He seemed relieved, taking her all over the island, although there was this one cove he never showed her, one that was just across from where he said his parents lived on Vinalhaven. He also had a different boat each time he showed up for their outings. Sometimes they were long and flashy, and other times rough and well used. She commented on it once, and he laughed, telling her he had to take whatever boat was left at the dock. She didn't remember seeing any other boats at his parents' dock that first day, but with all the friends they seemed to have, she guessed the others had been in use.

One day she thought she saw him walking on North Haven. He was carrying a large laundry bag like one of the ones her hosts would send to their laundress. She thought that was sweet, that he would come all the way to North Haven to help carry people's laundry. She called out to him, but he just walked faster, and she wasn't sure it was really him.

She asked him about it the next time she saw him, laughing about him having a twin brother. He grew red, and he wasn't in a good mood that day. She never spoke to him about it again.

However, she enjoyed their trips in the various boats he seemed to acquire so easily. He showed her places she could have never walked to, things that were wild and remote, and they'd seen creatures she never thought possible in her short stay on North Haven. She viewed him in a new light that month, and she was glad she'd never listened to all the rumors that had gone around at the university. She liked this Andrew, and she hoped one day she'd see him again.

ROCKY LOOKED back to his old truck, wanting to be inside and away. Fish had abandoned him for Bette, however, and he wouldn't leave without him.

Bette pulled him up the front steps and pointed to the sign above the front door. It hung unevenly, a bracket coming loose on one end. "See that, Rocky? You look hard, you hear? You see the name Royster up there? Your father built that sign. Your father. You know how?"

Rocky loved his grandmother very much, but he didn't love being reminded of his father. He'd been Mr. Success, a lawyer at the top of his game. At least until his heart attack. Yet, all the money in his accounts hadn't been able to stop his runaway car when his heart had started to go.

His father had reached the hospital, crashing into a light pole just outside, and destroying the front of the car. It seemed he'd hit several things along the way, leaving several streaks of paint and one of blood. He'd died before they got him through the door.

It was his father's money that had gotten Rocky into the Massachusetts Center for Children. If his father had been a dock worker or a fisherman, maybe they'd have spent more time together, and his life would be better. That school hadn't cured his dyslexia, but then that wasn't what it was about. His father had forced him to go there because he was ashamed of having an autistic son.

The autism was still with him, too. To Rocky, there hadn't been much point in the Center.

He glared at his grandmother, yet accepting that she would do this, demand this answer from him. He reached to the sign, then unhooked it and took it down, running one hand over the end that needed the new bracket installed.

"How, Bette?"

"His hands, Rocky. With his hands. You condemn him because he worked in that Boston office. You forget. He worked with his hands, too. You're too much like him to understand him."

"Like anyone could understand my father." He laughed, and

he knew how sour he sounded. It was true, though. He'd never understood him, and he didn't think anyone ever had.

BETTE GRASPED Rocky's hands, pressing them tightly around the damaged sign. They were strong hands, with long fingers. She lifted her hands to his face. His skin was unlined, although he was nearing thirty. He looked so much like his father. They were the same, and one day this boy would realize it.

She tapped the sign. "You take that with you. It needs repaired, and you can do that for me. Now, come with me, boy. You need to be reminded, and I have something else to show you." She moved to pull him around the house.

"Bette." He sighed. When she didn't stop, he called louder, "Grandmother! Don't you have some people showing up for a late lunch today?"

"Grandson, I was ready for them last night. You just come with me. I've got your keys, remember."

"I remember."

She also knew about the extra set under the seat, but she was satisfied when he let her wrap his muscular hand in her old worn one as he followed her to the back of the house.

She also heard him mutter that he wasn't sure exactly what she had to show him, but if it was in the barn, he didn't want to deal with what was out there.

Well, that was just too bad, now, wasn't it?

TRAMWICK SWUNG the boat shed doors wide.

"God, I love this." He drew in a deep breath. He enjoyed the fresh wood smell. At least this evening it was a fresh wood smell. Next time, it might as easily be paint or varnish. It was always a surprise. He didn't care. He liked not knowing, opening the boat shed door to discover the surprise he always knew he would find.

17

He took one of the bottles he had in the bag, and he unscrewed the lid. The smell hit his nostrils like a sledgehammer. It brought back memories of good times he had enjoyed with friends. Those good times were the cause of numerous black eyes, that and his perennially empty wallet. No little ankle biters, though. Thank God for that.

He sauntered over to the boat taking up a good portion of the cluttered space. It had good lines. As a seaman, he could see that it would go quickly in the water. Handle well, too, with minimal draft. The keel . . . Rocky had an eye for a good keel. This one would be a humdinger.

He climbed on the partially finished craft and stood in the cockpit. Rocky only worked with the best wood, and even from this angle, the boat was sleek with good joints. It would have true speed, unlike the workingman's craft he owned. His boat was fast for the design, that of an open-water fishing craft. However, it didn't have high-end construction, not like this one. His lobster boat was built for rugged, low-end power, giving it functionality in the rough waters off the coast.

"Ah, Rocky, my good friend, if I have the money someday to hire you to build me a boat with no expense considered, this is one I could like. Solid wood. Center keel. Inboard drive. Classic lines. No, instead, my own poor craft must be of affordable, practical fiberglass. That's a real pissah." He grinned.

Finding a cardboard box in the unfinished boat, he placed it where the pilot's seat would be. He smiled to himself. He could sit and see out the doors of the boat shed across the water where the view stretched to the horizon. He squinted, as though looking for Isle au Haut or Swan's Island, although they couldn't be seen from here. They were a couple hundred miles north, just off the Fox Islands, and that suited him perfectly. He imagined himself as the captain of a fine, sea-going yacht with all the money in the world to burn. In his imagination, he headed out to his remote island getaway or perhaps to a tall ships race.

He hit the imaginary throttle, and the engine gave a throaty purr. The water stirred behind his sleek craft, and all the girls wished they were his, as he danced the water among all the elegant tall ships.

He took a drink out of his open bottle. As the liquid fire hit his throat, he made a face and involuntarily yanked his head to the side, his eyes open wide. Wicked! That first taste always hit him hard, like a kick in the gut. Whew! It could peel the hair off a sea urchin's belly.

It was the second and the third taste he really enjoyed. The buzz hit his head fast, and he liked that. What he didn't like was the drinking alone. Rocky refused to drink with him, but he still made convenient company, and as an extra rabbit in the bag, when Tramwick passed out, as he invariably did, there was someone there to make sure he wasn't sleeping it off in the middle of someone else's yard. He had done that a time or two, once coming to with a ticket for disorderly conduct stuck in his shirt pocket. Thank God for a good friend like Rocky!

Now, if only he would get here. Tramwick had some really great news for him. His friend's woodworking skills, the best on the New England coast, were about to be put to the test. His electrical, welding, and boating skills, also. Tonight was all about Rocky's "secret" application for the renovation of Goose Rocks Light. Well, to Tram, it wasn't really a secret, was it, Rocky?

"Not much you can keep from old Tram, is there, Rocky?" He took another swig from the bottle. "I met up with Booger Burrows last night. I found out some stuff you want to know."

Jack "Booger" Burrows was a lobsterman, a fishing competitor, who had been a drinking partner of Tramwick's the previous evening. Booger's wife happened to be related to someone on the Beacon Light Preservation Society, the organization awarding the lighthouse contract. While the news wouldn't become public for several more days, the final applicant had been selected. All that was needed was for the Society to meet to make the approval official.

Goose Rocks Light was Rocky's baby, and he could start anytime he wished. The money was already on the way.

Chapter 2

BETTE SLAPPED on the old barn door to get it unstuck, and she pushed Rocky inside. She reached to the wall and palmed a switch, causing the old florescent lighting to flicker and glow overhead. The room was large and filled with all sorts of tools. Off to the side was a small wooden boat that looked to be in the final stages of completion.

"I haven't been in here for years," Rocky groused, dragging his feet. He had a disgruntled look on his face as if he wasn't sure he wanted to go any farther in, and he turned as if to make his way back out the door.

Bette pulled his arm, forcing him forward. "No, you haven't, have you? You haven't been in here for years, Rockland. That's exactly why we're here today." She looked at him as she narrowed her eyes, her use of his proper name a good measure of her irritation with him. "That's the whole problem. You *haven't* been in here for years." She walked to the boat resting off to the side, slapping her hand on it and causing dust to fly. "Do you remember this?"

He laughed, but it was sour. "Remember? I helped build it."

"And," Bette barked, "you walked off from it." She watched her grandson's face. It had grown somber once again, like a stove-up winter sled, tossed in the bushes and left to rust. She was hoping she would get through to him this time. He was so strong and independent, and he couldn't see that he needed to finish this if he was ever going to move on from that place in his life his father's death had locked him into. Rocky needed to deal with the undone things that had trapped him.

She continued, "For years, this has been waiting on your attention. You go down to that little boatyard you have, and you build your boats for those rich people who don't even know what they've got when they take delivery of something you've put your heart into."

Rocky muttered, "Some do."

He looked at the boat while he said it, and his grandmother hoped there might be something going on in that head of his, something that meant he was thinking about what she was saying.

"Your father loved you." She took his hand.

He retorted angrily, "My father loved his job. He loved books and standing in court in front of people, and he loved all the attention he could get. I can't even read the dipstick in my truck. I'm lucky to get the key right side up when I stick it in the ignition." He turned to look away from her, his eyes tracing all the familiar things lying around the building, his face red with emotion. "Do you know how many times I've had to throw out food because I couldn't read the directions and prepared it wrong? I'm everything he hated, and he was everything I can't be. We were never the same."

With those words, he bolted from the old barn, and when he stepped outside, he called, "Fish. In the truck, boy!"

Through the open door, Bette watched her strong, handsome, red-haired grandson stride around her house, that big black dog at his side. When she heard the truck start up, she knew she'd gotten through to him. He'd used that extra key under the seat, and that meant her little talk had struck a very deep nerve. Otherwise, he'd have come back to demand the set in her pocket. Rocky would deal with this. He might not like it, but he would deal with it. She would see to that.

She closed the barn door as she exited, and she stood for a moment in the afternoon sun. The day was turning out to be good, and she was looking forward to the folks who were arriving today. Tomorrow she had guests coming from Texas, and they came every September. They also brought her jalapeno jelly, and it was the only time each year she could enjoy that little treat.

This was going to be a fine weekend, indeed.

ROCKY GROUND his teeth and hit his steering wheel. Bette *knew* he didn't like to talk about his father. He had only wanted Fish to run free, and now this. Wasn't she glad to have him around, anymore? Or was she trying to drive him away because he hadn't offered to make any repairs on her old place?

That boat in the barn. He never should've walked around the house with that conniving old woman. He'd wasted the day up here, and he *still* had to drive the entire distance back to Massachusetts.

He wished he'd never come up.

His tires caught on loose gravel as he pulled out onto the road. They spun, spewing rocks into the air, and Fish fell in the bed of the truck with a yelp. Rocky felt a pang of momentary guilt at his actions, and he did look up to make sure his dog stood back up unhurt. His contrition was temporary, however, and the anger began to flood his veins once more.

Finally, flying down the highway, he glanced down to see

his fuel gauge was below the line. It had been full when he'd been at Bette's, and that made him angry, too.

"Pissant truck." He hit the steering wheel, jerking it off-center, and causing the truck to swerve before he corrected it, bringing it back into his lane. Someone had siphoned his tank. Why hadn't he installed that locking cap he'd looked at in the auto store the previous week? Then it dawned on him. It had been on empty all day. He shook his head to clear his anger. He couldn't even drive without risking running out of gas. His father was right. He was a loser who couldn't even read the gas gauge in his truck.

Pulling over at the next station, he sidled up to the pumps and killed his old beater. Holding the bare key in his hand, he cursed himself for being so angry he hadn't even walked back to get the regular set from Bette. He'd just wanted *gone,* and that's what he'd gotten, too. Now, his good keys were back in New Hampshire, and he was on the way home.

He threw open the door and cringed when it hit a concrete-filled steel post that was there to protect the pump from drunk drivers. Getting out, he checked his door. The scrape was small, and no one would notice it among all the other infractions that age had lashed upon the old truck. He walked back to flip open the filler door, only to feel Fish nuzzle him on his shoulder. He turned, his anger at Bette melting away in the presence of the dog. Fish might love food and Tramwick and running on Bette's place, but the dog loved *him,* too. He reached up and grasped the dog's face.

"Hey, boy! Did I knock you down back there?" Fish's tail went crazy with the attention. Rocky laughed. "Let's just get home, how about that? I need fuel, first. Gimme a minute." He pushed the dog away and reached for the nozzle.

When he unscrewed the fuel cap and stuffed it inside, he turned to the pump. He knew the order on the pumps he used at home, where he always chose the bottom button for regular unleaded. Here they were sideways, and he had to think which was which. As he looked at the letters, they seemed to jump. He looked at them a second time, glanced away, and then back again to make sure the letters hadn't changed places. Then he touched each one. He had to be sure. It was his engine at stake here.

Only then, he pressed the button and held the trigger until the pump cut off. He took a deep breath at yet another issue. Now he had to make sure the dollar amount really was what it looked like to him.

He turned to open the truck door and leaned inside. He picked up a pad of paper and a pencil, and turning to the pump, he wrote the number he thought the pump showed for the price of the gas he'd pumped. Then he held it to the readout to see if it matched. He changed one number on his paper, then read his new number aloud. Fish's nails clicked on the rail of the truck bed, and he turned to push him inside.

"Stay, Fish. I've got to pay." He tossed the pad into the truck as he walked by, and he stepped up to the cashier. He should be used to this by now, but he guessed he never would be. He didn't mind filling up at his usual station. He just pumped it full and handed the old man at the window a hundred. He never counted the change, either. The old man had worked there a long time, and Rocky knew he could be trusted. Here, who knew? With resignation, he handed the cashier a hundred just like he did back at home. As he did, he commiserated tiredly about how he should have made sure he had a full tank when he'd left home to go up to Bette's.

"Son, can't take no hundred." The cashier pointed to a sign that said *Small Bills Only.* "Got any twenties or fifties? I don't got one of those pens to check a hundred."

Rocky's heart froze. He had twenties, but how many did it take? Three, or four? He tried to remember the numbers from the pad. They were in his head; he could see every one, but they

25

kept switching places. He wished he'd brought the pad with him. He couldn't go get it now, not without seeming a fool, and he'd already done that enough in his life.

Perspiration began to run down his back, as he slipped the hundred into his wallet and grabbed the corners of three twenties. Then he knew that wasn't enough and grabbed a fourth, handing them to the man. He knew he always got one twenty in change, but he couldn't remember if it was ever two. Just as the man took the money, he knew. He *knew.* He always got two twenties back, and then some extra. He reached, but the money was gone.

Then, the man looked at the bills and back to the register. He glanced up at Rocky and grinned. "Too many bills, son. I only need three of these." He peeled one of the twenties off and handed it back. "Just a minute, and I'll get you the rest of your change."

Rocky's head spun. He hated this. He *hated* this. He was stupid, *stupid.* The only time he wasn't stupid was when he was working on his boats. Then, he could forget the world and all the problems it caused him. Time would fade away, and his boats would grow in his hands to whatever he wanted them to be. He hated to let them go when they were finished, but they were what paid his bills. He had to have money. He knew that, so he would agree to the next boat, and the cycle would start again.

For no good reason he could imagine, he thought of Bette, and he felt his head pound. She didn't understand. When he ran away, he ran for survival, and he hid for the same reason. His boats made him good money, but they were survival for him. Otherwise, the storm that swirled just out of his reach would drown him, and he had to be able to survive.

One other thing came to his mind, also. Tramwick and that lighthouse application. Tram had hounded Rocky about that.

"Apply, Rocky. It's a lighthouse. Think of the skills you

could use there. You'll also be all alone. You'll love that. Then, I could stop by with some fresh lobster and a couple of fifths. What do you think?"

Rocky had listened, too. He'd liked the alone part, and in a moment of anticipation, he'd applied for the project. Now, he hoped it just disappeared. All Rocky wanted was to go back to his little boatyard and work on his boats. The rest of the world could disappear, and he'd be perfectly happy about that.

THE DAYLIGHT had faded quickly, and Rocky pulled his truck into low gear as he approached the turnoff to his home. He'd have to get that one headlight replaced. It was shining off to one side. Or maybe it was going out altogether. This winter, the days would be short, and he'd need good lighting. His drive today had shown him that.

The items he'd stopped and picked up on the way rattled in the bed, as the truck's tires hit the rough spots just at the start of his driveway. Those were the rocks that had heaved out of the ground last winter. He couldn't ignore them any longer. Some of them would have to be dug up, if he wanted to continue to keep all his teeth in his head. When the soil began to freeze again, they would keep pushing up until he lost his transmission.

Pulling ahead until he could just get his hand into the mail-box, he slipped the shift lever into neutral and released the clutch. He flipped the interior lights on and felt to see what might have been delivered while he was gone. A check, he hoped. Bills, if he was right.

Then he saw the thing he dreaded most of all. Bette had told him it might be coming. He tossed the envelope on the truck's seat before flipping out the interior light. There were the hated words on the outside. Massachusetts Center for Children. He sat at the wheel, and in the darkness, he picked up the sealed envelope. Bette had received this—and forwarded it to him—even though he'd told her he didn't want it. He'd moved on past that

27

part of his life. He was no longer Rockland Royster, bedraggled teen of dyslexic and autistic attributes. No, that boy had endured having his spirit beat down by the ever-helpful teachers and staff who had encouraged him endlessly, while never offering him the cure that would let him measure up to his father's impossibly successful standards.

Then, his father was gone, dead in the car accident, and no matter what Rocky did after that, no matter how successful he became, there was no way to prove himself to his father. The boy who had been Rockland would always be inside him, a lonely, insecure mote struggling to shine in the light of his father's brilliant accomplishments.

He'd learned to compensate. Rockland the autistic boy had become Rocky the successful boat builder, and the Center failed to understand. Even the envelope made that clear. It was on the address. *Rockland Royster,* care of Bette's bed-and-breakfast in New Hampshire. His grandmother had marked through the address and added his in Massachusetts. Now, the postman had thoughtlessly delivered it, as if Rocky really were this *Rockland* he had cast aside a decade earlier.

Bette hadn't opened it, telling him they'd left a message on her machine. They wanted to do a follow-up to track the success of their top ex-students. Rockland had been their best. They really wanted him to come in for an interview. Bette had encouraged Rocky to go see them. After all, it wasn't far, and the teachers and staff had adored him.

Rocky hadn't adored himself, and Bette couldn't understand. She was much too practical. *Love heals all wounds,* and all that stuff. *Gird up your loins. What you don't get done today will still be there tomorrow.* He could quote a dozen, and that wouldn't even break Bette's ice.

He slammed the clutch to the floor and roughly forced the shift lever into first. This was the end-all to a humdinger of a day. Releasing the clutch too fast, the truck's tires flung dirt and

28

gravel, as the rear end fishtailed before catching and bouncing down the driveway over the rocks that had forced themselves through the soil. He snorted disgustedly as he heard a rough scrape underneath the truck. The beater's one good headlight illuminated the lower tree branches as the springs bounced down the drive, and the scene ahead finally opened to the clearing that included his home. Past that, it stretched to his shorefront boat shed and dock. Everything was quiet, just as he expected it to be. The house would be cold, even in late September. Summer didn't last forever this far north, and although the days might try to fool the populace by teasing them with the remembered warmth of languid summer afternoons, the nights were precursors of the winter days to come.

Then, he saw his boat shed. He never left lights on in the shed. Never. There was a glow there now, and that meant something was not as it should be. He pulled his truck behind the house. He would need to unload his supplies in case it rained overnight, but more importantly, if someone was in the boat shed, Rocky wanted to be the surprise that person would never forget.

Opening the truck's door, he grabbed Fish's collar. "Shush, boy. Not a sound. Stay." Then he felt his way in the darkness along the back of the house. Pulling the screen door open slowly, knowing just where it liked to squeal its complaints, he jiggled it against the hinges at the right spot. Its concerns pacified, he moved forward and opened the door. It wouldn't be locked. It never was. Anyone he knew—Tramwick, to be precise—would know to just go on in.

Once inside, he stepped to the sofa and felt carefully behind it until he could feel the rifle he kept there. He gingerly removed the mandatory safety device all stored guns in Massachusetts were required to have. Before going back outside, he reached to a drawer in the end table and felt at the back until he found several loose shells. He loaded the gun and heard it click sharply in the quietness of the room. With a deep breath of pending tension, he moved to the front of the house. Peering through a window, he could see the light still on in the shed. It was jumping, too, almost as if someone was having a party out there.

"What sort of leaf peepers would party in my boat shed? I might shoot them just for fun." He'd been through a very long day, from Bette's forced confrontation with his father, to the heaving stones in his driveway. Now this. He had no more patience.

He opened the front door, and stepping off the porch, he heard singing. As he silently moved through the door yard, he could tell his intruder was as drunk as a loon flying over a Vermont pond in mating season. Great sunken ships, he didn't have a leaf peeper out there. A certified *imbecile* was in his boat shed.

Then it occurred to him. The voice reminded him of . . . of . . . Fish! Fish and a certain night of torturous rescue—as well as mouth-to-mouth resuscitation! He reached to the chamber of his gun and released the ammunition, dropping the shells into his pocket. That was Tramwick in his boat shed, and if the moon were brighter, Rocky would be able to see his lobster boat tied up to the float or at one of the buoys out in the harbor.

A mischievous grin crawled across his face. He glanced down at the gun he held in the darkness. The ammunition was out, and it might be good to put a bit of fear into that drunken friend of his, if he could even call him a friend, what with him being intoxicated in the boat shed. Didn't the man know that Rocky's livelihood was under construction out there? Tram's behavior while drunk wasn't predictable, either. He was as likely to drink the kerosene Rocky kept by the jug, as remember it went in the portable heater's fuel tank.

A short whistle came from between Rocky's teeth, and after a moment, a large, black dog stood at his side. Rocky put his free hand down to work his fingers into the dog's fur. He knelt and whispered, "Boy, let's go and have some fun." With a chuckle, he stood and began to walk towards the glow he could see dancing through the boat shed window.

AT THE BEACON Light Preservation Society offices, senior management were gathered around a table.

"We can only close the lighthouse for a year." John Remington, the speaker, tapped one of the packets lying in the middle of the table. "Are you sure one man can handle this amount of work?"

"John," another man, Rand Walters, looked up at him and chuckled, "have you ever been out on a Royster boat? His motor yachts are fabulous. His sailing yachts are hand-built works of art. We're fortunate to get him on this project." He pulled the folder to him. Opening it, he flipped through the application inside. It was hand written in the blocky format of someone who didn't work well with letters. It was almost discarded when the selection process started, then Rand had deciphered the name. Lightning had flashed in his brain, and he had known.

It was a tightly held secret that Rand had put up the money for a Royster-built boat. He just hoped he could convince his wife to let go of the funds when it came time. It would be a lot. Then, when the boat arrived, he'd have to spend even more to have an engine installed, along with tons of electronics. However, it would be worth every dollar he spent . . . that *he and his wife* spent. A chuckle escaped him, although the others at the table didn't understand what it was for. He knew, though. It was his wife's money, and she would be the one buying the boat, not him.

A third man cleared his throat. "What do we say? We've already decided, then? We want him to start immediately. He's said he can do so. There's no wife or other family—other than a grandmother in New Hampshire. She runs a bed-and-breakfast out of the old family place, I understand. Rand, you've stayed there." He glanced that way to see Rand's acknowledgement. "According to this form, Royster helps his grandmother with maintenance issues at the old B-and-B. If he takes time to travel back and forth between Massachusetts and New Hampshire, does that mean he'll allow the necessary time to devote to the lighthouse?"

"I was thinking about that very thing. To do maintenance on a business in New Hampshire could be very time consuming, in travel time, alone." Another of the men, one with a balding head, seemed concerned. "You are sure he has time for our lighthouse? What if he has to travel inland to help his grandmother? How much will that eat into his time for us?"

"I think we'll be fine. If he has to be away from the Goose Rocks renovation site to maintain his own projects, he'll still be relatively close by. This looks good to me. Besides, it's late, and I have my wife's pot roast waiting for me at home." John turned his gaze on each of them in turn.

The other men chuckled. They'd heard of his wife's pot roasts, and they understood his desire to get there as quickly as possible. They all had their own reasons to be gone, and with a series of nods, John picked up where he left off.

"Good. This goes out tomorrow. He'll be able to access the funds immediately. Any other concerns? None? Good. Good evening, men, and have a great weekend."

Within a matter of minutes, even before the chairs had finished spinning, the room was emptied, and the lights were off. Rocky had his lighthouse, and the lighthouse had its retrofit on the way.

ROCKY TORE into the boat shed, his gun at his shoulder and his voice hard.

"You thieving scoundrel, whoever you are! My finger's on the trigger, and I'm firing now." He danced the barrel of the rifle across the room as if looking for anything that moved, as though the slightest motion would incite a rain of fire from the unloaded weapon. He continued his volley of words, "Only the lowest dog would break into a man's shop and steal his livelihood. Drop to the floor, or I'm firing now."

He froze the swinging barrel of his gun directly at Tramwick. The sound of breaking glass shattered the silence. After a moment, Tramwick's voice quavered in broken words, "Oh, my poor bottle of Scotch." With a hiccup, he continued, "I think I just peed myself."

"Tram, you're in my new boat." Rocky dropped the butt of his gun and set it aside, now really irritated. He walked up to see a dark stain spreading across his friend's crotch. "Get out, man, before you ruin the wood. I've already been paid for this boat, and I won't have it smelling like your sour, used whiskey just because you can't take a joke." As he reached to stand his friend up and get him out of the unfinished craft, his eyes caught sight of the shattered bottle off to the side. He muttered, "At least you threw the bottle out of the boat before letting it break."

Tramwick wrapped his arm around Rocky's neck, as he let himself be helped up. He kissed his friend roughly on the cheek, and Rocky groaned in disgust. The next words he spoke were blended so smoothly with his whiskey that they were hardly understandable.

"I enjoyed my boat ride, Rocky. I want one just like this. Just like this." His hand paused and slapped the gunwale as he stepped to the floor of the shed. "Can I borrow the john, old Rocky, my friend? I got more to go. Your gun just scared a tiny bit out, you see. There's a bunch more where that came from."

Rocky shook his head with resignation and grasped his friend's face in one hand. "Are you mine for the night?" At Tramwick's uncomprehending stare, he released the face. "I shouldn't even ask. You can't go anywhere like this, anyway. At least I've got a washer in the house. You can thank Bette for that. Phew, this stinks!"

Tramwick stumbled and grabbed Rocky's shirt. With thick words, he complained, "Thought you'd be here. Got some news for you, old Rock. Then I remembered it was Thursday. Thursdays, right? You go to Bette's, that's right?" He reached clumsily and wiped his mouth with the back of his hand. "You came home, though. We can party some more."

"News?" Rocky looked at his friend hard. "What news, Tram?" After his rotten day, he wasn't entirely sure he wanted to know.

Tramwick hiccupped. "News? The . . . the light . . . no . . . the lighthouse, Rocky." He grinned, apparently pleased with himself.

"Lighthouse?" Rocky stumbled as Tram leaned hard against him, and he spit out, "Help me out here, Tram."

"Yeah," Tramwick slurred. "Lighthouse." As if that said it all, he grinned and nodded several times in a row, almost upsetting his fragile balance.

Rocky shook his head. That made no sense to him, and he adjusted his friend on his shoulder and began to walk him to the door. He let out a sharp whistle. Before they could get outside the boat shed, a big black shape came bounding inside.

"Come on up to the house, Tram," Rocky encouraged his friend. "I've got a bathroom, and you need to use it—in more ways than one. Besides, Fish misses you."

Tramwick dropped to his knees and wrapped his arms around the dog's neck. "Hey, old Fish. I thought you drowned in the sea. What are you doing here?" He looked up at Rocky, and he slushed his words out, "Fish? This is Fish, right? You didn't go and get a different dog just to fool ole Tramwick, did you?" His expression was one almost of pain, as if Fish were already dead and gone.

Rocky laughed. "You're too soused to know your own dog. I should leave you here to sleep it off. I won't, though." His voice turned suddenly sharp. "Fish! Bite, Fish. Bite hard!"

Rocky hooted when Tramwick quickly clambered up with a look of terror on his face. That rapidly faded when the big dog jumped up on him and began to lick his face. Tram finally recognized the animal, and he dug his fingers into the thick fur around the dog's neck.

"Fish, it *is* you. You've been brought back to life by a miracle." He turned to Rocky, and there were tears on his face. "He's back alive again, Fish is. I thought I'd never see him again. Thank you for saving him, Rocky." He sniffled several times, and then his eyes started to close as he stood. When he began to sway, Rocky grabbed his shoulders and shook him.

"No, you don't, Tram. You've got a tub coming up. Plus, those clothes have got to go in the washer. Tonight! C'mon." It took a while, and it was dark navigating through the door yard and into the house. Before too much time had passed, Tramwick was installed in the tub, and his clothes were sloshing up a storm in the washer.

It was when he returned to the truck to unload it and get his mail that he was reminded of the letter. Once he stepped inside the house, he opened it. He saw the date they had scheduled for him to come in to meet with one of the school's nurses. Bevier. Miss Lisa Bevier.

He imagined this Nurse Bevier. She would be haughty and reserved, and her hands would be cold when they shook in greeting. That would be Lisa Bevier. Why, even the name sounded standoffish. He'd attended that school for more years than he wished to remember. He should know.

Glancing at the calendar above the table, he tapped the red diagonal crosses on each box, matching up the latest unmarked date with the one on the letter. Saturday. The meeting was Saturday morning. The Center may have sent this out long ago, but the letter had been forwarded to him. There was no telling how long it sat at Bette's place. She could have at least asked them *when* the meeting was set up while she was nosing into his business. Now, it was here, two days away, and that caught him up short. His head throbbed with the pressure of traveling to the Center. Filling out a piece of paper to return to them would have been bad enough, but they wanted him in person. They'd want to run some sort of test, or check his responses, or something. As a student there, he'd endured that for years, and he didn't want it done to him anymore.

Bette did, though.

He placed the letter on the table. For his grandmother, this one last time, he'd go. For his father, too, although that reason wasn't out of love. Rocky still had something to prove to the old man who'd said he loved him, then locked him away for nearly half his life.

He'd prove it, too. He'd show them he'd overcome all the problems they'd claimed he'd once had, even if it meant he had to lie on every test they put him through.

Chapter 3

LISA breathed in the leather and wood smell as she opened the door and slipped inside her car. She ran her hand over the steering wheel, enjoying the feel of the supple, soft-touch cover. The vehicle was new, a treat she'd splurged on after moving in to help her mother. She'd given up her home and sold all her furniture. This was her one indulgence, and she'd refused to listen to the naysayers who claimed it was extravagant. With a touch of the starter button, the engine purred to life.

Tapping the radio, a steady beat filled the car, and she stroked the control to lower the volume. She should have never held on to her rusty heap so long. It had been beaten up by New England's winters till the holes in the fenders were letting water and air through to the inside.

Just like the men in her life.

No matter how well she maintained her end of the relationship, they were still men, and they never held up their end of the bargain. Why was that? Male hormones. They drove them to be irresponsible. Maybe part of it was that musky smell they gave off, or their deep, resonating voices. Maybe, and she smiled as she backed out of the garage, it was those broadly muscled shoulders. All that masculinity *forced* them to be cruel and philandering brutes.

Andrew had proven himself to be that and more.

It was September 28th, the day of the wedding. In the weeks prior to that day, he was like a wind-up dime toy, his attention all over the place. She had it figured as pre-ceremony nerves.

She was very, very wrong.

When it grew close to the time for the formalities to start, no one had heard from him all day. The guests were arriving, and the minister was waiting just outside the chapel. Lisa had a bad feeling about the situation. Her mother tried to tell her it was pre-wedding jitters, but Lisa couldn't shake the feeling it was more.

Her cousin Steve from Staten Island, who was serving as Andrew's best man, decided to find out what was going on. Lisa tried to hold him off, reassuring him Andrew would show, but he told her this was her special day. He wanted Andrew to be present—and on time.

What Steve didn't tell her was that Andrew had been caught several times in the previous weeks partying with another woman. Steve had tried to strong-arm him into doing the right thing, but Andrew just didn't seem to get it. He'd promise to do better, that his high times were the last goodbye for an old flame. Each time he said his fling would be the last time he saw her, but he hadn't followed through on his word.

Andrew never showed up for the ceremony, and for some reason, although he certainly could have, he never filed charges against Steve, either. Apparently, he had intended to attend the wedding, because his tuxedo was out and ready for him to slip into. In the heat of the moment, his activities with his old girlfriend had skewed his attention to the clock, and when Steve arrived, Andrew was in flagrante delicto with a woman who wasn't invited to the ceremonies.

Lisa was horrified and extremely embarrassed. That was what she told everyone. What she really felt was heartbroken and angry. As the truth began to come out, she could see all the signs she'd missed, and all because she had *wanted* to be charmed by this man. She had wanted to see the best in him. She had wanted to find love.

Yes, that had her heartbroken. Even more than that, fury had torn at her. She was still angry, and with herself. She was determined she wouldn't let any man do that to her again. She realized Andrew had just been himself, and as awful as that day was, she was glad to have found out before the knot was tied. She also decided that if, and she knew it was a strong if, she allowed any man to get close to her again, he would have to prove himself first. She wouldn't make it easy for him, either.

She shifted her car into gear and pulled into traffic. At least she had her kids at the Center, and they loved her. Better yet, she didn't have to bring them home with her. She could be her bright and cheerful self, enjoy all the emotional attention they showered on her, and return home each night to the peace and quiet of her mother's house.

Besides, her mother needed her. There was no room in Lisa's life for children of her own, and especially no room for a man. She'd never admit that she sometimes dreamed of one. He haunted her dreams, although she didn't know him, only his records in her school's files and her one glimpse of him. He didn't know her, either. Besides, he might also be a brute, what with those brooding eyes. They had been very dark—dare she say morose—that day, full of angst and self-inflicted anguish.

So, children of her own? For that she needed a man, another one besides that handsomely brooding *Rocky* Royster. To get one, she had to have the other, and that was something she just wasn't ready for.

Not now, anyway. Not in September.

"HEY, JOSH Reynolds, how have you been this year?"

Lisa stepped to the boy and snapped an old-fashioned bulb thermometer back and forth for a minute to prep it for insertion in his mouth.

"I've been fine, Miss Bevier." He smiled.

"I haven't seen you since school started. You're about ready to graduate. You're intending to stay with us through graduation, right?"

As the school nurse, she didn't see every student every day. Many of the higher-functioning children were ones she interacted with only when they needed special attention or the campus was doing a school-wide screening. This was the boy from North Haven the summer she'd been taken in by Andrew. However, she'd put that away as her personal trauma. Today was for her students, and this moment was for Josh.

He had been an enjoyable fourteen-year-old that summer, skinny and tall. When she watched him closely, she could still see many of the mannerisms that had made him stand out to others as strange or odd all those years ago. She had to watch for those things, however. No one who didn't know him well would be able to tell now. He had matured marvelously.

"So, you're leaving for North Haven this afternoon. Last weekend of the summer, I bet." As Lisa grasped his chin in her hand, she smiled. "Open, Josh. We must get this checkup completed. We want your parents to feel comfortable taking you away for the weekend. With the latest forecasts, you just might squeeze in a beautiful few days, if the weather holds."

"You bet. I know how to do this. I already spit my gum out, too." His speech patterns revealed more of his struggles with autism and other life-threatening medical issues than his physical appearance. "I can't wait to get to the island, even if the weather gets bad. I remember the summer you were there. I especially enjoyed my vacation that year."

He glanced away as she pulled his chin down, and he raised his tongue in a smooth and practiced motion.

"Look at the far wall, Josh." As the boy glanced over her shoulder, she peered into his eyes. They were the clearest blue she had ever seen. She hadn't paid much attention to them in the skinny, oddly behaving body he'd lived in at fourteen, but that skinny boy wasn't Josh anymore. This handsome youth was now seventeen. She suspected he still thought of himself as he'd been then. He didn't see the newly muscled young man with the crystal blue eyes who would one day attract the girls like mayflies. Lisa could see it, and while she would love to tell him to stand tall and be proud of what he'd become, she bit her tongue. Her words would carry little weight with him. The attentions of a pretty girl were what he needed.

She put her hand on his shoulder to steady a series of muscular spasms in his hands. She didn't want his jaw to crush the glass thermometer he held between his teeth. When her hand touched his shirt, his eyes flashed to hers, and he grinned.

"Thank you, Miss Bevier." He talked around the thermometer, as he clenched his fist, calming his body's spontaneous, flickering movements.

"For what?" She knew. Another of the school's nurses might have simply told him to hold the edges of his chair, or asked if he wanted a plastic thermometer, instead. That wasn't Josh. He wanted to be the same as the kids who attended the public school system, those he saw on the street running home when their classes let out, or maybe even darting past on their bicycles. Some of them now drove cars, but he couldn't hope for that. None of the students were permitted to drive at the Center. Josh lived on campus in the Residence, and it was only during his bi-weekly visits home that he spent time with his family.

He smiled around the thermometer.

Lisa pulled the instrument from his mouth, and she held it up to the light. "Looks good! No fever!" She patted him on the shoulder and pointed to the examining table. "Step over there and have a seat. Shirt off. Don't forget your shoes and socks." Once he'd done as she asked, she had him turn to place his legs on the table. "Hmm," she murmured, picking up one of his feet, "I can see you've been working on that foot positioning. Have you worn your shoe inserts at all this past summer?"

He grinned. "No, I'm holding my ankles in. I'm paying attention. I don't even think about it much, anymore."

She looked at the soles of his feet. "Calluses, I see, and they're even, too." She looked up at him as she rubbed her hands over his soles. "You've spent some shoeless time with these feet."

He laughed. "On the island. Remember? You were there when I was a kid. You met Andrew, and he took you out in all kinds of boats. I remember Andrew. He must have been rich."

Lisa could see the blush of embarrassment in his cheeks. At fourteen, he wouldn't have thought to ask about Andrew and their relationship. At seventeen, his thoughts were shifting to personal interactions that had been unimportant to him before. He had grown up more than she thought.

His voice was tentative as he inquired, "What happened to Andrew?"

She turned to some supplies sitting on a counter, as if she were readying them for use in his examination. Josh had been enjoyable that long-ago summer, and she had become attached to him. She'd enjoyed interacting with him in the years since, as the adolescent boy dropped away to reveal the one in her office now. Today he was forcing her to relive memories of a time she would just as soon not have to think about.

She brightened her face and turned to him. "He and I had different interests. Stand up, Josh. Let's check your spine." Now was the time to reveal to this boy what he couldn't see in himself.

He looked at her, puzzled. "My spine? You've never checked that before."

"Scoliosis. We can't have you get that, can we?" She stepped in front of the mirror to point to where she wanted him to stand.

"Scoliosis? My spine doesn't curve at all." He jumped up and stood as tall as he could. "See?"

"Yes, I see. Just stand over here, please. Let's check your alignment. Then I can mark in your records that there's no curvature." With a smile, she waved him over.

He started towards her, his feet cocked on their sides. In a quick correction, he shifted to stand straighter and walked with his feet firmly planted, as if she might indeed find the flaws she was looking for. She smiled at him. He wanted to be seen as strong and healthy, and she would show him he already was. She moved beside him. He was a head taller than she was. She had him turn sideways and look at himself as she pressed her fingers along his backbone.

"Any tingles?" He shifted his shoulders and held himself steady. When he sucked in his breath and shook his head no, she released him and smiled. "What sport do you play this year?"

"Sport?" He glanced at her in the mirror.

"You've got an athlete's body. A runner, or perhaps a swimmer. Something you've done somewhere has built up these muscles." She was pretty sure this boy tried to hide from sports. He needed to know that he could be more than he was. She continued, "What sort of car do you drive?"

His eyes watched his image in the mirror. After a long moment of silence, his eyes looked to her as if startled that her question hadn't already been answered.

"I don't."

"You don't what?" She smiled and continued to look at him.

"I don't drive." He glanced down.

"You don't drive? Ever? You're seventeen."

He turned to face the mirror. He flexed one arm as if an athlete might pop out unexpectedly. "Not alone. I can't drive alone. You know. My seizures."

Lisa took his hand, turned it upside down, and pressed her thumbs into his palm, smoothing out his fingers until his hand was flat. Then she held it lightly and very still. For a minute, she just studied it, and then she looked into his blue eyes.

"See that? Do you see what your hand is doing?"

"Holding yours?"

"No, silly. It isn't moving. Not a bit." She dropped his hand and slapped his arm lightly with the back of her hand. She noticed a flush on his face and decided she had pushed him enough. She told him to put his shirt and shoes back on. When he finished, he sat on the chair, his hands twitching in his lap.

She picked up a clipboard, and she sat beside him. "Josh," she began in her most serious voice, "I know your records. Since you started your new seizure medication, you've not had one episode. You're qualified to get a license. Your school records show you've taken a driver education course. Have you asked your parents? Three years ago, they were talking about the car they wanted to get you. Has all that been put on hold?"

His features twisted, revealing his distress. "I've been scared something would happen. I remember that summer you were on the island with us. It was bad, wasn't it?"

It had been bad. She wouldn't relive that with him, though.

"I've watched you grow from a boy to a fine-looking young man. You saw yourself in that mirror. You can do anything you want to do. Now, get out of here and tell your dad you want the keys to the family car."

He did stand, and this time there was a grin on his face. He seemed to stand a little taller, too. He looked in her face, and he said, "I do have a car."

44

"What kind?" His unexpected admission surprised her.

"El Camino. That's a Chevrolet."

Her jaw dropped. "I know what it is. I also know they don't make them anymore. What year is it?"

"1959." He paused. Then he smiled wider. "When my father brought it home, it was rusty and in very bad condition. He hired someone to disassemble and completely rebuild it, and it looks brand new."

Lisa burst out in a laugh. "1959. Who would have thought? I love it. I want to see it someday. You should drive it to school at least once while you're in your final year."

His face fell. "Here? I can't do that. A car is for public school. I could drive it, if I transferred to public."

There was no reason he couldn't finish out his year in the public sector, if he wished. It would be a change, that was for certain, but he was bright and funny, and he rarely showed any signs of his autistic behaviors. He would do fine. However, she couldn't control his family's decisions in that arena. In the school environment, she could only offer carefully phrased suggestions.

"Josh, you could certainly do that. I see no problems with it. Would you like me to arrange a meeting with your parents to discuss this?" She patted his shoulder and smiled at him.

He took in a deep breath, and it seemed as if he was considering it. Then, he brightened and straightened his shoulders. In a very grown-up voice, he said, "No, Miss Bevier. I want to be an athlete for a while, first." At that, he laughed, and it was the laugh of a fourteen-year-old once again, showing the boy inside rather than the man who was slowly emerging. He waved when he left, but he was walking very tall; and his stride was that of a man.

Students like Josh were the reason she enjoyed her job at the school. She could become emotionally invested in them, but she didn't have to take them home with her at the end of the day.

Away from the school, she could indulge herself in laziness or self-pity or dreams for a man who wouldn't treat her as Andrew had. Then, her self-inflicted abuses sloughing away, she could arise in the mornings in anticipation of returning to the wonderful children she worked with at the Center. They were the ones who kept her spirit alive, and as long as she had them, she had no need for a man.

She told herself that, but deep inside she knew it wasn't true. Andrew had hurt her, and the sting had gone deep. It had gone deep enough, in fact, that she was even willing to proclaim that men weren't meant for her.

She sighed and looked at her list. Catrice was next. She pushed the intercom button. Catrice was a cutie, only eight years old, and Lisa looked forward to seeing her. Maybe she'd outgrown that twitch from last year. It annoyed everyone, and Miss Perot, one of her teachers, most of all.

"Miss Roberts, send Catrice Buffons in, now." Lisa looked up as the door opened. Her face continued to smile, but her heart fell inside. There it was, still. The arm seemed to be worse, too. Lisa would have some serious recommendations to make to this girl's instructors. Doing so was part of her job, and that was one of the ways she showed she loved the students.

"Come, Catrice. Let's have a seat over here." Catrice didn't smile, but she did comply. That made Lisa feel better. Not all the students were compliant when asked to do something. Catrice was a dear. There was no doubt about that.

BETTE FORCED her feet into a pair of her sturdiest hiking boots. She had enjoyed her company from yesterday, but today was special. Her newly arriving guests from Texas would want to visit the mountains as soon as they unpacked. Tomorrow, too, probably. It would be cold, but Bette didn't mind. She had the right clothing for it. She'd take her heavy jacket she'd had custom embroidered. Across the back were the words, *Four*

46

Thousand Footers Club, and the bottom showed an alpine meadow of flowers and running children. She'd have to leave it in the truck when the actual hike started, as it would be far too hot for a fall excursion, but it'd be fun to wear until then.

She stepped out onto the porch. The lunches were ready, and there was nothing else to do except wait for them to show; so, she shifted her focus back inside to check on the weather for the upcoming week. This couple reported they'd just gone through a summer of twenty-three consecutive triple-digit days, and they wanted to be outside in the cool of a New England fall every single day, if they could. No outlet malls, movie theaters, or driving tours for them. They wanted to feel the weather on their skin, the sun on their backs, and, Bette imagined, a few sore muscles as they slept. That was fine with her. She was active all the time. She didn't get sore muscles.

Earlier that morning, she'd had the television on, watching the station's meteorologist, him talking as if every word he said was true. That was about the only channel she watched, the only one she had time to watch, and she knew the personalities pretty well. That man was her least favorite. He was loud and muscle-bound, and he liked to sound like he was all that and more. However, he had pointed to a storm in the Atlantic. Of course, this was September, and there were always storms in the Atlantic in September. They usually fizzled out near Bermuda, zigzagged up and down the East Coast, or sauntered over into the Gulf of Mexico. They didn't worry her unless she saw the thunderheads building in her sky, and the storm's lightning flashing its fury against her lighting rod. It never hurt, however, to keep track of what was coming three days out, especially with company arriving.

For now, she was going hiking. It was Friday, a crisp September morning, and the sun would warm the day. She knew just where to find the best color popping up in the New Hampshire hills. She couldn't deny her true longings, either. That was where she wanted to be, and this was just her excuse. It simply made it better to have someone who wanted to go with her, especially when they would find as much joy in it as she would.

Then she remembered Rocky's keys. They were in her other clothes upstairs. She'd have to get them and remember to give them back when she saw him next. Take them to him? She thought not. He'd be back up in a week or so. He wouldn't be happy about the way she'd taken them, and next time, she'd have to find a different premise to get them in her pocket. Rocky didn't often fool twice the same way.

Just then, the sound of tires on the gravel outside grabbed her attention, and a sharp series of beeps broke the morning silence. Bette smiled. Her friends were here, and they would have jalapeno jelly with them, brought all the way from Texas just for her.

"HEY, BETTE, babe! You in there? It's been a long time—too long! How you been doing?" In the front door popped a wide-brimmed western hat. White, bushy hair and a thick moustache over a broad grin followed.

Bette rounded the kitchen door into the center hall. She loved that Texas twang—although she knew much of it would be exaggerated especially for her—and she'd missed it since last September. A smile burst across her face, and her hand threw the dishtowel she was holding onto a convenient side table, just missing a vase of fresh flowers.

"Merv? That must be you, you old Ranger, you! How was your trip up?" Bette strode toward the door and pulled it back to make an official welcome to the rest of the big man who was leaning into her home. "How is it you're getting here so late? I expected you hours ago."

"Rain at La Guardia held us up." The face grinned wider. He reached a rough hand and pulled his hat from his head as he stomped his boots on the front door mat. Sailing the big hat with

48

a practiced hand onto a nearby chair, he lifted Bette into his arms. As he hugged her, his voice boomed, "I should'a left Leetha home this year. I always forget how beautiful you are, Bette. This year I'm moving in."

She laughed and wrestled free, putting her feet back on the floor. "I say! Leave me on the floor, you charmer, you. Be careful. I might decide to keep you, too. However, even though our state motto might be *Live Free or Die*, here in New Hampshire, our men only get one woman at a time."

Just about then a woman's voice could be heard outside. "Merv, hon? I got me a ton of bricks in this here suitcase. Think you can lift it up these steps?" Leetha's feet sounded on the steps, and a gaily printed dress topped by a suede jacket appeared, backing through the door and highlighted by the late-morning sun. "Merv? Do you have your hands on Bette, again? I swear I'm going to box your ears." She turned to reveal a brightly made-up face, nearly bumping into her husband. "Oh, hon! There you are."

Then, as she saw Bette, Leetha let out a shriek. "My Gawd, Bette, you are a sight for sore eyes! Merv and I were talking on the plane, and we were saying to each other again in the taxi, why that Bette had better live forever, 'cause this is always the best week of our lives. Now, here you are, and you're looking better than I've ever seen you. Oh, I'm right glad we came."

As Merv winked at Bette and stepped outside for the bag, Leetha reached out her arms and gathered in her friend, giving her a hug that was more of a friend's embrace than a patron's greeting. It was, too. Bette considered Merv and Leetha to be better friends than many of the people she had lived around for decades, and she welcomed them as such. Of course, she would also present them a bill when they left, but in spite of that, the friendship was sincere.

Leetha turned to find her husband, muttering to herself, "Now, where is that old wild-cattin' man of mine? Not an oil well in sight, and still, he always wanders around and gets himself in the most out-of-the-way places." She stepped to the door to peer outside, only to unexpectedly butt into the man she was looking for. Catching herself on the frame, she reached her hand to his face, smiling, and her lips kissed him gently on one cheek. "You are a dear. You brought my case all the way inside. Merv, hon, will you carry it all the way up? Bette, do we have the same wonderful room?" She called her question without turning, all the while gazing into Merv's eyes.

Bette liked that about Merv and Leetha. It was obvious they were in love even while the prickles flew between them like thistles from a mower gone amok. There was nothing soft and precious about this pair, but there was plenty that was good.

"Baby, it's done." Merv licked his lips as he nodded. Then, as his wife turned, he moved his hand lightning quick to slap her on the buttocks, squeezing a bit before he released her to lift the heavy suitcase. He laughed. "That was just to give me a little pep, my dear. This case'll be a dove's feather to me with that memory against my hand." He began to whistle a little tune as his feet climbed the stairs.

Leetha turned to glare at him before looking back to Bette.

"He's been seventeen since the day I married him. Horny as a buck deer and twice as fun." She winked. "I wouldn't trade him for three jackrabbits and a West Texas frog choker. Now, how about that grandson of yours? I seem to remember he was a bit of a burr in your saddle. You were fixing to work on getting him back in that barn out back. There was a boat he needed to put a little spit and polish on. Give me a minute to think." She tapped her chin for a moment with a knowing look at Bette. "Now, don't try to help me lasso names. I need the practice. I seem to remember his name is Rockland, no, Rocky's what he wants to be branded with." She put her hand on Bette's arm and laughed. "I forget my own grandbabies' names, now that I'm no longer a spring chicken." She reached to brush her hand down the case of Bette's old grandfather clock. "I remember this, though. I love the sound when I'm in bed here. If you ever mosey to Fort Worth, Bette, you'll love the bells at First Methodist Church. They ring out all across downtown. That's what I hear in your clock."

Bette reached to rescue the towel she'd thrown aside as she'd come in earlier. "Fort Worth," she murmured and paused, for a moment wistful, then she sighed. "Someday, Leetha, when things slow a bit here. However, I'm just setting out our lunch, so we can get you two out on the trails for a few hours this afternoon. We'll have a late supper when we return. Follow me into the kitchen. You can sit and watch me work, and we can bring ourselves up to date on all our grandchildren."

"Watch, nothing. I'm washing up and getting my hands gritty. My cook at home shoos me out of the kitchen except when she's off for the weekends. You always let me come in and help. I love you for that, Bette." Leetha was on Bette's heels, and by the time she crossed the kitchen door, she already had her jacket unfastened and thrown on a nearby chair.

Bette laughed at her friend's words. Merv and Leetha paid to come stay with her, and that was what had to happen in order to keep the old bed-and-breakfast operational, but it was the feeling of family that kept them returning. As the prepared dishes emerged from the refrigerator, and plates and flatware gleamed under the overhead lights, the women laughed and talked up a year's worth of words. They told of grandchildren, and there were stories of Texas and New Hampshire neighbors never met, yet who seemed as familiar as yesterday's toast. From this visiting Texan, Bette even knew her Fort Worth gardens, as if they were right here in her own native New Hampshire state.

UPSTAIRS, MERV smiled at the words he heard filtering up through the floor. He looked around the room that was to be his home for a week. It was filled with family heirlooms that were worn, scrubbed, and polished. Just like the friends and gardens the women talked of downstairs, these furnishings were as familiar to him as the pieces his own Leetha had placed in their Southern home during the many years of their lives together.

After a moment, he pulled his hiking boots from his luggage, and setting them aside, he found a chair; the softness of the cushions brought back memories of familiar naps in their embrace. Before he knew it, he was lulled to a sweet oblivion by the familiar comfort of well-known surroundings and the muted sounds of a much-loved woman's words. Getting up at the crack of dawn to get to the airport hadn't helped, and his nap was well deserved. He expected his wife would wake him for lunch, and he would feel recharged for their afternoon hike.

Even if it was only for a week, and he would pay handsomely for his time in Bette's residence, Merv was right at home.

Chapter 4

JOSH FOLLOWED the rocks lining the shore along the Fox Islands Thorofare. They'd caught the last ferry to the island, and he'd rushed to get away from the house before the light faded completely. He was wearing just shorts and shoes. He'd had a shirt on earlier, and even long sleeves, but late September could still be warm on the island. Now, the sleeves were tied around his waist, and he enjoyed the warmth of the sun caressing his skin. He planned to hike down far enough to see Goose Rocks Light.

Looking just across the channel, Vinalhaven beckoned to him. Yet, he had no boat to traverse the short distance between the sister islands. He'd been to Vinalhaven dozens of times. When his parents needed something really badly, they took the small ferry that crossed the Thorofare and had a friend drive them to town at the far side of the island. It was a long drive, and there were only trees, trees, and more trees all the way there.

The ponds didn't count to Josh. Here on North Haven, there was already water everywhere, and he liked lighthouses, anyway. Not ponds or trees.

He pictured Goose Rocks the way it would appear in the middle of the Thorofare. It was a sparkplug lighthouse, one that was sometimes rented by tourists. He'd asked his parents about that one time, hoping they'd let him go there for the weekend, maybe go with him, perhaps. They'd given him their usual answer. *"What if you get sick? How would we get help?"* They hadn't liked his answer. *"At least I'd die happy!"*

He hiked to see the lighthouse every time they were here, if he could get away from the iron hands of his parents. They were always afraid for him, but Miss Bevier was right. He hadn't had an episode for years. He'd gotten taller, and his arms were strong. Maybe he was athletic and just didn't know. He'd never really thought that before, not until she checked his back for scoliosis.

He wondered why she hadn't married Andrew. Josh still saw him around the island. Josh's parents said something about Andrew's family being old money until the "old man" gambled it all away. Josh wasn't sure just what that meant, but maybe that was why Miss Bevier never married him. Maybe Andrew had been too embarrassed and had run away from her. Maybe that's why she'd never come back to North Haven with his family, either.

This would be his family's last trip to their place this year. They never came after the first of October. Josh's parents thought summer houses were for summer, and to stay in them any other time was middle class. Josh wanted to winter over one year just to see what it was like. It'd be cold, though. The lobstermen on Vinalhaven did it all the time, but Josh wasn't sure how many people wintered over on North Haven. There was a school, so he figured some must.

Then he saw it. Goose Rocks. It was out there, and the

whitecaps were breaking around the base. The sound of the water around the rock he stood on prevented him from hearing the churning waves against the lighthouse, but he could imagine. He'd researched it on the Internet, and it was scheduled for a renovation. The owners hoped to hire a famous boat builder to do the work. He didn't see how a boat builder would know how to renovate a lighthouse, but he wished it could be him.

Then, the cold, rising tide sloshed over the top of Josh's shoes, and he jumped back. Even with the sun shining and the warmth of the day, the early fall waters of the Atlantic were no friend to warm-blooded feet, and the soaking caused him to shiver. He reached to untie the arms of his shirt, and as he did, he noticed the sun already starting to dip below the tips of the trees. That was the only thing about September. The days were already short. Slipping his shirt over his head, he pulled it past his face. It caught on his ear, and he reached a hand to loosen the tight spot, causing it to slip easily around his shoulders.

He turned and headed back to his house, taking the sounds of the surf with him. He concentrated, making sure to keep his feet flat and level as he took each step. It would be quite a walk, and it might even be dark when he got there. He could feel the goose bumps popping out on his legs, and he reached down to brush them away.

He stopped and turned to catch a last glimpse of Goose Rocks Light. Running his hand through his sturdy shock of hair, he made a connection he thought very funny. Goose bumps on his legs. Goose Rocks Light. Maybe that was where the lighthouse had gotten its name. Maybe the sea floor looked like goose bumps just there where the lighthouse stood.

He turned back to home, but with the new bond he felt to this place he loved so much, his chest swelled just a little broader. The sea floor and his leg somehow seemed the same on this afternoon that had grown suddenly chilly. That they might be was enough for him.

LISA'S MOTHER, Terese, turned from the stew she was stirring, as her daughter set her things on the kitchen table. Her bag slipped, and the papers inside slid across the surface.

"Lisa, dear, let me help you." Terese wiped her hands on her apron and stepped to the table to help her daughter organize the scattered papers. For a moment, she paused to look wistfully at her beautiful child. This girl, so well educated, and working at that prestigious Massachusetts Center for Children. Yet, here she was living in her mother's house to help with her care. Terese appreciated it, but she also knew her daughter needed a man.

"Thank you, Mum." Lisa shifted the bag to keep it from falling to the floor and placed her purse beside it.

"What are these, dear? This young man, he's quite handsome, if a bit brooding." Terese began to straighten the forms, noticing they all seemed to concern the same person. She paused at one that held a photo of a boy at eighteen. There were several others of the same boy even younger. She handed the papers back to Lisa, and she apologized. "I'm sorry, dear. It's none of my business. These must be from the Center. I'm sure this must be a student there."

Lisa chuckled. "Was, Mum. Was. Many years ago. I have a follow-up interview with him tomorrow. The school wants to see how well their techniques carry over into the real world. Do the skills they teach hold up when the students become adults, that kind of thing. This is Rockland Royster. He's been out of school over a decade."

Her mother sighed as she picked up the paper and looked at the picture again. "I'd date this one myself, if I were only a few years younger." She pursed her lips, and she sent her daughter a look.

"Mum!" Lisa reached to grasp her mother's arm, and she chuckled. "You've never met him. He might be a wildly handicapped screamer for all you know." She pulled the papers out of her hands.

"You'll be careful, tomorrow?" Terese didn't like this idea of Lisa at the Center on a weekend.

"He's safe, so don't worry. I'm familiar with him. He's started a quite successful business."

Her mother barbed back, "Young lady, familiar with him? From just his records? They might lie in those papers. Funding. It's all about funding. You can't have met him before if he's been out of that school a decade. I've listened to your stories. For all you know, he might have run through the building jabbing holes in the walls with a pen. Is that in those records? Will someone else be there with you? Tomorrow's Saturday, I seem to remember, and I don't want you meeting someone alone."

With some of the Center's children, that might be a concern. Smiling at her mother's description, Lisa reminded her, "I have all that in his records, Mum. All the way back to when he was a small boy. He won't poke holes in my walls. And, for your information, I have, too, met him."

"Harrumph. Well, my pot's about to boil over." Terese stepped to pick up her spoon. Over her shoulder, she called, "Have you interviewed him before?"

"No, Mum." Lisa paused. "I saw him that summer I went to North Haven. He was in Rockland, that town where we caught the ferry out to the island."

"When you stayed the month with that boy's family. I remember. Well, is he married?" Terese turned to catch her daughter's eyes. When she didn't get an answer, she asked again, louder, "Lisa, is this ex-student married? Do you know that?"

Lisa groaned and stacked the papers off to the side to make room for dinner. "Not now, Mum. Here. I'll clear the table." She grabbed the cloth from the sink and wiped the top of the table.

When her mother tapped one of the cabinet doors, Lisa reached inside and pulled down two of her mother's oldest china bowls. A sweep of her hand brought up flatware from a drawer. When she stepped across the room for glasses, Terese put a hand on her arm.

"Daughter, he's not, is he?" For her Lisa's sake, Terese wanted her answer to be no.

LISA LOOKED her mother directly in the eyes. Normally, she'd have met a question like that with derision. Yet, this one was hitting entirely too close to home. She'd dreamed of this man, and for three years. She hoped she didn't dream of him tonight. Or, perhaps, she hoped she did. She would never admit wishing for that, though.

She did know one thing for certain. This afternoon, as soon as she'd heard of being assigned this meeting with Rockland Royster, her pulse had quickened. For that reason, she'd gone and taken every one of his files from the cabinet, and she'd slipped them into her bag to take home. She wasn't supposed to do that. To get permission required two weeks to go through the proper channels. Her meeting with Rockland was the next day. She'd needed them *tonight*. Well, not really. The interview wouldn't cover his life at the school, but rather his life since. Still . . . she'd needed the files . . . well, just because.

She had scoured them as closely as she could while sitting at lights and even in the driveway. Rockland had built quite a reputation in the boat-building business; several news clippings testified to his prowess, one containing a photo of one of his boats. He'd grown out of his autistic behaviors, it seemed, so much so that most people wouldn't recognize them. His dyslexia would always need attending do, but that would be something he could build a set of coping skills to deal with. He'd never been back to the campus since his graduation a decade earlier, although it was noted there had been repeated calls to a grandmother.

There was no suggestion of a wife. However, there was also no suggestion of whether he attended church or not, what his favorite foods were, or whether he owned a dog. For all these records showed, he could have had a sex-change operation, and a woman would walk in her door tomorrow.

When her face turned pale at that thought, her mother pressed her arthritis-twisted fingers to Lisa's forehead, remarking, "Dear, you've been working too hard. You should never have brought these papers home with you. Shame on that Center for forcing you to spend your evenings with that man who doesn't even attend there anymore. You need a man of your own to take your mind off that school. Now, go rest, dear. The food'll be ready in a moment. I'll call you."

Lisa waved her away. "It's all right, Mum. There's no record of a wife, so I'll just bring him home with me tomorrow right after our interview. Then we can call Father Tomas from down at the college, and he can stop by and marry us. You'll have a son-in-law by nightfall. How would that be?" She laughed, but she could hear it was hollow. This red-headed man whom she'd seen that one time exiting the ferry had spent many nights with her in her dreams.

"Lisa!" Her mother turned to her stew, as if irritated. "I did not say you had to *marry* him. I just asked if *he* were married. After all, a ten-year checkup. He'd be about your age." Her mother snorted her annoyance at her daughter's cheeky retort.

Lisa had thought about that. All his paperwork indicated a boy with no emotional problems other than those normal to all teens struggling to burst forth into men. She realized she'd become fixated on that one chance encounter with him from all those years ago. She blamed that on her devastation by Andrew. Andrew had hurt her deeply. In her dreams, this man, Rockland, had been quiet, romantic, and whatever she needed him to be. She had bounced back from her heartache with Andrew to her dreams of Rockland, *Rocky*, to believe her long-ago hosts.

Tomorrow, she would meet him, and she would know the truth of what he was really like. Would he be the man of her dream world? She doubted that. Could she hope? Certainly.

She was aware of one other thing. For years she had depended on him to be there for her at night. What if she found he was a rotten, cruel man? Then she'd have no one, not even her dream-world Rockland. As much as she hated to admit it, that scared the very socks off her feet. If that happened, she would be very lonely, indeed.

JOSH'S PARENTS went to bed early. They hadn't really wanted to come to the island this weekend, but he'd pleaded. His mother didn't ever really want to come, not since that summer when he'd had gotten so sick. His mother always thought he was going to die or something.

He knew better.

After that summer, the doctors had done more tests, and they'd found a new medication for him. He hadn't had another seizure since. Even Miss Bevier had told him he could transfer to a public school if he wanted. He did want that, but then he didn't, either. He liked to use his father for an excuse, but that was only part of it. The Center seemed safe. He wanted to be what Miss Bevier claimed to see in him, but inside, he still felt like the old Josh. While he'd seen some of what she'd suggested as he stood in front of that mirror with her, it was harder to see it when he was on his own.

Although it had gotten cold outside, the fire in the stove kept the living room warm. Josh removed his shirt. He stood and walked to the window. They were never covered, not here in the summer house, and in the blackness of the night, the windows were like ghostly mirrors. He ran his hand over his shoulders. It was as if he were touching someone else in the reflection, and in that moment, insight washed over him with a tingle. In his reflection, he became what Miss Bevier had described. He found some of what other people saw in him. He was the athlete who could run and kick a ball and row a boat. The swim team? Why not? The strong boy in the reflection, no, the *man* in the reflection could do all those things. A smile leaped to his face, and the man in the window smiled, too. *Swim team!* He flexed his arms, and he reached and touched the glass. He jerked his hand back. It was cold!

He laughed. Maybe not the swim team, not if he couldn't touch the window without being whiney about it.

The house was old and uninsulated, and if the glass was cold, it would be cold in his bedroom, and worse, the longer he waited. Besides, a tingle buzzed in his head, and that told him he was probably tired. He checked the wood stove to make sure the door was latched, and he turned out the lights except for one. Then he headed to the bathroom. Reaching to a small heater built into the wall, he flipped it on to warm the room, and then he remembered his medicine. The tingle was the feeling he used to have just before a seizure. He'd learned to recognize it years ago, and he hadn't been paying attention. He'd taken his morning medicine at home. Here at the summer house, his mother usually left his bottle on his bath counter so he'd remember his bedtime pill. It wasn't out, though.

He reached to the medicine cabinet, thinking it might have mistakenly been put inside when he'd put his things away. He rummaged about the items, at first not seeing anything. Then, at the very back, hidden behind several other containers, was a small prescription bottle that seemed familiar. He grinned when he saw his name on it. He popped the lid and dropped one tablet into his hand. It seemed a bit odd that it wasn't identical to the tablet he'd taken that morning. Still, it was a shape and color that felt very familiar to him. Relieved, he popped the tablet in his mouth and swallowed it.

Anyway, he had other things to think about. This was the

last weekend at the summer house, and he wanted to get to bed so he could get up early. Tomorrow and the next were all he had until spring. The day after that, Monday, would be mostly packing to get back on the ferry for the trip home. He wanted to have all of North Haven he could squeeze in.

As he flipped on the water and stepped under the spray, he failed to notice the tingle still prickled in his head. It had relaxed a bit, become a trifle better, but on this night, it hadn't entirely gone away.

He had taken his medicine, so he attributed the continued feeling to being seventeen, being on his favorite island for the last weekend of the season, and to being very tired. He didn't consider that the odd medicine might be one that was no longer his current prescription. He hadn't thought to check the date on the not-quite-right bottle. If he had, he might have awakened his mother for the correct medication. He was careful about that.

Instead, he was very pleased that he'd been responsible, and after he toweled off, he tied his towel around his waist and stepped into a very cold hallway to head to his room. There was no heat in this part of the house, and he tossed the towel to the side and shivered as he opened several drawers before finding the one where his mother had put his flannel sleeping pants. As he slipped them on, he glanced at his reflection in the window, and he imagined he was watching an athlete get dressed before a big game. That athlete was Josh, and the continuing itch in his head had to do with the fact that it was *cold* in the room, his skin was still damp, and his hair was wet.

He threw the comforter back, and he slipped inside. The sheets were like ice, and before covering himself, he lay a moment, letting the cold in the air bite his skin. As he closed his eyes and began to drift off, he shook his head once. The tingle nagged at him, trying to tell him something. Before it could get its message across, he was asleep.

Chapter 5

THE SUN hung low in the New Hampshire sky. Bette swung her massive old SUV up the road and into the drive. She paused directly in front of the house as Merv finished up a joke, and then he and Leetha climbed out to walk up and sit on the porch. The SUV's exhaust rumbled as the big machine made its way around the massive old house to the detached garage at the back. After turning off the engine, Bette sat in the dimming light for a moment. What a Friday! She was tired, perhaps the most tired she remembered in a long time. The three of them had taken off and hiked up one of the local peaks for the afternoon. Bette had thrown out a name when Leetha had asked her, but she hadn't been sure. Flume or Liberty or Washington. The mountains were just *fun,* and Bette no longer cared about what they were called. She had hiked all forty-eight of the 4000-footers, and she took great pride in claiming membership in the Four Thousand Footers Club. She just couldn't keep track of all their names.

Her guests were waiting on her, despite the fact that the day had worn her down, and she'd need to see them to a late supper. With a click of the handle, she swung the door open and stepped down, wincing as a twinge in her bad knee screamed at her. She'd walked too hard, and then she'd sat too long. She would need to work it out, and making her way to the house would do that for her. If she were alone, she would use the back entrance. With guests, she felt the need to meet them at the front and enter at the main door. That was only gracious.

Stepping around the corner of the house, she smelled the early fall flowers still blooming. She stopped for a moment to rest her knee and ran her hand along the blossoms. Soon, winter temperatures would take all this from her, and the only flowers she would see would be those in her little greenhouse off the garage. She would miss these growing out in the open. Inhaling deeply, she felt refreshed, and she stepped in view of her guests to call to them.

"Merv, Leetha." She waved, and her smile was sincere, even if tiredness caused it to be a bit forced. "How about cold roast sandwiches washed down with cider? I have fresh apple pie, too." She pulled herself up on the porch and reached to unlock the door.

Merv laughed. "Bette, how do you keep going like this? I was just telling Leet here that I want a bath and my bed. You fix me that sandwich for breakfast. How about that?"

As they stepped inside, Bette turned to Leetha. "You, Leetha? Can I get you anything?"

Leetha winked at her. "I'm joining Merv in the bath. You must be tired. You head on back to your bed, dear. If we get hungry, I know your kitchen. I can cut a mean cold roast. Even after all these years, I haven't forgotten that." She squeaked when Merv pinched her in an intimate spot. She slapped his hand, hissing to him, "Not yet, Merv. When we get upstairs."

Bette laughed. "I was young, once. You two go and have a

good time. I'll have that sandwich for you in the morning, Merv. You'd better wake hungry."

After making her way to her bathroom, she sank into her tub, glad for the break. She was more tired than she would want her guests to know, but that was all right. It was when she had no guests that she had time to relax, even though relaxing to her might seem very busy to many people. Still, all in all, that was fine with her. She didn't like down time too much, and having people around the house was her way of keeping herself occupied. If she also liked the people who visited and could make a little money in the process, it was all icing on the cake.

Finally, dressed for bed and her head on the pillow, she breathed in the aroma of her clean sheets, and she was gone. She rested like she lived. All or nothing. Bette loved life, and she loved making life better for others, even if that meant she had to take charge sometimes. She was determined that grandson of hers would experience some of that, because he needed his grandmother's help.

She might not remember in the morning, but that night Bette dreamed of Rocky. She dreamed of his father, too, a man much like Bette, even if her son was a bit too refined for her taste. In her dream she gave that grandson the direction he needed, and he worked out his issues with his father. He also worked out some issues with Bette and that drunken lobsterman friend of his. Most of all, he worked out those issues that kept him from finding a girl. He did it all with Bette's help, because taking charge was what made life fulfilling for the old woman.

Besides, she wanted great-grandchildren, and only Rocky could give her those—and then only if he hurried up. For that reason, the dreams Bette dreamed that night were especially fulfilling, even if she might not remember a one.

THE OVERHEAD lights in the room flickered then came on at full brightness. There was a slight buzz from one at the back corner by the filing cabinets. John paused with his hand on the light switch and let his eyes search until he found the obstinate fixture. He would have to get a report turned in about that noise. It probably meant the ballast needed replaced, but even more importantly, with the cooling nights of the fall season, the noise would get worse before it went out. Much worse.

Even so, he would be in for only a short time this evening. The night before, the members of the Society had given final approval to the work to be done on Goose Rocks Light. He stepped forward and reached to the stack of papers on the table. Sliding several aside with a bare finger, he saw the man's name on the one he wanted. The letters were hard to read, almost as if the applicant had labored to form them correctly. One was even reversed. John hadn't been sure of this candidate, but Rand had clinched this in his mind.

Rocky Royster. *Rocky.* John tapped the form. *Rocky.* Somehow the sound of that name just didn't ring right to him. However, his brain could be mismatching that connection from anywhere, what with being a member of good standing of several legal organizations in Boston. He was also on the board of the Massachusetts Center for Children. A lot of names passed in front of his eyes. Still, Rocky didn't sound right.

Putting those organizations together was when the light went off.

"Royce Royster. How could I have forgotten?" He slapped his forehead with the palm of his hand. "He was still on the team when I joined the firm. He was the best, too."

He turned as he heard the door open. A voice called to him, "John, is that you talking to yourself?"

"Rand?" The man looked rather rumpled, and Rand usually didn't look rumpled, but after all, it was the weekend. If Rand needed some slack, now was the time to give it. John smiled, "Partied after we left?"

Rand ran his fingers through his tousled hair. He looked

down at his clothes and chuckled. "No, I forgot my gate pass to get into the neighborhood last night. I had to sleep at my son's place. When I saw your car, I thought I'd see if the pass is here." His eyes jumped around the room, and then his face brightened. "There it is. The association charges two-fifty to replace one of these. Two hundred fifty dollars for this simple little device. I'd rather spend that on a good bottle of wine." He held out the small wand for John to see, and then he slipped it into his pocket. He looked up to catch his associate's eyes. "What was that conversation about? I didn't see any other cars out front." He winked.

John laughed. "I realized I worked with Rocky Royster's father at the firm. It was years ago. You might remember, Royce Royster." He picked up the form with Rocky's name on it. "The name Rocky doesn't ring true. A nickname, perhaps?"

Rand glanced up as he pulled his car keys from his pocket. "His name's not Rocky. I thought you knew. Hey, you're on the board for the Center just outside of Boston, right?"

"The Massachusetts Center for Children, yeah."

"Sure. That one. This Rocky character attended there. All the way through. His full name is Rockland." He chuckled as if admitting a fault. "I had to look it up myself." He grabbed the door, and as he was exiting, he turned. "Are you planning to post that approval to him today?"

"Sure. Already called. The delivery service is meeting me here." John waved absently as he responded to the question, his mind once again on the applicant's forms he held in his hand. Rockland Royster, dyslexic, autistic, wunderkind star of the Center. He remembered, now. The name Rocky had thrown him off. The boy's father had been wealthy, or at least well to do for a lawyer. He had wanted the very best for his son. As John remembered, he'd tinkered with boat-building himself. He'd even kept models of several he'd built in his office at the firm.

John tapped the paperwork, thinking, Rocky Royster, following in his father's footsteps. A boat builder, and quite exceptional, if Rand was on a waiting list to get one. This might work out fine. Better than fine, even.

He smiled.

A knock intruded sharply into his reverie. He could see the brown uniform of a package delivery service through the fading light on the other side of the glass. The world was pink with the pending sunset, meaning high clouds to the west. He grabbed the approval forms and dropped them into an envelope. These would go into a thin, sealed box. The delivery service would have the package at Mr. Royster's doorstep the next morning, and then things would really start to roll. Once this was taken care of, John's weekend could start. It was about time, too. He'd been swamped with work all week, and he needed a break, a good, long break. His in-laws were coming. Yeah, in-laws. A break was definitely in the works.

THE SATURDAY morning sun broke through the previous night's clouds and crawled into Rocky's bedroom long before it was welcome. With no curtains, he fought its arrival with his bedding tugged tightly over his head.

A rapid series of knocks insistently jarred him awake.

He pushed the bedding back, hardly alert yet, and definitely not focused; and he peered through the living room to where he could see the offending front door, all the while scratching underneath a bare arm. He groaned. He was supposed to get out of bed for this?

The knocks came again, and he knew he had no choice. He blinked against the morning glare and yawned, dropping his feet to the floor and standing. As he walked by, he kicked the end of the sofa with the side of his foot. Underneath a rumpled, flowered blanket, Tram lay on his back with his arms stretched over his head. His hands hung off the end, and he was oblivious to everything around him.

Rocky growled to himself when the man continued to snore. The fool was right by the door. He could have gotten it, if he'd just wake up once in a while. Fish opened his eyes from atop the sleeping man's legs, and they followed Rocky as he crossed the room.

Pulling the door open, he blinked into the face of a man standing just outside, and he shifted his position to let the man's brown-suited body cut the glare rippling off the water past the boat shed. Tramwick's boat hunkered at the dock while his own small tender bobbed at the float.

"Yes?" Rocky's eyes were gritty, and his brain felt like death.

The brown suit chuckled. "I have a delivery for a Rocky Royster. You him?"

"If I say so, do I have to sign anything?" Rocky hated doing that. His letters were slow and clumsy, the writing of a stupid, dyslexic kid, and he hated for anyone to watch him when he wrote.

"Of course, sir. By the way, this isn't Royster, the boat builder, is it? I see the shed down on the water."

Rocky growled at the attempted pleasantry. "If I say I am, do I still have to sign?"

The man held out a plastic box with a small window, persistently pleasant. "Sure. Right here. *Are* you the same?"

Pushing the screen door open, Rocky took the device and moved the plastic stylus as if actually making letters. They couldn't be read. It was just a scribble, and he expected the man to give it back to him, to tell him he needed to do a better job. He didn't even look at it. Instead, he kept his eyes on Rocky expectantly, with a grin on his face.

Rocky stepped out onto the porch. "Cold out here." His eyes went to the supplies stored up on his porch rafters, and he took a deep breath. Now that his signature was inscribed into the plastic box, he could relax, and he did like people. It was all the stuff that went along with them that grated on him. "Sure," he admitted. "I build boats."

The man laughed. "Excellent! Wait until I tell my cousin I met you. He has a scale model of every boat you've ever built. He'll be so jealous. Royster Boatyard, and I've been here. Wow!" He held out his hand to shake. "Now I can tell him I've shaken the hand that's built every Royster boat that's ever been made."

Rocky smiled at the idea of this place being a boatyard. All along he thought he had a dozen acres that happened to front on the water. He hadn't even built the shed. It was already here when he bought the place, although he'd had to shore it up and reshingle it.

The man's hand still hung before him. A handshake was less pleasant to think about. Rocky paused for a moment to decide which was the proper hand to offer in return, then, with aban-don, he took a chance and reached out. When the man took it, Rocky was relieved to see he had offered the correct one.

"Glad to meet you. I'm Rocky, and yes, this is my boat-yard." He chuckled to say it aloud.

The brown suit shifted his plastic box to his pocket as he held Rocky's palm. "Chet Abramson of Boston." He released the grip and looked at his hand, as if the touch of Rocky's palm had imbued it with magic of some sort. "My cousin will be so jealous. Thanks, Mr. Royster."

"Just Rocky. You said you had something for me?"

"Oh, this." Chet reached under his left arm to a thin pack-age. "It's from the Preservation Society in Boston. From John Remington, himself. I picked it up last night. I've got other deliveries, so I can't stick around, but I'm sure glad to have met you, Mr. Royster." He grinned, adding, "Rocky."

Rocky's head spun as he accepted the package. He knew he was turned down, and he wished he hadn't applied. It was one additional bad thing to add to his weekend. He watched Chet skip, stumble, and almost fall, as he tried to run to his truck, while looking back at Rocky at the same time. Rocky returned the man's wave as he pulled away and finally disappeared down the drive. Turning to the house, he stepped inside, and the screen slammed behind him. He glanced to see Tramwick jerk awake at the sudden noise, sending Fish off and onto the floor. Stretching, the man threw the blanket aside and reached to run a hand over his stubble-shadowed face. Wearing only a rumpled pair of borrowed boxers, he sat up and scratched his leg.

"Jeezum Rice, it's bright in here. Why'd you wake me so early?" He coughed and then rubbed his chest. "Clothes." He dug around under the flowered blanket. "Where are mine? I never sleep in just underwear."

"Still where you left them, probably. You've slept on that sofa for two nights, now." Rocky glanced to the side where a set of crumpled, paint-covered clothes—borrowed from Rocky—hunkered in the corner. The previous day, Rocky had sorted his friend's mess from the boat shed, making Tramwick earn his board by painting the dock railings.

About that time, Tramwick noticed the underwear he wore. His words came out in a disgruntled jumble. "My underwear? C'mon, Rocky! I'm wearing yours for a second day? I thought you threw them in the machine." When he saw Rocky dip his head in a Yankee nod without speaking, he fell back on the sofa. "This is a pissah! And after I spent the day yesterday painting on your dock."

Rocky turned to the refrigerator and pulled open the door, reaching to tighten the light bulb when it flickered. "Your clothes are in the washer. If you'd put them in the dryer like I told you yesterday, you'd have real underwear to put on. I've got an appointment in Boston." He tossed the package he'd been delivered on the table.

"Boston? On a Saturday?" Tramwick yawned, reaching to scratch an area that was only marginally covered by the borrowed shorts. He caught sight of the package. "That's who was at the door? What's in it? Bills? Must be big ones to be delivered right to your place, and on a weekend."

"That's about right. You were awake all along. Fool." Rocky made as if to toss an overripe tomato at him, then put it back in the fridge when Tramwick cringed. "Something from the Beacon Light Preservation Society. Special delivery."

Tramwick slapped the sofa beside him as a pained expression crossed his face. "Ah, frickin' pissah! They beat me to it. That's why I came by the other night."

Rocky pulled a can of beer from the refrigerator and held it out to Tramwick. When his friend shook his head no, he exchanged it for a soda and tossed it across the room, instead. "So, Beacon Light Preservation sent you to get drunk in my boat shed?" He grabbed an orange juice for himself.

The popping of Tramwick's can answered the question. The next sounds were the curse words that followed the overflowing carbonation that surged out of the can and directly onto the borrowed shorts he wore. He leaped from the sofa, kicking Fish and sending him scurrying with protesting yelps.

Rocky laughed, distracted from the missive on his table. "That's twice in three days, Tram. That's rich! There are more shorts in the bedroom. Feel free to borrow as many pair as you need. Be nice to Fish, though. He hasn't peed anyone's underwear."

Tramwick shot Rocky a look of irritation. "Who peed their underwear? This is soda." He brushed at his dripping crotch, pulling the fabric away from his body. "It's cold!" He glanced accusingly at his friend.

Rocky snapped his fingers to call Fish, and then he knelt to console him. Talking softly to the animal, he rubbed his fingers around his ears, speaking directly to the dog. "It wasn't soda in old Tram's shorts the other night, was it, boy? It was something rather more stinky. Tinkle-drawers, we might call them."

72

He looked up, but Tramwick had disappeared into the bedroom. An arm and leg could be seen as a wet pair of shorts was flung across the room, and he could be heard searching through Rocky's drawers for a clean pair.

Rocky called loudly, "Don't leave the wet ones on the floor. Lay them across the tub. They need to dry. Remember to put your clothes in the dryer, if you plan on going out today."

Tramwick walked in, this time wearing black boxers with a large, yellow smiling face on the crotch. Stepping to the table, he picked up the package, looked at the address for a moment, and held it out to Rocky.

"You've got the lighthouse, you know." He reached to rub a hand through his hair, yawning. "Goose Rocks. That's what's in this." He tossed it back on the table before pulling out a chair and sitting down.

"You can't know that. I haven't even opened it, and it just came."

Tramwick grabbed the package and held it to his forehead. He closed his eyes and hummed. Dropping it again, he said, "Now, I know. The lighthouse contract is yours. Tomorrow we're going out there."

"Yeah, right." Rocky snorted his opinion of that. The man couldn't know he'd turned in his application. In any case, he had business at the Center. He didn't have time to argue this now. "We can discuss it later. Today I have to be in the city. Bette let an appointment slip until I don't have time to cancel it, and I need to drive in. Southborough, to be exact. Want to ride along?"

He got a laugh in return. "In my yellow, smiling face drawers? Remember, my pants are in your washer." He frowned, puzzled. "Although I'm not exactly sure why I've been wearing your clothes in the first place."

"Figure it out." Rocky downed the last of his juice and tossed the container in the sink. "I've got to shave and get out the door. Don't forget the dryer, or you'll be in that smiley face all day. I've got clean work clothes on the dresser. Wear 'em if you want."

"Thanks. I can find the dryer, I think." Tramwick was stretched out on the sofa again, with his drink held in one hand.

"Maybe." Rocky laughed, as he disappeared into the bathroom.

"BETTE, I'D like to take a gander at that boat your grandson's finishing up on." Merv took another slice of bacon from the platter on the breakfast table and put it on his plate. "It seems that boy's boats get more famous every year. Even some of us Texas folk have heard of him. He might even be rightly famous someday."

Bette waved his remark away. "Famous? Irresponsible. That's Rockland. His boats might get more famous, but he's all over irresponsible like butter on toast." She reached for the emptied bacon platter and reloaded it from the skillet on the stove. "Eat up, Merv. I'll cook up more when Leetha comes down." She winked at him.

"Who's irresponsible?" Leetha walked in the room, her fingers plumping her hair. She reached to tuck in an errant strand before sitting beside her husband. "Oh, Bette! Look at these dishes. These are more beautiful than a diamondback rattler's scales. Where did you find these? Merv?" She held up hers for him to see. "Did you even notice?"

He smiled, reaching to plant a greasy peck on her cheek. "I was saving the praising for you, pumpkin pie. You know how to brag so much better than I do." He was careful to look away before he rolled his eyes, but Bette caught the look, and she laughed.

"I found those in the attic." Bette was extremely pleased that her friend had noticed. "That's my wedding china."

"No," Leetha exclaimed, looking at Merv. "Her wedding

china. Well! It hardly looks used."

"First time," Bette exclaimed. "This morning's the first food that's ever sat on those plates. I found them back in the spring, and I thought of you two. Merv and Leetha, I said. They would love these. Besides, I'm so old, and I'd hate to keep them all my life and never set a place with them. My husband hated them."

"Well," Leetha exclaimed. "I love them. Don't you, Merv?" She elbowed him to encourage his agreement. Bette laughed when she saw the motion, and she wiped her hands and walked to sit at the table while the fresh bacon sizzled in the pan.

"That's all right, Leetha. He doesn't have to love them. You're right about the diamondback. That's the pattern." She flipped one over to reveal the words on the reverse side. *Diamondback.* She had insisted on this pattern when she was married, and she'd gotten her way. Then there had been the moving and the raising of the children. The china had never quite gotten unpacked. Last spring while cleaning, there they were, fifty-five years in the boxes and never opened.

"I loved these when I saw them in the store down in Boston," Bette said, running a hand over the textured diamond pattern running around the lip of the plate. "My husband never loved them, and somehow, family kept getting in the way of unpacking them. We always had aunts or cousins running these halls, and finally we stocked up on the melamine. Near unbreakable. My husband passed on, but the young'uns never did. They just changed sizes, and the melamine endured."

Merv cleared his throat. "No little critters running the halls now. Is that it, Bette? The dishes might survive?" He grinned and winked.

Bette paused, looking at her skillet on the stove. "Maybe. I love these old dishes, but I don't care anymore about whether they break or not. Broken things can be fixed. If all a thing's worth is how pretty it is, then something's missing. That's what

I've come to think. My granny had a saying that I still remember. It didn't make much sense to me as a girl, but now it does. *Pretty is as pretty does.* I used to think my granny meant that if a pretty girl was mean, then she really wasn't pretty. I've come to think it means if an item isn't useful, then how pretty it is means nothing."

Leetha's eyes twinkled, and she laughed out loud. She leaned into her husband's embrace as she cooed, "Merv, what about me? Am I all pretty, or do you find me useful, too?" She brushed her hand against his chest, playfully toying with his buttons.

The tapping of a utensil against the bacon platter drew their attention. "I know how you can be useful, Leetha. Get off that man and take this platter of bacon. It's part of your breakfast, and with all the antics you two were involved in last night, I'm sure the both of you need all the nourishment you can get."

The twinkle from Merv's eyes told her she was speaking the truth, and he pushed his wife up to take the dish from Bette's hand. "Eat hearty," he whispered. "There's more antics on the agenda for this evening."

Leetha caught Bette's eye, and she just smiled when the other woman winked. After all, this was a vacation, and that's what vacations were for. At least, it was part of the reason, and it might very well be the most important of them all.

ON DISTANT North Haven, one ray of sunlight managed to find its way into the rumpled mass of bedding Josh had crumpled around his body. It crawled across his face, and he immediately withdrew deeper into his comforter. He had a headache, and it felt like when he was a kid. He hadn't known what the headaches were then, as if they were a part of everyone's day. His were just there, and the medicine he took sometimes made them fade. However, they never went away. At least they hadn't until he started taking the new medicine.

Now, this headache was just like from before. The only thing was, he'd taken his medicine, or so he thought, so this must be something else. It was the cold, or he might be dehydrated. He got headaches sometimes when he didn't drink enough in the summer. That might be it. Or maybe he needed breakfast.

He knew one thing. It hurt this morning. What had been a tingle was now a church bell, and it was painful.

He decided that if he took his morning medicine, it might help, and so he threw the covers back. The cold in the room bit his skin, but he didn't climb back inside. He put his feet on the floor, making sure they were flat. He wouldn't let them rock sideways, although it would feel better if he did. When he got to the bathroom, he grabbed roughly in the medicine cabinet and opened the bottle he'd used the previous night. With a shake, one of the tablets fell into his palm. Throwing it back into his mouth, he bent over and turned the water on. Drinking as it ran from the faucet, he raised his head and swallowed.

Wiping his face on a towel, he realized he really needed to use the toilet. With a practiced motion of his hands and a quick release of muscles, he aimed the collected water into the toilet and automatically flushed when he was finished. His head wasn't feeling any better, and he went back to his room to find his way to his bed's warmth.

When he crawled inside, his feet were immediately warmer, and he pulled the comforter over his head to snuggle in. Sleep proved more difficult than he could imagine. His skin tingled, and his head throbbed. To top it off, he felt nauseous.

He lay very still. It had been a long time since he'd felt like this, and he was starting to remember. It had been that summer he was fourteen. He'd been here on North Haven in this very room. The difference was that Miss Bevier had been with him that time, and she wasn't here now.

He wished she was. He'd begun to understand what was

coming, and he wished with all his might Miss Bevier was here right now. He knew how bad this could get, and the implications made his head spin.

Chapter 6

LISA TURNED into the parking lot directly off the turnpike. It was early for a Saturday morning, but this was when the Center liked to schedule its follow-up visits. She understood, although she didn't especially like being the nurse coming in on her Saturdays off.

It wasn't as if the campus was vacated. There were numerous students and staff in the residential program, and they were here 365 days a year. It was the day program students who were missing. In comparison to the total campus population during the middle of the week, however, the campus was virtually vacated. She did see two teen boys on the basketball court. They wore hooded shirts, and she didn't recognize their faces.

She scanned the lot to see if she could spot a vehicle that might belong to Rockland Royster. She had no idea what he would be in and wasn't certain he'd ever called to confirm their meeting. It seemed his grandmother had contacted the school, assuring them he would be present, and that she would forward the letter to him. It he didn't show, perhaps she would use the morning to get some shopping done.

Lisa stopped her car in her customary space. She glanced at the gauge and noticed the gas was holding up well. Her old one had used twice as much, and even though it wasn't really any cheaper to drive this one when she factored in the payment, the fact it was new made it worth the cost. Unlocking the door, she climbed out and gently pushed it to. It closed softly, barely making a sound, and she breathed deeply, enjoying that it didn't have to be slammed like the old one.

Once inside, she made her way to her office, and she began to prepare for her meeting. She would be checking for neuro-muscular responses during the interview, although they were the simple kinds, ones that involved the tapping of knees and walking a straight line. She wished the Center would put that in the letters they sent out, but as it had been explained to her, many people wouldn't understand that the tests were noninvasive, and they simply wouldn't show up.

She hummed as she worked. She noticed a flashing light on her phone, but it was Saturday, and she wasn't here to answer messages. There were other things to do. She could make herself busy even if her interviewee didn't show. Other ex-students had skipped out on their interviews before, and it hadn't hurt Lisa one bit, not really. Besides, while the school was advertised as twenty miles from Boston, it wasn't twenty from Lisa's house. It was only a fifteen-minute trip, and the leaves were already starting to turn. She had enjoyed the morning's drive, and that made the trip driving in worth her while even if she had to turn around and go right back home.

If she did, "Rocky" could live without meeting her, and then she wouldn't have to have her dreams of him spoiled. She didn't really want that. After all, how could she dream about someone who wasn't even dependable enough to show up for a simple

Saturday interview? For that reason, she hoped he was very prompt. Then she would at least know for certain, and that she needed. To keep this man in her dreams, she had to know he was as dependable as she hoped he'd be.

ROCKY SAT outside of his house in his truck. The stress of returning to the Center, the place that had been the bane of so many years of his life, burned through him. He held his key in his hand, and he couldn't remember whether it went in the dash on the left side of the steering wheel or on the right. He looked but couldn't find the slot. A sense of panic brought perspiration to his forehead, and he lifted an arm to brush it away. He couldn't start the truck unless he knew where to insert the key, and he would be forced to tell his grandmother he hadn't made it to the interview. He took a deep breath and grimaced.

Forcing himself to slow down, he studied the house. He thought about rolling down the window and calling for Tramwick. His friend would know what he should do, but then he remembered he'd fallen back on the sofa wearing those yellow smiling face boxers. He was already snoring when Rocky had stepped out of the bathroom.

"All right, Rocky. You can do this." He took a second deep breath as he talked to himself. Sometimes that helped him focus his way past the stupidity that wouldn't even let him start his truck. "Don't panic. It has to be on one side or the other. Just *look!*"

He dropped the key in his lap, and he reached his hands to the dash. He felt along the surfaces, his pulse pounding when he couldn't feel an opening for the key. He knew there had to be one. When he bowed his head in frustration to rest it on the wheel, he wrapped his hands around the steering column. Like electricity, the totality of his stupidity shot through him. There, under his hand, on the column, was the ignition slot for inserting the key.

He slumped back in the seat. He knew it was because he was nervous, or he wouldn't have blanked out like that. Deeper within, he also knew what had just happened was one of the reasons he was at the Center all those years. He lived there for a long time, only seeing his parents two weekends a month. That was hard, those years filling him with a sense of abandonment. He'd lain in his bed, certain they no longer wanted him, and when it came time for his biweekly visits, he was convinced no one was coming to pick him up. Panic would set in, and it was the same as now. Obvious things would be gone from him, things he knew how to do. His brain simply went stupid.

Well, at least he no longer threw things or banged his head against the wall. He could chuckle at that, although he still carried scars on his forehead. Most were buried in his hairline where they couldn't be seen. Others were more visible. When his hair was fuller, they were easier to hide.

Picking up the key from his lap, he inserted it and started the old truck. At least it fired up with no complaints. It had been through many salty winters and might not look like much— quite the junker—but it ran well. He was also glad he'd unloaded it the night before. Leaving now, he was confident he could just make his appointment. After he was finished at the Center, he'd still have the day to get his chores done. He'd have to get them all done today, too, if he was to believe Tramwick. That lighthouse was all the way up to North Haven—Maine!— and visiting it tomorrow would eat a full day.

Pulling away from the house, he navigated around the rough places in his driveway. As he eased up to the road, he flipped on his blinker, only to glance down and realize he'd turned on the wrong one. He changed it, and then he pulled out onto the pavement. It wouldn't take just a few minutes to get to the turnpike, and then the school was just down a ways. He'd been on this path enough times during his years there. Now he was going voluntarily, and he wasn't sure just why.

JOSH'S MOTHER put down the phone. Her heart beat hard inside her chest, and she was worried. Miss Bevier hadn't answered, and the Center had assured her she was scheduled to be in her office this morning. She had an interview on tap.

She looked at the offending bottle of tablets sitting beside the phone. She'd gone in to make Josh's bed, assuming he'd already disappeared into the island's abundant, rocky shoreline recesses, exploring as he usually did, only to find he wasn't gone. She'd found a mound of bedding on the mattress, and in the chill of the room, she had thrown the comforter and blankets back to find him, blank and shivering. It scared her. Here on the island without the Center's immediately accessible medical care, she always worried that he would someday die. She ran her hand over his chest, grateful to find him at least breathing. That had taken the first shock off. He'd been cold, though, and lying too still to be well.

Covering him again, she tried to wake him. His eyes opened, and he tried to speak, but she hadn't been able to understand him. She recognized that he was having one of the partial seizures he used to have years before. She also knew where partial seizures went. Eventually, they translated into the full-blown, grand mal sort.

The one thing she had gotten him to tell her was that he had taken his medicine, both the night before and this morning. This bottle in her hand, however. She always put it in his bathroom, except yesterday she'd forgotten. It was on the kitchen counter, instead. It was still there this morning, right where she'd put it when they arrived.

She opened the lid. Turning the bottle, she shook the contents into her hand. Then, her muscles shaking with anxiety, she cast the tablets across the top of the desk. Were two gone? Josh was so good at remembering to take them, and she couldn't recall how many there had been before they left on the trip.

She counted them out, carefully moving them one at a time to a separate pile. There were sixteen. It was the same as the previous time she had counted, and the five times before that. Sixteen.

Picking up the empty bottle, she looked at the date and prescription instructions. She tried to reason out how many he would have taken since this bottle was filled, and how many should be left before it needed to be refilled. She kept coming up with fourteen, and she knew Josh said he had taken two. That totaled sixteen, so she should have only fourteen. But then maybe she was wrong.

She raked the tablets back into one hand and slipped them into the bottle. Snapping the lid on, she set it by the phone. Her husband would be up shortly, and she hoped he would know what to do. In reality, he rarely understood Josh. He was glad when he was away at the school. Craig wanted Josh to be normal, to be a son he could brag about to his own friends. He loved the boy as much as he could. She felt that, and she trusted it, too. He bought him things and tried to find ways to interact with him. However, he ran out of ideas quickly where his son was concerned, and this? She feared he would have no ideas at all.

She walked to her son's bedroom and sat on the edge of his bed. She pulled her sweater a little closer around her, and she reached to his forehead. This time he smiled at her.

"Mummy, hi." He shifted under the covers, his voice slurred. "I was walking on the rocks, and the sun was bright. I thought I might fall." He blinked rapidly several times, and then he continued, "My head hurts, Mummy. Can you call Miss Bevier?"

She moved her hand to rest it against his cheek, and her eyes glanced away so he wouldn't see the moisture filling them. "I already have." She felt the skin on his face crinkle, and she knew he was smiling at her response.

"Is she coming?"

She took a deep breath, and she watched through the windows for a moment. The sky had become overcast, and some of the clouds in the distance were very dark. An unexpected shiver ran down her spine. "I hope so, Josh. I certainly hope so."

"Me too, Mummy. My head really hurts."

She looked back at him, and seeing his eyes once again close, she ran her hand across his neck. Then she slipped it under the covers to let it rest on his chest. It was comforting just to feel his heart beating inside of his body.

He was so beautiful, she thought to herself. Too beautiful to have to deal with this. Young, also, although she could see the man coming out in him. When he was at rest, he was the strong and perfect son her husband wanted so badly. All the quirks and close calls were just a memory that belonged to someone else, and Josh was perfect.

Not this morning, despite his recent successes. His mother had already admitted that. This Josh needed Miss Bevier. If the Center could get her here, her son would be just fine. It didn't matter what it cost. They just needed her here.

JUST OFF Samelton where Chase turns to Pine. Chet had been asked to drop off the confirmation that he'd delivered the package to Mr. Royster, just to slip it in the mail slot, and since he had to be back in Boston anyway, he was on his way to make the return delivery to the Preservation Society.

Looking out to the waterfront, he noticed the weather seemed to be kicking up a day early. The forecasters had said there was a possibility that the storm brewing in the Atlantic might turn this way, but Chet had expected it tomorrow, not today. Otherwise, he'd have stayed home to batten things down.

Oh, well, he thought, as he began to whistle. He reached to the dash for his thermos of coffee. Maybe it'd move on up into Maine. If it didn't, Boston could take a good drenching without any real harm. Bostonians were tough, and the city had been through a storm or two. Another one wouldn't do any more than wet the city's whistle. That was something Chet liked about his hometown. It was tough.

Besides, he'd shaken hands with Rocky Royster, the famous boat builder. He had reached his hand out, and the man had grabbed it. His grasp had been firm, too, not like some lawyers' hands Chet had shaken before. No, Mr. Royster's hand had been made of the firm muscle of a person who builds for a living, and Chet liked that. That told him something, too. Chet met a lot of people in his job, and he had learned to tell a lot in a handshake. That Mr. Royster was a good one. Just in a shake, he'd been able to tell that.

JOHN'S PHONE rang.

He'd parked his car, and he was about to enter the subway. He normally didn't take the T, but he always carried his Link-Pass. Today, it would come in handy. He intended to put the metro rail line to good use, although he would try to avoid the El. No sense in getting caught up there. This being the weekend, he'd be able to get on and off the T without all the working crowds. He didn't expect to be inconvenienced in the slightest.

He dug in his briefcase and pulled out the phone. He saw the number on the display was Rand's, and he punched the talk key. "Hey, Rand. What can I do for you?"

"Have you been watching the sky, John? Maybe we should wait to send that confirmation." The voice was a bit slurred.

"What do you mean?" He glanced at his watch. He needed to get below, and he was afraid he'd lose his signal as soon as he did.

"The lighthouse, John. All that money. You know, Goose Rocks. What if it blows over?"

With a bark of a laugh, John looked around to see who might be watching. He hated his laugh, a short, honking sound he'd never been able to change. He was glad there was no one. "Goose Rocks blow down? Come on, Rand. Are you in a bar?"

"Course, John. It's Saturday. On the TV it says that storm in the Atlantic just shifted direction. Coming fast, too. Gotta move that lighthouse, John."

John could hear a clattering noise as the phone on the other end was dropped and then clumsily retrieved.

"Sorry, John. Hold that package 'til Monday. Can you do that?"

John could see how this was going to go. Rand was soused out of his mind. Besides, the paperwork had already gone out, and he couldn't call it back. He quipped to his friend, "Too late, Rand. What's done's done."

There was a pause and then a hiccup. "It's all right. I tried. Loss of a lot of money, though. My drink's coming. See you when the storm's gone."

The phone clicked off, and John paused to look at the sky. Out towards the water, it did seem to have grown dark. Maybe it would hold off until he got home in the evening. If not, he'd just pick up an umbrella at a shop somewhere.

He chuckled. Goose Rocks Light blowing over. That was a hoot. It was sturdier than the Old North Church, and the church had stood for nearly three hundred years. Get a grip, Rand, he thought, as he chuckled once again.

Then, the wind suddenly picking up, he tucked his overcoat around him and quickly stepped towards the subway entrance. At least he would be warm there. Dry, too, if this storm did hit. Rand had just warned him, and for the head's up, John was appreciative.

"I GOT THAT grandson of mine in here, but all I did was work him up. He doesn't realize yet he's just like his father. He sure bristled when I told him that." Bette worked open the door to the barn, swinging it wide.

Leetha stepped in and drew a deep breath. Then she smiled and let the air out, with a refreshed expression on her face. "Give him a chance, Bette. Boys have to rattle the corral on their way to independence. That's the way they are. All ours did. No matter how much they love you, they have to fight and claw until they feel they make a mark that's theirs alone. Often it's just like the one their parents made, but they won't admit it." She drew in another deep breath and closed her eyes for a moment. "Do you know how good it smells in here? We have nothing like this in Texas."

"You mean you don't have dust down there, or you just don't have New Hampshire dust?" She turned a quizzical look at her visitor.

"No, it's this place. We have mud and dirt and dust storms and tornadoes. We just don't have barns that are a century and a half old, ones filled with hand-built boats and the smell of varnish. It's just wonderful." She laughed. "Our barns are filled with hay and pies, the kind cows leave behind." Leetha walked over to the partially finished boat. "May I touch it?"

Bette chuckled. "I wish someone would. That grandson, preferably. However, I'd love for you to. Then, if I can get him to come around, maybe you can help convince him to finish it."

"He should. You say his father worked on this?"

"Better than that," Bette muttered, her voice suddenly pensive. Leetha looked at her questioningly as she continued. "They started this together. Rockland spent the whole summer here with his father one year." She used the name his father had called him, the only one her grandson was known by when he was a boy. She realized it revealed her irritation over the matter. She pressed her lips firmly for a moment, remembering. "He was probably fourteen or fifteen. I don't recall exactly, now. He was already strapping by then. His back was nearly as broad as it is now.

"I think that was the only summer he thought his father

really loved him. Rockland just knew that if he worked hard on the boat, made his father proud, he wouldn't send him back to the Center. That was his school, you know, down just out of Boston. Rocky hated it." She paused for a moment as the memories of the arguments about the school, the pleading not to go back, and Royce's determination that only the Center could help his son came back to her clearly. She could have helped her grandson, if her boy had just left Rocky with her. No, the mother and son had butted heads too often when Royce was growing up, and by then her boy had his own hardheaded ways.

Rocky hated it all, the conflict, the arguing, and the being sent away. He'd sometimes admit that what he really hated was something else. It was the feeling that sending him to the school was his father's way of showing contempt for a son who couldn't quite measure up.

Her face stern with memories, Bette slapped the side of the boat. Then she moved back to the door. Being in here with the past floating around, mixed in with more dust motes than any barn should contain, distressed her.

"He never hated that school, you understand. Not really. Rocky hated being *sent* there. He always felt he was being punished for his flaws, that his father was embarrassed to claim him as his own. Rocky could never see past that, and that's why this boat isn't finished. Someday, though, I'll get through to that boy. Then, this boat'll float in all its beauty."

Stepping outside, she realized the sun was gone, and clouds filled the sky. She turned to Leetha, "You hear about any weather coming in?" Bette had watched her forecaster before Merv and Leetha had shown up, and she hadn't heard about any clouds.

Leetha tugged the barn door closed. "One storm way out to sea. It was predicted to miss land. Seems not, now. You might ask Merv."

"Stay out to sea, huh? Good! This must be the trailing edge.

The clouds might make it cool the next few days. Hope you brought some warm clothes."

Leetha wrapped her arm in Bette's. "You might have longer winters here in New England, but we get our share. Ours just blow in real fast, then summer hankers back along, reminding us that it's not really a true winter like you have up here. I'm looking forward to your New Hampshire fireplace. Ours in Texas is useless most of the year. If it cools, I'll have no problem. And, yes, we did bring warm clothes. You don't worry about us." She looked up at the sky, and she shivered for a moment.

"You get just a slice of winter, not the whole pie." Bette found she could smile about that.

"We like it that way."

That brought a laugh from Bette. "About March, I'd like a little hankering, too, whatever that is. The cold gets old by then, and I'd take a bit of Texas in exchange."

"We do try to bring you some. Oh! I almost forgot. Your jelly!"

Bette gave her a hug. "Thanks for remembering. Merv's already given it to me."

These two were certainly good friends to her, and she would miss them if they found another place to vacation. She would also miss her jalapeno jelly, but she would miss her Texas friends even more.

LISA TAPPED her pen against the stack of papers on her desk. Her eyes glanced at the clock on the wall, and she wondered about the man who would be walking in her door. Her stomach twisted thinking how she would meet him at last, at least if he decided to show up, as he'd been requested.

Absently, she opened the folder resting next to the papers. There was his name. Rockland. Rocky, if she'd received good information all those years ago. Rocky Royster, a quite successful builder of boats. Rocky Royster, a frequent, brooding visitor to her late night dreams, too.

She slammed the folder shut, frustrated at herself for the heat she could already feel rising from her skin. She had dreamed of this man, and now he would be sitting here in this office with her. She would hear him speak, and his voice would be deep and resonant, she was confident of that. He would frown as he answered her questions, and she would be encouraging. Then his face would brighten. She would reach to touch his skin as she checked his eyes and his physical responses to certain stimuli, and her heart would pound her roiling emotions in an audible drumbeat. He would *know,* and she would be mortified.

She stood abruptly and walked to the window. Where *was* he? Where was this man she had in her files on her desk, this man she'd seen in person only once in her life? She noticed the sky had darkened since her arrival. It seemed that the tropical storm the meteorologists had aimed toward the open sea had decided to hug a little more closely to land.

Then she saw an old truck pull into the lot. It was beat up, and only one headlight was working. Surely not, she thought. The successful Rockland Royster? In that old heap?

When she saw the lights flick off and the door open, she laughed. It was indeed him, the man she'd seen at the ferry terminal all those years ago. The look on his face was the same, too, as if the clouds overhead were here to torment him alone.

His old truck was a relief to her. If he'd driven a flashy SUV with his company logo scrawled across the side, she would have been impressed, but she also would have felt intimidated. This broad-shouldered man walking through the parking lot in his black leather coat had a human element to him, one that was almost endearing. He looked a bit forlorn, as if he were a child who was being punished by spending a Saturday morning in detention. Saturday school. That was it. The look on his face was that of a child who had attended all the classes he could stand, and then he'd been told he had to do one more, stealing away his Saturday of freedom.

"Poor Rockland," she whispered into the room. Then she corrected herself and continued, "Poor Rocky. I shall have to be very nice to him." After all, what child deserved to be punished by an extra Saturday spent at school, even if it was with the congenial school nurse?

Chapter 7

ROCKY STOOD beside his truck, the door open, and he looked up at the familiar buildings. He drew in a deep breath. At least he hadn't made any left turns when he should have gone right. He'd only pushed his blinker the wrong direction that one time exiting his driveway.

At one window, he thought he saw a face. The clouds were moving in, however, and as the reflections flickered across the glass, he couldn't be sure. Glancing at the sky, he was aware there would be heavy weather before tomorrow, if this continued. Tram wanted to go to Maine early in the morning, but with the weather, today might be better, if he didn't get hung up here too long. It would be a good excuse not to stay. He could mention it would take all day to motor to Maine, and he couldn't be here long. His imagined option for escape infused him with a surge of anticipation. It was real, too; he was ready to get out and have a closer look at his upcoming project. And if Tram didn't want to stay, he could drop Rocky off for the night and find a berth onshore.

This thing at the Center, though, wouldn't go away until he did it, so he might as well get it over with. With a hard push, he slammed his truck door, knowing it would only catch if he put his weight behind it, and he began the torturous walk to the building. Between the truck and the door, with each dreaded step, the summer he was fourteen washed over him. He and his father had worked on that hated boat in Bette's barn all season. It wasn't hated, then. Rocky had thought they might even get it finished. When he realized it wouldn't be, he had seen glimmers of hope, the crazy-stupid hope that if it wasn't done, he'd get to stay in New Hampshire to help his father complete it. He'd *have* to. The prospect had been his lifeboat away from boarding school and the residential program at the Center.

Rocky's father had dashed those hopes. When the end of the summer break had come around, he summarily set the boat aside, telling Rocky it would be there another year. It was time to pack for school. He would be getting his old room from last semester. His teachers were expecting him, and he wouldn't want to let them down, would he?

Rocky had known, then. The summer had been a sham. His father had been bored, the boat wasn't good enough, and he wanted to get back to his life in Boston.

That year Rocky had threatened and cried. He'd wanted to burn the boat he and his father had worked on. Bette wouldn't let him. She had hidden all the matches in the house. He'd looked, hoping, only to have tears burn his cheeks in frustration.

The night before he was scheduled to leave, something had tripped in his brain, and he'd spent hours sitting in his bed, banging his head against the wall. His father had walked out of the house in disgust, leaving Rocky's grandmother to deal with her grandson.

Rocky had tried to beat those words out of his head. *"It's what's best for you.* " The Center wasn't what was best for him. Being loved by his father was what was best for him. That night, not even Bette had been able to help, and the Center was called. Rocky might not have been able to stop his head from hitting the wall, but he'd heard the words Bette spoke into the phone.

"Banging his head . . . won't stop . . . might hurt himself . . . please come. "

His grandmother had cried as he was carried from the house hours later. Her face was a postcard flashing before his eyes, as if she weren't real. He was so absorbed with needing to get his father's words out of his head, that all he could do was fight the hands that held him as he was bundled to the van.

Fifteen years had passed, and now he was walking into the Center on his own. He twisted his face into a semblance of a smile, but it was one of a sour realization that he didn't have to be here. He could have called this morning when he got up. Tram would have dialed the number for him. He could have even done it himself, if he'd taken his time and entered one digit at a time.

No, Rocky needed to prove he'd moved on past this. The old Rocky from age fourteen wasn't him, anymore. He needed to show this nurse that the Massachusetts Center for Children had been mistaken. That's why he was really here. He was present to make a point. He was no longer Rockland, the name on the letter that had been forwarded to him. He was Rocky, a boat builder who enjoyed what he did, and it wasn't spending time in school at the Center.

His muscular hand reached for the door, and the knob was cold to his touch. He shivered as he turned it. He felt a brush of cold air at his back. Turning, he looked up at the sky. It *was* darker. Then, the cold lifted, and the warmth of summer enveloped him once again. He shrugged.

"New England weather," he muttered. "Don't like what you get? Just wait a minute."

He stepped inside, leaving the weather to the world outside. Taking a deep breath, he looked around. He knew this building. He knew just where to go. He stepped off strongly down a hall and was several doors down before he realized what he'd done. He had *known* he needed to go the other way, and he had no idea why he'd turned this direction. He'd looked down the correct hallway, and then he'd walked the opposite direction. That was stupid of him. He wasn't dyslexic, anymore. He could see the way to go. He'd just gotten mixed up.

He turned around, forcing a smile on his face. He could find the correct office. He could see it just down the hall. Everyone made mistakes like that occasionally. At least no one had been in the hallway to see him. He was grateful for that.

LISA WATCHED the display on her computer. At the Center, staff members were each tied in with the central video monitoring system. There were twenty-four individual feeds she could see at any one time. Tapping any one would bring up that particular feed, filling the screen for closer inspection.

She tapped the foyer feed when Rockland stepped through the door. As it filled the screen, she watched closely. Her heart beat faster at the sight of this red-headed man here in the building with her. In her folder, his was the face of a boy who had just blossomed into adulthood. On her monitor was the image of a man who knew his place in the world, or who at least wanted to show that he did. She saw the hesitant look in his eyes as he glanced around the space he thought he knew. Her nurse's eyes were familiar with the autistic children under her care, and dyslexia run amok was right up her alley. This man's files told of all that, but to watch him was to see it boldly scream its presence in everything he did.

She watched his muscles shift under his clothing as he started to go one way, and then he caught himself to take a different direction. She watched as he walked away from her office, only to stop. When he smiled, his eyes changed. They weren't brooding any longer. His face brightened, and it was just like in her dreams. She would say something funny, and he would laugh. Then, for some reason or the other, he would take her hand. Her skin would flush, and he would tell her she was beautiful.

She reached up and snapped the monitor off. She did not need to see this. Peeping Tom. Tom-ette. Shame on her. She was fantasizing about a man who had once been a student at this school. She didn't know him, and had only seen him one time, if she could call it really seeing him. Caught a glimpse was more like it.

She'd have to contain herself during this interview, to be completely professional. When he arrived in her office, she'd need to take his temperature, and that might mean she would have to place her hand on his shoulder. She couldn't help that, but she could maintain a professional demeanor. As a nurse, she was required to monitor his heart rate. He'd have to let her check that, and his shirt would need to come off. He would, of necessity, be the one to unbutton the one he was wearing. His fingers would grasp the buttons one at a time, and the muscles in his hands would flex with the intricacies of the motions. His chest would be exposed, and as he continued, she would see his stomach muscles reveal themselves as the lapels of his shirt fell farther and farther apart.

Finally, she would see his navel, and there would be a swirl of hair there, hair that disappeared into the waistband of his pants. Then, his body would flex as he shifted the shirt over one shoulder, exposing the nicely rounded muscle that only a man who worked with heavy tools would have. As his shirt fell free, he would stand, exuding all the masculinity a man could have, and she would take his shirt from him. She would show self-control, and she would tell him she needed to test his reflexes.

Her hands would grasp his arm, and as she bent it at the

97

elbow, she would ask him to close his eyes and take a deep breath. Then she would place her stethoscope against his chest, and as she did so, she would rest her hand on his skin to steady the device. His skin would be warm, and her hands would be cold. He would take her hands in his, and he would warm them for her. Then, with the slowest of motions, he would lower his head and place his mouth on hers—

She jerked to her senses as the knob on her door turned. She realized she was very warm, and her shirt felt distinctly damp. This man was walking into this very room. She must be circumspect. As she stood, she turned and grabbed a tissue to pat her face dry. She had an interview to conduct, and all she could think of was how his lips would feel resting against hers.

Heavens, this was shaping up to be a tough consultation. It was going to be the toughest she had ever done.

JOSH'S FATHER stepped from the bedroom, fresh from sleep. He glanced at his wife on the sofa, and talking through a yawn, asked, "I thought the sun would be up by now. How early is it?" He walked to the window to look towards the water in the distance before turning back to his wife. "Sea's growing rough. Did you remember batteries for the weather radio? They were flat when we were here in August."

"Two tablets over." She picked up the bottle she'd been holding off and on all morning and held it up for him to see.

"Extra tablets? That's good, right?" He reached to touch the glass in the window frame. "Cold this morning. I'm glad this is our last weekend here. It's time to get that Andrew fellow up to close down the house."

"Andrew's not dependable. Remember last year? Try the Watkins boy." A frown creased her forehead. "Craig, this medicine. Did you hear what I said?"

"Sure. Two tablets over." He was preoccupied with the glass, feeling along the edges. "Maybe we need to have the windows recaulked. Couldn't hurt."

"Are you sure we cleaned out all the old pills from before? Josh is sure he took his tablets last night and this morning. Yet, there are sixteen here. There should only be fourteen." Her eyes opened wide with understanding. "What if Josh found some of the old medicine? Craig, what if Josh took his old pills, the ones that didn't work?"

"Surely not. We destroyed them." Glancing at the wood stove, he clapped his hands together. "We'll feel better when I get the fire going. Before next year, maybe we can get a real furnace out here and installed." He walked to the stove. Picking up the poker, he knocked it against the interior to jar off accumulated residue. He coughed when ashes flew back in his face.

"Craig! Stop that. Your son might die. Don't you care?"

He looked at her with a frown. "He's not out on the rocks again, is he? It's barely light. Remember when he sprained his ankle?" He shook his head, and he picked up a handful of kindling to toss in the stove.

"He's always on the rocks. You know that. Right now, he's in bed, and I'm certain he's been having seizures." She walked to the window and held her hand over her mouth. Her eyes were red as she looked out the window at the water in the distance. It was growing rougher by the hour.

He stood to get her attention. "Seizures? It's been years since he's had one. I thought he was over those. How could he be having seizures?"

She shook the bottle at him, her patience gone. "He's taken the wrong tablets. I'm sure of it, Craig, and I'm frightened. This morning he was certain he'd been out on the rocks already, and he's not been out of bed. He used to do that, imagine he was somewhere doing something, when he was by my side the entire time."

"Have you called the Center? We had that Bevier woman here before. Maybe she still works there." He reached a hand to brush the side of her face. "We can fly her to Witherspoon's airstrip. She was good with Josh. He liked her."

She wrapped her arms around him. "I have. I'm waiting on her to return my call. I'm really frightened."

"I know you are. We're all afraid for Josh." He held her. He had no other ideas other than to call the Center, and his wife had already done that. He never thought to go to Josh's room to see how he was doing. That was someone else's job.

TRAMWICK BRUSHED his hand against the head of hair next to him. The heat of another body as it warmed him slowly came into focus, and he tugged the bedding over them both. It was morning, but that didn't mean he was ready to get up, and he turned to the person at his side. Then, he felt a damp nose at his throat.

His eyes opened, and he jerked back, sending himself off the sofa with his arms and legs flailing. Landing hard on the floor, he lay there in Rocky's boxers, his morning desire for a woman fading as quickly as it had come on him.

Fish barked, and he leaned his head off the sofa to lick Tramwick's hand. The dog crawled forward several steps, barked again, and laid his head down, with his eyes following the man's every move.

Tramwick turned his head and realized he could just see Rocky's television. He felt with his hand on the coffee table until he had the remote in his hand and pressed the power button.

"Well, Fish," and he reached and rubbed the dog's snout, "let's check what's on. Weather, maybe?" After a moment, the image came up, and it was a children's cartoon show. He watched for several minutes, and then he began scanning the stations to find something to tell him what he could expect today. He finally reached a station that showed a red bar blinking across the bottom of the screen. It flashed a few times, and then words began scrolling. He felt with his thumb until he found the volume button, and he turned it up. A voice was overriding the regular programing as the words moved.

"Caution is advised. Tropical Storm Christian is moving nearer the New England coast. Those on the outer islands should prepare for high winds and heavy rainfall. Coastal areas should expect overcast skies with possible thundershowers. Keep tuned for updates."

Tramwick shifted his position to lean against the sofa, as he sat up. Rocky's boxers caught on the floor, and he tugged the waistband up. He looked around the room for his clothing and remembered the dryer. Standing, he rumpled Fish's fur before walking to stand in front of the window. He looked back at the dog and began to talk to the animal. "You know, Fish, Rocky had better get his butt back here. If we're going to that lighthouse, we'd better book it to get there. I bet anything the weather's going south tomorrow. Yeah, today's the day, or not at all."

He looked back out the window. There was a chop on the water, already. It wasn't bad, but the cloud cover out to sea was pretty heavy. Still, he had a good boat. It had been out in much worse. He grinned. Today's weather would be child's play, actually.

Whistling to himself, he absently reached and scratched under his armpit. He needed clothes. He stepped through Rocky's kitchen and into his laundry out in the ell. Resting his arm on the top of the machine, he leaned over, popped the dryer door down, and studied the empty cavity.

"Fish," he called. "No clothes." He turned his head, and the big dog was right there; a red tongue reached out and slipped along the side of his face. Tramwick stood and pushed the animal away, irritated. "You stop that, Fish. I pulled you out of that sea, and I can throw you back in. I'm not the pushover Rocky is. Now, show me my clothes. If you can do that, I might let you live another day."

At those words, as if actually understanding, Fish jumped up and put both paws on the top of the washer. Tramwick laughed. "You're kidding, right? You knew what I was asking?" He pushed the dog off and opened the washer. Sure enough, there were his clothes inside.

The first thing he pulled out was a pair of whitie-tighties. His eyes moistened as he looked at the dog. "Oh! Real underwear. I want my whities back." Farther in, he found pants and a shirt. Socks, too. "Hey, these are what I had on day before yesterday." He piled them on the top of the dryer and turned to Fish. "These are all wet, boy. I guess that was me Rocky was talking to this morning. *I* was supposed to put these in the dryer." With a sigh, he raked them onto the dryer door and shoved them inside. Hitting the start button, he heard the drum start to turn. Kneeling, he grabbed the dog by the ears, and he looked directly into his face.

"Fish, how did you know my things were in the washer? How are you smart enough to understand a question like that? You might be prodigy material. Say clothes, and you know."

At those words, Fish barked and forced Tramwick aside. Then he jumped back on the washer. Tramwick looked up, and he saw what was going on. Above the washer there were dog treats. He laughed and pulled several down, tossing them in the air one at a time to see the big, black animal jump to catch them.

Tramwick couldn't go out, however, wearing Rocky's boxers. He had to have something else on. He might be willing to continue to wear his friend's pants, but not his underwear. He needed to find something better.

"Okay, Fish. Clothes—" He was knocked backwards when the dog leaped against the washer. "No, boy. Clothes, me. Not food, you."

Fish barked repeatedly as they wandered back towards the kitchen. The dog grabbed an item from the dirty pile of clothes from the day before, brought it to Tramwick, and began shaking it in his teeth. Tramwick took it from him and tossed it back into the other room, to have it land in the hall. Tramwick studied the door that opened to the stairs, and he saw the answer to his clothing woes.

"Royce!" Tramwick gleefully clapped his hands together and grinned. He remembered some boxes of Rocky's father's things Bette had sent down several years ago. Tramwick had helped cart them upstairs, because Rocky had refused to deal with them. Tramwick bet they were still right where he'd stacked them, and he also bet he and Royce were about the same size.

Moving into the hall, Fish at his heels, he twisted the knob that opened to the staircase, only to have the door refuse to open. Upstairs was a no man's land as far as Rocky was concerned, and Tramwick guessed the last time the door had been used, he'd been the one to open it. At first he thought it must be locked, but Rocky never locked his front door. Why this one? It probably just needed a little persuasion.

With a yank, flexing his lobster-pot-strong shoulders, Tramwick forced the door wide. Taking the stairs two at a time, he got to the top and called to Fish, "Here, boy. Come on up." The dog peered through the door, and then in several long leaps, came bounding up. "All right, boy. Which box might have whitie-tighties? I need pants and a shirt, too. They've got to be warm. Do you think old Royce had any clothes like that?"

He looked along the hall. There were a dozen or so boxes. He opened the first. Business suits. Those wouldn't do. In the second there were shoes like a lawyer might wear.

It was in the next-to-last box that he found old-guy whitie-tighties. He immediately dropped Rocky's boxers and kicked them down the stairs. With an expression of bliss, he slipped on the more supportive underwear that he preferred. Then, in the final box, he found work clothes. He had known they must be here, because Royce had been an avid boat builder. He couldn't very well do that in a suit. Tramwick pulled out a good pair of flannel-lined jeans, thick socks, and several heavy shirts. They fit very well. A belt, maybe. He'd need one of those to pull in the waist a bit, but he'd seen one in the box with the shoes. Soon, he was dressed and fit for business, and all he had to do was find his heavy work shoes downstairs.

Calling Fish, he leaped down the steps. At the bottom, he kicked the boxers into the hall and closed the door. Then he spied his shoes, just there in the kitchen. With a hoot, he ran to slip them on, his heart beginning to pound in anticipation.

"Fish, let's go ready the boat. Then if Rocky gets back, we're on the way to Maine. I can't wait to get up there. Waves are kicking up, and the sea's a calling."

He was out the door before his words were done. Fish came bounding after him. The dog only went as far as the float, where he barked continuously at Tramwick as he clambered aboard his boat. Fish refused to go aboard, as many times as Tramwick called.

"BETTE," Merv started, and he paused, studying the landscape, as if just now seeing something that had been there all along.

Leetha and Bette looked at him, waiting expectantly. It was warm on the west porch, and they were taking brunch outside. The day was beautiful, and from this direction, there wasn't a cloud in the sky. It was a perfect end-of-September day.

Bette reached off the porch to a flowering bush, and she brushed the blossoms. The aroma wafted up to her nose, and she inhaled deeply. "This day with friends is what operating my bed-and-breakfast is all about. If I could bottle this, my winters would be oh, so much shorter." She closed her eyes and smiled.

Leetha prompted her husband, "Merv, what were you fixing to say?" She patted his hand where it rested on the table.

He leaned forward, and he cleared his throat. "Bette, I've seen a lot of little critters come up around our place back home, and I mean the human kind. Space. They need space, and the good Father knows, you've got tons of it. An oilfield full."

"I've got enough to keep me busy, that's for truth. Go on, Merv."

"Well," he began, "your boy, Rockland." He looked up at her, and he twisted his napkin.

"My grandson. He's my grandson, that Rocky is. But sometimes I like to think of him as my boy." She smiled.

He grinned. "Your grandson. He went to that school in Boston. What did you say it's called? The Center?"

"The Massachusetts Center for Children, but we usually call it just the Center. Why is that?"

"All those kids. I was just wondering. Of course, it's none of my business, except I think kids are my business, since Leetha and I raised so many of our own, but those little buckaroos probably need a little room to roam."

Leetha laughed. "Bette, I'm catching on. What Merv's trying to say—"

Just then, an enormous gust of cold air came sweeping around the house and across the porch. The tablecloth whipped up, and there was a tinkling sound as a goblet fell over, rolled off the table, and shattered.

Leetha cried, "Bette! Your glass!"

Merv quickly raked the items he could reach into his hands, and he stood. "Bette, honey, you get the door. We'll help you get all this in."

Bette stood and opened it for him. "This way, Merv. Thank you, Leetha." When they were past her and inside, she stepped back to roll the tablecloth and place it on the floor just inside the house. Closing the door and sealing the sudden breeze outside, she laughed at Merv and Leetha's windblown look as she pulled her hair back into place. "That's New Hampshire, for you. It knows September's slipping away, and it wants to keep us on our toes."

"Bette," Leetha had walked to a window on the east side of the house, "are those clouds darker than they were earlier?"

Merv leaned in behind her, and he was certain they were. "I think so, dumplin'. You, Bette? You know this weather up here better than we do."

Bette laughed. "It's almost October. The coast is bad sometimes, and we can occasionally see the weather from here. It's nothing to worry us." Then she began to sort the things from outside, stacking them in the sink.

"Can I get a broom? I can clean up that glass outside." Merv hovered nearby.

"Let's get this put away. I'll sweep the porch later." Bette ran the water for a minute, rinsing the bottom of the sink. Her repeated glances out the window, however, belied her casual remark about the weather.

Still, right now she had guests, and they were her priority.

She finally turned to Merv. "You have a Texas-sized heart. You know that? You and Leetha, both."

"And what's that for?" Leetha grasped Bette's arm, patting it warmly. "And thank you, no matter."

"It's what Merv asked about my place. I'd love to have those children from the Center up here. It's a long way, despite what I want, and sometimes other issues get in the way."

"Honey, for love, it's never too long a way. Not even Texas to here." Leetha let go of Bette's arm. "Right, Merv?"

"You're right," Bette responded, before he could answer. "Merv, I'd love to have a house full of children again. Mine, yours, the neighbors'. Anyone who wants to run through these doors. I do miss that, you see." She stood for a moment, and she was quiet. Her eyes were moist.

Then, she brightened her face. "However, I have you two, and this week is perfect. The weather seems to have stirred up outside, but I have a game of dominoes waiting in the front room. Would you like to play a good game of forty-two?"

That was a favorite of Merv's. "Bette, I'm so pleased that you remembered. Hog-tie me if you're not the best hostess ever!"

LIKE ALL good hostesses, Bette knew her clientele. That was why people came back. People like to be special, and knowing what they like and don't like makes them feel that way. Bette was good at that.

It was trying not to worry about her Rocky that she wasn't so good at. What happened at the coast did sometimes make it to New Hampshire, and if it made it all the way up here, well, her grandson got it first. After all, he did live on the edge, right on the water. He was down there, and with those clouds, he wasn't likely to have a very good weekend.

THE SMELL of the interior of the nurse's office washed over Rocky, and the memories flooded back. He'd spent time here, and it hadn't always been pleasant. His illness; other things associated with a nurse's office; especially, he thought, when that person attended the Massachusetts Center for Children.

However, there were other memories, too. He could admit that there had been people at the school who'd cared about him, although that was something else he'd had to bury, along with everything else about the school. Mrs. Earle who had sat by his side for hours, as he tried to excise his father from his head. His coach, a man whose name he could no longer remember, who taught him that to dribble a ball was to learn to talk to a girl— slow and easy, one idea following after the next. Then there was Mr. Foster, a man Rocky had wanted to take the place of his father for the longest time. Mr. Foster had moved on, to a job somewhere in Toronto. Rocky had been left behind again.

These memories surged through his mind, and they immobilized his muscles. His emotions were compromised, and he couldn't bring himself to walk through that door. He stood, frozen, a man of two worlds. He was Rocky Royster, a successful boat builder, long absent from this school environment, and he was Rockland Royster, a fourteen-year-old who had just suffered a bitter betrayal from a father whose love he desperately needed to feel. Then, a voice broke his ice, and he was abruptly himself again, one in his body.

"Mr. Royster? Is that you? If so, you may come in."

With those words, a very pretty face appeared and took the door from him. The giant slab of wood moved away silently, the knob floating from his outstretched hand.

"I'm Miss Lisa Bevier, and I'd like to speak with you for a while. Thank you so much for coming in on Saturday." She smiled at him. Her tone was more intimate than he expected. The extra warmth was just the right thing for him. It somehow charmed him, and that he hadn't anticipated.

He coughed. "Yes? Miss Bevier? Miss, you say?"

He felt himself warming around the face, the sensation starting just above his collar and creeping ever higher the longer he stood there. He immediately knew how stupid he'd sounded. It didn't matter if she was a miss or a missus. She was a nurse at this school, and he'd be on his way as soon as he showed her he was strong and independent, no matter that he had once attended here a long time ago. This school no longer had anything to do with him. All he had to say was that he had a business meeting he couldn't miss this afternoon, and would she mind cancelling the appointment?

Then, he noticed she had her hand out to shake his in a greeting. He looked at her, and he glanced at his hands. Shaking was a stupid way to greet people. If he knew it was coming, he could choose a hand and have it ready. Yet, to be caught off guard, that was unfair. He stared at his hands, and he didn't know what to do. Left? Right? The same as she was holding out, or was it the opposite? He felt panic rising inside, and he couldn't breathe.

Then, she spoke to him, "Mr. Royster, I can see you have your keys in your right hand. Here, let me shake your left, instead." She smiled, and she immediately switched hands.

He looked down, and his eyes found the hand with the keys. He was to use the other one, his left. He looked up and held it out, trying to smile. He knew it must look forced, and he couldn't hold it. He looked away as embarrassment welled up inside, making his eyes burn. All the frustrations he'd thought so cleanly pushed aside were there just below the surface. Just this little scratch, and the old wounds were opened again.

LISA HAD done that on purpose, and she hated it as it was happening. It was a standard opening for someone with severe dyslexia. Autism, too. It was a way to test the person's coping skills without appearing to have given a test, just like the cameras in the corridors. Observation without appearing to observe. It was something the staff were trained to do.

She watched him as he reacted, and she saw the clinical things she was expected to observe. There was more, though, and as she invited him to have a seat, she also observed things that had nothing to do with the Center's evaluation. She observed his strong jaw line, the broad shoulders that seemed to reflect plenty of muscle underneath his black coat and flannel shirt, and a sense of grace in his movements, an ease of motion that superseded the awkwardness she had forced from him when she'd asked him to shake her hand. She also noticed how his skin felt against hers, and it was like an electric current, forcing her heart to race ahead of her mind.

She also noticed his question. *"Miss, you say?"* Those words were interesting to her, indeed.

Chapter 8

LISA'S MOTHER sat at the kitchen table, and she pulled her robe tighter around her. A small television chattered in the background. Its remote was on the table, and it was one that Lisa had special ordered for her. The numbers were large, and the buttons were spaced far apart.

The remote had nothing to do with her eyes. She had excellent vision. What she didn't have were excellent joints. Arthritis had eaten at them, and she couldn't manipulate the small buttons that came with most television remote controls.

She wasn't really paying much attention to the television. It was the paper she held in her hand. It had been placed separately behind several others on the table. Even partially covered, it was obvious this was one of the forms Lisa had been looking at the previous evening.

It was so unlike her daughter to be disorganized. Just to leave one when she had taken the others with her to the Center today? Her mother didn't think so. Her daughter had set this one aside purposefully, and there had to be a reason why.

It showed the boy who had attended the Center. Rockland Royster. This was the page showing him during his final year. His picture was at the top. There was a darkly handsome look to his face, even with the red hair and brooding expression. She would give him that.

Lisa's mother knew her daughter. When she'd taken her position at the Center, she'd done so even though there'd been other, more lucrative offers on the table. With her nursing credentials, Lisa could have taken a position almost anywhere—major hospitals, long-term nursing facilities, or even in private practice. However, she'd been enamored of the children, and the Center was the only real option she had considered.

Then there had been that fiasco with Andrew. He had torn her daughter's heart from her, at least the part that was interested in life outside of the Center, and now, Lisa was content to adore her damaged children, then come home to spend the evenings with her invalid mother. Andrew had done that, and even her mother's promptings hadn't convinced Lisa to step outside that shell she'd built around herself.

This man, though. He was her daughter's age. Also, that brooding expression on his face did make him strangely appealing. Listed on the paper were the commendations about his success in the school's programs. In Lisa's own meticulous printing at the bottom was a note that he was a successful boat builder, and that he went by the nickname Rocky.

She laid the paper aside and smiled as she rubbed the swollen knuckles that told of her damaged joints. Throughout her body, the arthritis had attacked her, but it was her hands that pained her most. She had so loved to sew, and that was no longer an option for her. She had a machine, now. Lisa had seen to that. It wasn't the same, despite everything. She could no longer stitch the designs, the embroidery that had made her creations

111

so special. Why, even the pearls on Lisa's own wedding dress! She'd so wanted to do those herself, and her hands had been unable to manage them.

As her eyes glanced back at the paper, she knew one thing. Her daughter had an interest in this man, and it was an interest far and above that of an interview with an ex-student from the Massachusetts Center for Children. His face was quite nice in his picture, but he'd have been seventeen or eighteen at the most when it was taken. Add ten years to those features. Lisa's mother reached to run a finger over the face. She imagined a sharpened feature there. A laugh line, or at least she hoped so, would form at the side of his mouth just there. There would be small creases at the corners of his eyes.

She touched the forehead that brooded so, and in her mind's eye, she brushed the hair aside. Her finger smoothed the crevasses between his brows, and she pictured a glint of amusement in his eyes. His skin would be roughened by the sharp, New England winters, and he would carry a new sense of character in those features, one that it was impossible for an eighteen-year-old to have earned.

This was a man she could picture for her daughter's husband. Maybe, Lisa, she thought, as her eyes studied the image she'd made of the picture. Maybe you've found something here. Be nice to him, my girl, and see if you can reel this one in.

Then, she laughed at her musings and turned her eyes to the television. Touching her phone, she turned the ringer down several notches so her program wouldn't be disturbed. Absently reaching for the remote, her thumb touched the outsized buttons, feeling for the one to change the channel. About that time, a special bulletin flashed on the screen. A meteorologist appeared and began talking to her television audience. Lisa's mother reached for another button, and she held it as the sound increased in volume.

"As you can see, this secondary storm system that was

expected to veer east and dissipate in the North Atlantic has abruptly changed course. We are monitoring its progress closely as it heads toward Tropical Storm Christian, currently safely out to sea, traveling north up the coast. Should they collide, Christian could be forced directly into the New England coast. Will this intensify Christian into a Category 1 hurricane? We are unsure at this point. Stay tuned to this station for further updates on the hour."

Lisa's mother turned the sound back down, and as she stood to look out the window, she noticed the darkened skies to the east. At least her home was on the west side of Boston. If the storm did hit here, the house was strong. It had weathered many storms, and it would weather this one. If Lisa got back early enough, she might be wise to go out and purchase a small generator. The last big storm had knocked out the power for nearly a week, and everything in the fridge had gone bad. It would be nice to at least save the food.

Opening the door and stepping outside, she saw a neighbor across the street, and she waved. Gathering her robe about her, she made her way to the mailbox. She saw there was nothing there and realized it was too early for the postal carrier. Glancing up, she noted the roiling pattern in the clouds. There was no rain, but it sure smelled like it.

She hurried back inside. It was cooling off, too, and the day was barely started. If this storm hit, it might be bad. She'd endured a lot of bad weather in her lifetime, and this storm didn't feel the least bit good.

TRAMWICK SET the engine cover aside. The boat rocked with the swells coming past the stone breakwater that protected Rocky's small section of the coast. With the heavy cloud cover, the air moving in from over the water was cold. He glanced back at Fish, who continued to run up and down the float, determined to warn him just how dangerous it was to be on a boat that was suspended in the water. The float was bad enough, but to actually be on a boat?

Fish barked louder.

Tramwick called out, "I'm safe, Fish. You can quiet down, now." He reached into the engine compartment to check the oil, and he muttered to himself as he did so, "You're getting on my nerves, dog. Five more minutes and either I'm heading out for more whiskey, or I'm drowning me a big, black dog." He looked over at the animal, and he snorted as he pulled the dipstick out. He'd have to add a touch, he saw. He put a lot of hours on his engine, and in rough weather, he used it hard. Maintenance was the key, and he was meticulous about that.

Inside a storage locker, he found a quart oil container. It was partially empty, and what was left seemed about right to add this time. He opened the filler cap and carefully poured in the thick liquid. Wiping a drip with his thumb, he absently cleaned it on his jeans, on *Royce's* jeans, and capped the empty container of oil.

Closing all that he'd opened on the engine, he reattached the cover and leaped to the float with the empty oil container in his hand. Fish snuffled at his feet, his voice quieted, as if glad to find Tramwick safe at last, the survivor of a great, risky adventure on the open sea.

Tramwick dropped to the dog's side, and he wrapped his free hand around Fish's neck. He dug his fingers into his fur as he whispered in his ear. "I need gas, boy. See just there? Just by the breakwater there's a fueling station. How about you ride over there with me?" He stood and chuckled. That would put the fear of God in the dog if anything would.

"Stay," he told Fish, and with quick steps, he was up the ramp, throwing the oil container in the refuse bin, one he'd built into the dock especially for Rocky. Then he turned to look down at the dog below, waiting patiently on the man he adored, listening for him to release him from his command to stay.

Tramwick's eyes narrowed wickedly. He glanced at the water stretching to the fueling station, and he looked back down to Fish. With an ominous chuckle, he headed down the ramp. It was time Fish learned to use his water legs again. He could pee all over the boat, and Tram wouldn't care. It smelled like a lobsterman's boat, anyway, and it could be hosed off. With Rocky gone, who was there to complain? A dog? Fish? Who would listen to Fish, anyway?

He called to the dog gently as he stepped down the ramp. He would need to take him by surprise. Lifting the dog would be no trouble. He was only a hundred pounds, one-twenty soaking wet, but if the animal spooked, that would be a different matter. It was holding him on the boat as he got it started and out on the water that would be the challenge. He had his lines to untie, the engine to start, and then he had to get away from the float, all without Fish jumping off.

Kneeling to play with the dog for a moment, he held him under one arm as he reached to the cleats to gently toss the lines back onto the boat, setting the bow line free first. Then he walked Fish to the stern. Holding the boat with one hand, and pleased the waves were pushing it up against the float, he ran his hand roughly up and down Fish's rib cage.

He leaned in, "Ready, boy? It's time to go for a ride."

With a sudden motion, he tossed the line in and grabbed the dog with both arms, lifting him off the float. He gave a powerful leap, then both of them were aboard the boat. Fish began to flail, and Tramwick latched a hand onto his collar, as he dropped him to the deck. Reaching to start the engine, he grinned as Fish started to wail his desperation at the trick that had been played out on him.

Pushing the throttle forward, the boat leaped forward as Tramwick released the big dog from his hold. Fish backed into a corner and trembled. Suddenly, the expected odor of urine permeated the craft, and the man laughed out loud.

"Scared the pee out of you, did I, boy? Welcome back to the sea. Here's where I found you, and you need to learn to love this. Watch!" With a quick twist of his hand on the wheel, the bow of the boat swung to starboard, and then equally quickly, it made a leap to port.

Letting the throttle off, he felt the boat settle until it rested in the water, and he knelt to the big dog. Grabbing the animal's face, Tramwick looked into his eyes. "Are you over your fear, yet? You've got to tackle what you're afraid of, you old sissy, or it'll always keep you down."

At those words, Fish seemed to relax a bit, and his tail even began to wag. As Tramwick reached to push the throttle forward once again, Fish stuck his nose out of the protection of the cockpit. As soon as he caught the smell of the ocean, his ears perked up, and his tail lifted. He turned to look at the man who had done this to him, and it was almost as if gratitude could be seen on his face. He was enjoying this, finally.

Tramwick watched him, and he could see the glee on that furry muzzle. He *was* a water dog after all, and he'd just needed to be given the opportunity to remember that.

As he pulled up to the fueling station, Fish didn't even try to leap from the boat. Instead, he ran back and forth on the deck, barking as furiously at the man's abandonment of him on the boat as he had earlier at his fear that Tramwick would drown by being aboard a floating deathtrap. He wanted Tram back aboard, and when they were underway again, he stood at the stern, letting the brisk airflow whip his fur back and forth.

Fish, it seemed, was glad to be back aboard, and he seemed to remember something he had forgotten for a long time. Being at sea was a good thing, and being on a good lobster boat made it even better. Tramwick was glad for that. He loved Fish, and now he might get to spend some real time with him—and possibly even lay claim to him as his own.

ROCKY WAS flustered. He hadn't expected to find this nurse here. Oh, a nurse, yes, but not this. She was warm and friendly. She was pretty, and she had even shaken his hand.

That had thrown him for an emotional loop.

He recounted the meeting so far, determined to keep events firmly sorted in his mind. When he'd first smelled the room, he was taken back years. The drowning feeling of fourteen had drenched him. Abruptly, the sound of her voice interrupted that. It hadn't been cold and calculating, the bored voice of a woman being forced to give up her Saturday for Center business. It was familial and encouraging.

Then, he'd looked in her face, at first furtively and quickly, expecting a matron, then with eyes that were unable to tear themselves away; her appearance had caught him off guard. He had acted stupidly when he'd shaken her hand, but then he'd been holding his keys in his right hand, hadn't he? Anyone would have been confused when she'd asked to shake.

The touch of her hand, though. For a moment, time had seemed to stand still, and he was able to think only of her touch. In that moment, he'd forgotten he was an ex-student of the Center returned to prove he'd grown past all this. He was just a man whose heart beat wildly in his chest and whose pulse pounded in his temples with the drumbeat of physical attraction. He never wanted to let go, and he'd felt his knees go weak. His body had simply *responded* to this woman he'd never met before. If she hadn't broken the touch, he felt sure he would have pulled her to him just to feel her against him.

Outwardly, he was sure he appeared calm. However, inside he was very frightened. He'd always steered clear of personal relationships with women, fearing they would know him for what he was: flawed; a mere shadow of what his father had been; unloved; cast out to grow up far away from his family. This woman was an employee of this school, and she would know him for what he'd been. It would be in his records, and he couldn't erase that. He would simply be a cipher in her notes, someone she had come to interview on an increasingly stormy Saturday morning. When he left, she would file him away, and he would be forgotten. He'd better remember that, because she wouldn't be interested in him in the slightest.

"Mr. Royster, are you with me? I asked you a question."

He looked up to see her peering at him with a smile on her face. She was still beautiful. He tried to return her smile, but he knew it was weak in comparison.

"Rockland? May I call you that?"

That did catch his attention, and it wasn't a positive thing. A frown crossed his face before he could wipe it away. In fact, when he heard that name, he didn't *want* to wipe it away. His reaction was as automatic as his earlier response had been to the touch of her hand.

"I hate that name. *Rocky*. Rocky's who I am now. Please call me by my real name."

THE FEROCITY of his response surprised Lisa. At least now she accepted the name he preferred. Josh's parents had been correct. She looked down and let a smile ghost her lips, quickly quelling the expression. She pulled a paper from a folder on her desk to give herself a moment to recover. She wasn't likely to get to the bottom of his reasoning in this interview. She would have to simply accommodate him.

"Rocky, then. How are you? Please call me Lisa. This is a voluntary follow-up interview only. You've been out of school for ten years, and the Center does like the opportunity to track the success of its ex-students." She looked up and smiled gratuitously. It was part of her training for these interviews, and although she felt butterflies in her stomach, she was able to remember that. "We like to evaluate the success of our programs this way. Could I get you to fill this out for me, please? Just the top section, if you don't mind. You can use the table just here."

She slid the paper to him and placed a pencil on the top. Quickly, she walked to look out the window. As she had handed him the form, the dismay on his face was obvious, but the requested action was another way she could observe him without seeming to do so. The degree of his continued battle with his dyslexia would become apparent both in how well he read the directions and in the actual writing he did on the paper. His frustration level would reveal how well he had outgrown his autism, or at least how well he managed to cope with it, to divert the impulses and integrate his feelings into acceptable channels.

Once at the window, she did turn to glance at him, to see how he was doing. She found she couldn't easily look away. In that moment, as she watched him, it occurred to her that she could have possibly looked him up on the Internet. She could have easily found out information about his current life. As a prominent boat builder, surely he would be there.

As she saw his hand holding the pencil, she realized he was gripping it tightly, more so than a person normally would. With a start, she saw his eyes jump to her face, and he attempted to smile. There was the obvious glint of moisture beading on his skin. Then, his brows knitted, and he quickly looked back to the paper.

In an instant, the pencil shattered in his hand, and he stood, a portion of it still between his fingers. His eyes looked around frantically before he visibly calmed himself. She watched him take a deep breath before he spoke.

"I'm sorry. Coming here was a mistake. I'm very sorry I took up your time, Miss Bevier." Looking down at the portion of the broken pencil lying on the incomplete form, he dropped the remaining piece of shattered wood on the paper, and he glanced to the door. He caught himself and corrected the name he'd used. "Not Miss Bevier. You asked me to call you Lisa. I'm sorry." Then, without another glance in her direction, he stepped toward the door and disappeared.

She looked in dismay at where he'd stood. He was just *gone*. She had dreamed of this man, he had come and shaken her hand, had even spoken her name, and then he was gone. Like that!

She walked to the paper and picked it up, brushing the broken pencil to the side. She looked at what he'd labored so arduously to write. It was his name and his address. He'd even put his phone number . . . all written perfectly in reverse. She smiled for a moment, knowing if she were to hold this to a mirror, every letter would be perfectly formed—backwards.

Quickly she rushed to the window to see this man one last time. He was walking to his truck. She blinked rapidly as her eyes moistened, realizing how much this one act must have taken out of him.

He opened his truck door. He stood there for just a moment before climbing in, and he stared back at the building, his look almost wistful, if Lisa could believe that, as if he had hoped to find something here, and he had walked out without it.

She didn't know what that might be, but as he climbed inside and closed the door, his headlights came on. One came on, anyway, and the truck began to move towards the turnpike. Just then, several splats of rain hit the Center's window. It was only a few drops, and while Lisa stood for a moment expecting more, the rain had already passed.

As she turned away, she realized her relationship with this man had been just like that rain. It had grown in anticipation, splattered for a few moments of interaction, and then he was gone.

Finally, she laughed. She couldn't fix this man's issues, not if he wouldn't cooperate. That wasn't what this meeting had been about, anyway. Besides, she would never see him again. He wasn't her concern.

However, her heart continued to beat faster than she would like over this simple few minutes out of her morning. She breathed deeply, attributing it to the abruptness of Rockland

Royster's departure, *Rocky's* departure, or maybe it was only the upcoming weather. Yes, she decided, the weather must be making her nervous. After her pulse settled and her hand no longer quivered, she took the paper he'd written on and printed her own words neatly across the top. *Interview terminated, incomplete and unsuccessful.* Then she slipped it in his file on her desk. It was time to go, and at least he had wasted little of her time.

The blinking light on her phone caught her eye. She glanced at her watch and decided she might as well listen to the message. How long could it take? It would be one less thing to do Monday morning, and she would be glad of that.

Lisa reached to her phone and picked up the receiver. With one long, beautiful finger, she reached to the button that flashed its desperation to her. She listened into the earpiece as a mechanical-sounding voice began to speak.

"To retrieve your current messages, please enter your password and press the pound sign. You may enter your password at any time."

She sighed, and she pressed the four digits that made up her phone password. Then she reached for the pound sign. The phone system at the school was very convoluted to operate, but she guessed she should be used to it by now. A new set of instructions came at her over the line.

"Thank you. To retrieve new messages, press two. For saved messages, press three. To start again, press four . . ."

She sighed a second time. She reached a finger to press the number two. Her pulse quickened once again when the next words were spoken. This time she knew the reason.

"Miss Bevier? Lisa? This is Josh's mother here on North Haven. You remember? Josh Reynolds? He's having an episode, and he wants you. Please . . . call me back as soon as you get this."

After that, all she heard were sobs.

ROCKY PULLED off the turnpike at the first place he could find. He pounded one fist against the steering wheel. His eyes were moist with frustration, and he knew he'd botched everything back in that room. He hadn't done what he had set out to do, and even worse, he'd found the nurse, that *woman,* virulently attractive.

He took a ragged breath, and he leaned his head back. Closing his eyes, he tried to calm himself. He'd let no one close to him, and he hadn't felt these emotions pouring over him in this manner since he was sixteen. That was the year he first kissed a girl. He was home for the weekend, at Bette's, not his father's, and the girl lived in the next town. There was a dance, and at the start, the grownups had taken the floor. Rocky had gone with the girl outside where the night was warm. They'd stood shoulder-to-shoulder just talking, and before long, he'd found his hand under her shirt. Then, in a quick motion, his fingers had been on her breast—her bra, really—and his lips had been pressed against hers.

His body had screamed its sixteen-year-old need to him, and he was sure she could hear its cry. It was certainly loud enough. Then, the music had stopped, and it was time to go in for the teen dance.

He'd made a fool of himself inside, his feet unable to find left and right, and she'd laughed at him. Mortified, he left the dance and walked all the way home to Bette's. He lied to his grandmother, telling her the dance had ended early, and that he'd had a great time. That night as he climbed in bed, it wasn't the dance he remembered. It was the touch of that girl's lips.

He felt exactly the same now. His body was betraying him, betraying *him*, and he had to admit he didn't know this woman. Opening his eyes and shaking his head to clear his vision, he reached to the truck controls and slowly pulled back into traffic. He hoped that when he got home, Tramwick had decided to put some clothes on. He might be Rocky's only friend, but a friend wearing nothing but Rocky's underwear was just too much to think about right then.

Besides, he needed to get to the lighthouse. He didn't care about the weather. The rain had splattered a few drops against his windshield, but then it had stopped. Tramwick wouldn't be deterred by a few raindrops. If he was, then he was a sissy, and sissies needed to be brought into line. That, Rocky could do for a friend. He could do it and mince no words in the process.

So, Tramwick had just better get ready. Rocky was on the way. They had a lighthouse to visit.

JOHN'S PHONE rang. He tapped the answer icon and put it to his ear. He reached for a French fry, and swirling it in catsup, he held it up, ready to put it into his mouth.

"Yes?" he asked.

"John? This is Trish. Are you on your way home, yet?" The voice had a bit of a whine to it, and John winced.

"What is it, sweetheart? I told you I'd be most of the day. You do remember, don't you?" Actually, he'd said he had a few stops to make. He'd wanted the rest of the day. His in-laws were scheduled to visit. He went ahead and popped the fry into his mouth and began to chew.

"I've been watching the news. The weather keeps coming up, and it says terrible things. Have you watched it?"

He could cover that. He grinned, although he knew she couldn't see it. "I talked to Rand. He rang me up. He's heard all about it, and I told him I'd buy a new umbrella. However, I'm as dry as a house mouse holed up in a wall." He laughed and picked up another fry. "I'll be home later."

"I've made my green bean casserole. You haven't stopped for lunch, have you? John! I told you I was making my casserole. You're eating, aren't you?"

"Just a quick snack. You know I rarely come into Boston on

123

the weekend. If I can take care of everything I've planned today, I can stay home next weekend. Baby, I'm doing this for you." He licked one thumb, and then he reached to his plate to wipe a large dollop of catsup onto his finger. He brought it to his mouth.

"What are you doing in Boston that you couldn't take me? I haven't been to town in weeks. I'd like to go with you sometimes."

"Your parents, remember, Trish? They'll be at the house with you all day."

"John!" She was clearly whining, now. "Didn't you listen to what I said? The news! That second storm is coming. When they collide, it might cause a real hurricane. John! You have to learn to listen."

"Trish? Two storms? What do you mean?" His ears perked up. Rand hadn't said anything about a second storm.

He heard her sniffle over the phone. "I'm scared, John. What if that tree in front blows down? I told you we should've had it taken out. It's already rained once."

"How much? The basement isn't wet again, is it?" This conversation was taking his appetite from him, and he pushed his plate away. He reached his hand into the air to signal for his check.

She was suddenly muted. "No, it just splattered on the glass, that's all. By the way, I told my parents they shouldn't come. With the storm, they might have to spend the night. They said they didn't mind, but I know you. I didn't tell them you don't like it when they stay over, just that it would be better if they didn't come. Was that all right?"

He dropped a twenty on the table and stood. He grinned at her words. He could cut his day short and head home if her parents weren't going to be there. All of his errands could wait. He'd just wanted out of the house for the day. He spoke into the phone, "I'll be right there. I have to catch the subway back to my car, but I'm on my way. You'll be fine until I get there, won't you?"

"I think so, if it doesn't rain anymore. Did you get your letter mailed to that man with the lighthouse?" The relief in her voice was evident.

"Yes, Trish. Last night. I had a courier come and pick it up. It was supposed to be delivered first thing this morning."

"John?" Trish's voice was once again full of foreboding.

"Yes? What now?" He felt a cringe creeping into his tone.

"He won't go up there, will he? Not this weekend with this storm coming in?"

John actually laughed at that one, relieved. "He's a smart man. He builds boats for a living. He knows the sea, and he'll be holed up safe and sound far from the water. You don't have to worry about him going out in this weather."

Her voice was very small as she asked one last question. "You didn't already give him the key, did you?"

"There's no key. It's a lighthouse, and it's in terrible repair inside. That's why he's renovating it. We'll put a lock on it *after* the work is done."

Trish could be such a trivial person. The things she sometimes asked about were beyond him. Her best attributes came out at night, and if her parents weren't there, they might even come out early. For that, John was fully prepared to make his way home as quickly as possible. Then, if a storm hit, they wouldn't even notice. They'd be stirring up one of their own.

Chapter 9

JOSH'S MOTHER jumped when the phone rang, and she looked at her husband. She had convinced him to go into Josh's room with her, and at her encouragement, they had brushed their hands against the boy's face and arms. He was so grown-up. He'd been sleeping again, and when he didn't wake, they'd left him alone.

The phone rang again.

"Answer it," Craig prompted.

She reached for it, and she slowly wrapped her hand around the receiver. With her eyes glued on her husband, she raised it to her ear.

"Mrs. Reynolds speaking." She held her breath, not sure who was at the other end. At home she had caller ID on her display, but here on the island, cell phones with their video displays were useless. The house phones were old, and there was no such luxury attached to them. She wouldn't know who was calling until the person on the other end spoke. Her face melted into tears when she heard the voice she needed to hear.

"It's Lisa Bevier, Mrs. Reynolds. Something is wrong with Josh?"

Josh's mother just sobbed, and her words were unintelligible. Her husband took the phone. "This is Craig Reynolds. Lisa? May I call you that?"

"Mr. Reynolds. I was surprised at your wife's call. Josh has been doing so well."

"Craig, please." He coughed into the phone, pausing as he phrased his answer. "I'm sorry, Lisa. My wife feels there's been a mix-up in Josh's medication. Josh is asking for you. There's no one on the island to help."

"Mix-up? What symptoms has he shown?" She paused for a moment. "Isn't there a full-time doctor on the island, Craig? I'm in Boston, and it would take hours for me to get there. Have you called him?"

He paused, and he looked at his wife. "Lisa, I'm sorry. I defer to my wife in matters concerning Josh, and she's insistent that you be the one to come and help. Besides, I trust you, too. You were here several years ago for a month, and you were exceedingly good with the boy. So, please, for Josh. On the island, there's an airfield near the house. I can make arrangements for you to fly up. The cost will be ours, and we'll get you home afterwards, for work on Monday if you wish. For Josh?"

HIS VOICE pleaded, and it sounded as if it were for Josh. Lisa knew Craig as well as his wife. After all, she'd spent a month with them. Clearly, this man loved his wife very much. Lisa suspected Craig ultimately cared more for his wife's distress than his son's. However, he did ask, and very nicely, too. And, if she could be back by Monday, then what was the harm? Some time on the island would be a welcome break from her disaster here at the Center.

She looked at the clock, and then she looked at her watch. The time was the same, and she didn't know why she looked at both. Habit, she guessed. She'd have to call her mother. There was no other reason not to go.

"Is Josh having seizures? I'll also need to know what medications he has with him." Her voice paused, and there was silence on the line for a moment. He had several he took, but only one for seizures. In a rush, she continued, "Oh, never mind that. I have his school files here. I also have a full set of his medications. I'll bring what the school has. You might call the island doctor just in case."

Josh's father let out a sigh of relief. "Lisa, if you'll go to the Marlboro Airport, I have a friend who can fly you here. She's based at Minute Man, and she can fly out of the airport there and meet you. Although, if you think Minute Man is better for you, I can have her wait there."

Lisa had to wrack her brain. She knew where Marlboro was. The airport should be simple to find. Minute Man was bigger, she thought, but the location escaped her.

"Marlboro, I think. It will take me half an hour, maybe more to get there. I have to gather Josh's medicines." She was already unlocking the cabinet where the medicinal supplies for the students were stored. She reached to the section reserved for Josh. She raked them all into a small satchel with a long strap that went around her neck. It was one she always used for transporting the students' medications. Made of the best quality, it was waterproof when sealed up.

After she finished her arrangements and hung up, she dialed her mother. Not receiving an answer, and not surprised since she often turned down the phone to watch television, Lisa just left her a message.

This was turning into quite a weekend. She grabbed her keys, Josh's medications, and headed outside to her car. It was when she stepped through the front door and looked up that she began to doubt this mission of mercy. The clouds were very heavy, and she remembered the rain on the window earlier. That *man,* and she gave a shudder of irritation, that man who had come to meet her and then run off had even turned on his lights before driving away. This wouldn't be a summer vacation experience. What did she expect? It was the last weekend in September, and this was fall. Pretty weather was a dream for next May. Perhaps Mr. Reynolds could arrange to get her back to the mainland this evening, if Josh's situation wasn't serious.

For now, though, she had a job to do, and it started in Marlboro, Massachusetts. She had transportation offered to her, and the Center would pay her for her time. After all, this was school business. Josh was one of her students, and she would be there at his parents' request. Josh's request, also. With a surge of empathy for the suffering seventeen-year-old who had so recently become an athlete, she considered Josh's request the one most important to her. Even if his parents hadn't offered to pay, she would have gone for Josh. He was her shining star, and she treasured him very much. He mustn't die. If she had to give up her weekend to prevent that, then it would be a weekend very well spent.

TRAMWICK WAS on the porch when Rocky drove up, and he was already dressed in his best slicker. Fish was beside him. There was rain spitting from the sky, and the water off the dock was dark. As soon as the truck stopped, Tramwick ran to open the door.

Rocky glanced at him with a sour expression on his face. He'd seen the weather worsening. He wouldn't even make it to the lighthouse this weekend. This hadn't been a good morning, not by any stretch of the imagination, and he needed food. He had no idea what Tramwick wanted.

"Rocky, let's go. You'll never believe this. Fish is a water-dog again. He has his sea legs back. I've got food on the boat, and I've even refueled. We have to book it, now."

Rocky glared at him. "Go where? And what's this about sea legs? Fish? He hates the water."

Tramwick pulled his friend from the truck. "Come on, I'll show you." He looked at the sky, and then he looked guilty. "Your slicker is on the boat. Sorry, Rocky. I didn't think. Oh, and I'm wearing Royce's clothes."

At that, Rocky took a deep breath to steady himself. Just the mention of his father's name was a taste of his past and how he'd felt abandoned. However, they were just clothes. His father was dead, and seeing them would tweak no memories in Rocky's brain. After all, how much time had he actually spent with his father? Almost none. Tram could wear every item Bette had brought down for all Rocky cared, as long as he cleaned them out of his house.

"Sure, Tram. You're welcome to them all. Now, where are we going?"

Tramwick stepped onto the porch out of the rain and turned to his friend. Reaching to rap him on the forehead, he squinted at him. "Now tell me who's been imbibing the whiskey a bit too much. The lighthouse, my friend."

Rocky frowned. "Lighthouse? Did you listen to a word I said?" He reached his hand to the water falling from the sky, and he shook it off in his friend's face. "That's rain."

Still, he remembered how he'd desperately wanted to go as he left the Center, and he looked longingly at Tram's boat. He'd also watched the clouds darken. As he'd driven in, he had bet himself Tram was still wearing his boxers while sitting in front of his television, lazy as the day is long.

Tramwick grinned wickedly. "Let me spell it for my struggling friend. L. I. G. H. T. H. O. U. S. E. Sometimes we shorten it to Goose Rocks, but that's just for us normal lobstermen, the ones who like to drink lots of whiskey when we're ashore."

Rocky finally felt his impatience melt, and he laughed.

Tram was in rare form today, and when he was like this, he was hard to redirect. "Can I at least leave my good coat inside and maybe get something to eat?"

Tramwick stepped off the porch and into the rain. "You can put your coat inside, but there's no food left in your kitchen. I packed it all in the boat. I figured you'd want to spend the night, so I have some kerosene, a lantern, and a heater. I'll drop you off and come back in a day or so. Or a week." He cackled at that as he began to head down the walk.

Rocky was already out of his coat, and he tossed it through the front door and onto the sofa. Before closing the door, he called, "Food for Fish. I have to leave him food."

"No, you don't. He's going with us." He pointed a yellow arm. "See? Waterdog! He's headed to the boat. He knows, and he's excited. Come on!"

Rocky took off at a run through the gathering rain, getting to the boat about the same time as his friend. Reaching into a locker, he took out a slicker and some boots. Pulling them on as he stood, the boat lines were cast off, and he gazed in amazement at Fish standing in the cockpit alongside them. Tramwick started the engine, and with a smooth surge, the craft began to push through the darkening water and out to the open sea.

Rocky knelt to Fish, and he grabbed him behind his ears. The black dog looked at him happily, his mouth open, and his tail wagging. Rocky questioned Tramwick.

"How'd you do it? This morning he was afraid of the rain. Now, he's happy to be here on your boat. Witchcraft?"

Tramwick patted the dog on the head. "Nah. He just loves me. We had a little talk, and we worked things out. Didn't we, Fish?"

Rocky watched as Tramwick flipped on the wipers. As they passed the breakwater, he could feel a distinct increase in the chop of the water, as it slapped against the hull of the boat.

"How long do you expect we'll be?"

Tramwick grinned. "Hours, friend. Hours and hours. We're on the water. That's what's important. I've got two hundred gallons of fuel, and we're on the way to Maine. The sky's spitting at us, and the waves are just right for a good ride. Man, there's no better life. Tonight, you're sleeping in a lighthouse. You are one lucky dog." He turned to Fish. "No offense intended."

Rocky chuckled. "All right, I'm along for the ride. There's one problem. I haven't been given a key to the lighthouse."

Tramwick slapped him on the shoulder. "Don't need one, friend. I checked. It's just sitting there, waiting for you to come enjoy."

Then, he looked ahead, and reaching to the throttle, he pushed it forward.

The rain hit Rocky in the face, and it was cold. However, Tram was enjoying this. The heavy weather made it that much better for the lobsterman behind the wheel. He decided he might as well enjoy it, too. It didn't seem he had any other choice.

THE LIGHTHOUSE stood in defiance of a century of nature's wrath. Its foundation was wrapped around bedrock that erupted along the sea floor, a fist of stone that thrust up to broach the surface of the sea at low tide. The lighthouse's sturdy footing both gripped the smallest of ridges as well as extended deep toes into the earth's surface. Its superiority against the onslaught of the sea had never been successfully challenged. Goose Rocks Light stood supreme, a symbol of protection warning ships of all sizes of the dangers skulking just below the surface of the Thorofare.

However, inside, rot had set in. One hundred years of storms had worked their tendrils into the sparkplug lighthouse. During the blistering gusts of wind driven by the sea's wrath, slender ribbons of water had writhed their way through the iron casing. Repeated wetting of many of the interior surfaces had severely rusted numerous joints in the beams that held the floors aloft. In other places, the metal flooring plates that had held strong for a double handful of decades had developed weak spots in their oft-painted surfaces, with rust bubbling through the multiple layers of protective coatings. Infrastructure that had been constructed of the highest-caliber materials had endured for tens of years against the onslaught of water and salt, as well as rodents seeking refuge from storms that would at times wash them from the shores of the nearby Fox Islands. Now, they suffered the ignoble disgrace of time and decay.

For years, the lighthouse was inhabited, and for many more, it stood vacant. Then, purchased by the Preservation Society, it had become a home once again, albeit a rustic one, for those who would be a keeper for a day or a weekend or a month.

On beautiful days, its worn interior shimmered with the light reflected off the sea, and in summer, the cooling breezes kept its outside porches and catwalks inviting. Always, there were the sounds and smells of the waters of the Fox Islands Thorofare. The views of both Vinalhaven and North Haven were as pretty as any ever seen.

During winter, the islands were coated with the brilliance of snow, and the seas pounded the base of the lighthouse. It was frigidly cold inside. Rarely did warmth brush the frozen surfaces of the lighthouse's bedroom walls or the wood that covered its metal floors. It was the automation of modern science that kept the warnings flashing from its beacon above. It was the concrete-filled caissons that kept it attached to the ocean floor below. It was the care of the Beacon Light Preservation Society that would keep it standing for many years into the future.

Now, it needed that care, and that was why the contract had been awarded to Mr. Rocky Royster, boat builder extraordinaire. When he arrived, he would find that there was no electricity, and the plumbing was in abysmal condition. Wooden floors laid over the damaged metal ones were no longer safe to walk upon, and the glass in the windows rattled under the blast of heavy weather's fury. Cast iron and steel trusses needed to be refurbished or replaced. This bastion of safety that was balanced in the crux of two islands and surrounded by many more needed to continue to stand, and to do that, it needed the touch of a man's hand.

The lighthouse needed Rocky Royster, and unknown to its stone walls, concrete foundation, and rotting wooden floors, help was on the way. Within a matter of hours, a rescuing hand would touch the double ladders that led up to the lighthouse's door. Light would once again shine against the damp stone walls, and heat would seep into the cold floors.

Yet, before more decades could once again grace this wonderful slice of history, the lighthouse had to stand strong against one more storm. Even though the men who were on their way didn't know it, the combined storms that would assault the Fox Islands were already headed their direction, and the spitting rain and the sea's merciless chop were only the tip of the proverbial ice-berg.

The forecasters had already made their determination. Both of the storm systems thrashing the summer-warmed Atlantic waters would collide. This would be a full-blown hurricane forced directly into the Maine coast, and Mother Nature would do her worst. In distant television studios, the warnings were already being prepared.

The lighthouse was strong, though, and it had laughed at storms before. It would laugh at this one, also, and it would offer its protecting embrace to anyone who dared the waters of the Thorofare to shelter under its roof. That would be the challenge. Safety could be found inside, but getting past the shoals upon which the lighthouse was built would be very difficult. Only those who were desperate would dare to approach Goose Rocks during a storm.

LISA WATCHED the sleek aircraft land. The props slowed,

and their rapid chop died in the air as the rumble of the engines took over. There was the continual burp of engine noise as the props sliced gently through the mild rain, pulling the craft across the tarmac.

This was no tiny puddle jumper. It might be small in comparison to the large jets that flew out of Logan, but she had expected a two-seater, one with a single prop and room for the pilot and herself. The outside alone told her this was a luxurious craft. Once it came to rest, the side of the plane opened, dropping down to form a stair into the interior. A woman leaned out to wave to her.

She was glad she'd grabbed her spare raincoat out of her office at the Center, and she always kept an umbrella under her seat in the car. Rain during New England's fall and winter seasons was more apt than not. Today was proving to be very apt. She checked that she had her satchel with Josh's medications, and she began to walk briskly toward the waiting craft.

This was a simple airstrip. There was no tower, and as soon as she boarded, she assumed they would be aloft again. Craig— *Mr. Reynolds*, she felt more comfortable saying—had suggested as much, as had the men in town when she stopped and asked for directions. As she boarded, she greeted the woman at the door. She hadn't expected an attendant for this unscheduled flight to Maine.

It turned out she wouldn't have one, either.

"Miss Bevier?" The woman reached to shake her hand. As Lisa grasped it, she was aware of the last time she had shaken another person's hand. This woman's grasp was much firmer than she expected, but it was very cursory and businesslike. There was no secondary layer of warmth that spoke to Lisa's emotional heart.

Earlier in the morning, that man's touch—Rocky's touch— had been entirely different. His had been the touch of electric fire, the flash of a storm's lightning through her skin, and she'd felt drawn to him, inexplicably drawn to him. She knew love couldn't happen in so short an interaction, but in her long-ago sighting of the man, she'd formed some sort of connection with him, one that had followed her through the years. He'd once been a notable student at the Center, giving her a point of reference with which to identify when she caught her glimpse of him. It made him somehow real to her, and then she had dreamed of him.

She never thought she would meet him, not until his name was shuffled to her for his follow-up interview. Then she'd shaken his hand. In that meeting of skin, her thoughts had gone all a jumble. In retrospect, she guessed the fire wasn't so inexplicable after all.

She'd found him to be quite handsome, just as she'd imagined, and he had that strong jaw line. His shoulders when he sat hunched over that form in her office were very muscular. Even when he stood at his truck before driving off, she'd seen a look on his face that had called to her.

Then, when he cut short the interview, disappearing from her presence with no explanation, she intentionally cast him aside, disappointed in his abrupt departure. She had felt an immense loss that this man's presence had been gifted to her and pulled away again, but she easily accepted that she would never meet him again.

This woman's touch was just that, a touch.

"Good morning." She smiled at the woman. "I hadn't expected to have a flight attendant."

The woman laughed. "Oh, you don't. I'm your pilot, Mary Jorgensen. You'll be alone in the passenger cabin, so choose any seat. You picked quite a day to head up to the islands. A storm's blowing in. A bad one, if what they say is true."

That concerned Lisa. The feeling of danger wasn't enough to refuse this request to help one of her students, but it concerned her, nonetheless. If a storm truly attacked the islands, she didn't want to be stranded there. She had nothing with her except what she was wearing, her phone, and Josh's medications.

"We'll be safe, both going and returning. Right?" She set her things in one of the seats and began to remove her raincoat. She checked her pocket to make sure her cell was off before letting Mary hang the coat.

The pilot laughed. "Going, I feel confident about. Your return? I can't vouch for that." At the look of concern on her passenger's face, the pilot continued, "I'm only flying you in. I won't be staying. I understand there's a water taxi, the Equinox, that will be ferrying you back to the shore, Rockland, I believe. There's an airport there, or you can rent a car, perhaps. The Reynolds can help you take care of that. This plane's time is too valuable to let it sit out on the island. Also, I understand the airstrip is very small. It'll be tight for me to land, and I'll need to be away to clear the space for other craft. I'm very sorry. Is there anything you need before we're off?"

"I'll be fine. What's our flight time?"

Mary smiled as she sealed the outside door. "In this? It's a guess. Half an hour, if I could fly like this plane's designed to go. Plan on an hour, at least. Don't forget to buckle up. Safety first, you understand."

The pilot disappeared into the cockpit as Lisa snapped her seatbelt around her. Almost immediately, she heard the pitch of the engines increase, and through the water-spattered window at her side, she could see the prop on the wing blur into nothingness.

With no one around her, her thoughts were drawn to one word Mary had said. It was no more than the name of a town, one she'd been to years before. However, it was also the name of a man she had met only that morning, and she wasn't putting him aside as easily as she thought she might. He'd written everything on that paper backwards. *Backwards!* He'd been so frustrated by it, that he had stormed out of her office with no explanation. No, she corrected herself. He hadn't stormed. He was polite, and he apologized for taking up her time. He exited quietly, and she was left with her day to spend as she wished.

His reaction to his frustration was what had impressed her most of all. This was a man who had made a name for himself in a field he had conquered as his own. Renowned would even be a good word to describe him. He was renowned within his field as a consummate craftsman. Yet, he hadn't been able to write his words correctly, and he'd apologized for taking up her time.

Lisa leaned her head against the headrest as the treetops of Massachusetts dropped away beneath her. Andrew wouldn't have done that. Andrew *hadn't* done that. He'd betrayed her on her wedding day, and then he'd disappeared without a word.

This man, this Rocky, was someone Lisa thought she could be drawn to. Maybe it was the nurse in her. She didn't know. Perhaps it was all the nights he'd come to her in her dreams. It could even be sympathy for a man who was still fighting through the painful effects of a problem-plagued childhood. His autism documented in his records? That was probably part of the reason he'd walked from her office so abruptly. Autism could do that, bring a gut response from a person, one that was only marginally under the individual's control, if that. She'd not had time to study his reaction in depth. He'd been gone too quickly.

Whatever it was, he'd somehow hooked her with his brooding eyes and that resonant voice. Now, she would have to work on forgetting this man who had flashed through her morning like a supercharged lightning bolt. Perhaps her command performance on North Haven would be just the distraction she needed. She could run up there, lavish care upon her favorite student, and forget all about Rockland "Rocky" Royster. She would focus on Josh, on making him well, and on the fact she would get to spend the rest of the school term with him. It was a good situation for her, and she had come to like the pattern of her life very much. On Monday that pattern would be back, and Rocky Royster wouldn't be part of it. Come Monday morning, her life would be normal once again.

However, she wasn't on North Haven yet, and Josh wasn't under her care. At this moment, Rocky was very much on her mind. The feel of his touch was warm on her hand, and his polite apologies were in her thoughts.

He'd hooked her, even if she fought against realizing the depth of it. He had hooked her right in her heart, and even Lisa had to admit, those were the most difficult hooks of all to remove.

FRANK BLASINGAME reached to his keyboard. The meteorologist hesitated. If he was wrong, there would be the devil to pay. Storms were unpredictable, and they could and would go where they wished.

However, it looked as if these two storms would combine within the day. The second system from the east was moving at an easy forty knots per hour. When it impacted Tropical Storm Christian, the tropical storm would be thrown off course, shifting directions to the west. That was the worst possible scenario he could imagine.

He had run the computations over and over with different forecast models each time. The end result was always the same. There would be hurricane force winds impacting all along the New England seaboard.

A mandatory evacuation was the thing to do. However, there was no time. When these storms collided, there would be hours, only. If people were on the road responding to an evacuation, there would be a greater death toll than if people stayed in their houses. If people tried to evacuate the islands, God forbid the deaths that would ensue.

The weight of this was on his shoulders, and it made his

139

head throb. Perspiration dappled the back of his shirt as he placed his fingers on the keys.

11:45 AM. Saturday, September 29. Weather alert. A strong secondary system is due to impact Tropical Storm Christian within the hour. Winds will increase to hurricane force. The storm track is expected to veer sharply west and will impact the New England coast from New York City north to Halifax, Nova Scotia. Those in the affected areas should find high ground if available. Remain in your homes if possible. Please keep all roads clear for emergency personnel.

Under no circumstances should those on the offshore islands take to sea. Secure your possessions and remain in your homes. Run extra drinking water and have emergency supplies ready. Please prepare now. Do not wait.

His heart pounded, and his vision was focused on one thing: his message and the enter key on his keyboard. People's lives would change with this information. If he was wrong . . . well, he just couldn't allow that thought. All the blame would fall back on him, Frank Blasingame. As a sheen of sweat erupted on his forehead, he tapped the enter key, and his eyes turned to the monitors lining the room. They showed the feeds from each station that carried the emergency warning from the weather service. He saw a red blinking line across the bottom of the display on each one.

When his words began to scroll across, he wondered who would *not* get his message. He knew it would be picked up by emergency weather radio broadcasts. That meant those who received it were either in front of a television or listening to a weather radio. What about those in private airplanes or already out on the sea? Others were in summer homes on the islands, and they might have no access to the warning. What of them?

Frank shivered. When a big storm comes in unexpectedly, some people die. That's the way of life. His job was to keep that number as small as possible, even if he couldn't prevent them all.

His eyes grew moist at the thought of those he couldn't save. God help him, he would save them all if he could. He'd save every last one.

Chapter 10

BETTE JUMPED at the sound of the weather radio. She was in the kitchen preparing an afternoon stew for her guests. She'd put meat in, and lots of it. The potatoes had been peeled earlier that morning, but the carrots had just come up from the cellar. They had to be washed and chopped. Merv and Leetha had borrowed her SUV to run into town for some shopping, and Bette wanted the house to smell appetizing when they returned.

Holding the knife motionless, she listened. The unit was tuned to the coastal broadcasts. She'd adjusted it that morning after seeing the distant cloudbanks in the direction of the sea. She knew from experience what coastal storms looked like, and she had developed a *feel* for them.

As she listened to the stilted, computer-generated words that crawled from her radio, her heart grew icy inside her chest. "*A second system . . . hurricane force winds . . . emergency supplies ready.*"

This was her grandson they were talking about. Rockland. *Rocky*. He didn't listen to a weather radio, either. He was constantly working on those boats, and his mind was in its own world.

Bette laid her knife down and reached for a towel. Wiping her hands clean, she reached for the phone. Punching in the numbers to his house, she waited for it to ring ten times before reaching a finger to close the connection.

She stood for a bit, thinking, and then she opened a cabinet to run her fingernail down a list of numbers until she came to one with the name Tramwick beside it. She didn't expect to be able to reach this man. He was probably on his boat or in a bar soaking up all the whiskey he could absorb. She would try, though.

When no one answered, she tried one last thing. The Center. They'd told her when the appointment was scheduled, and she had it marked on her calendar. She'd have told Rocky, but then he'd have come up with some excuse. He might still be there. Her fingers dialed in the digits, and after four rings, a machine answered.

"Massachusetts Center for Children. Miss Bevier speaking. My office hours are Monday through Friday, seven-thirty to four. Please leave your name and number. If this is an emergency . . ."

Bette knew the process. She punched in the number two, and the phone immediately beeped. She left her name and number, and then she hung up the phone.

It seemed her grandson was determined to look out for himself today. She'd done the best she could short of getting in her truck and driving around to find him. She knew she couldn't do even that. Her truck was in town with Merv and Leetha.

She sighed. That meant all she could do was finish lunch. With that in mind, she figured she might as well push her concerns from her thoughts. She picked up her knife. It was time

143

to put the carrots in the pot, and she couldn't put them in whole, now, could she?

THE ISLAND was coming up fast, and Lisa sighted it growing out of the haze. It could easily be dusk, but she knew her watch showed it to be closer to one. The flight had been an easy one, and Mr. Reynolds had said he would be there to meet her. She was glad. The weather was atrocious, and she didn't want to be forced to stand out in it for any length of time.

As soon as the plane landed and came to a stop, the pilot stepped back into the cabin. "I'm so sorry you had to ride alone. I've left the engine running, as I want to be off again and back on the mainland before the weather gets worse. I radioed in just before we landed, and your ride's waiting. If you look out the window, you can see Mr. Reynolds. I believe that black Range Rover is his." She helped Lisa unbuckle her seatbelt. "Let me gather your things while you put your raincoat on. You'll get wet out there if you're not careful. One warning: In this weather, you'll probably need to use a landline on the island if you wish to make a call, and expect it to be much colder than it was in Marlboro. The temperature's dropped at least twenty degrees."

Lisa smiled at her, trying to hide her renewed nervousness about the weather. The pilot's urgency to get back to the mainland wasn't helping, either. She slipped on her coat as she spoke.

"Thank you. I appreciate you flying me up here so suddenly. I know the Reynolds will appreciate it. Their son . . ."

Mary patted her arm. "I know Josh, and I've been told why you're here." Then she winked at Lisa. "Also, so you know, Mr. Reynolds is compensating me quite nicely. Don't you worry about *that*."

Lisa laughed, but it felt high-pitched and strained. "I won't. Thank you. I should have known."

Mary paused and looked at her passenger. Glancing outside at the weather, she gave her charge a quick hug.

"Don't you let me worry you with my comment on the storm. Safe in the air and safe on the ground are two different things. I know Mr. Reynolds, and I've been to his house. He wouldn't have his family here if he didn't feel secure. It's being in the air that's a problem. You're safe now, and the rest of your trip will be at ground level. Take care."

She stepped to the door and put her hand on the catches. She turned to Lisa.

"Ready?"

When her passenger nodded, she released the door and let it swing to the ground. Lisa was surprised at the wind that buffeted her as she headed down, and at the bottom, she turned to wave as the door closed. Mary returned the wave as she disappeared, and Lisa was alone on the field. She raised her umbrella and headed to the Range Rover.

As she began to walk that direction, she saw its lights flicker on, the bright beams of illumination directing her path. Growing colder, she was grateful when she saw it began to move toward her, and she waved at it. It was dark inside the vehicle, and it wasn't until she opened the door that she could see it was indeed Mr. Reynolds inside. She would make a point to use his name.

Closing the door, she spoke. "Hello, Craig. It's still all right to call you that?"

He reached to shake her hand. "Lisa. Of course. We're on equal footing, here. I really appreciate you coming. I know this is sudden and very inconvenient. This weather." He looked up and out the windshield at the rain that splattered across its surface. Then, blasting an intense spray of water across the glass, the airplane that had ferried Lisa to this offshore island flew by them, and it lifted quickly into the air.

Lisa took a deep breath. "She was in a hurry to get to shore. Bad weather, she said." She looked at him before turning her gaze back to the window. She wanted him to reassure her. She hoped he would.

CRAIG LAUGHED, brushing off the pilot's remark, but even he could tell his voice sounded tired. He was doing this more for his wife than his son. He loved Josh, but he couldn't handle the constant demands of the boy's problems. The last three years had felt almost as if the boy were normal, but this setback was like a bucket of cold water on that barely flickering flame of hope. There were fourteen years of desperation from before, and it had erupted in this one weekend and was washing over his family once again.

He looked at the woman in the car with him. She was beautiful. He'd seen that when she was with them before. She was even more so now, as if she were in love. He certainly hoped it wasn't that Andrew boy again. He was a loser. His wife had been right earlier to tell him not to call the man to close up the house. Last time there had been items missing. Andrew had blamed the locals who wintered over, saying someone must have broken in. Craig had been unsure, but the cost of the missing items hadn't been enough to worry overmuch about. The look on this woman's face was definitely the look of love, though.

He reassured her as best he could. "It always rains in October on the Islands, and we're dancing with the October devil. He's just a few days early."

"October devil?" She smiled at his reference.

As he reached to shift the heavy machine into drive, he chuckled. "I'm sorry. It's a personal reference. A family thing."

"You don't have to explain. I shouldn't have asked."

"No, it's Josh. He always wants to winter over up here. He loves it, especially that decrepit Goose Rocks Light. He'd hike out to see it every day, if he could. I'm always forced to set my foot down. I won't stay into October." He pulled ahead onto a road. The rain was picking up, and all Lisa could see in the pounding downpour were the blinding flashes of reflected light

146

on the road as the water droplets devoured the pavement. "Josh and I fight about it every year. The house is uninsulated and unheated. October is simply too much."

"I understand. Goose Rocks Light? What's that?"

"It's an old lighthouse out on the shoals. It's over a hundred years old, privately owned, now. Josh loves it. It's very picturesque, if you like that sort of thing. Sparkplug design, sticks right out of the ocean. It's scheduled for renovation to start as soon as the owners award the contract. Josh keeps me abreast on everything concerning that lighthouse, whether I wish to know or not."

"I think your son might have spoken to me about it before. He mentioned a lighthouse, anyway. It could be the same one. Is it near here? You said he could hike to it."

"If he spoke to you about a lighthouse, it was this one. Trust me." Craig laughed, remembering his son's frustration with not being able to reach the lighthouse to explore it. Back at home, he'd researched every detail of it on the Internet. He could recite every owner it had ever had, including the local doctor on the island, but Craig had refused to let him contact anyone about it. He had no intention of letting him make a nuisance of himself over that wreck of a structure.

"I'd like to see it, if I get a chance. If the weather clears while I'm here."

"I wouldn't count on that." He nodded at her knowingly, motioning to the deluge just outside the windows. "It's in the Thorofare, the passage between the two big islands. You have to take a boat to get there. We don't keep one on the island. If you're seriously interested, Josh can fill you in all about it. He has all the details memorized. Oh, we're here." He turned his blinker on, even though they'd seen no one else on the island road. "See? We're very close to the airstrip. Mary did tell you the Equinox is available to take you back to the mainland?"

"That's the water taxi, right? She mentioned it." She

paused, her eyes darting along the blowing trees, as the truck moved smoothly up the driveway. "It's very windy. Will the taxi be able to run in this? I know there's a ferry, also, but I don't have a schedule. Will I need to see about a ticket back?"

Craig pulled up to the house and under a large portico. The sound of the drumming rain on the truck's large glass roof ceased, and it was very quiet in the vehicle. With a practiced motion of his hand, he reached and removed his key from the dash, retracting the metal stiletto into the fob. The gentle murmur of the expensive vehicle stopped.

"Don't concern yourself about the ferry. This is Maine. Mainers are tough." He was from civilized Boston, and he spoke with a bit of rancor in his words. He didn't consider himself a Mainer. "It'll take more than a few rain showers to stop the Equinox. If this becomes a hurricane, then they might shut down for the evening. Other than that? Trust me. They'll get you back." He chuckled as he opened the door. "If not, I have some strings to pull. I'm not without a few tricks." He tapped his temple. "It's who you know, sometimes."

LISA SIGHED as he closed his door, leaving her in the silence of the luxurious vehicle. She gathered her things as she looked at the glass front door that opened to the brightly illuminated old house. It saddened her how his tricks seemed to be so important to him. She murmured, "Just not any tricks for your son. I know, Mr. Reynolds. Just none for your son."

She turned as her door opened, and Craig helped her from the truck. It was positively cold on the way into the house. She was beginning to wish for a real coat, the kind that had a liner, a warm collar, and buttons up the front. It was early in the day, even if it was growing darker by the minute. She reassured herself she had plenty of time to get home.

IN THE NEXT house over, one hidden in its own forest of trees, the windows were dark, but the weather radio, one that was high-tech and corded, had accidentally been left plugged in and turned on. It shrieked to life, and after a second warning, its mechanized voice began its announcement.

"First received at 11:45 AM. Saturday, September 29. Weather alert. A strong secondary system is due to impact Tropical Storm Christian within the hour. Winds will increase to hurricane force . . ."

However, no one was home to listen, and the Reynolds' house didn't have a weather radio, not one with fresh batteries, anyway. They never came up during the bad weather season, and to them this was just another fall thunderstorm. It would blow over in an hour or two or three. Storms on the island always did, and they weren't concerned in the least.

"TRAM, HOW can you see through this?" Rocky leaned in close, the rain and darkness making everything seem the same. The throttle was pushed nearly to full speed. "Shouldn't we slow down?" He built the boats, not drove them through storms and blinding rain.

His friend laughed, "No need. Seriously, I don't have to. See?" He pointed to several instruments mounted in the boat. "Depth finder. GPS. I don't need to see, what's outside, anyway. I can just watch these. Look there. On the radar, see? There's something I need to avoid. Simple. I just go around, making sure I have clearance underneath the keel."

"You're at the wheel. Be careful." Rocky shrugged and resigned himself to what he knew he had no control over. Just as the boat altered course to go around the blip on the radar, there was the sharp report of an air horn. Rocky leaned out to see where it was from. "Stop. I think that's a stranded boat."

"Stranded? Are you sure?" He pulled back on the throttle, causing his boat to immediately begin rocking wildly in the swells. When Rocky looked at him alarmingly, he grinned. "It's the push forward that keeps us steady. Stationary like this, we're at the mercy of the waves. It's always better to keep moving in rough weather. You should know that. You build these things, by dog." For the second time that day, he glanced at Fish. "No offense, big boy." Fish looked at him and swished his tail back and forth several times.

Rocky barked, "I build 'em, Tram. I don't take 'em out into deadly storms."

"Deadly?" Tramwick looked aghast at the man standing in his cockpit with him. "This is a gentle breeze. Wait until a real gale hits. Then's when it gets fun. Let's go help your friends."

As the boat turned, Rocky muttered, "They're not my friends. Every friend I have is on this boat." He looked at Fish, pointedly including him. "Every single one of them."

"Hey, thanks for stopping," a feminine voice called to them from the stranded boat. Underneath the hood of the slicker appeared a very pretty face, one certainly no older than twenty. "My friend and I are headed to her Gram's place on Green's, and my boat started running rough. I stopped it for a minute, and now it won't work. Not even the radio. I tried to send a mayday, but everything's dead."

About that time, another slicker appeared from below. The new face revealed itself to be about the same age. "Oh, Julie. Thank goodness you found someone. I'm glad you had that air horn." She smiled, but behind the facade skulked an obvious tinge of fear.

Tramwick looked at Rocky and grinned. "Here, Rocky, you take the wheel. I've got to be the one to help these poor girls." Then, in a quick step, he was gone across to the other boat. He turned with a practiced motion and secured the two boats with a line, then he pulled the engine cowling back. He seemed to know exactly what he needed to do.

He called to Rocky, "Turn on the lamps. The switch is just there on the dash. On your left." The blinding rain and the heavy

150

cloud cover made it like night underneath the cowling.

"Lamps?" Rocky had never piloted Tramwick's boat. He had no idea where a lamp switch might be. "What's it look like?"

"A toggle. You can't miss it. There on the left."

Rocky knew he could miss it, and very easily. Left? Right? When he was stressed, he couldn't figure out where to put the key to start his own truck.

He felt along both sides of the dash until he found a switch. He flipped it, and the cockpit filled with blasting music and multicolored strobe lights. In an instant, he heard Tram's feet on the deck behind him and felt a firm hand on his shoulder.

As he leaned in past Rocky to turn the music and lights off, he whispered in his ear, "Not that one. I meant the one on the *other* left." As he flipped it, brilliance flared from lights around the boat, illuminating the stranded vessel next to them. It also showed the driving rain that pelted the swells. "Be right back. I think I know what's wrong." Then, he was gone.

Rocky turned, and he saw his friend lean into the open engine bay. There was a flash of light and a loud curse, and the boat next to them came alive. Tramwick sat up and smiled.

"Loose battery connection. It's not firm, still, but if it starts and you don't kill it, it should take you in. Try the engine now."

The first girl they'd spoken with walked up to the wheel, and pressing a button, the engine fired right up. She looked at Tramwick and smiled. Glancing at her friend, she stepped forward and gave her rescuer a hug and a quick kiss on the cheek.

"Cover the engine," Rocky yelled, aware of where this kiss might go, and that there was no time for that. "Tramwick!"

"What?" Tramwick turned to see the cowling still off, and he looked longingly back to the girl who had just kissed him. "Oh, the engine! Yeah, I guess I'd better."

He knelt, and with an assured series of motions, it was soon reattached. He reached to release the line that held the boats together, and before he stepped back to join Rocky, he reminded the girls, "Have that tightened when you get in. Also, don't kill it until you're sure you're wherever you need to go. Keep it running." Then he stepped over the gunwale with his line in hand. He waved as the girls' engine roared, and the boat sped off into the choppy water.

He turned to Rocky and grinned. "That was well worth a kiss. Green's Island. That's not far from Goose Rocks."

Rocky grabbed his arm and placed his hand on the wheel. "It's on the other side of Vinalhaven, and you know that. Grow up, Tram. Those girls were eighteen at best."

"Twenty-one, Rocky. I bet they were twenty-one."

Rocky gave an exaggerated sigh. "I'll give you nineteen, but not a day over. I hope their parents changed their diapers before giving them the keys to that boat."

TRAMWICK PUSHED the throttle hard forward. He turned to grin at Rocky, making a dig he knew would get under his friend's skin. "I hope not. I want to change them myself." Then he cackled in mirth at the disgusted look on his friend's face. Rocky never could take a joke, and Tram liked to make them all the more for that very reason.

Besides, he'd never been with a woman who hadn't wanted to be with him. Rocky should know that. After all, they were good friends. They'd have to be, or he would've never put on Rocky's underwear in the first place. However, he wished he could remember just *why* he'd put them on. That had him mystified to no end.

It didn't matter, and he let it go. He didn't have them on now. He had on Royce's underwear, and that was an entirely different matter. Royce was dead. Tramwick would much rather wear a dead man's underwear than his friend's. Besides, they were whitie-tighties. Rocky's shorts hadn't given Tram any support, and he hadn't liked the feel of that one iota.

Like he said, wearing Royce's underwear was much better.

"RAND? Is that you?"

Ignoring the question, Rand scattered his things across the massive table in the entrance hall, blinking to clear his eyes as he walked into the study. After seeing John, then stopping off for a drink to clear his head, he'd had a time focusing on the drive home, so he'd spent a second night at his son's. He should have skipped the bar this morning, but he'd had a hangover, and the best cure for that was another drink. Opening a tall armoire, he rifled through a series of upright containers holding various oddities of information that were important enough to keep, but not something he had to access every week.

There was one item he especially wanted to look at. He touched a wooden box that was designed to look like a book. The spine was carved with the undulating shape of a hand-bound tome, and it was leather wrapped. As soon as his hand touched it, he pictured what was inside.

He sometimes told people he was on a waiting list for a Royster-built boat. He even convinced himself, forced himself to think of it that way. Well, he was waiting, wasn't he? Holding the box built to look like a book and opening the hinged lid as if lifting the cover to read the story inside, he reached for the plans he'd had drawn up. This one would one day be his.

He stepped to the ornate desk he called his own, and he laid the book-like box down, its hinged cover still open. Turning to the window, he touched a pad at the side, and the motorized draperies hummed as they pulled themselves into pockets at the edges of the massive, curved opening. When the slender drapery doors on either side of the window closed, effectively making the window coverings disappear, Rand turned the design on the paper to catch the muted light filtering in through the glass.

For the first time that morning, he looked, really looked at the sky. It was early afternoon, now, and he seemed to remember having called John that morning. Something about the light-house and it blowing over. However, the events were fuzzy, and he couldn't remember them all that well. He'd tipped a few back—well, maybe more than a few—and he'd been good to get his car in the garage.

At least this time he'd had his pass to get through the gated entrance. He wished the complex would keep a guard on duty twenty-four/seven like they'd done years before. Now, the gate-house was empty from midnight until six. He'd have gotten through even without his pass if the guard had been there. He'd have to push for that at the annual meeting, insist that the gate once again be manned around the clock.

"Rand? Oh, it's you. I missed you yesterday, and you never called. Why, look at you." His wife walked into the room. Her footsteps only carried her a short way inside. This was Rand's space, and he barely tolerated the cleaning woman in to dust and sweep.

He turned at the intrusion and smiled apologetically. "I've been at Seth's. I had to drive all the way to Worcester. I was glad he had room for me."

"I know." She moved a step or two closer. He didn't act irritated to have her past the door, and it emboldened her.

Rand raised his eyebrows. "Seth called you? He said he wouldn't. I misplaced my pass to the gate and couldn't get through. I left it at the meeting the other night and had to stop by and get it." The alcohol from earlier was finally starting to wear off. He'd wait a while before breaking into the liquor cabinet on the other side of the room. He didn't want his wife inside when he started drinking again.

"I thought the guard was on duty until twelve. Surely you weren't out past twelve? Rand!"

He looked out the window again, knowing he'd been out well past the hour of twelve. He laid the paper in his hand on his desk upside down.

"What's that, Rand?"

He glanced at it and then smiled guiltily. He tapped it twice and distracted her by stepping across the room to take her arm. His leather heels were soft against the distressed oak floors. As he pulled her to the window, her hard-soled pumps tapped dully.

"Look, Beth. My God, have you ever seen such a dark sky? I thought I'd never make it home. Have you watched the weather?"

She reached a hand to the glass. Rain had been striking the windows of the house intermittently, but now it was beginning to drive against the glass with increasing fury. However, it wouldn't be cold against her skin. The rare gasses filling the panes kept the outside temperature at bay. Besides, the windows in all the townhouses in the complex were triple glazed.

"I was worried about you, Rand. I love you. You know that, don't you? You never tell me you love me, but I know you do. You do love me, Rand?"

He looked at her to see her eyes glistening. Impulsively, he wrapped his arms around her, and he pressed one side of his face against her hair. Then he reached a hand to place it on top of hers. "Of course, I do." He breathed deeply as he thought of the paper on his desk. She was so needy, sometimes, that he wondered why he'd married her. He knew, though. She was very old money, as well as an only child.

"Say it, Rand."

He stood for a moment. He could see their reflection in the window, and he knew he'd better be careful of his expressions. Beth could see him as well as he could see her.

"Say what, Beth?"

She sighed. "Tell me you love me. I want to hear it."

He paused, not wanting to say the words. He hated it that she demanded it. He didn't hate Beth, and at times he even enjoyed her company. However, he hated when she demanded his love. Then, not letting the time that was passing tell the lie to his words, he whispered the phrase she so wanted to hear.

"I do love you, Beth."

She relaxed in his arms, and then she turned to give him a quick kiss on the cheek. She patted his chest and straightened his tie. Her fingers took the lapels of his coat and pressed them flat.

"Fresh clothes, Rand. These smell like a bar." Then she smiled, and her shoes tapped their way out of the room.

He turned to pick up the paper on his desk. Turning it over, he looked at the lines that represented the boat that was currently being built in Royster's boat shed. It wasn't finished, and he hadn't been up to look at it, yet. He was too nervous. It wasn't even paid for. Of course, Royster had received his money, but that wasn't money Rand had been able to pull from his wife's funds. He'd floated a loan on some of the stocks he managed, and it would come due in another six months or so.

He slipped the paper back into the box and closed it. His mind raced as he tried to think of how to best convince Beth he needed this boat. Then he sighed. She was very pretty, and she was available. If he spent some time with her, behaved romantically, and warmed her bed frequently in the next few weeks, she'd sign over the money to him. He was convinced of that.

She was just so demanding, and he didn't like giving what was demanded of him. He held his hand on the box that contained the plans to his new boat. It was a trade off, and he really wanted the funds. After all, it was already under construction, and the loan would come due in only more six months.

He picked up the box and slipped it back into the armoire. Closing the door, he paused, taking a deep breath to steel his resolve. He could give in to her on this. He would do this. It was for his new boat, the one he'd never seen before except on that sheet of paper.

"Beth," he called, "I missed you, too." He stepped out of his office into her part of the house. It was less formal, softer and warmer. She was curled on one of the sofas, and across the room there was a large flat panel television filling the wall. It was showing a movie that at a glance seemed to be a romance.

Rand touched a switch by the door, and the drapes began to slide over the two-story bank of windows opening to the pool. He walked up behind the sofa, and reaching to the remote sitting on the marble-topped sofa table next to it, he turned the television off. His hands began to massage his wife's shoulders.

"Beth, we've not had much us time together lately. I've been thinking about that, and I want to show you how much you mean to me."

At his words, she stood and stepped around to him, melting against his rumpled, bar-smelling clothes.

"I still need to change." He remembered her remark from earlier.

"I don't care about your clothes and how they smell. I care about you, Rand."

She probably knew this meant he wanted something from her, and if he was true to his words, she would gladly give it. There were tradeoffs in life. That was a reality they'd come to realize a very long time ago. If this was one they had to make, then it was well worth the price Rand knew they would have to pay, both of them.

With one hand, she reached and touched the lamp at her side. She tapped it with two short strokes and then held her finger against it. As she waited, all the lights in the room faded to darkness.

As the afternoon progressed, Rand remembered there was one thing he especially loved about his wife, and he loved it very much. Then he realized there was another and another. Finally, his passions fully aroused, he came to the full understanding that there was one place that was the best of all, and he couldn't believe he'd thought this was a tradeoff. It was no tradeoff. This was what life was all about, even if Beth didn't give him the money he wanted. She would, he was certain, but as he let himself be enveloped in that place, he no longer cared. He might later, but not at that moment. His concentration was focused only on her, and that's all that mattered for the moment.

AS LISA stepped through the front door, there was a fire crackling in the stove, and the room was warm and well lit. She noticed Josh's mother on the sofa in front of the fire, and she called to her, only to see her turn a red-eyed face her direction.

"Mrs. Reynolds, are you all right?" Lisa dropped her raincoat from her shoulders and let her things fall into a chair. Glancing at Craig, she saw him nod, then she stepped to sit by the distraught woman. "Josh, is he worse? I got here as quickly as I could."

Josh's mother reached her hand to reveal the bottle of medication. "Sixteen, Miss Bevier. There should be fourteen. What should I do?"

Lisa glanced to Craig. Josh's mother was making no sense, and Lisa needed to know what was going on if she was to help.

Craig stepped over to take the container from his wife's hand. He smiled at her as he grasped her fingers and curled them into a ball. Pressing them into her lap, he kissed her on the forehead.

"It'll be fine, honey. Help is here." He turned to Lisa. "My wife says Josh is certain he took his medication last night and this morning. However, we went to bed early, and the boy was on his own for a time." He paused and looked at the bottle. Then he handed it to Lisa. "If he took the pills, my wife is certain there should be only fourteen left. She's counted them repeatedly. There are sixteen still inside. We're lost as to what to do now."

Lisa looked at the bottle. In a quick glance, she took in the two people in the room with her. She knew them, or at least as well as she could get to know someone she'd spent a month with three years earlier. They were obviously affluent, although Lisa had no idea where their money was from. She assumed it was old money, but she never tracked the parents of the Center's students. She preferred to know her students just for who they were at the school. With Josh, it was a little different, and she had learned a little about his family. On one level, she understood they had a handicapped son they only saw twice a month. During those short visits, they could pretend there were no problems. Josh was dependable and independent. He took his own medication. Of course, even at seventeen, it was still doled out to him, but he always remembered.

Now they were talking as if this were an academic problem. At the Center, medications and the problems resulting from their use or misuse were urgent and handled with the utmost promptness. If Josh were her child, she would've had the island doctor on the phone at the first sign of trouble. This couple hadn't yet asked her to see Josh or even shared what they felt was really wrong with him. They were certainly lost in dealing with this. She'd have to forge ahead against their slack tide of indifference; that was all there was to it.

"Josh. Where is he?" Lisa stood and looked around. "It seems I remember he had a room down this hallway. May I see him?" She nodded towards the doorway leading to the rest of the house.

Mrs. Reynolds sat and looked at Lisa as if she hadn't understood the question. However, her husband jumped forward in a sudden motion, as if realizing he had forgotten something very important.

He had, too. His son.

"Yes! Come this way. It'll be very cold, still. The house warms very slowly in weather like this." He led Lisa down a wide hallway and opened a door. When she stepped inside, she could see the rain running down the unadorned glass in the windows. This room was especially chilly. Having windows on three sides probably caused that.

She sat on the edge of the bed and pulled the covers back to see Josh's head resting on two hands balled up under his face. His hair was tousled with a night spent pressed into a pillow, and his face was flushed. She placed her hand against the cheek she'd seen at school just the day before. His flesh was warm, and the skin was smooth. This was a face that had yet to roughen into a true man's face. He hadn't even begun to grow coarse whiskers. Only soft down covered his cheeks. She let her fingers brush his cheekbone where she could feel the adult inside struggling to make its way out. This boy would be wildly handsome someday. At seventeen, he was sweet, and perhaps beautiful, instead.

She looked at his father. "I brought a satchel. Would you bring it to me?" Seeing him move to the hall, she turned to the boy underneath her hand. "Josh?" She massaged the skin on his face, and the one eye she could see slowly opened, staring ahead. "I'm pulling the covers back," she told him. "It'll be cold. Are you ready?"

His eye turned to hers, and he rolled his head so his face was fully exposed. "Let me stop the car, first. It has a good heater." He smiled wanly, then it faded to a sleepy, bland expression.

"Your car, Josh? The '59 El Camino?"

He smiled, his focus sharpened, and he sat up awkwardly, forcing his elbows into the bed and sliding back. "I drove it to school. It's in the parking lot just outside. Do you want to see it, Miss Bevier?"

Lisa sighed. It seemed he was having a seizure right now. At least he knew who she was. She removed her hand from his face and pulled the bedclothes back to his waist. His arms and torso were bare, but he didn't seem to notice. Hearing his father returning, she reached for her bag.

"Thank you," she murmured. "Lie down again, Josh, please."

She made to cover him up, pulling the bedding over his

torso, but he tossed it off. She placed her hand on his shoulder and pushed him to lie flat on his back. Before doing anything, she needed to check his vital signs. She wanted to be certain this had to do only with the medication in that bottle before she decided her course of action. His skin was very warm, but she knew that was probably from being encapsulated underneath the mounds of bedding she'd pulled back.

"Take a deep breath, Josh. I need to hear the air go in and out." As he followed her instructions, she glanced at his father. "Has he been out of bed today?"

Craig looked mystified at the question. He glanced to the door as if his wife might know the answer, then he cleared his throat. "I don't think so. I could ask my wife. No, he must have gotten up to take his medicine. My wife definitely said he'd done that. Would you like me to get Dee?"

Lisa shook her head. It wasn't important, anyway. She looked back at Josh, and whispered to him, "You did great, Josh. I bet you did a good job driving your car to school today. You'll show it to me later?"

"Sure. Can I go back to class, now?" He smiled, although it was once again a bit vacant, as if he were still in his dream.

"Are you cold, Josh?" She was freezing, and if he wasn't, it was another indicator of his disconnect with reality.

"Not very. I have on a very thick shirt, today." He shifted in the bed.

Lisa rested her hand against his wadded bedding. He probably needed to cool off a bit. Despite the muscles she'd pointed out to him the day before, he was very thin. His stomach showed that. With her free hand, she reached in her bag and pulled out several items. She wanted to listen to his lungs a little more closely. She would check his ears and eyes, too. Then she would search the house. Josh was acting just like he had previously when he'd been on his old medication. If she could find any of that present, she would have some support for her suspicions. If

161

so, she could simply watch him closely until that evening, and perhaps getting him back on the correct dosage of his prescription would resolve this situation.

As she sat there with Josh's father at the door, she drew in a deep breath to calm herself and held it for a moment. Here beside this abandoned boy, this young man whose parents didn't know how to love and to care for him, she felt a sudden emptiness that was very strong; and when she released her breath, it didn't go away. She was very attached to this boy, and lying in his bed, he looked so young. That man, however, who had cast his hooks into her heart that morning had been very different from this one beside her. Rockland Royster was no longer the youth in the school picture she'd intentionally left on the kitchen table at home. His body hadn't been that of a schoolboy just experiencing his first taste of manhood, a boy whose parents would let him die in his bed simply because they were lost.

Suddenly overcome with longing for a man she'd only met that morning, someone she didn't even know, and certainly not as an adult, she stood and stepped to one of the rain-drenched windows. The clouds roiled overhead, and she could tell the room was strikingly colder next to the glass. It was even colder in her heart, and she wondered where Rocky was now.

Without turning, she spoke to Josh's father. "A portable heater? Are there any in the house?"

He shifted against the doorway. "Let me think if there are any extras. We have the one in our bedroom, but I don't think any more. Josh likes it cold in here. It's his winter, he says."

She turned to him. He had the strikingly handsome features of his son. She suddenly realized that. This was what Josh would look like at forty. The prettiness would continue to sharpen until this handsomeness came out. Oh, the girls would love this boy. However, she was very irritated at his father just now, and his handsomeness couldn't take the edges off that. This room was freezing, and there was a heater in another part of the house.

How could he not think to carry it in here to warm his son's room? The boy was sick, for God's sake.

She was polite, but she was firm when she made her request. "Please bring the heater in here, Mr. Reynolds. Your son will do better if this room is warm." She looked back to Josh's uncovered form on the bed. His eyes were closed. Resolutely, she faced the rain outside once again. She hadn't called Josh's father by his first name, and she realized she'd done that on purpose.

When she heard the portable heater being plugged in, and its small motor whirring to life, she turned. She saw Mr. Reynolds stand from his position on the floor, and she smiled at him.

"Thank you, Craig. I'd like to check Josh's vitals, now. Do you think you could look around the house while I do that? I'd like to know if there are any of Josh's old medications anywhere inside. Please check everywhere, even places you don't think they could possibly be." As he stepped away, at last having something to do, Lisa called to him one more time. He stopped and turned with a puzzled expression on his face. Her words to him edged on brusque. "Treat this as if your son's life depends on you finding this, Mr. Reynolds. He could die right here in this bed, and no one wants that to happen."

Josh's father stood for a moment, and Lisa saw him lick his lips as if he hadn't thought of that. Or, she wondered, perhaps he had, but hadn't dared wish.

Dear God, she hoped not. She really, really hoped not.

Chapter 11

CRAIG FELT caught out, and the heat of his embarrassment warmed his face. He didn't think of himself as excessively self-centered. Josh was just so broken. He refused to admit that when his wife said she'd called, he'd thought, just for a minute, that he wished she would've waited until he was up. He might not . . . but then there it was. The moment was already gone. Now, he could no longer refuse to help his son. He didn't see how this woman could know, but she seemed to read him like an open book.

His eyes glanced to his son on the bed. The boy's breathing forced his chest to rise and fall in a rhythmic pattern, proving he was very much alive. He looked completely normal as he lay there. This was what he should have been, what Craig had always wanted him to be.

"Mr. Reynolds? Medicine? There's no reason for this to be

happening to Josh. He excels at everything at the Center. We must find the cause, and we should do it now. We can't let Josh down. You can't let him down."

Excels? Craig had never thought of his son in that way. Now, seeing him there, his face a reflection of his own, and his maturity just now making itself known, the previous three years swept across his memory. Perhaps it was seeing Lisa at his side, and realizing the difference between then and today, he wasn't sure, but in that moment, he realized just how normal his son had become in the past three years. He no longer walked on the sides of his feet, and he'd not had a seizure in years. No sudden autistic outbursts, no emergency meetings at the Center, none of that for so long Mr. Reynolds couldn't recall the last one. For years, the sickness had blinded him to everything about his son, even the good times in between the bad. He blinked away unwelcome tears. This was his child, and not just when he seemed undamaged. This was his son, and how could he have forgotten that? It hit him with an intensity he hadn't felt since the boy's birth.

He remembered that his wife normally put Josh's medicine in his bathroom, and with determination, he stepped inside. Josh would have been in here the previous night as well as that morning. Reaching to the medicine cabinet, he opened the door. Right in the very front was a prescription bottle, and when he picked it up, there was his son's name, Joshua Jeromy Reynolds, right on the label. He saw the date and immediately recognized it as an old prescription.

"Miss Bevier? Lisa? I think I found something." He choked up before he could say anything else, and tears began to run down his face. He thought of the sixteen tablets his wife had counted out over and over, and how Josh, dependable Josh, hadn't known where they were. He'd searched and found his medication anyway, determined to be responsible. It was just the wrong bottle. His son might have died for the third time, the first when he was six and was rescued by the Center, then at fourteen, and this time lying in his own bed, and all for this.

"Mr. Reynolds?"

"In a moment. I'll be right there."

In spite of his words, it was a long time before the father of the boy in the front room stepped from the bathroom. When he did, he felt changed. Josh was going to be all right.

At least he prayed that he would, and with Lisa here to help them, he knew a new sense of hope.

"YOU'RE LOST, Tram!" Rocky slapped him on the shoulder with the back of his hand, now more than irritated. "You can't trust electronics, not in weather like this. Admit it, you have no idea where we are."

"There!" Tramwick pointed with his yellow-suited arm, to a red-and-white beacon flashing through the blinding rain. "The lighthouse!"

Rocky wasn't so easily convinced. The lighthouse he'd bid on needed serious repair. He had a long list telling all that was required—which he'd glanced at but not read—but he'd seen detailed pictures. It had been abandoned for years, and only in their attempts to make the structure into a paying rental had the new owners admitted it required a total rehab.

This lighthouse was operational.

"Tram, there's a light. Even you can see that. Mine was abandoned before the Preservation Society bought it. You've brought us to the wrong one."

"Did you read the paperwork?" Tramwick looked at him, then to the dog that had settled at his feet. "I bet you just looked at the pictures and decided this would be fun."

Rocky growled his annoyance at the slight. It cut, even if it was the truth.

Tramwick laughed, then turned back to his instruments. "I know, I know. It's all about the solitude. Well, I *did* read up on

166

all the information. That little stick of rock is solar powered. The light is automated. The Coast Guard keeps that part of it up. It's the inside you're here to improve. It *has* been abandoned, although there are those people who would probably consider it livable, I suppose, if they were desperate. Now, the Society wants you to take it back to better than new. Besides," he continued, "see this? My GPS tells me we're in the right spot. That's where you're spending the night." He throttled down his engine. "There are lots of tricky spots around here. This baby is built right on the shoals. At least we're coming in at high tide. It'll be less risky pulling up to the base of the structure. Wouldn't want to hole my hull. That'd be the finest kind of disaster, to go down in this weather." He looked appreciatively at his friend. "I'm telling you, if this wasn't in a protected spot between these two islands, it'd be plain numb approaching it even at high tide. At least being here in the Thorofare, the chop is less." He began to manipulate the boat's engines, working his way alongside.

The lighthouse emerged through the haze created by the rain. Tramwick pointed to several bumpers. "Drop those off the port side. Then grab the lines, there. I'll idle up alongside the ladder, and you look for cleats or rings in the wall to tie off to. I've got me a good lobster boat here, and it's easy to maneuver, but this'll be a bit risky, no matter how we do it."

The lighthouse could now be clearly seen. The noise was considerable as wave after wave surged against the solitary sentinel perched alone in the middle of the sea. Each time a wave hit, the lighthouse seemed to thrum with a low-pitched basso vibration that carried across the water. Then, with a great sucking sound, the water pulled back to make way for another crashing breaker.

While the chop was less here away from the open ocean, the water still created considerable spray against the base. About halfway up, a platform encircled the central tower. There was a solar array just visible in the fading light, and at the very top flashed a rotating beacon. Through the black and white paint were bits of red, probably an original color from decades before.

As they made their final approach, Fish jumped to the edge of the boat and began barking ferociously at the gigantic object in the vessel's way. Rocky pushed him back and slipped several bumpers off the gunwale. Then, grabbing the line, he poised himself to loop it around whatever he could find when Tram brought the boat close enough.

Tramwick, yelling instructions, and once pushing Fish out of the way, maneuvered his craft next to the masonry structure, and with a careful hand on the throttle and another on the wheel, he steadied it as Rocky tied the stern line down, then jumped and attached another from the bow. When he saw his friend was finished, he killed the engine.

Standing in the protected cockpit, Tramwick outlined his plan. "Lantern, first. Sun'll be down soon, and we've got to get you some light. Then, we'll haul up the rest." He picked up the kerosene-fueled light and thrust it into Rocky's hand. "Carry this. I'm bringing the extra fuel and a starter wand. We'll find out just what this place is like." He grinned. "Mikey might like it," he called out, referring to an old cereal commercial they liked to laugh about. He helped Rocky strap the lantern over his shoulder as he tied the fuel can to his waist.

As Rocky stepped from the cockpit with the lantern, the wind blasted him, whipping his slicker, and setting the bottom to popping against his legs. The rain was sharp on his hands as he reached for the metal rungs to climb to the platform above. Above him, the suspended walkway had a matching covering, but he expected that in this rain, the cover wouldn't make much of a difference. As he reached the halfway point, and moved from the ladder to a steep metal stair, he peered down to see the boat rocking perilously underneath him, and all around was roiling, black water. An expression passed across his face, and he didn't even realize it had come and gone.

GLANCING UP, Tramwick caught his friend's expression, even as it flickered across his face, and he chuckled. He called loudly enough to be heard over the weather, "This'll be fun, Rocky. A blast. Own up to it. This is your dream come true."

What he'd seen, however, was a look that said, "What am I doing here?" Tramwick appreciated it, too. Out in this storm, tied up to this lighthouse, with the weather getting worse and not better, he was beginning to think the very same thing. He couldn't let Rocky know that. After all, Tram might be spending the night ashore, but this was Rocky's home, for a while, at least, until it blew down in the storm.

Tramwick laughed and grabbed the ladder, and he began pulling himself upward, with the lantern fuel safely in one hand.

CHET WAS downtown, the waterfront just to his side; his van rocked precipitously, as he tried to call the main office. This morning when he'd pulled out, he'd seen actual sunshine. Even at Mr. Royster's boatyard, there had been only a hint that today might turn out like this. If the weather worsened all day, his garbage cans as well as his patio furniture would be all over the street. He really needed to get home.

He pulled his personal cell phone out. He wasn't supposed to do this, call in to take the rest of the day off, and he hesitated, his heart pounding. He let his eyes trace the white-capping breakers off to his side. Then, a wall of saltwater spray slammed against the side of his truck.

Without any further hesitation, he glanced down and pressed the number six, holding it until his employer's phone number appeared in the screen. When the line picked up, he immediately started talking, preempting the spiel he knew would start immediately.

"Sondra?" He waited breathlessly.

There was a pause. Then a voice came on. "Chet? Is that you?"

He cleared his throat. "Yes, Sondra. Chet Abramson. Do you know any other?"

"Chet." She giggled. "Now, tell me, Chet Abramson. Why are you calling in on this line? You know this is customer service, only. Besides, you didn't even let me give my phone spiel. I'm supposed to do that each and every time I pick up the phone. You know that. Company policy."

He chuckled. He liked Sondra. She had long, black hair, in contrast to his thick mop of reddish-blond curls. She was perfect with him, or at least she would be, if they could ever get together on a date.

"Do you want to give it now?" He smiled, even though he knew she couldn't see it.

"No." She suddenly sounded tired. "Everyone's been calling in today. With the storm coming in, no one wants to make the deliveries they're carrying. You know how it is. What can I do for you?"

He chuckled. "Well, I'm out here on the waterfront. Downtown. My truck's jiving like it's got top billing on Saturday Night Live."

She giggled again. "Jiving? Is that even a real word?"

"I think so. Jive talking? Let's go jive on the dance floor? You know." He watched the wipers in their valiant attempts to keep the windows clear.

She was quiet for a moment. Then a giggle seeped out. "Chet, you better look that word up. Oh, here on my computer. Hold on. I just googled it." She paused, and he could hear her mouse click a few times. "I apologize. It does mean what you said. Dancing, and the jive talking, too. It says here that another meaning is foolish."

"Well, since I got that right, how about you work me some quick time off?"

"Hmm. How long? Just for an hour or two?"

"Come on, Sondra. Have you seen the weather outside? The rest of the day. I've got to get things at home secured. I live alone, and if I don't get to it, no one else will." He leaned his head back against the top of the extra tall seat. "It's getting worse every minute."

"Sure, I'll call to the back and have Marcy do it. You owe me, though. Like a date, maybe."

He sat up, very pleased with the turn the conversation was taking. "You mean that? You'll do that, go out with me?"

She laughed. "I said so, didn't I? Next Saturday. You'd better not forget, either."

"Saturday. Thanks, Sondra." He hung up, and he had a smile on his face. Just then, another wave of spray hit his truck, and he swore. He had to get this vehicle back to the distribution center, and he wanted to get home as soon as he could. He had the rest of the day off, and he wasn't going to waste it just sitting around the waterfront.

However, driving back in, it wasn't the storm on his mind, and it wasn't having the day off. It was Sondra, and it was next Saturday. This was even better than meeting Mr. Royster. Well, almost better. He wouldn't know if it was better until Saturday, and then only if he could convince Sondra to come back to his place afterwards.

DEE WATCHED her husband as he held out the old prescription bottle to her. When she looked at the label and compared it to the one on the pills she'd been recounting all day, her breath came fast and hard. Then her eyes cut to see Lisa coming in the room behind him.

"This was in the bathroom? How? All the old medicine was cleaned out." Her hand began to shake. "Miss Bevier, the last time you were here . . . Josh was fourteen, then. Remember? He had that grand mal seizure. He's had none since then. He's

171

always taken the new tablets."

Craig stepped to the sofa and sat beside his wife. He looked up to catch Lisa's eyes, and then he turned to the woman at his side. He had shown Lisa the bottle first, and Josh had been able to tell her it had been in the very back of the medicine cabinet hidden behind everything else. He'd thought they were the right ones. Craig took his wife's hand and explained all that to her.

"Oh, my God," Mrs. Reynolds exclaimed. "It's my fault, isn't it?" She looked to her husband and back to Lisa. "I never taught him to look at the labels. I always laid them out for him." She gasped and grabbed her husband's arm. "Last night, we went to bed early. This morning the bottle was still on the kitchen counter. That's why he took the wrong one. I almost killed my son." She wrapped the bottle tightly in her hand and pulled it to her chest. Her face was blank with the enormity of what might have happened.

LISA WALKED up to sit on the coffee table just in front of Josh's mother. She reached for her hands, disentangled them, and held them in her own. However much Lisa might disapprove of how this couple were handling their son's illness, they were clearly troubled at the disaster they had narrowly averted. In their way, these people did care about their son. Looking Josh's mother in the eyes, Lisa spoke very gently.

"Mrs. Reynolds, no one is dying today. Josh will be fine. He needs to be watched, and we dare not give him an extra dose of his medication. We can't risk the complications that might arise with doing that. However, tonight he can take the correct pill, and he should be out of the woods." She looked at Mr. Reynolds. "I can stay the night with you just in case, if you wish."

An obvious look of relief washed across his face.

Dee grabbed at Lisa to pull her into a hug. "Thank you, dear. Oh, you have been Josh's salvation." She leaned back, and the woman transformed into the gracious hostess Lisa remembered from her earlier visit, even if it was a bit overly bright and forced. "We're so fortunate Craig was able to arrange for you to come. Josh adores you. You certainly must be aware of that." She stood and held the old medicine bottle out to her husband. "Craig, throw these out. I want to forget these ever existed. I intend to go in to see my son, and then I'll arrange something for lunch. It will be a very late lunch, but I'm famished. You, Miss Bevier?" She leaned in to her husband and gave him a kiss on the cheek. "Craig, you've not even had breakfast. You must be ready to drop. I won't be long with Josh."

After she was gone, Lisa looked up at Josh's father. "He's not truly out of the woods, yet. I hope you understand that."

"I assumed you were just reassuring my wife." He took a deep breath and closed his eyes for a moment. He looked up and attempted to smile. "Thank you, Lisa. I especially appreciate your willingness to stay. I know this is a very big inconvenience. With the storm outside, I can't even offer you the island." He walked to a window that in better weather opened to a distant view of the sea. The only thing that could be seen was a darker dark against the horizon. Without turning, he said to her, "I do love my son. I want you to know that. I've never known how to deal with his ... problems. It's been hard to find common ground." He abruptly turned to her. "I must know that you recognize where I stand. I do love him, although my wife sometimes thinks not. The Center. He's been gone so much of the time. When he's here, I'm lost."

Lisa looked through the windows at the rain and what she could see of the trees that surrounded the house. They were thrashing in the wind. She didn't really want to stay the night. She was afraid the weather wasn't simply a passing thunderstorm, and that it would get much worse. However, she couldn't abandon these people, not when she was the one they'd called as their only hope.

She smiled at Josh's father. "Your son would like to attend

public school. Has he ever told you that?" The look of surprise on his face told her he hadn't. "He'd also like to drive his El Camino to the high school parking lot, and he'd like to show it off to everyone."

Craig turned and abruptly wiped his eyes with his hands. "He told you about the El Camino? It was his grandfather's car. Did he tell you that? I had it rebuilt for Josh. I thought he hated it. He's never wanted to drive it."

Just then, his wife stepped into the room. She laughed. "Craig, what is with you? Josh is finally well, and now's when you cry. Don't be a baby." She walked over and pressed her hand to his face for a moment, and then she disappeared into the kitchen. Her voice called out, "Miss Bevier, Josh wishes to see you. I think he wants your permission to get up. He needs the bathroom or something. Will you check on him?"

Lisa smiled at Mr. Reynolds and stood. Yes, this was exactly like the last time she was here. However, she hadn't come for Mr. Reynolds or for Mrs. Reynolds. She'd come for Josh, and she had come to run away from Mr. Royster. She had gotten everything she wished, even if she'd had to brave a storm to do it.

After she helped Josh up and sent him down the hall, she stood at the windows in his bedroom looking out across the island. This was an interior view, and she couldn't see much. It wasn't the view that was important to her. In her mind, she was seeing a scene from earlier that morning, one that wouldn't leave her alone. Despite her proclamation that she had wanted to run away from Mr. Royster, she knew it was otherwise. She hadn't wanted to run. For that reason alone she was glad for this distraction from his pull on her. Perhaps being here on this remote island would shake him from her thoughts.

Still, she found herself searching in the darkness for the face from the picture on her mother's kitchen table. As hard as she stared out through the glass, she couldn't find that strong jaw line and those brooding eyes that had grabbed her attention. She wanted to, because now there was an emptiness inside that only this morning she had hoped that man would help her fill. However, he had disappeared as quickly as the morning sunshine, and that had been very brief, indeed.

She decided what she would do. She would fill the rest of the day with Josh. She would charm him, and he would charm her in return. He would take his proper medication tonight, then again in the morning, and tomorrow she could chase the good Mr. Royster with as much energy as she could muster. She laughed as she thought that, and she turned at the sound of Josh's feet on the wooden floor.

"What's funny, Miss Bevier?"

She looked at his bare feet, and they were flat on the floor. She glanced into his eyes, and she winked at him. "Because of you, Josh Reynolds, I get a two-day vacation on your island. You, young man, are my best friend ever." His face broke into a grin, and she continued, "Your feet, Josh. I'm very impressed. They're both flat to the floor, just the way they should be."

He grinned even broader. "Always. I practice. You're here just for me? You mean that?"

"Of course. If you feel like putting a shirt on, your mother is preparing lunch. Are you hungry?"

"Very!" His eyes had begun to twinkle.

Then, just for a moment, Lisa stepped to him and took his chin in her hand. She looked him hard in the face. It was a beautiful face, too, just as beautiful in motion as it had been earlier in sleep. "If you were ten years older, I'd ask you out on a date. I love you that much." Then she laughed and put one arm around him in a quick hug. "However, I have another man to chase."

He looked at her in dismay. "Andrew? He lives here on the island. Sometimes he closes up our house for us."

Lisa laughed at the idea she would chase a man who had

once cut her so deeply. However, she wouldn't tell Josh that. She hadn't even known he still lived here. Now she was glad she hadn't been back.

"No, Josh. Not Andrew. I have someone else."

He grinned. "Good. I don't like Andrew very much."

She laughed again. "I don't much, either. I like this other man much better." As Josh reached to a chest-of-drawers to pull out a shirt, she stepped out of the room. Only then did she finish her thought.

"Even if he doesn't know I exist."

MERV PULLED the old SUV into the garage where Bette had parked it the night before. He and Leetha had been out shopping for the morning, and the hardest thing had been to buy only things they could carry home in their suitcases. Today, they hadn't been successful.

Leetha turned around in the truck to survey what they carried in the back. She turned her eyes to her husband. "Merv, what will we do with a six-foot tall flying horse?"

His eyes sparkled, and he squeezed her knee. "It's not a horse. It's a wind vane. I'll put it on the roof, so everyone will know I'm flying high with love for you."

She laughed at the silliness. "And the association will force you to take it down. It'll have to go in the country on the farm-house. You know that."

A movement from the house caught their attention. It was Bette coming to greet them. Merv and Leetha looked at each other. Merv spoke first.

"What do you think she'll say about the horse?"

"She'll say we found the only unicorn available for sale in New Hampshire."

He chuckled. "A unicorn? I seem to recall a unicorn has a horn on its head. We have wings on our horse."

"Oh." Leetha smiled. "That's right. So, I guess that means

we bought a Pegasus."

Merv whispered, "I guess we did, if that's what a winged horse is called. You think she'll notice?"

His wife reached and gently pinched him as Bette stepped up to the window. Their winged horse was sitting in the back of their host's truck, and there was no way to hide it.

Bette laughed. "What do we have here? This is the biggest wind vane I've ever seen. Did you two steal it off someone's barn? It certainly looks original. It even has pigeon droppings still on it."

"Bette, don't laugh," Leetha started, as she opened the door. "Merv is planning to put this on our roof so the whole world knows he's flying high with love for me."

Bette walked to the back and opened the tailgate. She reached in to rub her hand over the patina that covered the copper vane, and she looked at Merv with a twinkle in her eyes.

"So, does this mean you enjoy horsing around, or you're a horse's rear end?"

Leetha laughed. She called to her husband, "She's got you there, Merv." Turning to Bette, she said, "I think you're right on both accounts. Where can we unload this until we can get some-one to ship it home?" She looked to the front seat of the truck where Merv was watching them in the rearview mirror. "Merv? Get out and help."

"Help?" he called. "You two ladies haven't wrestled it out, already? It just weighs a smidge."

It weighed more than a smidge, but between the three of them, they managed to get it out and to the back of the garage. Bette said it would be safe there until a shipping company could come pick it up. She knew who to call, and she would be on the phone that very afternoon. However, she had lunch ready. Then she hustled them inside for her fresh, hot stew.

"THIS WILL warm the two of you," Bette said, as she spooned

out bowlfuls for both of them. "Did you hit any rain out there?"

Serving herself up a hearty portion, also, she sat at the table alongside her two guests. It hadn't rained yet on her property, but the fact that she hadn't been able to contact her grandson nagged at her. He was right on the coast, and remembering what Merv, Leetha, and she had discussed about the Center, she was worried about that place, too. What if a big storm came in? It could easily disrupt services in all eastern Massachusetts. What would those poor children do?

Her guests seemed such close friends that she began to share her concerns. They could understand completely, they assured her. Would she like them to drive down with her? They'd be glad to do that. If everything was Jim Dandy, then they would have at least gotten to see the school where her grandson attended for so many years.

During the meal, several times Bette reached and placed her hand on Leetha's. This woman from Texas who had come to visit over a succession of years was a comfort to her hostess, and the touch of familiar skin seemed to settle Bette's nerves.

Rockland would be just fine, she assured them, although the nagging remained. She wouldn't admit that. Instead, she said that he was a big boy, and he knew the water. If anyone did anything stupid, it would be that lobsterman friend of his, Tramwick. Her grandson was too smart to let that scoundrel tug him into too much trouble. Thank God for that.

Merv and Leetha smiled in agreement. They went along with Bette wholeheartedly, repeating her sentiment.

"Thank God for that."

THE HINGES on the metal door refused to budge as Rocky twisted the handle and put his shoulder against it. He turned to watch Tramwick pulling himself up onto the elevated walk circling the lighthouse.

"You say they've been renting this out?"

"Since Moses wore knee pants." Tramwick sniggered.

"How'd they get in?"

Tramwick set down the fuel and chuckled. He pointed to the hinges. "It opens outward."

Rocky's face clouded. He turned the handle and yanked, and it still refused to move. Tramwick joined him, and in a quick pull of strong backs, the door screamed, then swung free. Tramwick fell against the railing, and he picked himself up and brushed off his pants. He peered into the dimness. The doorway revealed a shallow foyer, with staircases on either side, one leading up and the other down, but the interior was in near darkness.

"Not much light, Rocky. Where's that lantern?" There were windows, but they were either curtained or shuttered. Nothing could be seen clearly. "Watch your feet, until we know what we're dealing with."

Stepping through the door with the unlit lantern in his hand, Rocky reached for the starter wand the other man held out to him. He pumped the fuel up, and with a click of the wand, light blazed into the room. He adjusted the fuel flow until the flame burned steadily and evenly.

"Open the blinds, Tram. It seems someone put every window covering known to man in here. Shutters. Curtains. We have it all. Let's get some outside on the inside."

Tramwick pulled one back and chuckled. "Doesn't make a real difference. They're all filthy. You can't see much from these."

Rocky sighed. "Well, there's at least some furniture."

"If you can call it furniture, my friend." Tramwick kicked a table leg, only to have it crumple sideways. He jumped forward to keep the whole thing from crashing to the floor. "Let's get the things in the boat hauled up, and then I want to see upstairs. This place has three floors, I understand. Maybe there's even a bed."

"Like I'd want to sleep on any bed in this place. I'm thinking this might not be such a great place to spend the rest of my weekend. It's filthy."

Tramwick slapped him on the shoulder and grinned. "You're planning on staying here for weeks when you're working on it. Toughen up. I might even get some of my friends and bring a party to you. If they get too drunk, we can just push 'em overboard."

They turned and looked at each other as the lighthouse began to vibrate with a low-pitched hum. Then, a louder, anguished wail took its place.

They knew. It was Fish.

Rushing to the door, they clambered out and peered over the rail. There he was huddled in the protection of the cockpit, his snout turned skyward, with a high-pitched howl emanating from his throat.

Tramwick ginned. "I guess he doesn't like the storm, either that, or he just wants to sing along."

"I don't guess we can bring him up," Rocky lamented. "Tram, let's get the supplies up here, so you can get back to shore. You're right. I need to tough this out. I've got light and a heater. You've packed food. I can do one day. I don't know about the night," he laughed, "but I guess I'll survive that, too. You've got a bag or a rope to hoist with?"

"All in the boat. Let me set this fuel inside. You're gonna want that before morning. Then we'll get you all loaded up." At a new, higher-pitched wail from his boat, he yelled over the rail, "Fish! Quieten up! We'll be right down."

Rocky backed onto the first section of steep steps. "I'm headed down. Meet you there."

At the boat, Fish was very glad to meet him. He jumped on him, and with the rocking of the vessel, he nearly went into the sea. Falling back to sit on the gunwale, Rocky pushed the big dog away.

"Down, Fish!" Tramwick leaped from the ladder onto the deck of the boat. "I'll lock you below if you keep on." He grinned at Rocky. "That'll get him quiet." Then he pointed and indicated the items that needed to go up. He pulled a rope from a locker. "The ice chest'll be awkward. I'll tie it shut, and then I'll go up top. I'll pull, and you can steady it underneath." He twisted the rope around the container, and with a deft movement of his wrist, the knot was secure.

Tramwick reached to grab the ladder, and he scrambled aloft with the rope in one hand, calling back, "Ready, Rocky. I'm pulling. You keep it from blowing around."

The ice chest did make it up fine, and bagged and tied, the rope soon had all the other items inside the lighthouse, also. Poor Fish howled again as he was left behind once more, louder when the men disappeared inside with the light so they could explore.

With only the lantern's illumination, much of what must be old and worn couldn't be seen. It was musty and cold. The steps were sturdy, at least, and two sets of feet made their way to the next level. Passing a window, Rocky rubbed his hand against a rattling pane of glass. He noticed moisture leaking around it and running down the inside.

"Here's one fix I'll need to make," he said, looking at the man standing beside him. "Gotta stop the water damage from getting worse. The frame probably needs replaced."

"Piece of cake for you," Tramwick called back, as the light-house began a subtle moaning sound. Then Rocky touched the glass again, and the noise stopped.

He laughed. "Air pressure against the glass. It's creating a resonance." He let go, and the sound started up again. "It might get nerve wracking before morning."

Tramwick topped the stair and exclaimed, "Wicked! A real bed!" He laughed.

Rocky joined him. There was a pair of bunk beds built right

into the wall. The wood they were made from was old, and in the lantern's light, initials were carved all over them. He walked up to shake the frames. They seemed sturdy enough. He hit one of the old mattresses, and dust billowed.

He turned to Tram with a grin. "Needs aired, I think."

Both men were still wearing their slickers, and the storm's water made dark spots on the floor as it dripped. Tramwick stepped up to Rocky and draped a yellow arm over his shoulder. He leaned close to his friend and tapped him on the chest with his fist.

"The floor seems pretty soft. I hear it's good for the back." Tramwick kicked his foot along the floorboards, and when dust flew up, he laughed. "A little dust never hurt anyone. Besides, there's a sofa below. I couldn't tell if it was all there, but you can always give that a try. Let's see up one more floor."

The next level was empty, and there was obvious damage to the floor. A wooden plank surface had been laid atop the original metal, and it was rotted in places, and missing in others. They stepped around the weakened spots to find a ladder. It led to a small room that opened to an equally small outside catwalk. Tramwick grinned, pointing to another ladder leading upward.

"The lantern room. There's where I'd spend the night. A good bottle of whiskey, the light for company, and the occasional toot of a foghorn to keep me from getting bored. You should try it."

Rocky took the rungs two at a time. Reaching the top, he unlatched a trap door into the glassed-in lantern room, and he crawled inside. He was surrounded with walls of red glass interspersed with clear. A low door in one wall opened to an uncovered, outdoor platform surrounding the room. He shielded his eyes as the light turned his direction.

"Come on in, Tram. I thought it'd be roomier than this." There was the sudden blast of a foghorn—a strangled honking noise—and Rocky covered his ears. He looked down through the opening, and he saw his friend laugh. Rocky dropped back through and pulled the door closed. "Why'd the foghorn go off?"

"The weather. Lack of visibility. I'm surprised it hasn't started before. It'll probably be every ten seconds from here on out. Are you ever going to have fun!"

Rocky wasn't quite so pleased. He slapped Tramwick on the chest, chiding him. "You knew about this? You brought me here, and you knew this would happen?"

Tramwick backed off, laughing. "Not knew. I sort of expected it. The weather and all. If fog comes in, I can promise you it'll stay on. Otherwise, you *might* get a few hours' sleep here and there. It'll be better down below. The walls and the floors should muffle it quite a bit. Be a good sport, Rocky. What would Bette say?"

Rocky began to retreat sullenly down the series of rooms. "She'd say I'm crazy to be out here with you. She'd tell me to get a real friend, not a drunken lobsterman to hang around with." He glared at Tram. He'd wanted to come, and he knew Tram hadn't forced him to tag along. This weather, though, made him jittery.

Tramwick leaped past the final few steps, and his feet slammed down at Rocky's side. The floor shivered, and Rocky gave him a stern look of disapproval. Tramwick grabbed him around the shoulders, involuntary ducking as the horn sounded once more. When it was over, he grinned broadly.

"My very good friend, I guess that's too bad for your grandmother. It seems you got me, and Bette gets to live with that. I don't think I'm too awful. Why, it seems to me like yesterday you were at Bette's in New Hampshire far from the freedom of the sea. Today, you're here on a lighthouse with your good friend and your dog. My dog, actually, if we let him have his way. Besides, who got you to the island?"

Rocky grudgingly answered, "You did, Tram." The wind

183

began to whistle through the loose pane of glass.

"That's right." Tram pulled his arm tight, squeezing his friend to him to emphasize his next point. "Who's planning to come back to get you tomorrow?"

"You are, Tram."

The foghorn sounded once more, and Tramwick released him with a flourish. "There you go. I'm the best thing that's ever happened to you. So, while I love Bette as much as you do, I don't trust a word she says when it comes to me." He stepped to the final set of stairs, and with another flourish, he leaped down them in two bounds.

Rocky studied the dark recess where Tramwick had disappeared, and he leaned to pick up the lantern. Tram was right on the money. Despite his occasional irritation with the man, that was exactly why he considered him his friend. It was also why he didn't listen to Bette one whit when it came to Tram. Tram was good for him; he pulled him out of himself when he'd hermit otherwise in his boat shed; and he was the best friend he'd ever had. Sometimes he thought he was his only friend, at least the only person who'd ever truly felt like a friend.

He moved to the steps and started down. "Tram," he called, letting his irritation slip away, "you need to get Fish back to shore. You're staying in Rockland tonight?"

When he crossed the final step, the wooden plank under his shoe squeaked. He found Tram in front of the open door. He was silhouetted against the stormy sky outside, and in his yellow slicker, he looked the iconic image of the lobsterman he was. The rain lashed the floor at his feet, and the moving lantern made shifting shadows dance around him. From under his cap, his face was strong and grizzled with a day's growth of beard. He turned as he heard Rocky on the steps, and he nodded towards the storm outside, calling over the noise, "Come grab the door, Rocky. You'll want to try to keep this place as dry as you can. Get that heater going, too. I'll be back for you tomorrow, me and Fish." He looked around the room, and he let out a sudden laugh. "By the way, thanks for Royce's clothes. His underwear is much better than yours."

Then he was out the door and on his way down the ladder. Rocky made his way out and held onto the railing as he watched him board the boat. Fish jumped on him with undisguised pleasure as he climbed aboard, and Tram pushed him away.

Rocky paused as the foghorn split the air, and he remembered the borrowed slicker he had on. He yelled down, his voice fighting against the wind, "Your slicker. Do you need it?"

Tram called back, "I can't wear two. Return it when I come to get you. Anyway, it's not like it can get lost. Who else would you give it to? I don't see any beautiful women rowing up in distress, do you? You're the only one here." He laughed again, and reaching to start the boat, he untied the lines that held him secure and was gone in a gurgling spray of water.

Rocky stood for a few minutes and watched him disappear into the storm's haze, his friend's boat tearing through the choppy sea. He looked up as the horn sounded once again. Turning and closing the door, he found that inside it was indeed much quieter, and he knew he would eventually tune out the repetitive horn, the same as he'd tuned out his grandmother's old hall clock when he was growing up. It had tocked and chimed, and all the years he lived there, he never heard it. Although, now when he returned, it was all he could hear. He knew this would be much the same.

Adjusting the light to consume as little fuel as possible, he explored one more section of the old building. Down a floor was the cluttered and debris-filled remains of an old kitchen and the lighthouse's only toilet. He refused to enter the space, as it was a safety hazard in its current condition. He returned to the main floor and pulled the heater to him to check the reservoir. He'd need to shut the upper floors off so only this space was warmed. He eyed the sofa. It might do for sleeping. It didn't seem Tram

185

had thought to bring any linens, so he'd be in his clothes all night. At least he'd put on fresh ones for his meeting with Miss Bevier that morning.

As he prepared to light the heater, and without the hurry of the day to distract him, his thoughts returned to the start of his day just outside Boston. It was hours ago, yet it seemed like a week or more. He knew why he'd broken the pencil, and he knew why he left in such a rush. It wasn't his dyslexia, either, or the autism that sometimes controlled the way he responded in certain situations. Both those were frustrating to him, and he'd be happier if he had neither. However, the real reason for his bumbling actions that morning had been of a more personal nature.

When he stepped into that room to find Miss Lisa Bevier waiting on him, the rush of attraction had overwhelmed him. He'd been able to think of nothing other than the beautiful woman with him. That was the reason his dyslexia had written his words backwards, and that was the reason his autism had forced the pencil to break in his hand.

He hadn't known how to recover from his stupidity. In the rush of emotions, he'd only known the woman in the room with him; and the sudden, intense memory of being laughed at when he was sixteen was there all over again. He'd kissed that girl. He'd been attracted to her, and she'd laughed at him. He'd run that time, too.

While he was on the boat with Tram, the sea had taken his attention. Now, however, he sat alone with only the heater to warm him. The wind whistled around the structure that held him safe, and the moaning from the loose windowpane echoed down the stairwells he hadn't yet sealed off.

In this solitary location, with no one else around, Rocky had nothing to do other than think, and all he could think of was Miss Bevier. Lisa Bevier. He knew nothing about her, except that she worked at the Center and was a nurse. That she was beautiful. Plus, she had a kind voice. And he had taken her hand.

He sat in the warmth of the glow emanating just in front of him, and he looked at the hand that had touched hers. This day it had driven his truck home, it had run through Fish's fur, and it had held on as Tram's boat fought the waves. It had climbed the ladder into this lighthouse, and it had hoisted his goods aboard. However, as he looked at it, he could see only one thing.

Lisa had held this hand. She'd reached to him, and he'd reached back. Her warmth had seeped into his skin, and it had shot like fire into his heart. He'd run from her, not from the paper form he'd mutilated with that broken pencil. He had run from his body's sudden attraction to her, and he wished he hadn't.

He was suddenly lonely. He'd accepted himself years ago. He hadn't always liked himself, but accepted, that he had done. He knew his life would never be shared with a woman, not being inferior goods as he was. He'd made every effort not to need a woman to share his life.

Now, though, his desire for this woman was out of his control, and he knew there would never be an opportunity to see her again. She was in Boston, and he'd never return to the Center. He couldn't. This morning had shown him that. There were too many sour emotional ties there he'd never cut. He could never return there, and she would never find him here. This weekend, he had only his lighthouse for company.

He sighed and stood. He also knew he would have dreams of her, this woman he didn't really know. Those dreams would haunt him all weekend. He had dreamed of that girl at sixteen. He knew he would dream this time, too.

Walking to the steps, he closed the upper floors off. Now this room would warm, at least enough to be tolerable. He slipped the slicker off, and searching, he found a series of pegs on the wall. He positioned the slicker on one to finish drying and began to walk around the room. That's why he was here. It wasn't to think about Lisa. He needed to see just what needed to be done to the lighthouse. He'd catalog the needed repairs in his head, and when he returned next time, he would be prepared to work. He was very good at keeping track in his head.

His ability to keep track using only his mind was also his downfall. It was the very reason his thoughts kept coming back to Lisa over and over. Growing up he had been forced to train his brain to work that way. When he was at the Center, his teachers had given a name to the way his brain remembered certain types of things. Photographic. He'd never really known what that meant, just that he didn't forget easily. Faces, anyway, and shapes and boats and things that mattered to him. What he saw he remembered.

He'd seen Lisa, and he'd been drawn very strongly to her. He couldn't forget. As hard as he tried that night, he just couldn't get her face out of his mind.

Chapter 12

LISA SAT on a side chair of supple leather, with her feet propped under her. It wore low arms, something transitional that was probably in style a decade before but too expensive to throw out. She found it very comfortable but didn't remember it from her earlier visit. She supposed it was one from the Reynolds' city home that had been relegated to summer status. She rested and watched the fire in the stove. It was nice here, even if the rain seemed to pelt the house with more and more force. The wind had picked up, too. Despite the lashing the house was forced to slough off outside, it remained warm and dry inside.

She kept her eye on the bathroom door down the hallway. Earlier Josh had been at a table by the front window working a puzzle that was set up. He had eaten the late lunch his mother fixed, and his father had joked with him. Josh had laughed, his eyes sparkling. Then he had sat at the table to work the puzzle.

His mother had been reading a book—was still reading it,

totally absorbed—and periodically, his father stepped up to adjust the fire. Occasionally, he added more wood.

Without warning, Josh had looked outside with a smile and stood. *"It's nice out. I think I'll go get ready."* Then he'd stepped to the bathroom.

His parents hadn't paid attention, except to watch him walk from the room. Lisa had watched more closely, though. Just going to the bathroom was normal. Josh's words weren't.

With his actions, she recognized he might be having another seizure, though if so, it was a small one, the kind that affected his mind and not the rest of his body. Through the Center, she had become very familiar with them. He wouldn't convulse or fall to the ground. Only grand mal seizures would cause that. These small seizures would cause him to do unusual things, odd behaviors that might seem funny at first, but that could develop into something dangerous. These were the seizures that made him dangerous to himself.

She knew she was correct when he walked into the hall. From where she was sitting, she saw him first, before his parents caught sight of him. She prepared herself for his parents' reactions.

He had stripped down to his boxers. A towel was in one hand, and a bright smile was on his face. His expression turned to dismay when he walked into the living room.

"Come on, Mum, Dad. I always go by myself." He seemed to suddenly catch sight of Lisa. His expression brightened. "Miss Bevier! Will you swim with me? The water always warms best when the sun's bright. Did you bring a suit?"

Lisa glanced at Josh's mother and father. When they sat dumbfounded, she spoke carefully, "Is that your suit you're wearing, Josh?"

He looked down, and his upper body flushed with embarrassment. "I must have left it at home. I looked, and these were all I had. I hope you don't mind."

Lisa stood and put her arm around his shoulders. "Josh, can we swim later? I forgot my suit."

He was immediately crestfallen. "But . . . it's so hot outside. The sun . . . and it's summer, Miss Bevier." He turned to look out the window. "Please, go with me. Mum and Dad never do."

Lisa looked at them, and she saw the emotions in their faces that she hoped meant they understood what was going on in their son's mind. She turned and touched his chin, moving his face to look directly into hers. "Tomorrow. Let's swim tomorrow. It's already getting dark outside."

He edged away from her. "Excuses. Don't be like Mum and Dad. They always have excuses. They call them reasons, but they're just excuses. I'm going to swim. Come if you want, Miss Bevier." He moved to the back door, and before anyone could react, he had it open and was gone into the shadowy torrent whipping against the glass.

The sounds of the wind and rain drummed in the warm and well-lighted room, and finding entry through the open door, the floor began to darken with the storm.

THE RAIN pummeled Chet's car. It was a very small vehicle, and the sound of the water hitting the metal outside resonated in the interior. If he wasn't mistaken, there were small bits of hail in the mixture.

The light up ahead burned steadily, telling the traffic to wait patiently for others to go. He observed that while lots of people were lined up with him to go forward, there was no one going across. The other light was green, but there were simply no cars. He couldn't understand why the light remained so long when no cars were going through.

Then green clicked on, and the red faded. He put in his clutch, and before engaging the transmission, he slid the shifter into second gear. He wouldn't have to shift as soon, if he could ease out in second. As he accelerated, he could hear the beat of a song, and he looked outside at the cars surrounding him, surprised that he could hear anyone's music through the rain. Then, glancing at his dash, he realized the music was his.

Reaching a hand to turn up the volume, he heard the engine rev too high and dropped his hand to shift to third. After a moment, he recognized the song. It was one he'd downloaded and written to a CD before he realized it was a tweener's song. Pulling a new CD from the visor, he pushed the eject button and pulled the old one out as it rolled from the radio. The traffic speeded up around him, and he dropped both disks on the seat next to him in order to shift. As he did so, the radio began to broadcast through his speakers.

"... *winds are now up to seventy-two miles per hour at the center of the storm. While still offshore, the secondary storm will force Tropical Storm Christian toward the New England coast sometime tomorrow. Wind speeds will increase, and we expect Tropical Storm Christian to become a full-blown hurricane* ..."

As Chet pushed in his replacement CD, he thought about what a smart decision he'd made earlier. He could stay home for the rest of the day, and the storm wouldn't bother him. All he had to do was get the trash cans and the patio furniture inside.

Finally, pulling onto his street, he groaned. All three of his cans were in the middle of the road. He'd have to come back out in the rain to retrieve them. His blinker flashed, and with a quick motion of his feet and hands, his car was parked safely underneath his carport.

He opened the car door and sighed with relief. He'd spent extra money to add a carport on his house, and today it was worth every dollar. Other people might get soaked, but he had a dry spot to get out. Glancing back to the street, he could see no one else, and that meant his cans were okay for a minute. He needed to use the bathroom, anyway. All this water was making the morning's coffee go right through him.

Inside the house, in the dimness of the room, the first thing he noticed was the blinking light on his phone. No one left him messages except the schedulers at his job. Usually it was when there was something out of town that he needed to pick up after his regular hours. His finger pushed the button, and he stood impatiently. He'd just gotten the rest of the day off. If he had to go directly back in, he'd be very upset. Sondra had promised.

"Pickup request for Chet Abramson, ID No. 76903. Location: Waterville Valley, New Hampshire. Requestor: Bette Royster. Timeframe: Within the next week. Chet, please call to confirm." Then there was a giggle. *"Chet, how did that sound? This is Sondra. You really do have to call if you want this one. It's something big, and I get to ride up there with you. I told Mr. Boenker it might be heavy, and you'd need an assistant. Call me, Chet, and I hope you're enjoying your day off. I'm still here until the sun don't shine. That was about seven hours ago, I think. Bye!"*

He grinned. Good old Sondra. The name Royster had a familiar ring, the same as the man he'd met that morning. He wondered if the two could be related, and then he decided probably not. He'd get to ride with Sondra, though. For that, he'd take the pickup no matter what it was.

He took the house phone and dialed in. When the line picked up, he recognized Sondra's spiel. He let her run through it, and then he spoke to her. "Sondra? Chet. You bet I'll go."

On the other end he heard a very happy squeal.

EVEN LISA was uncomprehending for a moment.

Josh's father immediately ran to the open door. He leaned into the darkness, letting the rain pelt his shoulders, and finally yelled, "Josh!"

Mrs. Reynolds sat immobile on the sofa. Her book was still open, and she was holding her place with one finger. She looked dumbfounded.

Lisa knew this family didn't get it quite yet. Josh's medication was off, and he couldn't come back. He actually thought it was the middle of summer and the sun was shining. His brain was telling him that, no matter what his eyes saw or what his skin felt.

She took a deep breath. Someone had to go get him, and his parents weren't making smart decisions.

She threw herself towards Mr. Reynolds and ducked under his arm. Turning her head to look him in the eyes, she spoke softly but with authority, "Your son's having a seizure. He can't simply return. We must go get him." Without waiting, she stepped into the maelstrom that was assaulting the island.

As she moved forward, unsure of where to look, she was relieved to hear Josh's father at her side. She had stepped out of the house confidently, but she immediately realized she didn't know her way. Too many years had passed since she'd walked this place, and she had never done it in the blinding rain.

It didn't take long to find him. He was at the water's edge, and he was sitting on a large stone that jutted into the surf. The tide was high, and the water roiled with the wind. Spray showered his exposed skin. He held the towel at his side as if he would use it once he left to head back inside.

Lisa reached him first. "Josh, you must come back to the house." She blinked as the cold ocean spray showered her. If anything, it was colder than the rain that had chased her as she searched for this boy.

He looked at her with distress in his eyes. "Miss Bevier, you didn't wear your suit. It's just as well. The water isn't as warm as I expected. I might as well go back with you." He looked at his father. "Dad won't swim, either."

As he stood, his father stepped up to put his arm around his son, and Lisa let him take over. "Thank you," he mouthed to her.

She followed them back to the house, shivering in the cold

rain.

IT WAS when Josh was in a hot bath that his eyes suddenly jumped from side to side. He looked up to see his father and Lisa in the room with him. The world had shifted without his awareness. He'd been working the puzzle in the living room, and now he was soaking in the tub. He hadn't fallen asleep. He'd *lurched* from one scene to another.

Miss Bevier. She was wearing one of his mother's house robes, and her hair was wet. In that moment, he felt all his successes at the school unraveling. Now he knew why Miss Bevier had come to the island. It wasn't a vacation. It was to watch over him. He was having seizures, and he couldn't be alone with his parents. They wouldn't know what to do.

He closed his eyes and sank deep into the water, letting the warmth cover his face to hide his embarrassment. He reached his hands to cover himself, and he was relieved to find he still had his shorts on.

His father lifted him by the shoulder. "Son, what are you doing?"

Lisa interrupted him with a touch. "Craig, I think he just came out of his seizure. He's a smart boy. He knows. He was in the living room, and now he's here. Let me step out. When he's warm, he can get dressed." She looked tenderly at the boy in the tub, speaking to him before she left the room. "Josh, I enjoyed our adventure very much. Thank you for letting me go with you. The sea was beautiful in the rain." She winked at him and got a smile of relief that played at the corner of his mouth.

Mr. Reynolds turned to her and whispered, "Your words are magic to him. I don't see how you do it."

She just patted him on the shoulder with a smile, and she closed the door after her.

"Dad—" Josh began.

"Not now, Son. Just know that I love you very much, and

195

Miss Bevier and I are going to make sure that you're fine."

Josh felt tears begin to run down his face.

LISA MOVED into the living room to see Mrs. Reynolds with her book still in her hand. She stepped to sit beside her.

"Josh is fine. He's warming up in the tub, and your husband will stay with him as he dresses. He's over it now."

Dee looked at Lisa, and tears gathered in her eyes. "Why, Miss Bevier? It's cold and wet outside. Couldn't he see that?"

Lisa patted her hand. "No, he couldn't. Let's wait to worry until we get him back on his correct medication. It should have an immediate effect."

"When, Miss Bevier? When can we give him the correct tablet?"

Lisa looked at her watch. "Eight, maybe. If he took one at eight this morning, then no sooner than eight. There are side effects at higher dosages. Watching him is better than risking that. I'm here, and I deal with this every day. I deal with *Josh* every day. I know him. He'll be fine."

His mother closed her eyes and sighed heavily. "Thank God for that." Then she turned back to her book, and she began to read. As Lisa stood, she wasn't sure if she was reading for a distraction, or because she didn't care. It didn't really matter, she supposed. Josh was all right, and next week he would be back at the Center in trusted hands. Hers.

She went to stand at the French door that Josh had earlier stepped from into the stormy darkness. She knew he'd truly seen the sun shining through the glass, and he'd felt the heat of summer on his skin. Two pills. He had taken two incorrect pills, and his life had skewed out of normal just that fast.

She studied her face in the reflection the glass threw back at her. Her day had been the same as Josh's, skewed all out of normal, she thought ruefully. Her two pills had been different, though. Her first had been that man who had taken her heart with his apologies, and the second had been a blinking red light on her phone. Together, they had thrown her onto this island during a storm, and she was babysitting this man and his wife who didn't understand their son.

She turned to see Josh walk into the room. His hair was tousled and wet, just the way a teenager would leave it after being in the tub. His skin was pink where his flannel shirt left it exposed. His feet were bare at the bottom of his flannel sleeping pants, and he was a wiry scarecrow in his loose clothing. She smiled at him.

He grinned and walked up beside her, and he simply stood there. He was taller than she was, and in the glass's reflection, they could have been very much the same age. He smiled his crooked grin as he reminded her of her remark as he lay in the tub.

"What adventure?" He glanced behind him to see his father, and he looked back at Lisa. "We didn't go outside, did we? This weather's awful. Dad wouldn't say."

She chuckled and put her arm in his, and they stood, Josh in his flannels and Lisa in his mother's robe. She lifted her arm touched the reflection in the glass, and then she took his hand and touched it to the reflection also, holding her hand over his.

"Josh," she said, in the way a parent would introduce a favorite bedtime story, "can you touch yourself there? Can you touch me?" His reflection was there. Hers, too. The glass was like a mirror, and their reflections were sharp and clear.

He stood, comfortable and secure in her presence. "No. It's only the glass. It's cold, too."

She smiled, and she felt moisture in her eyes at his simple answers. He would follow her story, and he would get her meaning. Whether he would accept it was up to him.

"So, where are the people in the glass?" She removed her hand from his and placed it flat on the cold surface. It was as if their hands were attempting to touch the hands of the people in

197

front of them, their reflections.

He thought for a moment. He was taking her question very seriously, and she was glad for that. His words to her a moment ago had also asked a very valid question. *"What adventure?"* Her answer as he had lain in the tub had been meant to reassure him. Yet, the seventeen-year-old in him wanted the explanation behind her words. Still, it was vital he not be demeaned for an illness he couldn't control.

He pulled his hand back to touch his chest. "I'm here, and I'm not touching the glass. When I touch the glass, I can't reach the reflection. I can't touch the me I see there." He turned to look at Lisa to see if he had answered her question.

"So, Josh. Where are the people in the reflection? You're here." She reached and placed her hand on his chest. There was the minutest quiver of his muscles, those small spasms that she knew he worked so hard to control. "Yet, you're reflected there." She pointed. "You say you can't touch the reflection. Tell me, then, where is it?"

He touched the glass and grinned. "It's past the glass." He looked at her, pleased to have worked out her meaning so easily. "It's outside."

"Is the reflection you?"

He paused. "Yes and no. It looks like me, so it is me. I can't touch it, so it's not me."

"Very good, Josh. Are you cold?"

He looked at her with his eyebrows raised. "No, of course not. The fire's going."

She laughed. "Is the person you see in your reflection cold?"

He laughed at that. "Of course not. It's me. It's just outside."

She patted him on his shoulder, and she looked at the reflection of his face next to hers in the clear panes that held the cruel weather at bay. "That's the adventure we took. We went to the shore for a swim, and it wasn't cold. Outside, the sun was shining, and the air was warm. Do you remember any of it, Josh?

198

You invited me for a swim."

"Did you go with me?"

She hugged his arm. "No. I didn't bring a suit. I would have, though. Next summer. I'll swim with you, then. All you have to do is ask."

Mr. Reynolds walked past, and he whispered one word before continuing out of the room.

"Magic."

She turned to watch him walk away, and she smiled. It wasn't magic. She loved this boy as if he were her own. He was, in a way, and sometimes she thought he loved her, too.

However, it was not a boy's love she needed, not today. It was that of a strong-jawed man with wide shoulders and red hair, one who felt the need to apologize even when no offense had been given. There was only one man she could think of who fit the bill, and he was nowhere near North Haven Island.

She looked at Josh. This boy would have to do for now. Tonight, when she was alone in a strange bed, then she would deal with Mr. Royster. Perhaps he wouldn't run from her then. Perhaps he would rescue her from her own inner roiling sea. He might reach out with his strong arm and pluck her from the storm raging inside of her, and they would huddle against the fury of the night.

She shook her head. She was getting silly, now. She turned to Josh. "I'm hungry. Can you make a sandwich?"

He grinned, shifting topics with the ease of seventeen. "The best. Wheat or white?"

"You pick. Put anything on it you want." When he was gone, she stepped to see how his mother was doing. She leaned to her and touched her arm. "Are you all right?"

Josh's mother looked up from her book with red eyes. "I almost killed him." Then, vacantly, she looked back down at her book.

Lisa glanced and realized she hadn't turned a page in all that time. She gave the woman's arm a gentle squeeze and turned to the kitchen. As she stepped inside, she heard Josh's voice.

"Milk?"

Nodding, she pulled up a stool at a counter, and she watched the seventeen-year-old perform at something he felt very confident at. She was his audience, and he was on stage. When he was finished, she would gobble up his performance in praise, and he would know he had done well. He was so adorable. It was too bad his parents couldn't see it. They wanted him to be perfect, and he was just Josh.

Lisa knew they would see him as perfect, if they only knew how to look. He was excellent at being himself, and that was all he needed to be.

In fact, he was a faultless version of exactly who he was meant to be.

"DID YOU bring me a cup of coffee, too?" Bill Taggert looked up from his computer monitor. It was nearly midnight, and the station always ran slowly this time of the night.

Lexi Rollmann rolled her eyes. "Nooo." Her voice twisted up on the end as if her response was a question, but it wasn't. "I'll watch things if you want to go get your own." She set down her coffee along with the box she was carrying, and she began to remove her coat. She'd worked at the station for two years, the last six months on nights. She hoped for a promotion up the ladder soon. The upcoming hurricane might be just the ticket for a motivated girl. Bill? Yeah, she liked him, but she didn't plan to let anyone get in her way.

Bill laughed. "No thanks. I'll take yours." He snatched it from her while her hands were busy.

She glared at him with a look that could have pierced armor plate. Then, her demeanor changed, and she laughed. "In that case, I'm glad I brought two." With a deft movement, she reached into the box and pulled out a second cup that was twice as large as the first. "This one was yours, but since you claimed that one already, I guess I should keep this for myself."

He looked inside the box. "What else is in there? Ah! Donuts. You're God's gift to this station, you know that?"

"Of course." She reached to claim one before he took them both, as she nodded at the displays around the room. "What about this storm? Look at that. Christian and that other one. They finally combined. Has Christian reached hurricane force, yet?" She walked up to sit on a desk right in front of one especially large monitor, taking a big bite of her donut.

He leaped to the monitor in excitement, almost spilling his coffee. Putting it down, he reached out, actually touching the image.

"Right here. See this? A hook. I think there might even be tornadoes in this. Over here, this is the remains of the secondary system that's now pushing Christian west. Christian has simply absorbed all the energy. See here? Look at the wind velocities. Right there. It's *over* hurricane strength. Just not at the eye."

"Not the eye, huh?" She looked at him, lifting one eyebrow.

He returned to his seat, shaking his head at her lack of enthusiasm. "By 9:00 AM. All the models show that. That's about the same time the eye should start to move over the outer islands. It's a big eye, too."

She looked at the display. "Who would have thought? All of a sudden like that. This just came together." She took another bite, finishing her confection in two mouthfuls. "That was a ballsy move of Frank's this morning, wasn't it? I envy people who can just *feel* the weather patterns. They have no sense of doubt. Someday I'll be Frank, and I'll make ballsy predictions. I'll go out on a limb, and I'll issue evacuation notices. People will flee, and I'll know I've saved lives."

Bill laughed. "Sorry. Can't happen."

"Why not? I can be as good as Frank."

He looked at her and raised one eyebrow. "You might be as

good as Frank one day. Ballsy? No way. You have to have balls, first." Then he grinned.

He should have ducked, because he had left his donut within her reach. She hit him upside the head. Or, for that matter, maybe he did duck. She used to play girls' softball, and she had been an all-state pitcher. Maybe it was just her good aim, but that donut was his, right on his temple.

He laughed about it, but it did hurt. Not only did she have good aim, she also held the state record for high-speed pitches.

She was very good.

ROCKY TURNED on the sofa. There'd been a high tide during the night, and he's sworn the spray off the breakers was crashing against the lighthouse windows.

He felt under his back. Yes, he was certain about something else. There was a hole in the cushion. The sofa smelled bad, too. Very bad.

And he was hot. He had all his clothes still on, and he was warm and sweaty.

He knew one other thing. The foghorn had gone off most of the night, and no, it hadn't been the same as his grandmother's clock. He hadn't been able to tune it out and not hear it. He'd endured it all night long. Every ten seconds.

He sat up and put his feet on the floor. The building vibrated with the force of the water. He'd thought so during the night, and now he was certain. Standing, he walked to the heater. He blinked to clear his eyes, and he looked at the red glow that was keeping the room warm. Tram had brought a good one. Maybe too good, as indicated by his sweaty back.

Reaching over his shoulders, he pulled at his shirt until it came over his head. That was better. He debated on stripping down further but nixed that idea. He'd have to remove his shoes, and he didn't want to be barefoot, not when he didn't know just what he was walking on.

He stepped to one of the windows. Rubbing it with his hand, he looked out, and in the distance, he could see pinpoints of light. In the thrashing rain, the lights seemed to twinkle off and on, but they were houses, he bet. There were islands close. He'd seen Tram navigate them yesterday, and besides, he knew the map of the Fox Islands. He'd been here several times over the years, usually by way of the state ferry. That meant he knew where this lighthouse was in relation to his surroundings. If it were pretty weather and the water were warmer, he could probably swim to either North Haven or Vinalhaven. However, that would be a near impossibility in this weather. The cold would bring hypothermia within minutes. No, there would be no swimming to either one of the big islands. None of the smaller ones, either.

He rubbed his arms, feeling his hands slide along muscle that came from working with the wood from which he built his ships. He was surprised to work his fingers into several that were sore. The boat ride up from Massachusetts? Possibly. The water had been rough, and he'd had to hang on the entire way. That sofa hadn't helped. He was glad Tram would be back today. Before he came out to spend any more days here, he'd want a better place to sleep. Those bunks up top, perhaps, if the mattresses were aired. One of them might have been a better choice last night, even.

While he didn't know the time Tram was returning, there was one thing he did know: the call of nature. He needed to find somewhere to let the mother goddess have her way. He hadn't seen any facilities other than the one down below, and he was certain it didn't work. That meant he had to improvise, perhaps outside on the walkway that surrounded the structure. He could barely see the shore, just that there were lights on across the water. Who would see anything he did outside? If they were smart, in this weather, they wouldn't even be looking.

Peering through the window, he snorted, nixing that idea.

Foam flicked repeatedly against the glass, making it clear the wind was pushing spray to this level. He glanced at the ceiling, remembering the outside walk around the lantern room. He could take care of his business there. It wasn't like there weren't tons of water already coming down out of the sky, not even counting what was crashing around the lighthouse at its base.

Working his way up the steps, he made a point to close the first floor off to keep it warm. The cold air on the second floor felt good to his bare torso for a moment, but by the time he got to the lantern room, he discovered he was missing the warmth of his shirt. He located the small door that provided egress to the outside. He set the lantern aside and worked until he had it unfastened.

He wanted to be on the side of the lighthouse out of the blast of the storm, if he could. That sounded reasonable to him until he looked out and realized he would get wet no matter what. With the increased noise of the water's onslaught and the unexpected sharpness of the foghorn's indiscriminate blast, his body suddenly gave him no choice. He would go out there, or he would go where he stood.

He tightened his groin as he scrambled onto the walk. He was almost dancing, and he refused to let the light flashing past distract him. This had become a pressing need, and not even the pelting rain that whipped past the protection of the tower lessened his determination to relieve his overloaded bladder. He took a deep breath as the pressure eventually subsided, and slowly he became aware how hard the rain was hitting his shoulders. This was no mere shower, and it was being driven hard by the wind.

As he readjusted his clothing and refastened his pants, he turned and was blasted in the face by needles of rain. Stepping to the side a bit, the wind caught him, and he was reminded how dangerous it was to be outside the lighthouse on this walk. These winds were strong enough to tear him off, and they would, if the main structure of the lighthouse wasn't protecting him.

He shivered, and it wasn't just from the cold or how wet he was getting. This was more than any simple tropical depression or storm. It was nearing hurricane strength, if it wasn't already there. He glanced at the beacon light flashing past, and he could see the water tearing from the top of the building. He grasped the door to step inside, and a piercing blast of the foghorn startled him. As he slipped through and closed the panel, he couldn't stop shaking. Looking down, he realized he had completely drenched his pants. He sighed. He guessed the shoes would come off, after all.

Picking up the lantern to look around and find the cleanest place to sit, he removed his shoes. When he felt his socks, he realized the shoes had filled with water, and the socks had to come off, also. Then, trying to be quick and still keep them from the floor, he slipped out of his pants. Feeling around his shorts, he was glad to discover the water had only dampened them slightly. Slipping his feet back into his shoes, he carried his pants and socks in one hand and the lantern in the other as he started back down to the warmth of the main floor. He hoped Tram gave his pants time to dry before he showed up. He remembered the slicker hanging on the peg where he'd left it. He knew then he was an idiot. He could have worn the slicker and remained perfectly dry. Now, here he was in a strange lighthouse wearing nothing but his boxer shorts and a pair of shoes. God help the angels who decided to fly past and look in his windows. They might get an eyeful more than they bargained for.

As he stepped back on the main floor and reached to hang his pants on one of the wooden pegs to dry, he caught a glimpse of himself reflected in the uncovered window. He laughed at the strange image of the man standing in nothing but his underwear and shoes. He hadn't expected that view of himself. He was glad he was the only one on the lighthouse. If someone came to the door and knocked, he'd have to pretend he wasn't home, unless it was a stranded mermaid swimming in the sea. Or a beautiful woman. Her, he might invite in, even reach down to pull her from the water. Yeah, even in his boxers. That wouldn't be too much to ask of him, not if she was drowning.

Then he laughed at himself. No woman was going to be out today. However, idiot or not, Tram had better get here. He'd promised. He'd better not fall in, either. Tram was no woman, and that meant Rocky could think twice before jumping into the sea to pull him in. He would be on his own.

He wouldn't be, but Rocky didn't need to voice that. It was as good as written on his soul. Friends didn't abandon friends, not for any reason.

Period.

Chapter 13

THE WIND whistled in the room, and Lisa snuggled deeper into the softness of the bed. This was also as she remembered from all those years ago. This house had the most comfortable mattresses and the most sumptuous linens she had ever slept on.

The whistling noise was atrocious, though. She threw the covers back, and she looked outside the windows. All of them were uncovered. That had surprised her that long-ago summer, but she'd come to enjoy waking to the brilliance of the northern summer sun. However, she was now finding herself waking to the darkness of an island storm.

It was not quite dark. The outline of the trees against the roiling sky told her night was over. She peered at what she could see from each window. At one, she found the culprit that had awakened her. Pressing down on the lower casement, there was a sucking sound, and the room was quieter.

As she made her way back to the bed, she knew it was

quieter only in comparison. She could hear the pelting of the driven water slamming against the glass. Somewhere in the distance blared a foghorn. It was mournful with its repeated, short blasts. She realized it had been singing its song most of the night. She smiled to think it might be Mr. Royster calling to her.

She lay in bed, and as she drifted to the edge of sleep, she imagined a stranded sailor, one awaiting rescue, perhaps soaked from the storm. He was alone and on an island. No, she was already on an island. The image in her mind changed. He wasn't on an island. He was in a boat. Then she realized that a sailor with a boat wasn't stranded. However, he could be on a lighthouse. He was stranded high above the water, and there was no way off. It was in the middle of the ocean, perhaps even that lighthouse Josh was so fond of. Chicken Stones, or something like that. A sailor was stranded in Chicken Stones Lighthouse. He was there because a wild, drunken orgy had taken place, and when two young, beautiful women had been rescued from a shipwreck, the captain had claimed them both for himself, stranding the handsome young sailor in the lighthouse with only enough food and water for one day.

He wasn't even provided clean clothes to wear.

Lisa was having fun with her pretend sailor as she lay in her bed. She stretched and pointed her toes, pulling the bedding taut, before releasing her indrawn breath. Her limbs were lithe and sleek, and while she was not *bosomy,* back in her formative years, she'd known no lack of compliments in that area. Now, as a woman, she felt she was a comfortable size, and it was easy to find clothes that fit just right. She did have to pull them in at the waist sometimes, but a belt did that for her just fine.

Here for an unexpected night in a stranger's home, she was sleeping in one of Mrs. Reynolds's gowns. Lisa had laughed when she saw it. It was as if she was wearing nothing at all. It might be perfect for a married woman who wanted the advances of her husband, but for a school nurse attending to a seventeen-year-old boy, one who was quickly approaching the man his body already claimed him to be? She at least had the robe she wore after Josh's outdoor excursion. Wearing the robe covered a multitude of sins—or at least flimsy nightgowns.

Josh had taken the correct medication promptly at eight the night before. The entire family had been up to eleven or so, and Lisa was certain Josh knew they were watching him like chicken hawks in a barnyard. However, with the proper medication in his system, there hadn't been even a hint of a problem.

Lisa had gotten up to check on him twice during the night. The first time he was sleeping quietly. The small heater had been running softly in the corner, and he'd been uncovered to the waist. In the light filtering in from the living room, she had just been able to make out the shadowy whiteness of his body as he lay face down, his arms wrapped around his head. He'd been breathing softly, and his shock of hair had flung itself all directions as if trying to escape his scalp.

The second time, he'd been on his back. She stepped in, and pausing, she watched him for a minute to see if his breathing was regular. As she turned, he softly called to her.

"Miss Bevier?"

"Yes, Josh? I didn't mean to wake you. We've all been concerned." She stepped to his bed where they could talk quietly.

He slid to the side of his bed to make room, and he asked her to stay and talk for a minute. "I took the wrong tablets, didn't I?" He lay back and put his hands behind his head. As her eyes adjusted to the dimness in the room, Lisa could tell he was watching the ceiling and not her.

"Maybe, Josh. Your parents aren't sure." She was, but it wasn't the boy's fault. There were probably a hundred layers to this situation that had brought her here. Josh had thought he was doing the correct thing.

His eyes turned to her. "You're sure, though, aren't you, Miss Bevier?"

She took a breath. "What's that lighthouse you like so much?" She hoped this might divert his attention.

He settled back into the bed. "Goose Rocks. I can see it if I hike down to the end of the island. It's not far."

She pushed him for more. "What makes it special to you?"

"Goose Rocks stands all by itself. If you ever get the chance to see it, it's out there in the water surrounded by these big islands. Yet, the islands can never touch it. It's safe. And the thing about Goose Rocks is that it's important. Even people who never think they pay attention to it still do. They just don't know it. They sail by, and it's there. It tells them to go left or right, port or starboard." He laughed at that. "Port or starboard. My dad doesn't even know what those mean."

He turned on his side and propped his head on one arm. "Another thing is that Goose Rocks never needs help. No one has to baby it or worry about it. It's just there. It's always strong, standing tall in the water, unlike some of us who take the wrong tablets and have to be fussed over for two days." He fell back onto the bed and returned his hands under his head.

Lisa saw his fascination, now. The lighthouse was really all about Josh's life and the issues he dealt with. She looked at him, and she so wanted to reach out and place her hand on his face. She wanted to tell him he was already strong, and that he should be glad of who he was. However, not in the middle of the night. She could change the subject, though. He had shared something important to him. She would share something important to her.

"Josh, do you remember me telling you I was looking for someone?"

"Just not Andrew, right?" He grinned at that.

"No, not Andrew. The man I'm looking for is a man who graduated from the Center, just like you're going to do." That got his attention.

"He has autism? Do you have autism, Miss Bevier?"

"No, Josh. I don't. Does that matter?"

"It does to people who don't have it. Why would you want someone with autism if you don't have it yourself?"

That made her think. She had never considered that the students at the school would think their autism made them unlovable. Especially not Josh. He rarely showed signs of it, anymore. His bigger problem was the seizures, and they had been well under control—until he had taken the wrong tablets.

She pulled one of his arms down and held his hand. "Josh, if you have autism, it doesn't make you loveable or unlovable. It's like your blue eyes." She leaned in as she teased him for a moment. "You know, those eyes you carry around are so deep I feel I could fall into them. Should I love you just for your eyes?"

"If you want to. I'd let you do that."

She smiled, and she shook his arm back and forth to chide him. "You know what I mean. Your autism is part of you, and if I love you, I love your autism."

He was quiet for several minutes before he responded. "My father doesn't. He doesn't love my autism, or my medicine."

Lisa's heart nearly broke inside of her. She wondered if Rockland had ever thought that of his own father. What a horrible thing for any child to endure!

"You need to give your father another chance. I think you may find he sees you differently from now on. You know he's the one who sent for me. He hired a private plane and everything. He did that just for you."

The boy at her side wasn't yet ready to give his father that much credit. "My father has lots of money. He won't even notice what it costs." Then he returned to his subject. "This man you're chasing, and you said chasing earlier, does he have anything else wrong with him? Besides his autism?"

"Like your seizures, Josh?" She saw him nod his head. "Yes, he does. Do you know what dyslexia is?"

211

"People see things backwards."

"Well, the man I want to care about has it really bad. However, he's very successful in spite of it, and I'd like to try to get to know him."

"Does he want to get to know you? I would if I were him."

She laughed at that. "I'm heading back to bed."

He grabbed her arm before she could stand. "You're sure about the pills, aren't you, Miss Bevier?"

She had to be honest. "Yes, Josh. I think you did. It was by accident, though. You mustn't blame yourself. It can't happen again. All the old medication has been thrown away."

"It was all thrown away last time, too. Did you know that? Now I know better. I'll never be fixed, will I, Miss Bevier?"

She leaned over to kiss him on the cheek. "You do not need to be fixed, Josh. You're the same Josh I've come to love during all the years I've known you at the Center, and if you were any different, how could I love you the way I do? Besides, you make a mean sandwich. Who else in this house can do that?"

He squeezed her arm before he let her go. Lisa couldn't tell in the shadowy light, but it seemed as if his eyes glistened more than they should, and she thought she might have witnessed the start of tears. She wouldn't ask him, though. It was what he said next, just before she exited the door, that was very special to her.

"I love you, Miss Bevier. I'm glad you're here." His voice cracked as he spoke. As she left the room, she turned to look at him one more time, and he was once again lying on his back with both hands behind his head.

She had left the boy's room and made her way back to bed, taking a long time to fall asleep, and now it was morning. Still half in her dream world, she thought about her man stranded in his lighthouse. It should be Mr. Royster. It should. How he would get there, she didn't know, but he should be the one there. This storm would go away, and she and Josh would hike down to see it. They'd see a man high on the lighthouse, and he would be yelling for help. She and Josh would abscond with a boat from someone's dock, and they would row out and rescue the man. Then she could introduce him to Josh, and Josh would know it was all right to be autistic, that enduring all the problems he was used to having tagged onto his life didn't mean the end of the world.

That was her plan, and as she lay in bed, she laughed very loudly and to great length. There was no way to pull this figment of her imagination off. It had been great fun to imagine, but Mr. Royster was far, far away, and she was here on North Haven. Chicken Stones was an impossible dream, and she was being ridiculous.

"Silly girl, you need to climb out of this bed and stay up. Up, silly girl." She did get up, too, but it was the sudden smell of bacon wafting in from the kitchen that convinced her. It drew her like a moth to a flame.

THE PATTERING of the rain was soft and seductive. Bette turned to look at the clock on the bedside table. It was blinking, and she wondered how long the power was off. She let her eyes rove to the windows that ran down one wall. The blinds were closed, but it was definitely morning. She could see soft light filtering through.

Throwing back the covers, she sat up, pulling her gown around her. She moved one leg at a time to force them to hang off the bed. It was chilly in the room, and she would need to let the furnace run for a bit today. She wouldn't leave it on long, not with company upstairs. It might feel wonderful down here, but the upstairs rooms would grow hot very quickly.

Her leg was bothering her today. It might be the rain outside. She sat for a minute thinking about that. It might be the rain inside of her soul. Without being able to get Rockland on the phone, she'd started to worry again. She had pushed him with the old boat in the barn, and he'd been very irritated with her when he left. Now, she couldn't locate him.

It wasn't Rockland she had missed during the night, though. Miles, his grandfather, had been gone a long time, and Bette knew how to live on her own. Sometimes, though, on nights like the one she'd just gone through, she would wake in the dark and reach for him. The old buzzard! In that unconscious nightly movement, there would be an emptiness that would surge through her, and the storm of emotions that had engulfed her all those years ago would leak out of her eyes once again.

She scolded herself. "Get busy, Bette. You know that's the cure. You love life, and you have good friends for company. This old house may be empty again next week, but you can't be a pitiful, old, lonely woman today. There's no time."

Then she smelled coffee. In her own home. God, she missed that, Miles up before dawn getting the coffee pot on. No one had done that for her in years. It must be Leetha. She always talked of how she missed her own kitchen back home.

Putting her feet on the floor, she felt around until she found her slippers. Her hand reached to the bedpost, and she stood. Moving to her dresser, she flipped on a lamp and reached for the brush she had left out the night before. Looking in the mirror, she froze. The face looking back at her was unfamiliar for a moment, and in that instant, her connection with Miles was gone. She was no longer forty, and he was no longer preparing her coffee. She was a grandmother with a bad leg that hurt when it rained, and her guests had arisen before she did. Pulling the brush harshly through her hair, she opened a drawer and laid it inside. Reaching for her robe, she pulled it around her, tightening the cord around her waist.

She smiled as she opened the door. She made the few steps down the high-ceilinged hallway towards where she could see the kitchen light spilling out through the door. The coffee aroma pulled her forward, and as she rounded the doorway, she was surprised. It was Merv standing there with a cup of steaming brew in his hand.

He pushed a second cup across the big island towards her. "I heard you getting up, Bette. Join me, won't you? A cup of the old black stuff is what makes dreary mornings something to look forward to." He watched her take the cup in her hands, and he was smiling when she closed her eyes to inhale the steam rising from the top. "Out in the oilfields, there were cold winter mornings I missed my Leetha so much the money didn't matter one whit anymore. The only thing that kept me going was the blackest coffee I could find. Cowpoke black, we'd call it. I'd consume it by the thermos full."

Bette smiled. "I'm glad you found my cinnamon roast this morning. However, I'm sorry you must do with less than the best. I rarely make it plain and black."

"Black? You think I miss it?" He chuckled. "Don't get me wrong. In the field, black's all there is. I learned to be a connoisseur once my wells started making me some money. Leetha taught me that, and I have no desire to go back." He raised his cup and sipped it for a moment, and then he looked at her. His next words came out in a near whisper, "Have you heard from your grandson?"

Bette sighed. "Not a word." She looked into her cup to see the brown inside making a dance of the overhead light. "Two days, and with this storm." She stopped speaking and just watched her coffee. She looked up and brightened, but it was hard. "Got some new people coming in for a night. They'll be across from you. Rand and Beth Walters. It was on the machine. They've been here before, though not usually in the fall. You'll like them, though." She sighed and leaned against the counter, her brightness fading.

Merv cleared his throat. "I'll look forward to meeting them." He took a sip of his coffee, then set it on the island. "I had the television on earlier. They say it's bad on the coast.

215

Some evacuations are in place, but mostly the storm came in too quick. They're telling people to sit high and ride it out."

Bette nodded. First Miles, then seeing herself in the mirror. Now, Rockland taking himself out of circulation. Merv and Leetha might be paying her for her hospitality, but she would be drawing strength from them today.

She brought the cup to her mouth. "The coffee's good, Merv. You do make a right good cup."

A voice interrupted them from the doorway. "What? I don't get a cup?"

Bette smiled as Leetha joined them. By the time she reached the big island, Merv already had a third steaming brew ready.

Bette knew one thing. With her friends, this would turn out to be a good day, no matter what. Somehow, she never considered how all her days were like that. Then, that was how she dealt with life. She turned her bad times around, and she let the small joys of life make each day into one that was something to treasure.

FRANK HAD been up all night, and it was obvious to look at him. His hair was askew, and his clothes were disheveled. He stood and watched the display in front of him.

People were telling him he'd made a very good call the previous morning. He'd felt less than confident about it, though. His sigh of relief when the storms followed the path he'd outlined in his warning had been a mixed blessing. He'd rather they'd been driven out to sea, or that they'd simply dissipated.

No, now the eye wall was sitting over the eastern half of Penobscot Bay. What would those people on the islands do when the storm subsided for that thirty minutes or an hour? Those who had no radio or television access might assume the worst was over. It wouldn't be. When the second wave hit, it would be worse than the first, and the winds along the eye wall would come from the opposite direction. That would throw a lot of people off.

He brooded. He turned as someone touched his arm. There was a fresh cup of coffee and a donut waiting for him on the desk at his side. He smiled absently and looked back to the board. How many people would die out there? No one, he hoped, but he knew that was an empty wish. The winds had passed hurricane strength long ago, and that meant some people wouldn't survive.

He reached for the pastry and took a bite. The sweetness made his eyes open wide with surprise, and he quickly took a sip of the coffee to cut the sugar's taste. It had been a long night, and he knew it would likely be a very long day. He was here for the duration, though, because this was his baby, and he had to see it through.

LISA RAN her hands along the sculpted edge of the dresser in her room. It was an exquisite piece of furniture, one that saw use only a couple of weeks a year. Outside the windows, the water lashed the exterior of the house, and it was nearly dark. Inside, however, the lights were working, and her clothes from yesterday were freshly laundered. Josh's mother had done that for her, thrown them in last night, and now she could get dressed.

Removing the gown that was not much of a gown, she felt goose bumps rise on her skin. As she rubbed her arm, she chuckled at herself. Chicken Stones. How she had come up with that she had no idea. Goose Rocks was the name of the lighthouse where poor Mr. Royster was stranded. Now she would have to get with Josh to see if there was a rowboat they could borrow. After all, the dyslexic Mr. Royster wouldn't be able to tell his left from his right, and he just might swim to the wrong island, if he felt the urge to jump from his prison to the sea below.

She chided herself as she began to pull her clothing on. She had no right to tease, even to herself, about someone's disability. Besides, there was no one on that lighthouse, and how would she get there in a rowboat? She'd seen the water when she went with Mr. Reynolds to retrieve Josh from his outing. A small boat would be swamped immediately.

Finally dressed, she stepped from her room and made her way to the kitchen. Stepping inside, with her words prepared to greet Mrs. Reynolds, she was surprised to see Josh at the stove, turning the bacon in the pan. He looked up as she entered.

"Good morning, Miss Bevier." His face split into that crooked grin she loved so much. "Could you smell breakfast in your room? I've got some bacon already cooked if you're hungry. It's under that plate beside you." He nodded to the counter where one plate was turned upside down on top of another.

She pulled up a stool, and she slipped out a slice. She was, indeed, hungry, and she never had bacon at home. Sausage was what her mother liked to prepare. That reminded her. She should call her mother, and she would in a bit.

"So, Josh." She paused and looked at his lean form moving confidently among all the kitchen utensils and appliances. "You do more than a mean sandwich. Is my breakfast being catered by a renowned chef, the likes of which North Haven has never seen?"

"It's just breakfast, Miss Bevier." He grinned in embarrassment, but he obviously enjoyed the compliment. He went to the refrigerator and pulled out a carton of eggs. He glanced through the door behind her before whispering, "My parents sleep late, and the breakfast smells bother them. They always want me to eat cereal. You're here, so they won't complain."

She smiled at that. She would enjoy this boy's efforts, and she would once again gobble up his symphony of exertions in praise of his skills. First, she needed to make a call.

"May I borrow the phone? My cell doesn't have a signal, and I need to call home to let my mother know where I am."

"My parents' don't work here, either." He reached to slide

an old, rotary, corded model to her, and he smiled as he did so. When she chuckled at the oddity, he explained, "I think it came with the house when my grandfather built it. Nothing up here ever gets replaced unless it breaks. Sorry."

She lifted the receiver. "All it has to do is work. I've just never used one of these."

He reached a slender finger and moved the dial. "Just spin it like this. It's easy when you get used to it."

She looked at him, and she could see seriousness in his blue eyes. He truly thought she would find the phone confusing. He was being very helpful in the charming way seventeen-year-old boys did, even if his explanation was unnecessary.

"Thank you, Josh. Will your parents mind if it's long distance?"

"Everything's long distance from here. Don't worry about it. I'm going to put the eggs on. Ham omelets." He held up a wooden cutting board covered with diced ham. "Would you like cheese on yours?"

"Sure," she replied, as she began to dial her mother's number. She was relieved when the line picked up at the other end.

"Yes?"

It was her mother's voice, and Lisa smiled. "Mum? It's Lisa. Did you get my message yesterday?"

Just then the house went dark. After a few moments, the hum of a generator could be heard, and all the lights came back on. Lisa caught Josh's eyes, and he grinned. She spoke into the phone.

"Mum?" However, it was silent.

"Sorry, Miss Bevier. The phones won't work until we have power again. When the power goes, everything goes. Even the phone. It cuts a primary relay in town or something." He reached to the stove to adjust an omelet he had just put in the pan.

"The power's out? We have lights."

"We have a generator. Lots of people up here do. It automatically turns on when the power goes. It does that a lot up here. It'll come back on sometime. Onions?" He had a bowl in his hand, and he was ready to add it to the pan. She shook her head, and he set it to the side.

"Josh, your father said there's a boat that can get me back to Rockland today. The Equinox, I think he called it. Is there a way to contact it to schedule me in?" She took a bite of the bacon slice she'd pulled out earlier.

He tested his creation on the stove, and with a practiced hand, he folded the omelet in half, raising the pan to let it slide onto a plate. "Without the phones? No. Someone else might possibly take you, though. Dad knows lots of people around here, and I bet he could call someone."

She smiled as he slid his completed creation in front of her. "Thank you. This looks excellent. How will your dad call without the phones?"

He paused, then a smile touched his lips. "Drive. He can drive to someone's house to ask. I'll see when he gets up."

"This omelet is huge. Do you think you'd like to share?"

He glanced at it, and then at the eggs he had yet to crack open. He pushed them to the back of the counter and got out a knife.

"Sure. I like them fine without onions. I'll cut, and you pick the half you want."

She didn't care which half she got. She was beginning to have some concerns about getting back home. She had work tomorrow. Josh and his family could take an extra-long weekend, but she couldn't.

Then there was that lighthouse. It seemed the probability of getting out there to rescue the obstinate Mr. Royster was slipping further and further away. At least she could enjoy this breakfast that had been prepared for her by this seventeen-year-old chef of consummate skill.

She did, too, and just for a moment, she forgot about Mr.

Royster. She was with a boy she loved, and he was quick and smart and perfect. That was just what Lisa needed to survive the morning, and it was enough to get her through.

ROCKY FELT of his pants, and he sighed. They weren't even pretending to dry. The room was warm, but the walls were still bleeding dampness. It would probably take days for the temperature in the thick masonry walls to equalize, and until then, the moisture in the air would continue to bead up on them. He did appreciate that long ago someone had thoughtfully driven the pegs into the walls, but anything wet hanging there clearly took forever to dry. They were almost useless. Still, it was better than dumping his wet pants into a corner.

He had found an old broom. Working around the room, he'd cleaned the floor enough that he no longer minded walking across it in his bare feet. He was finding some things about being in this lighthouse that were even better than being at home. Here, he could leave his windows uncovered, run around in his underwear, and scratch his armpits all he wanted. If he grew hungry, he could just break into the ice chest. He didn't even have to worry about delivery personnel knocking on his door. He was free to be as indolent and scruffy as possible.

That made up some for his wet pants.

His socks were slowly drying, too. With the floor clean, his shoes were out to air along with everything else. Padding to a window, he peered out at the sky, glad to see a break in the weather coming up. Perhaps it would be the end of this mess, and not just a temporary respite. If so, Tram would probably arrive soon, so he'd better keep a watch out.

However, he wasn't here yet, and there was equipment to maintain. He shook the lantern, hearing plenty of fuel inside, and with a quick snip of his knife blade, he shaped the wick. Better wick, better light. Less fuel, too. He'd leave the lantern here when Tram came, and any fuel he could save was fuel he wouldn't have to haul up next time.

The same was true with the heater. It was doing a very good job of keeping him warm, and he was quite comfortable wearing almost nothing. Still, the less fuel he used, the less he had to bring next time—and it was nearing October, the start of Maine's cold season.

He moved the heater a little closer to the sofa, adjusted the flame lower, and sat down to enjoy the sounds of the storm. With the upper levels closed off, his moaning windowpane wasn't nearly so loud, and it gave the old place a nice ambiance. He was getting used to the repeated vibrations when the waves hit, and the past few hours, the foghorn had even quieted its cry.

Drowsy in the absence of activity, he propped his feet up on an old chair; and with one hand, he brushed his leg and scratched. He couldn't do that if Miss Bevier were here, that was for certain. There was one other thing he could do since he was alone, and that was dream about her. If he couldn't have her, he could at least do that.

His eyes closed, and in the soft glow of the lantern, he drifted off. As he did, he found he was back in Miss Bevier's office. He was shaking her hand, and his blood ran hot in his veins. He called her by her name, Lisa, and she smiled at him. With a flourish, he filled out her forms, and every letter went the correct direction. He was warm and charming, and she understood that his time at the Center had been a mistake. He was a successful craftsman who had never really had autism or dyslexia. He had been misdiagnosed all along.

Finally, she said she was hungry, and he told her he knew of a great place to eat. They took his brand-new truck, and they drove to the waterfront where Tram was waiting. On the deck of his boat was a table covered with a white tablecloth, just like Bette would have prepared for a summer brunch on her porch; and boiling in a pot of water were lobster tails, fresh from a pot on the floor of the ocean.

Tram motored out to the middle of the bay, and as afternoon turned into evening, the sun dropped behind the Boston skyline. Whenever they were hungry, they dropped another fresh lobster tail into the pot of water, and they never ran out.

Back in the lighthouse, safe from the battering of the storm, Rocky lay on the sofa, and the kerosene heater kept the chill of the storm at bay. Deep in his chest, something else helped keep him warm inside. It was the warmth of a heart in love. The woman he dreamed about was charming and inviting. She laughed at his jokes and admired his accomplishments. When he mentioned his years spent at the Center, she leaned against him, wrapping one arm around his neck and the other across his stomach. She whispered in his ear that she never would have sent him there. She would have kept him at her side always. She wished his father could have seen him through her eyes, because to her, Rocky was quick and smart and perfect.

In his dream, that's what he became.

THERE WAS the noise of a slamming door as a junior staffer ran into the room. He handed a warm piece of paper to Frank. It was just off the printer. Then, breathing hard, the staffer turned and was gone.

Frank looked at it, and then he turned to carefully study his staff sitting around him. They were fresher in appearance and possibly in smell than Frank. However, not in mind. He reached to a nearby keyboard and typed in several lines of information. The big display shifted, and it showed a direct satellite feed.

Frank called out, "Look at this, people. NOAA. This is direct from the space station." He walked up to the display and touched one area. "This is the eye, people. Right here. Tell me where this is and how long they have before the second eye wall hits. How fast is this storm moving? Hop to it, people. Let's save some lives."

There was a buzz in the room for a few moments, and then

several answers were called out. The consensus was that the storm was still over Penobscot Bay off the coast of Maine. The eye wall had just approached the Fox Islands out from the town of Rockland. The storm system had seemed to stall for the moment, and everyone agreed the islands would see perhaps an hour to an hour and a half of clear weather. Then, the backside of the eye wall would hit, and the storm would resume in all its fury.

Frank put his hand over his eyes and then dropped it to cover his chin. "How many people will think the storm is over? They'll be unprepared for phase two. They won't even know the storm is only half done. My God, could it get any worse than this?"

Chapter 14

MR. REYNOLDS CALLED to Lisa. She looked up from the card game she was playing with Josh, and when she saw him motion with his hand to join him at the window, she smiled at her partner and placed her cards face down on the table.

"I'll be right back, Josh. Let me see what your father wants."

His crooked grin lit his face. "I might peek."

She grabbed her cards, reaching to rumple his hair. "Not on my watch." Holding the laminated paper in her hands, she stepped to the other side of the room.

"Look out there, Miss Bevier. I think I see clearing sky." He looked at her and smiled. "You get to go home after all." After a pause he offered, "You could stay another night. We'll be leaving in the morning. I have a reserved spot on the ten-twenty ferry." He cocked an eyebrow. "Josh would love to have you here for the entire day, and you could return to work on Tuesday."

She demurred, "The Center needs me on duty. Besides, Josh hasn't had another occurrence since taking the correct tablets last night and this morning. The rest of the weekend should belong to your family."

He sighed. "I guess you're right. You do realize the phones are out, and I can't contact the Equinox. I should be able to find someone locally who has a boat, however. There are plenty of fishermen around here. Don't fear. We'll get you ashore just as promised. See?" He tapped the window with his knuckles. "The rain has almost stopped. I'll take the Rover and see what I can drum up. You might want to be ready when I return, because they'll probably want to go right away."

Josh called to her, "Miss Bevier, you're not staying? You can ride over with us tomorrow."

"My duty at the Center calls, Josh. They'll need me there in the morning. I'll see you on Tuesday." She quickly stepped into the bedroom she'd spent the night in, and she grabbed the one medicine satchel she'd carried with her. Looking around, she realized she had nothing else but her raincoat. She felt in the pocket and checked her phone, to see it still had no signal.

Returning to the living room, she saw Josh seated at the table, and she held up her cards, smiling. "Is this game still in play?"

He grabbed his own and waved them at her. "Sure. How are you getting to Rockland? Did Dad say?"

"He's finding someone for me. He says there's no way to reach the Equinox until the power returns." She winked. "You were right." Moving to the table, she pulled one card from her stack to lay down.

He snickered. "It'll probably be Andrew. He seems to be able to come up with a boat anytime he needs one. We don't think they're always his, though." He put one of his own cards down.

She groaned. "Andrew. Why don't you just beat me with a

stick? Then I can get the misery over with all at once." She smiled and fanned out her cards.

At the beep of a horn, Josh looked out the window. "It's Dad. He's back, and he's waving to you to come outside." He chuckled. "That was quick. Don't be angry, Miss Bevier, but I bet it is Andrew." He jumped up and ran to the door. Opening it, he called, "Dad, can I ride along?"

His father reached his arm out the window and waved him along. Josh turned to Lisa. "Come on, Miss Bevier. You get to go on a real boat ride instead of the ferry. It'll be fun." As they stepped from the house, dappled sun filtered through the trees, and the wind had dropped to a full calm.

She teased him. "First let's see who it is. If it's Andrew, maybe not so much fun."

He ran to the truck and opened the door. "Dad, who's taking her?" He looked back at Lisa with a grin.

"Hang on, Josh. Let Miss Bevier get in." When she closed the door, he put the vehicle in reverse. He spoke to Lisa as he pulled out of the driveway. "Your ride'll be at the Crabtree's dock."

Josh interrupted with a grin, "That's right by Andrew's house."

"Josh, let me speak." His father looked to the left and right before pulling out onto the road, and in the sudden sun, he lowered his visor. "Miss Bevier, Josh has told me about you and Andrew. I talked to several men, but most of them have already hauled their boats in for the season. Andrew did say he could get one."

Josh reached between the seats to touch Lisa's shoulder. "I bet it's not even his. Right, Dad?"

His father shot him a look in the mirror and reprimanded him, "We don't know that. Miss Bevier?'' He looked at her, and she noticed he had Josh's infinite blue eyes. "You can still stay with us another night. We can get you home tomorrow."

227

She laughed. "The sun is shining, and what bad can happen? What will it take, an hour or less? I can endure Andrew that long. It's been three years since I've seen him."

"An hour? Less," Mr. Reynolds said, "if he has a decent boat. There's a taxi service in Rockland that can get you to the local airport. Also, if you would rather drive to Boston, here's the number of a car rental agency." He handed her a folded slip of paper. She started to slide it inside her satchel when she noticed it was thicker than it should be. She opened it to see a number of very large bills inside. She looked to Josh's father.

"There's money here. What's it for?"

He chuckled. "You've given up your weekend for us. You have a taxi, a car to rent, also, and gas to buy. An airplane ticket, perhaps."

She held it out to him. "This is far too much for all that. I have money of my own."

He turned to his son. "Is it too much, Josh?"

"No way," he grinned. He reached to spread the bills between his fingers. "You can buy me ice cream every day for the rest of the year when I get back to school."

Lisa smiled and pushed his hand away. The truck slowed and pulled into a driveway that was obviously private.

Craig turned to Lisa. "I've already paid Andrew. This money is yours. Don't let him ask for more."

Lisa looked at him, and her expression was one of amusement. "You don't know the whole story between Andrew and me. Trust me, he'll get nothing more from me."

"Good," Mr. Reynolds said. "Josh will see you Tuesday."

Josh opened his door and jumped out. Just then a very small lobster boat pulled up to the float at the base of the dock. When Lisa got out, he hugged her before taking her place in the front seat. He rolled his window down, "Bye, Miss Bevier. You'll go right by Goose Rocks Light."

She turned to him and laughed. "Will anyone be home?"

"No, it's abandoned. The only light will be the beacon. It might still be on. Watch for it."

Then Andrew was calling for her. She steeled herself. She had made light of this, but it wasn't something she was looking forward to. As the boat bobbed at the float, the name could be clearly seen on the stern. *Duty*. Underneath it was the word *North Haven*. Josh pointed to the name and laughed, calling to her from the truck.

AS THEY pulled away from the Crabtree's dock, Josh looked to the horizon far in the east. There was a wall of dark that was once again building against the blue sky overhead. He turned to his father.

"The storm's over, isn't it, Dad? Miss Bevier will be safe, won't she?" He noticed the sudden frown that clouded his father's face.

"I think so, Son. I hope so."

Josh's expression soon mirrored his father's. "I hope so, too, Dad."

ROCKY WAS startled awake. Miss Bevier, Lisa, had been with him, and now she was gone. Quiet surrounded him.

He squinted at the filtered sun that pierced the inside of the lighthouse, forcing its way through the clouded windows. Perhaps the storm had blown itself out, and the rest of the day would be nice. He walked to the door, and he pushed at it until it released its hold on the frame. He swung it wide and stepped outside. He could tell the air was still cool, but there was no breeze, and the sun was warm against his skin. He closed his eyes and stood against the railing for a moment. Then he opened them and looked around. Any houses were far away, laughably small, and surely no one could see him. He did locate one small boat just now peeking out of the Thorofare, but it was very slow. It was probably just checking for storm damage. It would take it a long time to get close to the lighthouse, if it even headed this direction. He was more aware of a dark bank of clouds still off the horizon, but the sky overhead was brilliantly blue.

He stepped back inside and reached for his pants. They were still damp, and he decided to put them on the rail in the sun. They would dry better there. He could like this. As rough as the previous night had been, he could look forward to spending time out here alone.

Stepping back inside, he turned the heater to its lowest setting, then dimmed the light in the lantern to a mere glow. Kneeling by the ice chest, he pulled out a drink. Then he rummaged in one bag until he found a can of meat with a pull top.

Sitting on the floor, he snapped it open and began picking out the meat with his fingers. After a short time, the room began to dim. Through the door, the bank of clouds had begun to eat the day. He groaned. He'd seen enough rain, and with that thought, he could sense his drink had gone right through him. He needed outside before the storm hit again.

By the time he got to the door, rain was pinging against the outside walk, and he knew he'd better hurry. He cursed. His pants, almost dry, were spotted with moisture. Priorities, however, had to be stacked in the order of importance. He could wear wet pants. He would not wear *wet* pants. He glanced out to see that the boat was drawing closer. It would go near him but was certainly headed to another destination. He was confident he had time to relieve his needs unobserved, if he went to the opposite side. In a flash of impulse, he grabbed the pants from the rail and threw them through the open door. After all, he'd swept the floors the night before, so they were reasonably safe.

Finding a spot where he wouldn't be seen, he stood at the rail and let his liquid offering to the sea fly. The weather was changing rapidly, though. From his start to his finish, the wind picked up and began whipping his stream against the side of the tall building. In the quickly darkening sky, he could see the dim glow of his lantern through the door, and he ran for cover, grabbing his pants from the floor as he stumbled inside.

He pulled the door mostly to, pausing when the hinges began to drag, and he reached to turn up the light. Now his boxers were wet, but he had no intention of going naked. These might be wet and sticking to him, but he'd wear them until they dried.

He shook his pants out, placing them back on the peg, and with a sudden squeal, the wind beat at the lighthouse again, flailing rain wildly through the partially open door. As Rocky stepped to work the door closed, he noticed a light in the darkening morass outside, and it was not the one on top of the lighthouse. It was jerking up and down as the waves kicked up, and it was from that boat he'd seen.

He noticed something else. It was coming right at him, and it wasn't slowing down.

"GO BACK, Andrew," Lisa cried, panicked. The skies had been clear when they set out, but the boat they were in was plainly one of the slowest ever built. Then she'd seen the wall of approaching darkness, and she had known they wouldn't make it to the mainland.

He laughed at her. "You've hated me for years, haven't you?" He forced the boat into the rising swells. The small craft attempted to best them, but the waves were rising faster than the small boat could manage. It seemed as if the weather had leaped from clear and calm to sudden ferocity with no warning.

It had, too. The boat Andrew had borrowed—as Josh had suspected, without asking—was only designed for close-in motoring, and in calmer weather, at that. With a larger motor, it might have vanquished the rising waves. It was a good design. However, no sea-going craft, underpowered as it was, could expect to conquer the decimating fury of the storm that had begun to rage once again.

"Andrew, I don't hate you. I'm frightened of this storm. It was over, we thought. Well, it isn't. Take me back, now." She reached for her satchel, and adjusting the shoulder strap, she secured it against her body. She pressed its inner seal closed so that none of Josh's expensive medications would be damaged.

"And lose the money Mr. Reynolds paid me? I know his kid, by the way. Goes to that autistic school of yours. Loves that lighthouse up there. Did he tell you we'd go right past it?" He looked at her. "I saw him hug you. Kinda young, isn't he? Although, surely he must be eighteen, by now. At least he's legal."

"Seventeen," she said. "He's seventeen, and you're being stupid, Andrew. I know what you're suggesting, and he's not like that. He's a student at my school."

Andrew laughed. "Well, sweetheart, I've been with a few students before. They're better when they're young. A few of the summer people have had pretty daughters out for the season, and I've sent them on their way a little wiser when fall rolled around."

"That's disgusting." She looked at the quickly blackening sky, and she shivered. "It's getting bad fast. Oh, please turn around."

"I don't think so. Besides, we haven't passed the lighthouse, yet. You can't give up now. It's just ahead." He snorted with laughter.

The boat was small, however, and it was intended for calmer waters. With its good design, a better pilot might have been able to control it against the onslaught of the waves, well enough to make it back to the closest shore, anyway, even underpowered as it was.

Andrew was not a better pilot.

As he turned it sideways to an oncoming wave, the gunwale slipped underwater. Within minutes, the engine sputtered to a stop. The small craft was at the mercy of the sea, and it was sinking. The water began to rise, and soon it covered the deck.

That was when Lisa began to scream.

ROCKY STOOD at the door looking out at a scene he couldn't believe. Where blue sky had hovered, there was now only roiling darkness. The sun that had warmed his arms and legs now sulked behind the black cloudbanks. He could barely see the water below.

Within minutes, faster than he could have imagined, the storm had returned in its fury, and the small boat had not run for safety. He watched as it fought for its life, and for all he could imagine, he didn't know why it was still coming his way.

However, he understood now why the weather had cleared. It had been the eye wall of a hurricane. The storm had come directly over this lighthouse, and now it was headed toward land. All that he had endured was only half the storm.

The small boat's light flickered as it rose and fell in the sea. He hoped he would see it turn away, back to where it could find a safe resting place. It had survived the first half of the storm without damage. Surely there were places it could find protection for what was still to come.

The waves in the sea picked up, running even higher, and wind whipped into the open lighthouse door. He couldn't close it, though, not with this small boat in his view. In a quick motion Rocky found incomprehensible, the pilot turned the boat sideways to the waves. He watched the scene as a wave crashed over the side, and in the aftermath, the small craft was frozen in its forward thrust through the water. Then, it was as if it were cast adrift and at the mercy of the gods. He couldn't see any propulsion, and he knew the engine must be dead. This boat would founder, and he had no choice but to watch it go down.

He watched it drift closer and closer to his bastion of safety, and as the rain battered his feet, Rocky heard an unmistakable

233

cry. It was the high-pitched wail of a woman's plea for help.

"SIR, THESE are early damage reports. The outer islands have fared well. People were already prepared for upcoming winter storms. The closer in the storm gets, however, the more ominous it is. All of North Haven is without power or phone service."

Frank looked at the paper in his hand. "What about Vinalhaven?" He had a cousin who lived there. Her house was out on a point. He hadn't been able to reach her.

"Spotty, sir. They have power in the town proper, though."

"Deer Isle? Isle au Haut? Islesboro? What about Frenchboro and Matinicus?" He named off the islands that came to mind.

"It's hit or miss, sir, and some we haven't any reports for. The surge will run high out on the islands, but it's when the surge hits the coast that we expect the most damage. Flooding is bound to be rampant."

"Are there any reports of people who thought the eye was the end of the storm and took their boats to sea?"

The staffer had a relieved look on his face. "None that have come in."

Frank breathed easier. "Thank God for that." He placed the report with all the others that had been coming in.

"Yes, sir. Thank God for that." The staffer softly repeated his boss's words.

THE WATER came in over Lisa's feet, and it was *cold.* Frantic, she looked around for anything to grab hold of, a life preserver or something that would float. She was wearing the waterproof satchel with Josh's medications inside, its leather strap secured around her, but she didn't think that would help her to stay afloat. Not much, anyway. The raincoat she hadn't had time to put on washed out to sea as she watched, carrying her phone with it.

"Andrew," she yelled over the roar of the storm. "Help me!"

Glancing towards the sky, she was acutely aware of the lighthouse's beacon flashing overhead. As she stood in the sinking boat, that one moment of awareness seemed to stretch on forever. Here she was, and this was the lighthouse Josh had so often wanted to visit, Goose Rocks Light. She had gotten here before him, and she knew now it was the last thing she would ever do.

The lighthouse was abandoned; she understood that. She had been told so by Josh's father, and as she started to grow cold standing in the water filling the boat, she wondered if Josh had also mentioned that important detail to her. Her thoughts grew muddled with the increasing cold that numbed her, but she was clear on this one thing.

She knew something they didn't.

Josh and Craig were both wrong, and she'd discovered something they weren't aware of. She smiled as she pictured their surprise when they realized what she now knew. Someone lived in the lighthouse. The windows glowed a golden yellow, and the door was open. It seemed very welcoming, a warm, homey place, with the smell of baking bread. There would be bread baking. It was what her mother would do when she wanted company to feel especially at home. Lisa knew she was welcome, because yellow light spilled out, and there stood a man. He had to be an angel, because only an angel would be on an abandoned lighthouse in the middle of a hurricane. The glow surrounding him must be a light from heaven.

With a clarity that she couldn't imagine she'd missed, she understood something now. This was a hurricane. The wind and driving rain, and then the break of clear weather. This was the second half of the storm, the same hurricane that had lashed the Reynolds' house on North Haven. She had gotten into this boat with Andrew, and she had allowed him to carry her directly into the fury of the storm.

Then, her body numb from the cold, the ship disappeared from under her, and the icy attack of the sea was like a thousand knives all over her torso and face. The water swelled around her, and she vanished beneath the waves. Through the water directly over her head, she could still see the beacon on top of the lighthouse, and it flashed as it circled round and round. Dimmer, she could see the yellow glow from the lighthouse's door.

She had lost Andrew. He had jumped as she stood in the boat, and she had watched him start to swim for the shore. She hoped he made it. She really did. She didn't hate Andrew. She just wished he had helped her when she'd asked.

Then, the world around her blurred, and she could see nothing at all.

JOSH PACED the floor. The storm was back. He had watched the boat leave, and it seemed very slow. It couldn't have made it to the mainland in time.

Just before the second wall of weather hit, the electricity had come back on. Almost immediately, the phone rang. He grabbed it and spoke into it breathlessly.

"Josh Reynolds speaking. Yes?" His mother looked at him, and she frowned. He slowed his words down and asked politely, "How may I help you?"

The voice on the other end was hesitant. "This is Terese Bevier. I got a phone call from this number, and I was cut off. I've been trying to call back for hours. The caller was my daughter, Lisa."

Josh held the phone to his mother as she reached for it, but he couldn't contain himself. He yanked it back, and his words came out in a jumble. "Miss Bevier, that's my nurse at my school. She's been with us for the weekend, but she just left. Andrew took her. They went to Rockland. They were going past the lighthouse, but it looks like the storm is back. Have you heard from her?" His face was hot with need, and he wanted to hear that she was all right. Just then, with a sudden blast, the storm struck the house with a ferocious blow. The lights blinked off for a moment, and then came back up again.

He stared at the dead phone. "She's gone, Mum." He looked outside, before he reached and hung the phone on the receiver. "When's Dad coming back?"

"In a bit, Josh. He's checking on the neighbors' places."

"Will she be all right?"

"Who, Josh?"

"Mum, do you have to ask?" Anguish filled his words.

WITH THE TEARS in Josh's eyes, Dee knew just who he meant. She didn't have an answer for his question. She hoped Josh's nurse would be safe, but right now, having her son still alive was what mattered most to her.

She patted the sofa. "Come sit. Keep me company." When he did, she put her arm around him and hugged him close. She breathed in the smell of his hair, and she remembered something she had forgotten. Josh's hair smelled just like her husband's, and it always had. Josh was Craig made over. Even his build was what Craig had carried at seventeen.

She stroked her son's arm, and she whispered to him, "We don't do church much, Josh, but you could say a prayer for Miss Bevier. I'll be glad to listen, if you'd like to do that."

"Mum, I don't know how."

She did, though. When Josh had been smaller, she'd prayed for God to change him, to make him different and better. She knew now she had been praying for the wrong thing. She should have prayed to love him as he was. When he'd gotten so sick this weekend, she'd truly been frightened, and she'd felt the fault was hers. She had prayed as she had sat looking at her book. She hadn't done it aloud, but her prayers had been there the same. God had come through, too. Her Josh was still alive. She could help her son pray for Miss Bevier. Surely God cared about her, too.

"Josh," she began. "It goes like this."

Within a few minutes he was sending up his earnest words for the person he had watched head out into the waters the storm raged over once again. His mother smiled as his deep voice spoke his concerns to the room. Her boy truly cared about this woman, and that made Mrs. Reynolds care, too. When he finished, she added her own words.

"Let there be an angel of mercy out tonight. Let Miss Bevier find a beacon to lead her to a place of safety. In the Father's name, we pray." She opened her eyes and looked at her son. "Better, Josh?" She felt him relax against her, and she knew she needed no answer. His body told her all she needed to know. She hugged him tightly and pressed her face into his hair. He was her son, and he cared about other people very much. What more could she want than that?

Chapter 15

ROCKY WAS compelled to watch as the sinking ship washed closer and closer to the base of the lighthouse. He was hardly protected from the rain and wind on the covered walk, and it seemed that he would be forced to witness this disaster, no matter how much he wished it away.

In the flashes of the beacon overhead, he watched a man jump from the sinking ship. He was quickly lost to view in the churning waves. Nevertheless, the woman stood on the deck of the boat, and she looked up at him as the water swirled around her. Finally, as the boat disappeared, she sank into the sea.

Rocky cried, "No!" With a sudden intensity of emotion, one that he had no control over, he did something he couldn't have imagined himself foolhardy enough to do. He threw himself down the steep stairs to the small landing just above the surface of the surging water. His eyes tore through the churning maelstrom, straining against hope that he'd be able to see where she'd gone. She had to be saved.

Then, something black caught the light of the beacon as it flashed in its circular ritual, and Rocky leaned out and grabbed at it. The force of the water surged against the lighthouse, sending the wave over his head. At the same time, whatever he held came with it, nearly forcing him from his perch on the metal rungs.

As the water dropped and surged again, he realized the thing he had grasped was attached to the woman, wrapped around her somehow. He let her body roll against him, and he pulled her next to him, curving her into his embrace as the sea tried to pull her from him. He held her tightly, looking upward at the climb. If they stayed here, he would soon lose his grip, and they would be washed away.

Struggling to ascend the near-vertical metal steps that led upward, Rocky moved one foot, and then he slid his free hand up the rail a few inches. Once his hand was secure, he moved another foot. Gradually, he inched to where only their feet were being swamped by the highest swells. Then, with a final push of his limbs, the water was hitting them no longer.

The wind was, though. It had been cold as he'd stepped to the rail when all this started, and he'd been quickly soaked. This, however, was the chill of an ice water bath. Then they were on the metal walk that circled the structure he'd called home for the past twenty-four hours. He laid the woman down, and he reached to pat her face with his hand. She was chilled, and her skin had no color. He felt he should know this woman. How, he didn't know. He knew no one here on the islands.

Then he realized she wasn't breathing. Putting his cheek to her nose, he felt for the warmth of breath. There was none. In panic, he tried to remember what Tramwick had done with Fish. Seven-Eleven. The convenience store. That was it!

He put his hands together and pressed them to her chest. He felt ashamed, but he couldn't help noticing the feel of her breasts

240

just underneath his palms. Then he pressed rapidly seven times. Remembering Tramwick and Fish, he pressed his lips to the woman's, and he blew eleven times into her mouth. He sat up and looked at her, unsure why she was still lying there. This had worked with Fish. He remembered, and he groaned. Fish had been breathing all along.

He reached to the woman's chest and pressed seven more times. Unexpectedly, she coughed, and water poured from her throat. Rocky quickly rolled her to her side so that the fluid could drain from her mouth. Then, she gasped and moved her hands, reaching unsteadily to balance herself.

"I'm freezing," she mumbled. In that instant, hearing her voice, Rocky placed her. This was the woman from the Center. Just the day before, she'd touched him, and his mind had been able to think of nothing else. He had broken her pencil, and he'd run from her. Then he'd wanted to go back, and he'd been here on this lighthouse, unable to go anywhere. How she had come to be here, he couldn't even guess.

"It's warm inside. Let me help you." He reached under her shoulders to help her stand, and together they made their way into the warmth of the lighthouse. Rocky slammed the door shut, forcing it totally closed this time, and he helped Miss Bevier—Lisa, he reminded himself—to the sofa. Grabbing the heater, he moved it directly in front of her, turning the control up a notch.

As she sat there, she lifted her hand and forced it through her wet hair, shivering violently. She looked at him, and an expression of recognition came over her face. Then, through her shivering, she laughed. The sound was broken yet amused.

"I know you. You're Rockland Royster. From the Center. I didn't know you were a sailor."

"Rocky," he muttered. "And I'm not." Irritation crawled across his skin. He had just saved this woman, and now he was once again being reminded of all his years at the Center.

Her voice chattered out her next words. "Rocky. I remember, and I'm sorry. I'm Lisa, and I'm freezing. Do you have any towels or anything?" She wrapped her arms around herself, and anywhere she touched her clothing, water dripped to the floor.

He was cold, too, and he was wearing only his very wet boxer shorts. He looked desperately around the room. He'd brought only what Tramwick had packed, and that wasn't much. All he had were his drying clothes. His shirt was good, but the pants had gotten more rain.

She needed them, though. He could sit in front of the heater and eventually warm himself. She couldn't. Also, she had to get out of her clothes. He rubbed his arms as he walked to the pegs where the things were hanging.

"I have these. Except for the pants, they're dry. The pants are only wet on one side."

She took the clothes as he handed them to her, whispering, "I should wear these?" She glanced at him, then looked longer, clearly taking in his half-clothed appearance. "Are you sure? You do have more?"

Her voice chattered with the cold. When he shook his head, she made to give them back. However, no matter what, he knew she had to get out of her things. "You have to change, or you'll catch something." He motioned to the clothes.

"Towels? Do you have anything to dry with?"

His bare shoulders shrugged, and he repeated his earlier offer. "Nothing except those."

She looked around, her body beginning to shiver violently. "Where?" Her voice wouldn't let her get anything else out.

"I'm sorry," he said, suddenly aware there was only one room on this floor, and she would have to remove her clothes to put his on. "I'll go upstairs. You'll need privacy to change. Let me know when you're finished." He made his way to the steps and took the passage to the next level.

He discovered how dark it was without the lantern. There

was a small window, but the sky outside was nearly black, and he could barely see. He hadn't swept this floor, either, and he couldn't tell what he was walking on. He made his way slowly to the bunks, and he sat on one, pulling his feet underneath him.

It was freezing in the room. There was no heat of any sort, and he was dripping from both the sea and the rain. His one piece of clothing was so wet and so cold that he could barely stand for the fabric to rest against his skin. He desperately tried to think of anything he had seen in the lighthouse that he could wear besides just his wet shorts. Lisa was putting on everything of his that he had with him, and that left him nothing. He could wear the slicker, he guessed. He would at least be covered. He just didn't know if the slicker would be better than his wet boxers. Not, was his guess. He sure wished she would hurry. She might have nearly drowned, but he was up here in this cold room, and he was freezing. All the heat was downstairs, and he needed some of it.

After a few moments, he heard her call, and relief washed over him. His teeth chattered as he reached the steps to the lower floor. Right then, he just wanted to be warm. He didn't care what he was wearing. He simply needed that heater, and he needed it more that he had ever thought possible, no matter who huddled in front of it with him.

ANDREW WAS in pain. His leap from the boat had been a desperate act of self-preservation. He hadn't cared about the woman he'd betrayed. Why should he? It had happened long ago. Anyway, she was simply another in a long line of betrayals.

He thought of the boat he had taken, although he knew stolen would be a better word. He always returned the vessels he borrowed. They might be a little lower on fuel, but that was a small price for the owners to pay. This one would never get home.

The water was freezing, and it kept piling up around him,

washing over his face and into his mouth. He choked with the effort of trying to breathe. However, one arm after another was all it took, and he could swim to shore.

He turned to look back at the sinking boat, and in the reflection of the beacon against the water, he could see the pilothouse as it slipped beneath the waves. Then, there was only the lighthouse standing in the storm with the waves crashing at its base. He turned and began to swim.

He never should have stopped. He might have continued to make progress had he kept his body prone to the surface of the water. However, his legs were now lead weights, and they dragged after him, tiring his arms faster and faster.

As his face began to sink more and more often, panic surged through him. In the cold of the stormy sea, he could no longer feel his limbs. His arms began to flail, and his heart pounded. The final time he went down, he no longer knew he was dying. He only knew the silence of the sea.

EVEN WITH the disaster than had befallen her, Lisa was appalled at how cold her rescuer looked. "You cannot still be wearing those wet shorts. Surely you have something you can change into."

He stepped the rest of the way into the room, closing it off and making sure the heat was trapped inside. He rubbed his arms against the chill bumps that had collected there.

"Goose Bumps Light, they should call this," he managed to chatter. "I have goose bumps all over. May I come to sit in front of the heater?" He didn't wait for her response.

Dropping to the floor in front of her, he pulled his knees up to him and hugged them tightly. With a quick movement, he pulled the heater closer.

"Sorry," he mumbled. "It was cold up there."

Lisa pulled Rocky's shirt tightly around her. She'd hung her clothes on the wall where his had been, and she glanced at them, feeling very guilty. Looking to the window, she was aware of how close she had come to death, and it frightened her. Then, this man sitting at her feet had rescued her, offering her his only suit of clothing, and that left him with almost nothing to wear.

A low-pitched moaning sound filled the lighthouse, and she felt the structure vibrate. Her heart caught in her throat. The storm was getting worse. She was certain of that.

"The man with you, who was he?" Rocky's voice was deep and melodious, even in his chilled state. Against the sound of the storm, the words fought to be heard. He looked up as the foghorn started. He reassured her, raising the level of his voice. "You'll get used to that sound. It'll go off about every ten seconds until the storm passes." He paused until the horn quieted. "That man in the boat. He won't be able to swim to shore." He reached his hands to the flames to try to soak up the warmth they put out, his constant, agitated motion revealing just how cold he was. "Was he close to you?"

That question hit a nerve with her. Andrew had been close to her three years ago. At least she had thought so. She had sewn her own wedding dress with plans to marry him. She hadn't wanted to be in that boat with him, though. He had told her things she would rather not have heard, and then when she'd cried to him for help, he'd abandoned her.

This man at her feet hadn't. He had somehow pulled her from the tempest outside, giving her safety and warmth. His clothes even smelled like a man. There was a muskiness about them that made her feel protected and safe, even though she knew there was a storm beating at the exterior of the building, a rough structure barely keeping her alive. Although he sat at her feet wearing only his underwear, she felt this was a man who would treat her with respect. He'd already risked his life for her.

Breathing deeply, she tried to remember exactly how she had gotten inside. Andrew had jumped, and then the water had risen. It had swirled around her, and she'd found herself on the lighthouse walk, lying wet and cold. It must be how Josh felt when he had one of his seizures, that jarring that took him from one event to a new *here* in that jolting instant of awareness.

"The man," Rocky prompted again through his chattering teeth. "Who was he?"

She answered the question quietly and without emotion. "He was someone I used to know, but that was long ago. He was just piloting the boat." She turned at the sound of water slapping against the door. "Does it normally do that, hit the door like that?"

"Some. At least it did last night when the tide was high. There'll be a storm surge. This is a hurricane. It must be. What else could cause this?" He stood. "I'm warming up a little. Thank God for that." Stepping forward, he pulled a sack from his stash. "I have food. Not a lot, but I'm willing to share. I have some canned meat left, and there's probably other things in here I don't know about. My friend, Tram, packed all this. He's the one who dropped me off here."

Lisa smiled at the man's sudden burst of energy, and she recalled her imaginings from earlier that morning with a clarity she wouldn't have thought possible. Her pretend tale of a story flashed through her mind. "Is this friend a fisherman? A lobster fisherman?"

He stopped and looked at her. "How did you know?"

She laughed but didn't elaborate the details. She couldn't tell him she had dreamed it, or maybe fantasized about it would be a better way to describe it. "Did he recently rescue two stranded women?"

Rocky stepped back to the sofa, and he sat on the edge. He looked into her eyes. "How can you know that?"

Hiding her mouth with her hand, she smiled. This was entirely too much like her pretend scenario. "He left you here with this food and no clean clothes, didn't he? So he could go party without you."

Rocky leaned back on the sofa, and hearing her words, laughed in amazement. "You know Tramwick, don't you? Then you must know Fish, too." He looked at himself and adjusted his drying shorts. Glancing at the slicker on the wall, he made to move that direction, then he hesitated. "He did leave me one thing." He rubbed his arms, finally stopping with his hands resting on his shoulders. "I should put it on. Then you wouldn't have to be embarrassed looking at me." He stood, only to have her catch his arm.

"I wish you knew how grateful I am." When he sat back down, she continued, "I really thought the storm was over." Her eyes moved to the slicker, and it looked like it would be very uncomfortable against his skin. Her own clothes were dripping puddles next to it. "You were here in your lighthouse before my boat came at you, determined to sink literally on your doorstep. You may continue to wear whatever you wish. I won't be bothered."

She knew otherwise. She would be far from unbothered. This man was one she had dreamed of for years, and who had run from her with his apologies. She'd been afraid she would never see him again. Now, in the most bizarre turn of events, he was sitting next to her in the barest of clothing. She could see the curve of his arms, and when he breathed, the muscles in his belly moved. His waist was firm, and his legs were long. He was actually speaking to her this time. He was carrying on a conversation of sorts, and he'd laughed at what she said.

She could tell he was charming her, and she wasn't sure if it was because he was all that charming, or if his heroic actions were causing her to sense charm where there were only good manners. As she sat curled up in his clothing, her body warming, it somehow seemed that the yellow light of the lantern as it shifted the shadows in the room, and the roar of the storm outside, were just what she required. It was like a rebirth from that watery grave to which she had nearly succumbed.

It was also a rebirth from three years ago, one that she hadn't even known she'd needed.

ROCKY GRINNED at her generous comments, and his explanation tumbled out.

"I don't usually run around in my shorts inside abandoned lighthouses. There are no facilities, see, and when I stepped outside, my clothes got wet. They were almost dry, too, when the eye of the storm passed over. I thought the weather was clearing, and I hung my pants outside. The rain wet them again."

"Is that so?" She smiled. "You were outside to use the facilities, and the storm caught you."

"Um, when you need to go . . ." Even as he told his story, he realized Lisa wouldn't be able to take care of her personal needs as easily as he had. He looked at her, and he glanced away. Embarrassment overwhelmed him as his neck warmed, and he dropped his head.

She smiled at his bumbling. "I'll try to drink very little. Perhaps we'll be rescued before then."

"My friend, Tram, is in Rockland—"

"Tramwick, you mean?"

He nodded. "—and he was supposed to pick me up today. I don't think he'll make it. No one could." He didn't mention what had just happened to Lisa's boat.

She stood and went to feel her clothes, shifting them for better access to the air. "If he doesn't show up, do you have enough supplies for another night? Oh," she turned in realization, "your supplies. You surely don't have enough to share, do you?" She pointed at what he had. "I know you offered, but you really didn't plan on me. Is there more?"

"I was only planning on one night, last night, but yes, there's enough. We can certainly have something tonight, and we can have breakfast, maybe, if we're still here. There are drinks in the ice chest."

She smiled and shook her head no.

Just then a massive shudder shook the structure. They looked to see water seeping in under the door. Lisa looked at Rocky, and he could read the expression on her face. She'd nearly died out in that, and seeing the water again was too much for her. He stepped to her, and then he realized how it might look with what he was wearing. Unsure what to do, he stopped and stood in the middle of the floor. She laughed haltingly.

"The water. It came in under the door. Will it do that anymore, do you think?" She had gone pale. "Will it?"

He tried to sound reassuring as he moved to the window. "The storm's blowing something fierce, but this lighthouse is over a hundred years old. It should stand a few more."

"But will the water keep coming inside?" Her voice quavered, and her eyes were red. "I nearly drowned. I must know."

He had seen the water level outside, even in the darkness of the storm. It was nearing high tide, and the storm surge must be compounding that. The waves were washing over the walk, sending the big ones to find their way inside. The door didn't provide a watertight seal. He suspected that before long, this lower floor might be wet and uncomfortable.

He pulled himself together and turned to her. "It'll be a long night, tonight. We might as well start getting comfortable. There are beds upstairs." He glanced at her, and he saw her startled look. He clarified his suggestion. "Bunk beds. We should take our things up and try to warm that room. Do you feel like helping?"

"It's not warm up there, and you went into that to let me change?" Her expression softened. "I would like to help. What should I carry first?"

TERESE SAT in a chair beside her kitchen table, and she held the phone in her hand. This was twice in one day, and she still knew very little. North Haven was off the Maine coast, right

249

where the storm was battering New England.

It was also where Lisa had met Andrew.

She thought of her husband, injured in that hit-and-run accident so long ago. Andrew had been no accident, and that was unforgivable. Terese looked for the paperwork her daughter had left behind. Sorting through the things on the table, she pulled it out. His was just a boy's face in the picture. She hoped for her daughter that she might meet a man like this. She set the paper aside and hummed for a moment as she opened and closed her arthritis-ridden hands. Then she reached twisted fingers to massage her distended joints. The rough weather outside had picked up, and she hoped the power stayed on. Then, with determination, she stood and opened her cabinet doors, searching for containers to fill with water. If the power did go, she wanted to be prepared. She could never tell, not in a storm.

Terese hummed some more, and soon the water jugs and pitchers were filled. Satisfied she had done all she could, she gathered her flashlight and moved to the living room. Turning down the phone ringer several notches, she picked up the remote and switched on the television. She caught the tail end of the weather report, but that wasn't what she wanted to watch, anyway. A voice spoke as she looked for the proper buttons to change the channel.

"The eye of Category 1 Hurricane Christian is currently estimated to be eight miles off the mainland, centered directly in Penobscot Bay. Those along the coast will experience a substantial storm surge coupled with the storm's arrival at the month's highest tide. Please be prepared. Your life may be at stake."

By the time the message was finished, she had found the buttons for her game show, and the image flickered and changed. She laughed and was distracted by the contestants, and that was what it was all about.

WHILE THE ice chest was the most awkward to carry up, it was the fuel can that concerned Lisa the most. It seemed far from full, and the cold in the room above made her very aware of how bad things could get if the heater were to fail.

"Rocky," she asked, as she was handing it up to him, "is this all the fuel you have?"

"We'll conserve however we can," he reassured her. "We can run the light lower, maybe turn the heat down. I never thought I'd be staying a second night, much less playing host. Tram was to come rescue his stranded friend today." Grinning, he quipped, "Maybe he was partying too hard with those women he rescued to bother with his old friend, Rocky."

"You can joke about this?" Lisa looked up at the man who crouched above her. She was very aware of the feeling in her stomach that told her this situation was far too intimate for her own good. Yet, she was equally aware of its unavoidability. To be rescued by this man was beyond her wildest dreams, but she still hadn't managed to find out just what had brought all this about, how he could be here at just the moment she had needed him. He seemed to enjoy skirting every question she asked of him.

"JOKE? WHAT DO you mean?" From the top of the steps, he threw her question back at her, grinning as his words were swallowed by the tune of the foghorn that continually interrupted everything they said to each other.

For the first time in his adult life, Rocky felt confident in his interactions with a woman. As he had moved about the lighthouse and warmed, his embarrassment had lessened. If asked, he couldn't have said whether his self-confidence arose from the heroic act he had performed, or whether it was that this woman had been forced into his world, and she was completely dependent on him. If Lisa were making the call, she might have said he was in his element, in the physical world he felt comfortable in.

251

He could move things, fix problems, and rescue helpless women, and those were the things he was best at.

"Aren't you the least bit frightened?"

"Tell me, is this lighthouse about to blow over tonight after standing for over a hundred years?" When she glanced away and whispered it wouldn't, he continued, "Think what it'll be like to tell your grandchildren you lived through a hurricane in an abandoned lighthouse with only a strange man for company. Who else in this storm can say that? At least you're warm."

"I'm not sure I can say that. I've already passed up the heater, and that's what's been keeping me warm." She laughed. Her face relaxed, and her expression became warm and inviting.

He grinned at her and gave her a thumbs-up sign. As he stood and shook the fuel can, he frowned as he turned to put it away. It was indeed very low. He hadn't realized how much had already been used. He turned as he heard her give a startled yelp.

"Rocky, my feet are getting wet."

He scrambled down the steps only to land in water. It was very cold. He grabbed the lantern from the step and held it away from the window so he could see outside. The highest swells were nearly up to the glass, and the walk was submerged. The wind was peeling the tops of the breakers away, and the spray was being carried far across the sea. They had to move, and immediately. He glanced at the door to see water pouring in around the lower part of the opening.

"Grab what you can. The storm surge is here." With his feet splashing seawater, he ran to the clothing hung on the far wall, while she wrestled the rest of the food packages into her grip. "This might get bad," he called. "We may not be able to come back down, not until this is over."

SHE STOPPED and turned to him as she made her way up the steps, and her voice shook. "This lighthouse will stand, you're certain of that? One hundred years. Right?" She needed to hear him say it again. He had no real control over whether this place washed into the sea, but she needed to hear it.

He looked up from the bottom of the steps. "It'll stand. It's done so since 1890. It'll be here tomorrow and the day after. However, this water coming in is very cold. I'd like to go up." He looked at her earnestly. "Please."

She stood frozen, taking one last look at the black water on the floor, and then with a shattering sound and a crash of water, the window broke. Dark water poured through as the lighthouse shuddered, and Rocky yelled, "Lisa!" The wind howled through the opening.

His voice jerked her into action, and she scrambled out of his way. Before he closed off the first floor, they looked down, and holding the lantern over the steps, they could see the water swirling through the lower room. As the lighthouse shuddered with the onslaught of each new wave, water surged in torrents through the broken window.

Lisa turned to Rocky. There were real tears in her eyes. She licked her lips before speaking to him, but when she did, the emotions in her words were clear.

"Rocky, I need you to hold me. Please." She shivered and looked away, wrapping her arms around herself. "Hold me and tell me again everything will be all right."

HE WRAPPED his arms around her, and even in the onslaught of the raging storm on the other side of the lighthouse walls, his body responded to her, and he wasn't sorry to be here in this storm. He hadn't forgotten the electricity of her touch back at the center. He also remembered on the deck when he had given her Seven-Eleven. His hand had rested between her breasts, and he'd felt guilty for thinking of her that way.

This time, his words reassured her, and he felt no reason for guilt. His arms were wrapped around her as he held her in a tight embrace. His body fit perfectly against hers, and he'd endure all

253

the hurricanes on Earth to hold her next to him.

If he had to do that to have this woman at his side, he knew he would never regret a one.

Chapter 16

TRAMWICK HELD Fish at his side. Through the glass of the ferry terminal, he could see occasional glimpses of his boat tied up to one of the town buoys. The storm was ferocious. The water fell in sheets, with wind peeling the rain from the tops of structures in long, trailing feathers. The ferries had been secured long ago. At least the breakwater was damping the worst of the sea's onslaught.

The storm surge was threatening to swamp the wharf, though. Waves occasionally washed over, and the spray blown off the top of the swells slashed against the glass. He was glad he'd been stopped from going after Rocky when the eye passed. No one would ferry him to his boat. The sun had been shining, and he had cursed those around him.

Now he knew he would likely have gone down. His boat might have survived the trip out, because he was a good pilot, and his vessel was a good design. However, once he reached the lighthouse and cut the engines, he'd have had no control, and the power of the storm would have wrenched the ship whichever way it desired until it was taken to the bottom of the sea. If he'd tried to tie up at the lighthouse, the waves would have battered him unmercifully.

Either way, his boat wouldn't have survived.

Tramwick had to trust the old lighthouse. He did, too, but he could hardly stand the thought that his friend might feel he'd been abandoned and left to die. All he could picture was Rocky huddled without food or fresh water, the kerosene run dry, and him in the dark, cold and feeling forgotten. This storm would rage for hours, and Rocky would be alone.

He turned to the two girls standing with him in the terminal. They were both about nineteen—or twenty or twenty-one—and they hadn't been able to make it to Green's Island after all. Instead, they brought their boat into Rockland Harbor. Last night they'd huddled in the terminal, sleeping among the chairs scattered around the room.

Tramwick brought them food before the last of the stores closed down. They were ecstatically grateful, showering him with hugs and kisses, and the three of threw a little party. In the things he brought, Tram had stowed a bottle or two of whiskey. Maybe it was three. He couldn't remember, now. They'd all enjoyed it, hiding it so no one would see them imbibing in that very public space.

Eventually, their laughter had rung out, and the few people who ventured through the building were invited to join them. One or two had, but most just smiled at the intrepid trio. That hadn't mattered to Tram or the two maidens he'd rescued. When the storm was wild, the party must be wilder, and the one they threw that night was the best of all. The hurricane outside paled in comparison, and the night passed without taking any of their cheer from them.

The next morning caused them to reassess the events of the

evening before. Their heads hurt, and a more somber attitude prevailed. They peered through alcohol-fogged brains at the raging weather outside the glass, unable to comprehend the rising levels of potential damage that surrounded them.

When the sun unexpectedly came out, they took the opportunity to visit the small park just outside the ferry landing and talked of the craft moored in the harbor, and just why the ferry hadn't readied to pull out for the islands. Tram declared that if he could get to his boat, he'd take them to rescue the friend of his they'd met the day before, but no one would give them a ride.

Now, the storm was worse than ever, and he just hoped the mooring under his boat held. He'd need it to get out to Rocky. The two girls next to him looked as worried as he felt.

With a sigh, he pushed Fish aside and reached to the duffle at his feet. He rummaged inside and felt for a moment. Then, his hand pulled out what might easily be his fifth bottle of whiskey. He looked at the girls and grinned. He was certain they were twenty-one. They had promised the night before, and he had no reason to doubt them. He twisted the lid on the bottle, and after the hissing release of its seal, it opened quietly. He raised it to his lips, and just before drinking, he smiled and spoke, "Cheers, ladies."

After a moment, they took their turn. Each raised the bottle, and each called the magic word. Then the bottle continued its rounds, and the whiskey disappeared one additional cheer at a time.

LISA LISTENED as Rocky shifted on his bunk. She imagined him adjusting the slicker over himself for warmth. The heater was on low to stretch the fuel as long as possible, and the heat simply wasn't enough to warm the room adequately. In the dim light from the lantern, she shivered on the bottom bunk. Her wet clothes were across the steps leading to the top floor, drying very slowly in the chill dampness.

"Rocky," Lisa ventured. "Are you awake?"

"Freezing, but yes, awake."

"When my clothes dry . . ." She paused. She was very aware that she was wearing the only ones he had. "Tell me something of your family."

He chuckled. "There's not much to tell. I have Tram, a grandmother, and Fish. Fish lives with me, Tram might as well, and I see my grandmother when I can, usually when her house needs repair."

Lisa reached her hand to touch the bottom of the bunk above her. The man who had pulled her from the sea lay just there. She would have to ask him more about that later, but the horror of what had nearly happened to her was too intimate just yet. There were other questions she could pursue, though. She wanted to know more about this man who had attended the Center for his entire life, who had received its highest praises, and who had apologized so profusely before suddenly abandoning their meeting. Then, of all the impossibilities in the world, he was here in this abandoned lighthouse to pluck her from the sea. She knew she couldn't expect to uncover the entire story at once, but she wanted to know some of it.

"I know a little about Tram, and your grandmother I can picture. I don't understand Fish. Is it *a* fish, or someone named Fish?"

Rocky shifted on his bunk, and his amusement was clear. "Both. Well, neither, actually. He's a dog, and he was pulled up in a net out at sea. The funny part is that Tram thought he was drowning, and he gave him mouth-to-mouth."

"This is Tramwick, your friend? He gave a dog mouth-to-mouth resuscitation?"

The bed over her creaked, and Rocky's face and one bare arm peered over. "You have to know Tramwick. His favorite beverage is whiskey. I tried to tell him the dog was still breathing, but he was convinced the animal was already a goner. He still thinks the dog would have died if he hadn't done that." Rocky rolled back over in the bed. "That dog never liked being on the water after that. Then yesterday, Tram worked some sort of magic with him. When I got home from our meeting, the one at the Center with you, Fish was jumping at the hook to get out on that boat. I don't know what Tram did. Magic. That's all I know."

Lisa was reminded of Mr. Reynolds and what he'd said to her. *"Magic. Your words are magic to him."* She knew there was no magic. She'd just understood what to say. This Tram was probably the same with Fish. He'd *felt* what to do.

"Who's Fish with, now?"

Rocky laughed. "Tram. I claim Fish as mine. The dog thinks he belongs to my friend. They were on the boat together when they abandoned me here. I guess they're holed up on the mainland somewhere safe and sound."

"With two girls?" Lisa smiled as she teased. She was growing increasingly comfortable with this man, and she felt he would take no offense.

The bed above her creaked again, and she saw Rocky's bare legs drop to her bunk. Then, in one motion, he was sitting at her feet, pulling his slicker up over himself.

"I talk better face-to-face." He smiled. "I know this is a horrible situation, this lighthouse and the storm outside. You nearly drowned when your boat went down, and now we're low on supplies. We've been flooded out of the bottom floor, but I'm enjoying this. Freezing, yes, but enjoying this."

That caught at her heart. Earlier she'd wondered why she felt charmed. Now she could see what it was. This man was being open and sincere, and she understood exactly what he was saying to her. He was enjoying her.

"Tell me about the girls." She sat up. "May I sit next to you? We'd both be warmer." He moved the slicker, and he motioned for her to slide up next to him. Pulling the slicker around them both and tucking it in, it did feel better. Warmer, too, but mostly just better.

Rocky pointed to the one small window in the room. "It's about dark. The light from outside will be gone soon."

Lisa leaned her head on the bare skin of his shoulder. It felt just as she thought it might. It was muscular and firm, and each time he breathed, she could feel his shoulder flex against her face. She couldn't be afraid while she was against this man.

"Tell me of the two girls."

Rocky smiled as he slipped his arm around Lisa's shoulder. "On the way out, there was something on Tram's radar. We came from Mass, you have to know, and all in one long shot. The storm was already here, I guess, and we didn't know it. These two girls, nineteen, maybe, were sitting stranded in the chop, and Tram pulled up to them. He jumped into their boat and in minutes had them up and running. One of them gave him a kiss."

"That's sweet. What were they doing out in the storm?"

"They said they were heading out to Green's Island. It's on the other side of Vinalhaven."

"Vinalhaven. That's the island next to North Haven, right?" She thought she remembered that right. However, it had been three years.

She wondered what else she didn't know, both about this man, and about this storm. This lighthouse, also. She clung to the important thing: he was with her, and she felt safe in his arms.

ROCKY RAN his hand up and down Lisa's arm, enjoying the sensation as the fabric of the shirt slipped beneath his fingers. Her arm was underneath that fabric, and his body warmed with the touch. He murmured, "Vinalhaven's the big one. However, there are about fifty islands out here, I think, scattered all around."

"Fifty." Lisa's words weren't much louder. "How does anyone avoid running into them?"

Rocky whispered, "Lighthouses. You're in one."

Her voice was small. "Oh. I guess I should have realized that."

He just squeezed her, and for a time they sat quietly listening to the sounds of the storm dancing around them. The foghorn provided the musical accompaniment, and the beacon could be seen flashing through the rain as it rotated in its circular sweep.

It was nice, too, just the two of them, and no distractions to tear them apart.

For just that moment, they were glad they were together, and they wouldn't have traded to be anywhere else.

THE LIGHTS in the house blinked out, and the hum of the machines that kept it functioning smoothly ground to a halt. Only the thrum of the rain on the windows broke the silence. John looked around, and in the muted light through the blinds, he imagined he felt the start of an imperceptible cooling in the room. "The power's off," he said, stating the obvious. Then, the jarring ring of a phone broke the silence. He picked it up and growled, "Who's this, and how are you getting through? We just lost power."

Laughter came from the other end. "It's the phone system, John. They carry their own power. You have to lose power to the phone system for it not to work."

Rand? John's irritation faded as quickly as it had begun. "Forgive me. I knew that. Rand, right?" He didn't sound drunk, so it was hard for him to tell. John had tried to call his home earlier, but he hadn't gotten an answer. "Where've you been?"

"Beth and I, well, we're making up for lost time. We've come up to a bed-and-breakfast we sometimes frequent. It's raining here, but apparently nothing like in Boston. You and Trish should get out of there."

"Sure, Rand." There was no power. He couldn't get away if he wanted to. How would he know if the traffic lights were red or green? "What can I do for you? Whatever it is, don't expect it to get done soon. Remember, no power."

"Yeah, well, that's part of it, John. We've got power here, and after we unloaded, I sat down with one of the other guests. There's this one in particular. You'd like him. He a real Texas character with the prettiest wife. Anyway, we were watching the storm reports. I'm glad Beth and I got out when we did."

"Your point?"

"Remember Royce? Royce Royster from the firm? I'm at his mother's place in New Hampshire. Stay with me on this. Remember Rocky Royster? The lighthouse? Goose Rocks. You just sent him the contract." Rand laughed. "It's the same family. Royce's son is named Rockland. He attended the Massachusetts Center for Children."

John looked up to see Trish walk through the room, and in the dimness of the muted light filtering in from outside, he waved his drink at her. She smiled back. She had told him repeatedly it was good to have him home.

"I remember." Some of that, anyway. "I wasn't the one who was drunk on Saturday."

"Yeah. Well, sorry about that. Anyway, when the power comes back on, check out the reports. That school Rockland attended, the Massachusetts Center for Children, well, it's already taken a hit. The reports are all over the news. Flooding, and a tree damaged one of the buildings. It seems one of the school's nurses is missing, somehow. They're also having to scramble to find places to board the children who live in the residence and can't get home."

"It's the middle of the storm, still." John frowned. "I can't do anything now. Can't they just call their parents? Or postpone school a few days? I'm sure the kids would like some time off."

"John, you're not getting the point. It was the residence building that was damaged. You're on the board there. You can help." He chuckled. "Beth and I think we might have found part of your solution up here."

"I may be on the board at the Center, but you're certainly drunk. You're making no sense." Rand could be heard talking to someone in the background, and John decided he was calling from a bar. "I'm hanging up now."

"No, John! You can't hang up. Call the Center if you can get through. I've been talking to the owner here. You know, Royce's mother. She's got this big old house, and it's mostly empty during the fall and winter. We can bring some of the kids from the Center here, maybe a few teachers, and this could be a temporary satellite campus. She *wants* them."

John paused. He needed to process this.

"What do you think, John?"

"Bette Royster." John remembered her name from Royce's days and stories he'd told of his youth. His words were less a question than an interlude to give him a needed moment to think. "As in Rocky Royster."

"So, John? It's only two hours from the city."

"You're serious. You know, it's not as easy as you make it out to be. Even if all this is the way you describe it, and we make plans to do things this way, we'd have to get certain formalities out of the way. Also, nursing staff for the medications. We'd have to have that."

"That's what makes it so great, John. Do you see? This woman's *grandson* went to the Center for his schooling, all of it, in the residency program, nonetheless. Now he's a renowned boat builder. What could be better for the Center's image?"

John began to figure in his head, speaking aloud as he did so. "Let's see. There are about eighty in the residency program, and I'd say we'd be able to contact maybe seventy-five percent of those parents, as most of our families are local." As an active board member, he received regular reports. He read them, too. "The other twenty-five percent are from out-of-state families, or their parents could possibly be traveling, which would leave twenty needing housing." He questioned into the phone, "If all this becomes necessary, could she handle twenty?"

Rand could be heard talking to someone in the room with him, and then he spoke back to John. "If she does three to a room, fifteen, at least. She'd need portable beds to do more, but she might be able to make some storage rooms double as bed-rooms. If we could provide the beds, she could handle the entire twenty."

"A nurse? There has to be room for a nurse."

Rand laughed. "You have to meet this woman, John. She's got you covered. She wants those kids up here. Her grandson, remember? She's got what it takes. You won't regret this."

John drew in a deep breath. It was still dark outside, and the room was definitely cooling. Without power, he had no way to check the news reports. However, if it was as bad as Rand said, the Center would need to have a backup plan in place.

"I'll check with the Center. If it turns out that they need the space, and we can pull all the approvals together, I'll get back with you."

"Thanks, John. You won't be sorry."

After he hung up, Trish walked into the room. "Who was calling in the middle of this storm?" She sat on the arm of his chair and reached to stroke his hair. "Was it important?"

He smiled. "Something about the Center."

"The Massachusetts Center? Oh, I love those kids. They're all so special. Do they need help in all of this? I want you to take care of them."

"I know, Trish. That's what the call was about. We're plan-ning to take care of them all."

TRISH SLIPPED off the arm of the chair and squeezed in beside her husband. She was glad the electricity was off. This way there was nothing to do besides spend time with each other. She began to rub John's arm. When he didn't resist, she moved her hand farther down. Then, she began touching him in a way she wouldn't consider if anyone else was present. They weren't, though, and she was enjoying it very much.

It wasn't long before John felt the same way.

"LET ME tell you about my father."

Lisa spoke her words to break a growing silence. Talking helped distract her from the sounds of the storm. The room had finally warmed, although she wasn't sure if it was from the heater or from Rocky's warmth. She knew the butterflies in her stomach came from being wrapped up under this waterproof coat with him.

"I'd like to hear that."

"My father was a wonderful man. He enjoyed the outdoors, and he and my mother worshiped each other."

"Worshipped?"

"There was an accident. He was walking, something he did every day. A driver hit him, we think. Hit-and-run." She took his hand in hers and rubbed the backs of his fingers as she leaned her head against the wall and paused for a moment. After all these years, it hurt less to talk of it, even though she was certain the pain would never completely go away.

"He was killed, I take it."

"No, not immediately. That came later. It's the in between that was so hard to take."

A CHILL came over Rocky. Hit-and-run. He thought of his father. Rocky had been a teenager when his father had suffered his heart attack. He'd been in his car, and from the reports, he'd struggled with the controls, wrestling his car all the way to the

265

hospital. The whispered accusations suggested that someone might have been hit along the way; however, his father's car had impacted a tree and was mangled, and any real evidence had been lost.

"Hit-and-run, you say." Rocky whispered the words.

"He was only injured, we thought at first, and not badly," Lisa continued, brushing Rocky's arm to reassure him it happened long ago. "However, he never walked again. My mother cared for him as long as she could, and then he was sent to a home with around-the-clock nursing care. It devastated their resources."

"When?" Rocky let his eyes search the growing darkness. He realized the fuel in the lamp must be running low, and he'd added the last of the kerosene to the reservoir. In the darkness, he thought about how he'd felt about his father. Rocky had felt hated as a teen, but he would have been devastated to have known his father was dying from injuries inflicted by a careless driver.

"It was a very long time ago. I was still a teenager."

"Twelve years ago?" It was when he'd lost his father, and he didn't want the two to be the same.

"You're right. It *was* twelve years ago. That's very good."

The answer numbed him. He felt his gut twist as he asked his next question. "You never learned who did this?"

"I let it go long ago. My mother, too. We had to. We couldn't chase this and live, too. No one could. Bad things happen, and life has to go on."

"What if the man who did this is no longer alive?" If there was any connection between the two accidents, he dreaded what that might mean.

"It was just a story, part of my life that's over and now a memory. Don't worry about it. Tell me of your father, instead."

That brought silence from the man at her side. He had nothing to tell that he could say positively. His father had sent him away, and he hadn't felt loved.

"Rocky, what was something you liked to do together when you were growing up?"

"I grew up at the Center. My father and I never spent time together."

"Never? Surely, at least once you did something together. Over a summer or during a family vacation?"

He thought about it. There was that one summer. He'd worked on that boat with his father and had felt loved. However, it had all been in his mind. His father had been killing time until he could send his son away again.

"Rocky? Anything?"

He sighed. "I built a boat with him once."

She laughed. "How wonderful! That's where you learned to do what you do now. Right?"

"Hardly. We never finished it. It still sits in my grandmother's barn."

"Doesn't your father want to complete it with you? Surely he'd get with you to finish it, if you asked."

"I never asked. Now I can't."

"Why not?"

He leaned his head back. She would drag this from him, and he wished it to be forgotten. All the issues of his childhood and teen years were just below the surface. He'd found that out in the past week, first at Bette's and then at the Center, running from this woman.

"He's dead. He died a long time ago. A heart attack while driving his car." He thought of her father, wondering again if there could be a connection. "Besides, he hated me."

She sat up and looked him in the face, the image beside her bathed in shadows. "No, Rocky. He couldn't have hated you."

He glanced at her, and one side of his mouth drew back in a pained smile that he was certain revealed the irony of his answer. Then he looked away.

"He loved me enough to send me to the Center. He didn't want me to live with him. I couldn't even stay with my grandmother." His voice turned sour. "Sure, he loved me."

"I can't imagine how you must have felt."

"I'm dyslexic and autistic. You of all people must know that. Of course, he hated me." He yawned and smiled, changing the subject. "I didn't sleep well last night."

It was his signal that the conversation needed to move on.

LISA DIDN'T know how to respond to this man's sudden honesty. She simply leaned against his shoulder, and when she did, she found tears in her eyes. Her thoughts were of the words Josh had spoken to her, and the answer she had given him back.

"Do you have autism, Miss Bevier?"

"No, Josh. I don't. Does that matter?"

"It does to people who don't have it. Why would you want someone with autism if you don't have it yourself?"

She was seeing this man in a new way, one that had been explained to her by a seventeen-year-old boy. His life hadn't been healed by his time at the Center. He had needed more than what his teachers and the support staff could offer. He had needed his father, to be loved by him. She saw that in Josh, and she had been irritated at his parents, people who saw the handicap and not the child. Now she was broken for this man. Although ten years away from his time at the Center, he still dealt with the same issues as that seventeen-year-old boy.

She whispered into his shoulder as she raised her hand to rest it across his chest, "I would want you, Rocky. I'd want you with your dyslexia and autism." When she raised her head to look him in the eyes, she saw his were closed. Then she realized his breath had deepened into the even pattern of sleep.

She put her head back on his shoulder. Her hand stroked the muscles of his chest, feeling the downy hairs that grew there. She felt several spots that were damp, and she realized they were

268

her tears.

She whispered once again, "I'd want you very much, if only you'd be mine."

This man was someone she was learning to want very much. She only hoped he could feel the same way about her.

FRANK WAS spread across the sofa in his office. It had been thirty hours, and night reigned across the Eastern Seaboard. His snores cut softly into the room. A small light on his desk glowed warmly against the grain of the wood.

A new crop of staffers was on duty. Several were qualified meteorologists, and even more were those who ran under them to keep the minor detail gods satisfied. A new face, one fresh from home, looked through the glass wall at the man sleeping there.

"What will we do when Frank decides he can't take the pressure any longer? Almost no lives have been lost. People stayed in their homes, and that was all due to Frank." The staffer shook his head and turned to the room full of Weather Service workers and monitors displaying the progress of the storm. Large, the central display showed the swirls of clouds that had progressed across the New England coastal regions. The eye was now undefined, and there were no symbols identifying it as a hurricane any longer. As it had climbed onto land, it had slowed and dissipated, its wind speeds dropping at first to tropical storm strength, and then slipping quickly through that of a depression and even lower.

The water hadn't all subsided, but it would. High tide had come and gone, and as it had rushed back to sea, it had carried much of the storm surge with it. The New England coast was built for sturdiness and withstanding the battering of fall storms. The people were even sturdier. They would buckle down, clear the damage, and life would be ready for winter when it came.

To give those sturdy New Englanders assistance, once daylight returned, rescue crews would be out. At sea, there was the Coast Guard, and for them, many would be thankful. Others would depend on the state ferry services. Just as many would wait for friends and family to come to their aid.

On land, the National Guard would step in. The Red Cross would set up shelters if needed, and churches would do what they always did, providing food and housing to those who were displaced.

Frank would go on, too. Another storm would come, and he would find a way to save lives. He would always doubt himself, and others would know and wonder why, or they would see him as an infallible weather god.

In the distant future, he might go on to other things. Retirement, maybe, but for now, he was the best thing the Weather Service had. His staffers knew that, and they were grateful. Others would have been, if they knew. All Frank cared about was the number of people who died. He wanted that number to be as small as possible.

LISA JERKED awake. The lighthouse was silent. There was no foghorn, and the wind didn't whistle and moan through the loose panes of glass. It was cold, though.

She snuggled next to the man who had saved her from the sea. She moved her hand over his skin, and it was warm and moist. He shifted with her touch.

He hadn't awakened since his eyes had closed the night before. She knew he must have been exhausted. However, she needed to relieve her bladder, and she needed to do it quickly. She hadn't been since that horrendous accident the day before.

Carefully sliding out from under the slicker, she reached to the heater. It was cold. It was then that she realized why she could see. There was a stream of sunlight coming in from the one small window that was uncovered.

She didn't dare hope. This was certainly sunlight, but she

wasn't sure she could trust it to last. Yesterday's break in the weather had led her to a near disaster. Near? It hadn't been near for Andrew. She didn't see how he could have made it to shore. The water was so cold, she couldn't have swum if she'd wanted. Quietly, she crept to peer out the window. Her tension relaxed as she smiled, seeing the water was calm, and the sky was clear. Then, her breath quickened when she remembered the reason they had climbed to this level.

She reached the steps to the lower floor. With a pounding heart, she made her way down. Pausing and leaning against the wall, she was relieved to see the water had subsided. Perhaps the possibility of escape today could be theirs, after all. She felt the air coming in from the window that had broken the previous night. It felt crisp and clean. It was as if no storm had scoured the islands, and as if God had stepped down and kissed the beautiful land she could see through the opening. The soft sound of the surf coming in also reminded her that nature continued to call.

Stepping to the floor, she was careful to watch her feet. It was still damp, but it seemed safe enough to walk across. She looked in desperation for a toilet, but quickly realized there was nothing available. Off to one side was a used food tin. With relief, she rushed over and picked it up, hoping she could manip-ulate this into a makeshift bucket. Looking around, she saw the window was inset into a small alcove, and she could back into a corner just to the side for at least the semblance of privacy.

Finished, she stood and adjusted the too-large pants she wore. She looked down at the steaming can and knew she couldn't just leave it there. Moving to the door, she decided she could dispose of the offending fluid into the sea.

Tugging at the latch, she managed to get it loose, but the door wouldn't move more than a few inches. Finally, with her hands into the crack she had created, she pushed with all her strength until it gave a loud squeal and flew back against the outside wall.

"What?" A sleepy voice jarred her attention, and she froze. "I pull you from the sea, and you want to jump back in? Did I rescue a mermaid instead of the school nurse? Or, has a rescue ship come?"

Lisa turned to see Rocky standing on the steps. With that glance, she knew she was as near in love as she could fall with this man. His hair was sticking straight up, and his boxer shorts were rumpled. His muscles were rounded and firm on his frame, and a smile that he was trying to control rippled across his face.

Her eyes slipped to the still-steaming can at her side, and she was mortified. She couldn't leave it there, and if she reached to pick it up, he would know what she'd been doing. There was only one thing she could do.

"Rocky," she pleaded. "Please go back upstairs. Just for a moment. I desperately need you to do this."

He looked at her with puzzlement in his eyes. Then he shrugged. "Will I be able to come back down?" He laughed softly. "Today, perhaps?"

"Rocky, please. Of course, you'll be able to come back down."

He teased, "It got nippy the last time I had to hide up there. There's no heater this time. The fuel is gone."

Her voice wailed, "Rocky!"

"Hey!" He held up both hands. "That tone just convinced me. This floor is yours." He chuckled and backed up the steps, rubbing one hand over the side of his face and yawning as he did so.

As soon as he was gone, Lisa grabbed the can of fluid. Her first realization was that it was warm, and her hands were very cold. Then she stepped to the walk outside and dumped it over. She stood for a moment and let the sun wash across her face, glad for its warmth.

"Lisa," Rocky called to her from inside the lighthouse. "Can

I come out and play, yet?"

She looked at the can in her hand. She hated to throw it in the sea, but she didn't know what else to do. She had no water to rinse it. Looking at the gentle waves, she thought of the boat that had gone down. Then, she cast the can into the water, knowing it was only a small thing in comparison.

Returning to the inside of the building, she called, "You can come down. I'm finished."

With a quick scrabble of feet, he was down the steps. He rubbed his hand through his hair. He grinned and asked, "Did you enjoy your once-in-a-lifetime opportunity to relieve the call of nature outside?"

Horrified, she glared at him. "I did not go outside!"

He laughed. "Well, I will. I'm not so prudish." He leaned against the wall, and he crossed his arms. "For your prudishness, I can wait, but not too much longer."

She shook her head, but her heart beat faster. He was so handsome, and he was right here with her. This was the view the woman he married would see every morning. For this one breaking dawn, it was hers.

"I thought you had to go badly." She smiled as she turned to look out the door.

"I'm now being prudish. I have an audience who might find me crude. I'm allowing you the generous option of exiting upstairs while I engage myself in my own private activities. Besides, there are dry clothes waiting. You might want to change."

She gasped with the realization that the urgency of the storm was gone, and he might be embarrassed with what he had on. After all, he couldn't go around in what he was wearing, and he certainly couldn't wear her things.

"I'm so sorry. I didn't think. Your clothes have been so comfortable, and I've gotten used to what you have on. I no longer noticed . . . er, I no longer minded . . . that is, I *have* noticed, and I think you look good in whatever you have on, just

273

the way you are. After spending the night with you, I no longer think of you as naked." She froze, mortified that she had so easily put her foot in her mouth. She whispered, "May I please just go upstairs?"

He bowed and motioned to the steps. "My queen. Please enter your chambers by permission of the court jester, one Rocky Royster." He remained bowed as she passed, but she caught him looking up at her as she climbed the steps. It was when he winked that she realized he hadn't been offended. He seemed rather pleased with her stumbling rendition, almost as if he'd wanted her to notice him in that very certain way.

She liked that. She liked him, and it made her heart soar to think he might feel the same.

Chapter 17

JOSH LAY in bed and looked out the windows at the shadow line of the horizon silhouetted against the sky. The storm had ceased during the night, and now there were rays of morning sun breaking through the trees. He threw back his covers and stepped to the glass. Dimly he could see his reflection, and he remembered how Miss Bevier had described him. He felt a man. Sort of. He knew he felt he had a man's job to do. Miss Bevier had gone out as the storm had hit once again, and he needed to know if she made it safely to shore. He had no idea how he could do that, but surely he could do something. His father had finally returned the night before, and he'd refused to go out again. This morning, he couldn't refuse. If he did, then Josh would . . . he would . . . he didn't know what he would do, but it would be something, that was for certain.

He turned and ran to the bathroom. Flipping on the light, he heard the generator gently click on. As it hummed its even tune, he opened the medicine waiting for him on the counter. Then, stopping, he looked at the packaging. He grinned when he saw the date, and that it was current. Pulling one tablet out, he put it in his mouth, and it was gone.

A shadow appeared at the door. "I thought you'd be up early. I think we need to go check on our friend. What do you say?"

Josh looked up, and in the mirror, he could see his father standing behind him, warmly dressed. With a sudden rush of relief, he turned and threw his arms around the man he needed to love him. When his father hugged him back, Josh squeezed him as hard as he could.

"Whoa, Son. Save a little for your mother. Your tablet, it's down?"

Josh grinned. "Checked the label, too. It was the right one."

His father laughed. "Then we're good to go. Get your clothes on, and I'll head out to warm the truck. I've got some sandwiches and a drink. Binoculars, too." He stepped out, leaving his son to join him as soon as he could.

Josh was very quick, and as he stepped into the front hall and pulled on his coat, the first rays of sun found their way through the windows. Outside, the air was still and crisp. He heard his father honk the horn, and he ran to climb inside.

"Where do we head to check on Miss Bevier, Josh?"

It surprised him that his father asked his opinion. Usually, Josh was just told what his father intended to do. He smiled and said, "Maybe the last place we saw her. At the Crabtree's dock. What do you think, Dad?"

His father nodded. "It's as good a place to start as any. Since the power's still out, that might mean there could be downed lines. Keep an eye peeled."

"Sure, Dad." He watched out the window as his father turned the truck and navigated to the road. They found leaves everywhere, and once saw a giant spruce with its roots standing high in the air. Larch branches littered the roadside. The roads were mostly clear enough during their short drive, though, and after a few minutes, with only one detour onto the grass, the Crabtree's dock came into view. Out in the Thorofare, Goose Rocks Light stood tall, just catching the morning sun, and the water lapped softly at its base. At first glance, things looked pretty much the same as always.

Once they stepped out of the truck and walked down to the dock, they could see the damage was more than they had thought. The dock was still there, but the float had been torn away. It was washed far up on the shore next to the pilings. It seemed this area had been protected during the first part of the storm, and then when the winds had turned during the second half, a great deal of flotsam had been pushed this way. The shore was littered with debris.

"Dad? Is that part of the *Duty*?" Josh grabbed his father's shoulder and pointed at a painted board lying on top of the jumble deposited by the storm. When Craig turned, he put his arm around his son, pulling him in and hugging him tightly.

"I see it," he whispered. "It just looks the color of the boat Miss Bevier was on. Don't be too quick to jump to conclusions. Lots of stuff washed up here. My guess is this little cove was catching everything. It could be any one of a hundred boats."

Josh struggled out of his father's arm. Leaping down to the flotsam that scattered the shore, he reached to the board and flipped it over. He looked up at his father. The words were clearly written: *Duty*, and underneath that, *North Haven*.

"Dad?" His voice choked. Then the sound went higher. "Dad?" With a scramble, his father was at his side and had his arms wrapped around his son.

"We don't know. No rush determinations until we find out more." He looked back at the truck. "The binoculars, Josh. Go get them from the truck. We can see what's out there better that way. There may not be anything, but we can search and hope."

When the boy returned, Mr. Reynolds scanned the scene with the glasses. Not making out any movement, he handed them to his son. Josh put them to his face, and the first thing he focused on was the lighthouse.

"Dad," he ventured. "I don't know if this is important or not . . ." His voice died away.

"What, Josh?" He glanced over to see his son handing him the glasses.

"Just look, Dad. There's a man peeing off the lighthouse."

His father slapped the glasses to his eyes. Sure enough, on the walk that encircled the tower, there was a man in his boxer shorts, and a stream of water was shooting over the side. Mr. Reynolds lowered the glasses and looked at his son.

"It doesn't look like Andrew."

Josh grabbed the glasses and looked again. The man was finished, but then, after a short wait, a woman walked out the door. Josh knew those clothes. He knew who had worn them just the day before. He also knew his father had to get a boat, because they had to get out there. Miss Bevier needed to be rescued, and he and his father were the only ones who could do it.

"Can you get in the Crabtree's boathouse, Dad?

"Why?"

"I just saw Miss Bevier out there on the lighthouse."

"Let me see." His father took the glasses. He looked across the water, and then he turned to his son to see him grinning from ear-to-ear. He smiled, also. "I think we can sure try."

"Good, Dad. Miss Bevier needs us."

Craig reached and rumpled his son's hair. "Then, we have no choice but to get out there somehow and rescue her."

Josh grabbed his father's arm, pulling it off his head. "Thanks, Dad. I love you."

"I love you, too, Son." Craig sounded like he meant it, too.

TRAMWICK TURNED to Fish. "Sit, boy. Stay."

He glared at the dog until his tail stopped wagging, and then he turned to the man he had located untying a small boat at the dock. Tram was disgusted at what he was being forced to do, but he knew he had no other options. He had finally been reduced to pleading.

"My boat is right there. I just want you to drop me off. Please." Tram held out a fifty and turned to the two girls at his side. He felt sorry for them. It seemed their boat had come loose from its mooring. It was now high and dry in the parking lot. He hoped to give them a ride to Green's Island, so they could check on their families there.

The grizzled man cocked an eye at Tramwick. "All three of ya'?" He sighed and made as if to cast off anyway. Tramwick added a second fifty to his offer. The man clicked his teeth this time. "The dog, too?" Another fifty finally convinced him to let them onboard.

The small boat rode low, but it did get them to Tram's vessel. Throwing his duffle on first, he leaped aboard and called his dog. Barking, Fish jumped after him. Tram leaned over to help the girls aboard, and without a please or do you mind, their ride was gone.

The first thing Tram did was to look over his boat. It had survived quite a blow, and he needed to see that all the equipment was in functional shape, as well as that the structure of the craft itself hadn't been damaged by flying debris. Fish was at his side each step of the way, and Rocky finally pushed him away, telling him to go below.

One of the girls laughed. "He's a sweet dog. His name is Fish, right? Here, Fish. Come to Katie." She made a smacking sound with her lips, and the dog ran right to her. She smiled. "You just have to know dogs, isn't that right, Susan?" Her friend knelt and rubbed Fish's ears.

Susan called, "Can we play that music from the other night?

279

I kinda liked it."

Tramwick looked at her, puzzled. "Music?"

Katie laughed. "Sure. This." She stepped over and flipped the lever on the dash. Lights, not so bright in the morning sun, began to flash, and thumping music began to throb. Tramwick rolled his eyes. He might have bitten off more than he wanted to chew.

JOHN MADE his way through the shambles that was now the Center for Children. Rand couldn't be here of course, but several of the other board members were. This situation had to be resolved quickly. Half the students in the residency program had been at the school over the weekend, and they had no place to stay. The flooding had been relentless here, and just like Rand had said, a large tree had severely damaged the residence building. The children had to be placed, and today, if possible.

Already connections were being made with frantic families. Several students had been picked up already, and those who had been home would not be allowed to return until repairs were completed. The day program would be up and running by the end of the week, and students could return for classes. It was those who had no family close by who would need Rand's offer.

John pulled out his cell phone. Thank God the towers still stood. Otherwise, he'd get nothing done. He pushed his speed dial and waited for it to pick up. When it did, John spoke as soon as he heard the connection engage.

"Rand?"

"John? John, is that you? I've been waiting for your call." The voice over the phone bled concern on steroids. "How bad is it? Like I thought?"

John looked around. "Worse. You should see this. I'd never have thought it possible this far inland."

"If it's that bad . . . the bed-and-breakfast has only so much room, and if the damage to the Center is worse . . . how many children will there be? I hope this place can handle the number displaced. What's your verdict on the total damage, John?"

"Hundreds of thousands, at least. A million five, perhaps. We're insured."

"No, John. How many children are coming up here?" Rand laid out his primary concern. He whispered his next words. "I don't really care about how much the school costs to repair. I want to make Beth happy, and she really wants to make Bette happy."

"One moment. Let me think." John ticked off certain students in his head, remembering what he'd already discussed with the other board members present, and he finally came up with a number.

"Seventeen. Can your bed-and-breakfast do seventeen? I'll have to get someone up there to approve the facilities. State regs, ones you may be unaware of. However, for the short term, I'd like to send the kids today, if this woman can take them. With this disaster, the state can't fault us there. Our clientele have to be housed."

Rand could be heard yelling to someone in the background. *"Seventeen! Seventeen are coming today!"* Cheering echoed back, and then he spoke into the phone, "Beds, John. We need beds. Six singles, no, make it eight. Bedding, too. See you this evening, John. Bring all seventeen."

John hung up, and he went to find another of the board members. She would get the word around. Transportation, the beds, too. She would arrange to get those together. She was in supply management, and that was her forte. All the children would be placed, at least for tonight. Tomorrow was when John would worry about the state bureaucracy and its myriad regulations. This storm had torn the Center apart, and today's worries were enough for today.

ROCKY STOOD in the room where he had spent his second

night out on the lighthouse. While outside, Lisa had come to join him on the walk, letting him know his clothes were on the bed upstairs. He looked at her wearing her things, and he realized once again how beautiful she was. He had ached with sudden need to put his arms around her. He hadn't, though. Instead, he'd stepped inside to find his clothes.

In the upstairs room, he reached to the items that Lisa had worn during the night. He pressed them to his face, and he inhaled. Her smell was in them, and he closed his eyes.

Dear God, he thought, as tears burned. *I held her in my arms, and she's with me now. How can I keep this woman? How can I make her mine?*

He knew one thing. He should kiss her. Once he got dressed, he must go down the steps and kiss this woman who had washed up at his door and had taken his heart as her own. If he kissed her, she'd know what was inside of him, and she would have to stay.

Then he laughed as he reached the back of his hand to wipe the moisture from his face. They certainly couldn't stay here. This was an abandoned lighthouse. Thankfully he had a home in Massachusetts.

That thought made him freeze. He knew he used to have a home in Massachusetts. It was right on the coast, too. The storm surge here had driven the water into the lowest floor of the lighthouse, ten feet above the level of the highest tide. What had it done there?

His focus suddenly shifted, and Rocky's heart pounded as he began to pull his clothes on. How could he have forgotten his home? The boat under construction, and the money he'd already been paid for it. It would all be wasted. And where was Tram?

Suddenly, this storm was more than just an opportunity to spend time with a beautiful mermaid dragged from the sea to spend the night in his arms. It was his livelihood in ruins, and he had no way of knowing anything about the condition of his current project, the one he was building for Rand Walters. Then there was his boat shed and all his tools. He might have lost everything. *Everything.*

Then, as his body warmed the items he'd put on, the smell of Lisa wafted from his clothes, and he remembered her. He sank on the bunk they'd shared, and anguish overcame him. He was being pulled two different directions, and it tore at him. This woman needed his help, still. He'd pressed his hands against her chest, and his lips had touched hers. They had huddled underneath one of Tram's slickers to ward off the cold of the night, and she had been inside the clothes he now wore.

He should kiss her. He knew that. Before he did anything else, he must find her and let her knew his heart. There was magic in a kiss. There must be. There was certainly magic in this woman. She'd been at the Center two days ago, and in one look, she had placed him under a spell. It was a love spell, one of the strongest kinds, one that draws lovers together across the very distances that the harshness of life can impose on them.

Then, thrown apart into impossible situations, her magic had drawn them back together again, and he had plucked her from the sea. She had been his for the night. There was no one else who even knew they were here. He could go down the steps, take her into his arms, hold her, and tell her what he'd felt over the past two days. He could tell her his sense of who he was had been ripped from him, and he could only be the man he needed to be if she stayed at his side.

Rocky pulled himself to his feet as he looked around the room, and before he could take a step, his internal rudder, already weakened by his traumatic life, his perceived short-comings, and his fragile self-image, snapped free. Unwelcome words tumbled over and over in his head.

Massachusetts. His boat shed. His livelihood in ruins.

He dropped back to the bed, his exultation stripped from him, feeling as if his opportunity for a new life had been carelessly wiped away by the storm. What did an autistic man, one who also carried the burden of dyslexia, have to offer this beautiful woman? Not even a home, because his would be in ruins.

He picked himself up and moved sluggishly toward the steps. Even as he felt himself drowning in despair, he tried to hold on to his thought that he really should kiss her. Then the thought evaporated like the morning mist in the sun, as new waves of despair flooded over him.

"WHO WOULD steal anything from here?"

Mr. Reynolds wrestled with the lock on the boathouse door. He continued, muttering, "Do the Crabtrees think someone is going to get a boat and travel twelve miles out to sea, just to sneak into their boathouse and steal their little tender?" He looked at his son and tugged at the bracket one more time. "Any ideas, Josh?"

Josh glanced up to the house at the top of the rise. Other than some downed limbs, everything looked pristine and undamaged. Winterized. Screenless. He also knew of Mr. Crabtree's complaints about one of his windows that consistently failed to lock properly. He turned to his father.

"Dad, I think I can get into their house. They keep the keys in a can on the kitchen table. Can I try?"

At a nod from his father, he bounded up the hill, working at the windows across the back of the house. After a moment struggling with one, he whooped with success, raising the sash, and shimmying inside. The house was quiet, except for the drip of water through the building's guttering. He ducked into the kitchen and pulled the can from the table. Then, he unlatched the front door, threw it back, and headed at a tear down the slope.

"Dad! Keys!" With excitement, he pulled a keyring from the can and flipped through the metal pieces, looking for one that might match. Then, he fumbled, and the ring flew to the ground.

"Josh, here. Let me help." His father reached to pick up the keys, and flipping through the ring, he selected one. "This one, try it."

Excited, the boy slipped the key in, and removing the lock, the father and son swung the doors wide. Throwing back a canvas cover, they found the small boat they knew should be inside.

"Oars, Josh?"

Looking inside the boat, Josh grinned. "They left them inside. Dad, let's get it to the water. I can lift one end, if you can get the other." When his father didn't move as quickly as his son hoped, with a burst of adrenalin, Josh jumped to the bow of the boat and lifted it high in the air. His father laughed.

"All right, Josh. I see that you can. Grab several of those preservers, and let's get it down to the water." As his son walked by, Mr. Reynolds impulsively reached his arm out and grabbed him. "I love you, Son. I don't know why I've never said it much to you, but I really love you."

Josh flushed with the words. "I love you, too, Dad. Miss Bevier's still waiting." He pulled away, but there was a smile on his face. Without another word, his arms flashed in a sudden movement. Four life jackets were added to the boat, and with a quick bunching of shared muscles, the tender was on its way to the sea.

Josh was exhilarated with knowing his favorite nurse was alive, and now he was heading out to the lighthouse he'd long ago claimed as his own. His enthusiasm couldn't be contained, as proved by the smile on his face.

HIS FATHER steadied the boat in the water, and after his son was aboard, he pushed off, joining Josh with a quick step inside.

"Grab the oars, Son, and you row. I'll watch to keep you on track. You'll finally get to visit that lighthouse you like so much."

"Love, Dad. I *love* that lighthouse."

"That lighthouse you love. If we can, do you want to see the inside while we're there?" His father smiled. It was warm outside, the sun was shining, and his son was magnificent. For the first time, he felt he truly saw things as they were. He knew Josh would enjoy a tour of the building, and if that was indeed Miss Bevier, then there should be no problem with him getting a look around. Knowing she was safe had taken the urgency off the events of the morning, and getting to see the interior of the lighthouse would make Josh's day complete.

Josh rowed with enthusiasm into the flat, calm waters of the Thorofare. The grin on his face told Mr. Reynolds he was right. Seeing the lighthouse up close and personal would make Josh's day.

THE MORNING sun flickered off the waters behind the breakwater. What remained of the glass in Rocky's boat shed caught the sun's rays, and in brilliant rainbow sparkles, flashed them back out to sea. His dock was gone. Rather, it was broken and tumbled around his house. The float blocked the drive.

Inside his home, the sofa Tramwick had slept on was in the kitchen. The table was turned over on top of it, and one leg was missing. The missing leg was sticking out of the sink. Dog food from an overturned bowl was piled up around the edges of the room, and a rat flicked its tail as it nibbled at the generously offered tidbits. No one was home, and it was taking this day to feast. Its muscles were tired after having swum through the floating debris during the storm, and all it wanted to do was eat and sleep. Then, if no one was home when it awoke, it would eat and sleep again.

Outside of the house, the sun tickled the vegetation that remained, assuring the plants that they would dry and live again. The bed of Rocky's truck was filled with water-borne debris, and it would need new wiring and a battery before it would run again. A late swallow swooped down and onto the top of the broken boat shed. Its home was high in the rafters, and that end of the shed was still in one piece. The bird landed on the edge of the opening, and in a quick flash, it disappeared inside.

Its world had remained safe, far above the rising waters of the storm surge, but the world below had been decimated. One wall of the shed was completely gone, and the doors that opened to the bay were hanging. Rand's boat, once safely inside, was nowhere to be found. It had simply washed out to sea, or perhaps onto someone else's property. No one would ever know amid all the storm debris that covered the Massachusetts coast.

Broken, Rocky's property awaited his return. It *was* broken, too, and it would need repairs before it could be functional again. It would take more than Rocky to do what was needed. It would also take the help of a friend.

TRAMWICK'S BOAT skipped across the flat water. Music blared, and the girls had thrown their hoods back to revel in the brilliance of the freshened day. The air was cold as it tore at their hair, but the storm had worn their resistance down. They needed the sun.

Tram had offered to take them to Green's, but in the excitement of the clearing skies, they decided to visit the lighthouse. Off in the distance, the islands grew closer, and Tram steered to starboard to take the Thorofare from the south. He could cut between North Haven and Vinalhaven, and it would lead him directly to Goose Rocks Light.

"Girls," he yelled. "Do you think the music is a little loud?"

Susan shook her head in the breeze, and strands of her hair whipped across her face. With her hand, she pulled them aside and opened her eyes. She blinked in the sun and glanced to Katie. Then she smiled.

"It sounds good to me. Katie?"

Katie didn't even open her eyes. She just smiled and waggled her fingers in the air. Then she placed her hand back on Fish's head and gently massaged his fur.

Tramwick sighed and reached to the radar. He would need it when he got closer to the islands. There might be flotsam from wrecked ships floating unseen at water's level. Then he flipped on the depth finder. He had noticed the tide line, and the water was very low. Rocks that were ten feet under at high tide would be at the surface, and he wouldn't even know they were there. He was also concerned about approaching the lighthouse. He didn't have a tender onboard, inflatable or otherwise, and he'd hate to force Rocky to swim. However, Rocky would have to do whatever he had to do. He was a man, and tough. If he wasn't tough, then he was a sissy, and making sissies tough was what living on the sea was all about.

Finally, Tramwick smiled. He decided he was glad it would be slack tide when he arrived. Rocky wouldn't wash away when he had to swim to the boat. *Come to me, Rocky. Come to Tram. Be a good boy.* He laughed, and the girls with him didn't understand why.

WHEN ROCKY came down the steps, Lisa could see that something had changed. He had his clothes on, but it was more than that. It was in his walk and in his expression. That brooding look was back.

"Rocky? What is it?" She stepped to him.

He looked away, and in a sudden movement, his eyes found her face. He licked his lips and moved his arms as if he were intending to take her in his grasp. Then, in a change of expression, he stepped to the door and onto the walk.

Lisa followed him in a rising panic. "Rocky? Is it your clothes? I'm sorry they're no longer clean."

He took a deep breath and held it for a moment before letting it out, and he answered with careful precision. "My clothes are fine." He leaned on the rail, letting the sun wash his face.

"My clothes are fine. My life is not."

Lisa looked at the man standing in front of her. She could see a flinching around his eyes as he dealt with some inner turmoil. She didn't know what had caused this sudden change. Just moments ago he had charmed her, and with a wink, he had taken her heart into his hands. Now, this crushed her newly emerging confidence in him. She'd opened herself to this angel who had rescued her from the disaster that had been Andrew. Now, he was pulling back, and the reason was unknown to her.

She reached to touch the arm she'd held wrapped in hers during the night. "Rocky," she began. She drew back as she watched him flinch. "What is it, Rocky?"

ROCKY'S GUT wrenched with indecision. What he hadn't said was the real problem: his home, his livelihood, his dyslexia, and his autism all wrapped up in one ugly package. *Him.* He couldn't get all that out. It was too close to the surface. He wanted this woman, and at the height of the storm, nothing else had mattered. He hadn't been flawed then, and he'd been able to offer her safety and protection. Now, all he could think of was how much he was flawed, deeply and irreparably flawed.

"Did you see the water last night?" It was a safe topic, one that was neutral and easy.

She blinked back her tears. "Of course, I did."

"It's twenty feet below us now. Last night it was here where we're standing." He sighed and leaned onto his arms, his hands gripping the rail. His head was bowed, and he watched the gentle movement of the water below. His words were leaving his mouth, but they weren't the ones he wanted to say, *needed* to say. He knew that, but he couldn't say the important ones.

He warred inside, wrestling with who he was, and with what his life had made of him, even as he stood next to this woman. He wanted to turn to her and tell her that he was still the man he'd seemed to be last night. He wasn't that boy in her files at the Center. He wasn't dyslexic and autistic and fatally flawed beyond redemption. He didn't forget how to put the key in his ignition, write his letters backwards, and break his pencils when life didn't go his way. He wasn't Rockland. He was Rocky, a successful boat builder.

However, the storm had come, and he knew. If this much water had risen here, he didn't have Rocky, anymore. All that he had worked to become had been smashed from him by the wind and waves.

The ledge upon which the lighthouse rested could be seen through the still water. There were urchins and patches of seaweed. A starfish clung to the rock. He looked over and pointed to something submerged underneath the water. It was the remains of the boat that had carried her to him. In that gesture, he hoped to tell her about how he felt they'd magically been given another chance together; how much their time during the storm had meant to him; how much he'd been drawn to her; and how he wanted her to be by his side always.

What he said instead was, "There's what's left of your boat. Not much remaining, is there?"

LISA LEANED forward, not caring about the boat. His comment about the level of the water still pulled at her. It had taken over the main floor of the lighthouse. How could she not have seen it? What did any of that matter, anyway? Her heart was breaking. She had held this man last night, and he had been open and sincere with her. Now, he was somewhere else, as if they had found each other only for the duration of the storm, and with the rising of the sun, they were being torn apart.

"No, there's not much left, is there?" She looked down, seeing the seafloor and not seeing it, and not knowing how to force her way through his new shell.

"The rest will be there, on the shore of North Haven. The storm will have pushed it that direction." He had yet to look at her. He squinted, then pointed, "Another boat. See? Maybe they won't be blown here by a storm. Or maybe they will." He laughed, and it was very sour. "It's a rowboat. Idiots."

Lisa looked at him sharply. This wasn't the Rocky who had taken care of her the past day. This was another man, entirely. She made a desperate try to reach him. She couldn't let him simply lock her out.

"Rocky," she tried again. "What's the matter?"

"Did you listen to the storm that trapped us here, see the water that forced us upstairs?" His voice was bitter, and his face was suddenly hard. "I build boats. That means I work on the water. If twenty feet of water rose here, what's left of my boat shed? I have one project nearly complete. It'll be destroyed. My home. It's there, also, and ten feet of storm surge will have flooded the lower floor. That's what I'll go home to. Nothing. All that's who I am. It'll be gone. I'm nothing, now."

His voice had become tight, and Lisa desperately wanted to put her arms around him. She hadn't thought of this. She had her school, and her mother's house was far inland. Her life would resume, as if the storm had never occurred, and this man had lost everything.

Her hand reached to him to take his arm, to comfort him. As she did, he pulled away, and like a light switch, she was certain she understood the cause behind his sudden distance. It was Josh's question become real. He wasn't willing to be *touched* by her, to feel the *sympathy* of someone who wouldn't want him with his *handicaps,* the *condescension* of someone who knew he had nothing to offer except his flaws.

She didn't feel that way, but as she looked at him, she knew he was gone from her. If he wasn't already gone, then he was running, and she didn't know how to follow. She had reached out to him, and he had withdrawn where she couldn't find him. The students at the Center did this, and sometimes there was nothing that could be done. She had held him for one night, and he was no longer hers.

Standing there on that lighthouse, suspended far above the surface of the sea, the sun was warm, and it felt good. However, the brilliance of the day wasn't important. It could have been storming and dark, and she wouldn't have cared. She knew one thing, and somehow she knew it would have been the magic that would have kept him at her side. She should have kissed him. Lisa turned and walked to the far side of the lighthouse to where she could no longer see Rocky's idiots in their little boat. Perhaps they weren't idiots. Perhaps they were coming to rescue her. How could he know? Irritation surged through her at his presumption and the cruel words he had lashed at those people.

Underneath her irritation, she knew she should have followed through on her feelings, and she should have kissed him. He would still be here, the man she'd spent the night with, holding him in her arms. That was all she could think about as tears ran down her face.

She really should have kissed him.

THE LIGHTHOUSE towered ever larger over their heads as Josh rowed closer to their destination. The man they had seen earlier was there, and he had clothes on, now.

"Josh, slow." Craig leaned over the side of the boat and cautioned him. "There's a ledge just below the surface." He looked up to the man leaning against the rail on the lighthouse, and he called to him, "We're looking for Lisa Bevier. We thought we saw her through our binoculars." When the man gave them a disinterested look, he called again, "Do you have a woman here with you?"

Just then, Lisa's face appeared. She gave a look of surprise, and a laugh of relief came out.

"Josh! Mr. Reynolds! How did you know I was here?" She ran to the ladder, turning to Rocky, "I know these people. They've come for us. Can I climb down?"

ROCKY'S EYES burned, and he could feel them tighten with impending tears of frustration. This woman was someone he couldn't even vie for. She had friends who had searched for her, who loved her. He couldn't even write his letters properly, and he had nothing to return home to. However, he couldn't cry, not now. He'd cried when he realized his father no longer loved him. He was fourteen, then. Half his life had been gone, and in front of these strangers, he wouldn't be weak.

He turned away before answering. He understood that he was more than simply autistic and dyslexic. He was also a fool. He had called these people idiots, and here they'd come to rescue this woman with whom he had thought he might find love. With that one word, he had destroyed any chance he might have had with her. He was the idiot, and he wanted to melt into the walls of the lighthouse. He wanted her to get in the boat with these people and be gone. He wanted to wash his handicaps from his brain, from his *life,* and he wanted to be lovable. He wanted Lisa, and he knew he was flawed beyond repair.

"Sure." His muted word was barely loud enough to reach her.

LISA PAUSED, looking at Rocky. Was he going to push her completely away without even a second glance? Had his rescue of her been that awful? Did he want her to just get in the boat and leave?

"Rocky," she tried one more time. "Please? Talk to me?" She was torn. She had this man who wouldn't communicate with her. Yet, she must deal with Josh and his father. They had come to rescue her. She was being forced to choose. In one last desperate ploy, she hoped she didn't have to.

"These are my friends, Rocky. They've come to our rescue. Come and go with us. There's plenty of room in the boat, and I've stayed with them in their house. They have room for you until you can get back home."

ROCKY WAS blind with misery. He would only make a bigger fool of himself. Besides, Tram was coming. At least he hoped he was. What would his friend do if he showed up, and Rocky wasn't here?

"I have a ride on the way." He squeezed his eyes for a brief moment, then blinked his frustration away. He refused to look at her. He couldn't. "I'll stay. Go with your friends and don't worry about me. Please, don't force me to speak to them. I called them idiots, and I can't face them."

"They won't know. I'm the only one who heard you."

"I heard me. I'll know. Please do this for me. I can't face these friends of yours who have come to rescue you."

Tears had begun to run down her face. "Look at me. I beg you. You saved my life. I can't just run from you as if nothing happened."

He stood for a minute, and his emotions roiled inside of him. He wanted to turn and grab this woman. He wanted to yell at the people in the boat to go away. He wanted to keep her here forever, and he wanted to huddle with her under a yellow slicker every night of his life. Yet, her friends had come for her. There was no food or heat in the lighthouse, and he was confident he no longer had a home to go to. He had nothing to offer this beautiful woman who had such caring friends that they would come for her the morning after a hurricane.

He only knew one thing to say.

"You owe me nothing. Your friends are waiting. Please go." His head felt as if it would explode. He knew what was coming. His autism hadn't affected him this way for years, but the feeling was one he had lived with as a boy. His muscles had begun to quiver, and he felt his emotions draining away. She had to go and go now. She couldn't see him like this. He would be cruel if he had to be.

He turned to her with a hard look on his face, and he demanded, "Go, Lisa."

SHE TURNED and fled to the ladder that led to the water's surface. She knew facing Josh and his father after this would be the hardest moment of her life. It would be worse than after Andrew. Then, she'd been able to cry, and everyone had understood. Now, she must put on a bright face for these people who had come to rescue her. She couldn't do it, and yet she knew she must. She must do it for Josh, no matter how awful she felt.

Looking down, she could see Craig in the boat at the base of the lighthouse. Just then, Josh came bursting out of the door, looking for her.

"Miss Bevier! There you are. I looked for you inside. You slept in here? This is so cool. I went up to the light. I wish I could have been here." His enthusiasm was written all over him. "Was it scary? Could you hear the foghorn?"

Lisa blinked her tears away, and she smiled. "It was very scary, Josh, and the foghorn was very loud. Is your father ready to go?"

"Probably. He said I could come look. Also, you might have to stay another night with us. Dad said the ferry might be out of commission." He paused and took a deep breath. "The man who was with you, is he the one you were looking for?" He smiled in anticipation, his expression telling that he was certain the magic that had put her here must have carried her to the love she'd wanted to find.

"Did you see all the lighthouse?" He nodded his head. "I have my black satchel inside. I'd like to go, now. Will you get it for me?"

When he disappeared inside, Lisa looked out to the sea. This morning, it had been magical on this old structure. Now, she just wanted away.

Josh stepped back outside, his eyes alight with the very idea

295

of actually being on the lighthouse he'd loved for so long. "Was it him, Miss Bevier?"

She turned and smiled at him. He was so young, and his eyes were so blue. Her words were pleasant, but her heart was heavy.

"I thought it might be. I really did. However, I don't think so any longer." This boy would be her beau for today, and they would charm each other. They would be chauffeured across the glassy sea to a grand old house built by this boy's grandfather. She would join his family for the day, and for another night she would sleep in luxurious linens amid the grandeur of old money.

She would do all those things, and she also knew that once she was alone, she would soak her pillow with the tears of heartbreak. Josh wouldn't know, and his parents would never find out. Lisa would keep her tears for herself. She would cry them, though, and they would flow for a very long time.

ON THE LIGHTHOUSE, Rocky sank to sit on the walk overlooking the sea. This was what he'd known was coming, and it was what he'd known she mustn't see. His back was against the masonry structure's exterior wall. The sun was bright, and one bird had returned to call out against the sky, proclaiming its victory over the storm.

Rocky saw none of that. He was in his head, and his emotions were locked deeply away. He rocked his head back against the masonry lighthouse wall, and with every driving beat, he tried to force his loss from his mind. Lisa had gone, and he had let her get away. Lisa had gone, and he had let her get away.

No matter how hard he hit the wall, he knew what he'd done. Lisa had gone, and he'd let her get away.

Chapter 18

TRAMWICK HIT the beam with the sledgehammer. It slid a few inches, and the roof of the boat shed was that much straighter. He stood, and sweat streaked his back. It was warm on this October day, and even stripped to his waist, he was hotter than hot. He looked at Rocky, who sat cleaning some of his salvaged tools with a wire brush.

"I still can't believe you didn't hear the music when we showed up. I had to wade up to the lighthouse across the shoals just to get up there."

Rocky's hand stilled, and he looked at him expressionlessly without answering. After a moment, he breathed deeply and returned to the rusted tool once more.

Shaking his head, Tram checked the beam for alignment, then pulled the sledgehammer back and slammed it again. He turned to his friend and looked at him, puzzled, his hands resting on the handle of the sledgehammer, absently rocking it from side to side. "Rocky, tell me again how you slipped and hit your head on the side of the lighthouse. That was a lot of blood."

Enough time had passed that Rocky needed to snap out of whatever was going on. He might *live* in the Commonwealth of Massachusetts, but he didn't have to *act* like a Masshole.

"I NEVER did tell you how." Rocky hadn't slipped, and he also knew this friend didn't need to know just why that blood was on the wall. It was still there, too. He knew he'd have to go back. He had that contract. He hadn't been able to convince himself just yet. The pain was still too fresh.

"All right, my friend. I just thought you might decide to own up today. Could I get you to help me with this last support beam? Once this is in place, we can get the walls back up. If we can get the boat shed sealed in, I can pull mine in here and repair that damage from that ledge out there at Goose Rocks. It sure took a hunk out of the bottom. Leaks some, too." He pointed to his friend. "All to rescue you, my friend. Your fault." He grinned. "It was worth it, too."

With a shift in his weight, Rocky stood. "I think I'll go in."

Tram was immediately in front of him. "No, you don't. I'm here talking up a storm, making repairs to your boat shed, and you hardly say a word. What happened out there on that light-house? You haven't told me a single thing. You need to get your mouth open and talk to me." When Rocky stepped forward to brush past him, Tram put his hands on his friend's shoulders. "No. I'm your friend, here. What's going on? It's been two weeks, and it's like you don't even care if I'm around."

For a moment, Rocky stood there, his breathing growing more and more rapid, and then he jerked around, flipping Tramwick's hands off his shoulders. Then, his actions once again under his control, he wrapped his arms around his torso, breathing heavily.

"Sorry, Tram. Let's get that beam in place." He turned, but

he had a frown on his face. "You're right. Your boat is my fault." He shifted his weight to step around Tram, and walked to pick up the sledgehammer. He grabbed it and slammed it into the post time and time again.

Tram ran over and grabbed one arm as he was lifting the hammer to swing it once again. "Well, there, Rocky. I wanted help to rebuild it, not tear it down. Stop, already." He took the heavy hammer from his hand and set it aside. "What's with you, man? It's like you're not even there, and then when you are, there's so much of you it's scary. Call 'em, Rocky. Cancel the deal on that lighthouse. It's not worth whatever happened out there. They can award the contract to someone else."

Rocky slumped down to sit against the beam. He put his hands over his face, and then he leaned his head back against the wood. "It wasn't the lighthouse. I died out there. That's what happened."

Tram squatted across from him. "Talk in English. You can't have died. I'm here with you now."

"Tram, you're my friend, right?" Tram snorted at the question. When no other answer was forthcoming, Rocky repeated his question. "Well, are you my friend?"

"God, Rocky. How can you ask that? There's nothing I wouldn't do for you. We're like brothers. At least I hope so."

"Then trust me. I died out there. I can't live again, yet. Maybe not for a long time. Just put up with me, all right? Can you do that?"

Tram stood, and he grunted. Then he said, "For a brother, I can do that. Come on, brother. Let's go to the house. At least the kitchen is working again. I'm hungry."

TRAM REACHED an arm to pull his friend to his feet, and slapping him on the shoulder, he followed him to the house. He was glad there was an upstairs, too. He was spending the night, and the sofa was no good. However, the bed in the upstairs room was perfectly fine, even if Rocky had pulled the extra mattress downstairs. That was all right. There had been three mattresses on it before. Now there were just two. Two made it just right, and Tram wondered why he had ever slept on the sofa in the first place.

"DAVILLA, LET me see your eyes. Look right at me." Bette took the hand of the girl standing in front of her. "The steps are off limits. You must stay on the porch. Touch this rail." She placed the girl's hand against it. After a moment, having all the skin contact she could stand, Davilla jerked her hand back.

"I don't want to touch it," she whispered in her little girl's voice.

Bette smiled, but her response was firm. "You already have, sweetie. You can't go past that rail. Only if I'm with you, or one of your teachers." Now that the contact had been made, the boundary would be in the girl's mind the next time she approached the steps.

Along with the children, Bette was glad to have the teachers there. Five had been willing to come up until the residence at the Center could be made habitable again. One slept on the sofa, but that was fine with Bette. They had revealed all sorts of techniques for achieving success with different behaviors Bette might encounter. This was one.

"Bette," Davilla said, "can I play on the whole porch? Even on the side?"

Bette smiled. "Let's go touch that rail. Then you'll know how far to go." All the students called her Bette. Even the teachers. She supposed some of them knew her last name, but Bette was all she had been called for the past two weeks, and that was fine with her. She hadn't been asked by anyone except the inspectors who had come up to give their endorsement to her house. They had passed it with flying colors and given it their seal of approval. She hadn't been surprised. It was her home, after all, and Rocky had been her first autistic boarder.

She turned at the sound of a car in the drive. It was that pretty Lisa from Boston. Bette waved as she got out.

"Hi, Miss Lisa." Bette turned to Davilla and released her with a whispered admonition before turning back to her visitor. "I'm so glad to see you. You're so fresh and pretty. I've got a grandson you need to meet."

Lisa laughed. It was a bright laugh, but it faded quickly. Bette noticed that, too. This girl had something galling her, and Bette suspected it was a man. If she could get Rockland up here to meet this girl, Bette thought that'd solve a good part of the problem.

"YOU'LL HAVE these students calling me by my first name when they get back to the Center." Lisa chided her host for her insistence on only first names, but she did enjoy this plain-spoken old woman. This slightly weathered bed-and-breakfast was a place she wished she'd discovered long ago. It felt warm and homey.

Bette grabbed her hand and pulled her into the house. There were children's things spread about, toys and clothes. A Mono-poly game was on the coffee table, and a pile of bedding was folded neatly on an end table. The place smelled of warm bread.

Lisa stopped and shook her head at the disorder. The children knew better than to leave their things out. "I can ask the teachers to help the children with their organization skills. They seem to have completely forgotten how to put their toys and other items away."

"Never mind that, Lisa. I can call you that when the children aren't around, can't I?"

"Only in private, please." Lisa smiled at the concession. "I will someday have to work with these children back at the Center. I can't let them become overfamiliar."

Lisa had insisted the children call her by her more formal

last name, even though this wasn't their regular school environment. Bette disapproved, but she knew there was a certain amount of consistency the children needed. "Miss Bevier" was part of that.

"You must come see what the older students are working on. It's such a warm October day, and we won't have many more. I can't have you staying inside this stuffy house. Come with me." Moving into the hallway, the smell of baking bread grew stronger, and Bette drew in a deep breath.

"It smells wonderful in here," Lisa said. "Lovely."

"The bread will be done before long. I want you to have a slice when we come back in." They stepped through the kitchen, and Bette turned to her, her eyes red with emotion. "I've always loved children in the house. These from the Center have been a godsend. I want to thank you and your school. My grandson once went there, you know."

"Oh?" Lisa hadn't been aware of that. She smiled for a moment, having grown genuinely fond of the old woman. "I might know him."

Bette smiled as she patted Lisa's arm. "I don't think so. It was a very long time ago. He lives off, now. I get him home when I can, but he's grown. Grown men do what they want, and they don't listen to old grandmothers as they should. Do you have a grandmother?"

With another brief smile, the younger woman mused, "I seem to have found one in you, Bette."

The old woman laughed. "Good answer, girl. You should come stay here. It must be a long drive each day."

"My mother, I live with her. She has an illness, and without me, it would be very tough on her."

"Ah, I understand. Now, here's the barn. Look at what's going on inside." Bette grasped the door and forced it open. Inside were half-a-dozen teenage students working on a partially finished boat. One of the male instructors from the Center supervised from behind a leather apron. He acknowledged the women's presence and returned his attention to sanding on a wooden beam.

Lisa looked at Bette in amazement and stepped up to put her hand on it. "They've done this in two weeks?"

Bette joined her, talking to several of the students before answering. She seemed to have a special interest in the boat, as well as in what the individual students working on it were doing.

"Not in two weeks. My grandson started this years ago. He's not worked on it since."

Lisa exclaimed in dismay, "It's beautiful! Why did he leave it unfinished?"

"He's stubborn and rotten." Bette laughed. "I tried to get him out here just weeks ago, and he stomped off mad. Said it was his father's boat, and not his. He's a corker."

Lisa paused and reached in between the students working on the sleek craft, running her hand across the wood. "I knew a man who built a boat with his father once. He never finished his, either." She turned her eyes to Bette. "I guess fathers and sons have a way of doing that."

Bette smiled. "That's what these children are good for. Next spring, I want every one of them to come back and take a ride in this boat." Several of them looked up at her with hopeful expressions on their faces. One or two had grins of anticipation. Bette turned to Lisa. "Now, my city nurse, let's go in for a slice of fresh bread."

TERESE PATTED her daughter's hand. "How much longer will the children be in New Hampshire? You're wearing yourself out with that drive."

"A couple of weeks. Not long." She slid her dinner plate away and placed her elbow on the table, resting her chin in her hand. "The Residence should be habitable before long. At least I hope so. Winter will set in soon."

303

Lisa's mother sat beside her and took her daughter's hand. "Daughter, I know you, and something happened during that storm." She reached to the back of the table and brought out a single sheet of paper. She laid it in front of her daughter. Reaching a finger, she tapped it. "This is what's going on, isn't it? It's this Rockland Royster."

Lisa felt her eyes grow moist, and she knew there would be tears if she wasn't careful. "Rocky, Mum. Not Rockland."

Her mother smiled. "So, it is this man. You had that meeting with him, and then that storm happened. What else happened?"

Lisa had held this inside. She had told her mother some of what had transpired, the part with Josh's family. However, the lighthouse had been skated over as very thin ice, and her mother knew little of that, other than that was where she'd been rescued. With this paper in front of her, she could no longer keep it back.

"The man who pulled me from the water, do you remember, Mum?"

"I couldn't forget, dear. I was both horrified and grateful. I thought he must be the keeper of the lighthouse. Was he?"

"In a way, I guess, but not really. The place was an abandoned wreck. It was this man, Rocky. I never learned just why he was there, either. I was freezing and had to wear his clothes."

Terese chuckled. "It's good he had extras with him." Lisa looked at her sideways. Her mother understood immediately. "He had no extras?" She put her hand to her mouth in dismay. "Lisa!"

Lisa laughed at her mother's offended sensibilities. "There was no intimacy, Mum. You know me better than that. We were both soaked, and there was only one suit of dry clothes. He let me have them. I thought he was very gallant. He did have on his undershorts. He was perfectly decent."

With a wistful look, her mother smiled. "Your father was always gallant. I called him that. Not many people use that word anymore. Thank you for letting me hear it."

"I loved Daddy, Mummy. I still miss him sometimes." Her mother hugged her and stood, picking up the paper to look at the picture closely.

"What happened with this boy? If he didn't try to take advantage of you, why this mopey face for the past weeks?" She peered closely at her daughter. "Tell me, girl. Even after Andrew, you were never mopey. Angry, yes. Tearful? Absolutely. Mopey? Not one day."

"I really don't know." Lisa stood and walked to the door, looking outside. She reached to the knob, twisting it, but she left it closed. She looked back at her mother. "He came into the Center that Saturday, and he walked right out again—"

Terese interrupted, "Was he angry? Upset, perhaps?"

"Upset, maybe. He was a student there, remember, and the students at the Center have handicaps. He filled out one form backwards, broke his pencil, apologized like he'd done me some terrible injustice, and just disappeared. He was only in the room for a few minutes."

"Did you have words with him?"

Lisa knew what her mother meant by that. "We shook hands, and then I asked him to fill out the forms. The next thing I knew, he was gone."

"Was that it? Do you think that caused the problem?" Then her mother grinned wickedly. "Did you find him devilishly attractive?"

"Mum! Grow up! I didn't even get to see him more than ten minutes." She had, however, although *charmingly attractive* was a better choice of words.

"Daughter, I'm old and nearly crippled. However, I remember how long it takes to fall in love. Less than ten minutes, if the man is the right one." She nodded at her daughter in emphasis. "After ten minutes, you can know."

Lisa dropped into her chair, sitting pensively for a time, and then she pursed her lips, fighting a smile. "You intend to drag this out of me. Don't you?"

"Yes, dear. You can make it easy or hard, but I want to know it all."

Lisa needed to tell it all, too. She had hidden it, thinking that if she kept it inside, it wouldn't be real. It would become just an interlude on a lighthouse, a weekend she could tell her grandchildren about, just like Rocky had said. However, she knew it had been more than that. She had fallen in love. It had started that Saturday morning when he came to the Center, and then it blossomed that night in the lighthouse. All her years of dreaming? That had been fertile ground, but it hadn't been love. That first touch was when it had begun. That first touch of their hands on that stormy Saturday morning.

Now, all Lisa wanted was to hold him again, and she didn't know where he lived. She didn't even have that paper he'd filled out. It had been destroyed in the storm.

Lisa told her mother all that, and she told how he'd suddenly changed that last, clear morning. He had told her to go, and he had hardly looked at her. He had simply insisted that she leave.

The one thing she didn't tell her mother of was the night they slept under the yellow slicker. Lisa had held that man in her arms as he slept, and for that time, he had truly been hers. She had stroked his skin and felt the muscles in his arms. He had been warm, and the storm had been so long. If that man had asked her for more . . . well, she didn't know what she would have done. Refused him, probably. Refused him, for certain. She would have kissed him, though. She *should* have kissed him. That was the one thing she should have done. She didn't tell her mother that. There were some things even a mother didn't need to know.

TRAMWICK WAS at it once again, and he hit the beam with the sledgehammer. It slid a few inches, and the roof of the boat shed was that much straighter. He turned at a sound.

"I thought I did that for you." The words were growled, but at least Rocky was speaking.

Tramwick grinned, glad to see his friend. "You overdid it. I'm having to knock it back in place a bit. Come to help?"

"I haven't been to Bette's for a while. Forecast says an early snow in the mountains might be on the way. I need to get the storm windows on. I might be gone a while. Overnight, if it goes slow."

"You're welcome, Rocky." Tramwick rocked on his heels, with his head cocked in the air, and a smirk on his face.

"What do you mean?" Rocky gave him a mystified look.

"For rewiring your truck and getting it running. Man, do you notice *anything* around here?" He grinned, however.

"Yeah, thanks. Can you keep Fish?" Rocky's sentences were short, choppy, and close to brusque.

"Take him. He loves it up there."

"Fish is staying here. I'll be back tomorrow."

"Remember that Bette has all those kids there."

Rocky closed his eyes in dismay and blew out a heavy breath. "I forgot. I'll be back tonight." He turned and trudged away.

Tramwick watched him go. He called to him, "Rocky, buddy, I'm wanting to help. I have to know what's wrong, though." Then he turned to the beam and decided it was straight. He took a large spike and began to drive it into the wood. He was determined this shed would hold up if another hurricane hit. It was his reputation at stake. For that reason, it was important that it did.

THE BATTERED truck drove past several unfamiliar cars, pulled up outside the garage, and parked just behind Bette's old SUV. Bette looked out the kitchen window and smiled. Turning to the adults who were in the room with her, she announced, "My grandson's here. Take over for me." To the boy who was

307

helping her with the stew on the stove, she whispered, "Not so fast. Count to five with every stir."

Bette threw off her apron and went outside, stepping roughly down the steps. She found the day was getting cold. "Rockland," she cried. "Three weeks, it's been. I've missed you."

He smiled, but it quickly faded as he looked around at the old place. It was becoming rather lived in. There were toys strewn across last summer's grass, and the clothesline had children's clothing hanging to dry.

"Happy, Bette? They're making a mess of things." His words were clipped, and his tone was sour.

She snorted, snapping, "You could come and help me keep it clean." Pausing, knowing she wouldn't reach him that way, her words softened. "I saw a man who knows you the other week." She stooped to pick up a ball out of the drive and tossed it back towards the house. When he didn't respond, she prompted his memory. "Made you a delivery. He came to pick up a wind vane from behind my barn."

"A wind vane?"

"A wind vane. You heard me, Rockland." She peered at him, wondering why she bothered, sometimes. Because she loved him, she guessed. He was her favorite, even if he didn't act like he knew it. "Said he saw you in Mass, right before the storm. Said you were an important man, boat-building important. I laughed. I said you were my grandson." She fought a smile, but not very successfully.

Rocky shifted the subject back to the grounds around the bed-and-breakfast. "You could make these kids pick this stuff up."

She chuckled and tugged his arm. "Come with me, you sluggard. You just come this way."

When he saw she was headed to the barn, he pulled his arm loose. "No. You still have my keys from last time. I don't need

308

this."

Bette put both her hands on her hips, and she riveted him with her gaze. "Rockland Royster, don't you dare say no to me. You may be nearing thirty, but I can still tan a hide. These children staying here know so, and so you do. I've tanned yours a few times." She took his arm again.

"Sure. I only drove up to help with the windows before the snow arrives. I can endure another trip to the barn if you insist. I won't work on the boat, though."

When she opened the door, several teenagers were inside, and the boat was nearing completion. A staff member stood at the back, showing a girl how to hold a hand sander. He looked up and nodded to Bette. Rocky looked at his grandmother and then back to the students, several of whom came up to greet her. One or two of the girls looked him over as if in hopes he might be there to stay. A big boy came to shake his hand and introduce himself, quickly making his way back to his job.

Rocky whispered to Bette, "So, does this mean I'm free from this boat? I need to get the storm windows done. I have to get back tonight."

"Rockland. Why have you even come up here? I didn't see Fish, either. You didn't bring him? I wanted the kids to get to play with him. Shame on you, grandson." His grandmother looked at him hard, disappointed she'd not yet gotten through to him. It seemed he intended to keep even her from getting through his shell.

"Bette, please." Rocky made a face and growled. "My life isn't going well right now."

"Rockland, life never goes well. What is it that's so bad about your life right now?"

ROCKY SIGHED. He hadn't discussed this with Tramwick, and he wouldn't discuss it with his grandmother. He could distract her, though.

"How many children do you have here?"

She slapped his arm, all semblance of amiability gone. "Go count them yourself. You cannot distract me with that. I give up for now. If you're here to do the storm windows, then get to it. The house gets cold this time of the year. I want to be warm, and I also have the furnace to run. That costs me money, and money I do not have. I'm heading inside. Stay for dinner if you want." With that, she walked away, leaving him in the barn with the teenagers working on the boat.

He did step up to see what they were doing. After all, this was what he did for a living. He watched them and even reached to help one boy grab a tool correctly. Pointing out a place that needed an extra touch, he smiled at one of the girls and was amused to hear her giggle.

It was the windows he had come to do, though, and they wouldn't get done in here. He was glad the unfinished boat would no longer be here to haunt him. He wanted it gone, and it appeared it soon would be.

Heading to the garage, he began to wish for a coat. The wind was turning cold, and he had a lot of windows to do. Pulling out a ladder, he stood it against the house. The storm windows that would replace each of the screens were standing neatly on a shelf, and there was a blanket keeping them clean. He pulled the blanket off and slid down the first one. Carrying it to the front of the house, he planned to start with the ground floor. Next, he would head up. Many of the upper floor windows could be reached from the porch roof. Others would require him to move the ladder one window at a time.

Rocky set the window by the front door and slipped off the first screen. He had to start somewhere, and this wouldn't get done unless he did that. He reached to hang the window, and clipping it in place, he set the screen aside.

One down, and thirty-three to go. He wiped his hands on his pants, and he headed to the garage for another.

LISA'S HEATER was turned up, and her feet felt toasty. Reaching to feel the glass, she could tell it was growing very cold outside. Glancing in the rearview mirror, she slowed to let a big truck pass.

Her mother had insisted she pack her clothes. *"Stay the week, daughter. I'll see you on the weekend. Stop this driving back and forth."* Lisa would be glad not to have this two-hour drive each way. She just hoped Bette really did have room for her. If not, then her mother would have to stop her complaining.

The car shook as a sudden gust of wind blew a plastic bag across the road directly in front of her. She smiled. This was New Hampshire, and this was October. It would be November in only days. It was time for winter to hit.

The gravel crunched as her tires bit into the driveway at the bed-and-breakfast. Her coat was beside her, and she wished she had it on. Just to run inside, it seemed silly, however. She might freeze, but she could make it. Grasping the fabric firmly, she pushed the door open. As the wind caught it, she gasped. It was every bit as cold as she had thought, and if anything, colder. It certainly hadn't been this frigid when she left Massachusetts, but then, these were the mountains, and cold was what being in the mountains was all about.

ROCKY HAD finished the windows at the front of the house by the time Lisa's car arrived. He heard it but didn't see it. It parked out front, and he thought nothing of that. His grandmother had people coming and going all the time. Rocky was used to her guests being about when he was working on the house. He just kept installing the windows. It would take him most of the day, and it would be late when he returned home. That was fine with him. He had nothing else to do, and no one to do it for. Today was just taking up time he wished he didn't have on his hands.

He tried not to think about that weekend at the lighthouse,

311

but the kids here were all from the school he'd been forced to attend. Every time he saw one, distorted, unwelcome thoughts ran through his mind. Lisa knows these kids. She's touched that one. That one has talked to her. Another one has probably given her a hug. They all had Lisa, and he didn't.

In his misguided opinion of himself, Rocky knew that was as it should be. He was who he was, and he'd never been able to rise above that. He couldn't even finish that boat he'd started so many years ago. Some kids from the Center had to do that for him.

In his self-abuse, he was glad the wind was blowing and he had no coat on. He was freezing, and as he shivered and his nose ran, no one could tell just why. He knew, however. He knew very well. He hated his life, he was feeling sorry for himself, and he wanted Lisa.

He knew something else, too. He wasn't good enough to have her. Even if she should have a reason to come up here, she wouldn't want to see him. She would make a point to leave without talking to him. He wouldn't blame her, either. After he had made a fool of himself during those final minutes on the lighthouse, he would be surprised if she ever wanted to see him again.

It was the cold that kept anyone from knowing what was going through his head. The cold kept his eyes red, and the cold kept him sniffling that day. If anyone was watching, he wasn't crying. It was simply that the day was so incredibly cold.

LISA RAN for the door, holding her coat at her side as a buffer from the wind. It was only a moment before the door opened, but she felt nearly frozen by the time she stepped inside.

A small arm closed the door, and an equally small voice called out, "Bette!" The child was about ten. Lisa rubbed the hair on her head. She knew this one as she knew all the children here. At the Center, she had known some better than others, but

312

in the past few weeks, these had become her charges. Each one was very familiar to her.

As the owner of the bed-and-breakfast appeared, Lisa tossed her coat to a chair and reached to hug her. "Bette, it's so good to see you. The drive up was warm, but the walk to your front door was freezing. How have the children been? How have *you* been?" She had grown to care immensely for Bette. She was the grandmother Lisa had never known.

"My grandson is here." It was an announcement she seemed anxious to make. "Did you see his truck outside?"

The change of subject didn't interest Lisa. She was well aware what Bette wanted, and Lisa didn't need a new love interest. She'd been disappointed by her previous one, and it was something she was trying very hard to forget. She would be polite, though.

"I parked in front. There were no trucks. I'm sorry. I'm certain the children will enjoy his attention." Hopefully, that would be all of that topic. Another man had taken her heart, broken it, she would sometimes tell herself, although she knew that wasn't entirely true. It wasn't broken, because if it was, she wouldn't still long for him. With another man tugging at her heart, this grandson had no place in her life just now.

Bette wasn't to be distracted, however. "Would you like to meet him, dear? He's working just outside. Perhaps you saw him on the way in."

"Bette, it was very cold, and I ran to the door. I didn't look. I'm sorry." Lisa glanced up to see two of the children chasing each other down the stairs. She nodded at them. "They love it here, don't they? You offered me the opportunity to stay here instead of driving back and forth. Do you still have the room?"

Bette perked up at Lisa's question. "I'll find the room, even if I have to sleep on a cot and give you my own bed." Hearing the children on the stairs once more, she called to them, "Children, this is the last time. You'll answer to Bette if you run up and down again. Go up or come down. Then stay." She turned to Lisa as she grabbed her hand. "They have to have boundaries. Now, let's get your things inside. Then, I have a grandson for you to meet."

Lisa didn't know about that. Maybe this was a bad idea. Maybe she shouldn't stay. However, she had already asked, and the drive was long. Too long. She could meet this man, she guessed, if there was no way to avoid it.

Chapter 19

ROCKY MOVED his ladder to the front of the house. Several cars were parked to the side. Out front sat a new one, with Massachusetts plates, like the others. When he saw a Center parking decal, he knew this was most likely a business visit, and Bette would be occupied. He wouldn't return to the house. He didn't want to meet this person.

Carrying one window with him, he climbed the ladder. He released the screen and let it fall to the ground. With a quick motion, he had the storm window in its place and the catches attached at the bottom. He stood and rubbed his frozen hands together, and he wished for his coat.

As he clambered down the ladder, he noticed movement inside one window. He kept his eyes averted, respecting the privacy of those inside, and in any case, uninterested in seeing who was inside. He was just here to put up the storm windows, and this would be his final one. What went on inside the house was none of his business.

Rocky rubbed his arms again as he turned the corner of the house to retrieve the last window from the garage. The sky was turning gray, and as he looked up, he knew what would happen soon. It would snow. It would begin today, and he wanted to be home before it did.

"LOOK, MY DEAR. There he is." Bette moved the curtain aside. "My grandson is on the ladder just in front of the house. I'll introduce you."

Lisa glanced out the glass to see a man's legs coming down. Just then, a small body bounded into the room, wrapping itself around her waist. She disentangled herself and knelt.

"Hello, Meagan. I've missed you. I've come to stay with you for a few days. Would you like that?"

Bette looked at Lisa with a smile. "You'll be good for this house, you know that, dear? You have a magic touch with these children. I'm glad you're staying." She moved the curtain aside to see if Rocky was still outside. "However, let's get your things in the house. Then we can meet that grandson of mine. That is, if we can find him."

Lisa smiled. She remembered Mr. Reynolds' words. Magic. There was no magic. There was only interest, concern, and love. She had no magic besides that.

It was cold when they stepped out to her car, but at least this time Lisa was wrapped in her coat. So was Meagan, who had begged to help. When Bette looked to find her grandson, the ladder was empty, and the wind had picked up, driving their full arms back into the house.

ROCKY DID get his final window up. After returning the ladder to its place in the garage, he did one other thing before he got back in his truck to drive away. He reached behind the seat, and he pulled out a wooden sign. It was the one his father

316

had made, and it had the name Royster carved into it. Rocky had repaired the damaged bracket, and he walked up to the porch and hung it in its place over the front door. Bette would see it there and know he had returned it.

Then he climbed in his truck and started the engine. He hoped it would warm soon. It was a long drive home, and he still had no coat to put on.

As he backed up and pulled away, he didn't see the curtain at the upstairs window move aside. He was just glad he had avoided meeting anyone at the house other than those in the barn. He'd enjoyed that. His own boat shed was unusable, and even Tramwick hadn't been able to get it all back together. His house wasn't completely repaired, either. Tram had worked some on that when Rocky wouldn't. The kitchen was functional, that and the bathroom. However, Rocky no longer cared. The slow pace of his repairs wasn't for lack of funds, either. He did have insurance, and it would eventually pick up much of the tab. Rocky's problem was lack of interest. The damage could get repaired or not, and it would make no difference. He'd been given a chance at love, literally had her washed into his arms, and he'd let her get away.

As he drove down the road, he could only think of one thing. He knew his life would be different if he'd only kissed her. The tears began to form tracks down his face as that thought ran repeatedly through his mind.

He really should have kissed her.

"OH, DEAR. He's driving away. He failed to get his keys from me." Bette looked through the window at a truck pulling out. "You missed him." She turned to Lisa and held the curtain so she could see.

Lisa glanced out. "Your grandson?" She saw an old truck driving away. Then it disappeared around a bend in the road. She was glad, actually. She found the children to be a distrac-

317

tion, and to be falsely bright to a man she didn't wish to know was more than she thought she could take right then. "Another time, Bette. At least you have your storm windows, now. He must be a good grandson."

Bette barked a laugh. "He's obstinate and doesn't listen to me. He's a good man, though. He should have worked out his issues with his father. He never did. My son had his heart attack in that car of his. Hit a man, we think, but no one ever knew." Then she reached to plump up one bed. "I hope you don't mind sharing, dear."

Lisa walked to the window looking out where the old truck had disappeared, pulling the curtain aside. Something nagged her about this grandson of Bette's, but she couldn't tell exactly what. After all, she'd never met him, and there was no real reason she would want to.

However.

There was that old truck, and the grandson's father died from a heart attack? In his car? That seemed eerily similar to what Rocky had told her.

Still, Lisa knew the world was large, and with the students at the Center, circumstances in their lives often followed familiar patterns. Two fathers dying of a heart attack wasn't a coincidence. Two fathers having that heart attack while driving a car? Maybe.

Then she remembered her own father. How very different his death had been, although it was similar in one way. A car had hit him, but then that wasn't the same as a heart attack.

Lisa turned to Bette, letting the curtain fall. "I don't mind sharing. This room is beautiful. Meagan gets to share with me, too." She put her hand on the girl's head and smiled at her. "Who else is in here with us?"

THOSE WORDS made the little girl ecstatic. Her voice began to burble from her in her excitement, and Lisa could barely keep up. Bette smiled and left them alone. She was glad this woman was here with them. She should have stayed weeks ago. Now, Bette's household was complete.

Except for that grandson. He should have stayed to meet this girl. He would have really liked her. He didn't know what he was missing. She didn't know what had brought on that cloudy mood he'd been in out there in the drive, but this girl would have brought him out of it. Rocky just hadn't learned to listen. That was his problem. He didn't know how to listen to her or anyone else.

Bette paused at the top of the steps and smiled, glad for one thing. Rocky rarely listened to that drunken lobsterman, Tramwick, and the good Lord knew, she could be glad for that.

CHET KNOCKED on the door at the waterfront boatyard, as he zipped his coat a little higher. He looked around at the door yard that had been so pristine just weeks ago, and he could tell the hurricane had hit hard here. At least some repairs were under progress on the boat shed down on the water. A hired man in a heavy coat was banging on some beams with a sledgehammer. He was glad to see Mr. Royster was getting that done.

The area past the house was still a mess. At first Chet had thought he wouldn't be able to get his delivery van down the drive. It looked as though the float to a dock had washed all the way up to the road. He had cut the wheels tight, however, and his van had just made it.

Looking up, he noticed the supplies stored over the porch had survived. High and dry. Then he smiled as the door opened.

"Mr. Royster?" Chet's smile turned into a broad grin as he watched the man standing before him. Before, he'd answered the door in a pair of rumpled boxers and hair that stood on end. That hadn't changed. How many people would ever see this prominent boat builder looking like this? Not Chet's cousin, that was for wicked certain. "I'm sorry to be here so early. I have a letter for you. I'm glad to see you're getting your property back together. The damage must have been very severe. How high was the water?"

Rocky opened the door and stepped outside. As they heard the man on the shore call out, Chet turned, along with Rocky, to see what he wanted.

"It's about time you got your lazy backside out of bed. Come on down and help." Then there was the thump of the sledgehammer on one of the beams.

"Sounds like he's in a mood." Chet chuckled.

"He's angry at me. He needs to use my shed for some repairs. Thinks it's my fault. What's for me today?"

Chet held out his signature box. "Insurance proceeds, it looks like. I'm delivering them up and down this part of the coast. Hope yours is a good one. Hey," he said, changing the subject, "you have a grandmother in New Hampshire? Waterville Valley?"

That brought a wry grin to Rocky's face. "If so, do I have to claim her?"

Chet laughed. He handed Rocky the box for him to sign, watching his hand make a scribbling motion. "I picked up a wind vane there just after the hurricane. She didn't have any damage, it didn't seem. She had a houseful of kids, though. All ages. Said they were from some school outside of Boston that was damaged in the storm. I recognized the name Royster. She almost didn't claim you, either."

Rocky smiled. "That's Bette."

Taking the box back, Chet handed him the letter. "Oh, by the way, have you watched the weather, today? Up in Waterville Valley, there's a blizzard. No one's getting in or out. It just dropped without warning. I thought of your grandmother and all. Thanks, Mr. Royster. See you next time."

Rocky stood and watched the truck drive off. He looked down to see goose bumps all over his skin. That made him think of Goose Rocks Light and someone else wearing his clothes. He stepped back into the house. It was still a mess and smelled of dampness in the walls. He had heat, though, and it was warm. Still, his goose bumps didn't go away. He needed to be warm in his heart, and he didn't think he'd ever be that again.

Rocky headed to his room, grabbed yesterday's pants from the floor, and slipped them over his legs. When he buttoned the waist, he looked down and realized something. These were the same ones Lisa had worn. For a moment, it seemed that she was with him. However, almost wasn't something he could wrap his arms around, and almost couldn't warm his heart.

He needed Lisa, and she was nowhere around. He looked up to see Fish raise his head to watch. When Rocky sat down on the bed, his emotional exhaustion taking his strength from him, the big dog crawled forward and placed his oversized head in Rocky's lap. Rocky stroked his scalp, and the animal's body warmed his hands. However, not even Fish could warm the ice that chilled him inside.

FRANK REACHED to his keyboard. He hesitated. If he were wrong, there would be the devil to pay. Storms were unpredictable, and they could and would go there where they wished.

However, this one was already dumping an enormous amount of snow directly onto central New Hampshire. The moisture in that warm southerly had slipped right over the Arctic front, and the results were causing chaos. Blizzard was a big word, however, and it was one that might cause people to panic.

The meteorologist felt it in his gut, though. This would get worse before it improved. His fingers flew across the keys, and with a final, unconscious flourish, a thick forefinger punched the enter key. He saw the message scrolling across the screens on the walls around the room.

11:45 AM. Tuesday, October 23. Weather alert. A strong

Arctic front will continue to bring heavy snows from Central Vermont to Maine. Winds will increase to blizzard strength. The storm track is expected to knock out power and block any rescue efforts. Remain in your homes if possible. Please keep all traffic lanes clear for what emergency personnel can make it through.

Under no circumstances should anyone take to the road. Secure your possessions, run extra drinking water now, and have emergency supplies ready. Please prepare immediately. Do not wait.

Frank sat back. The storm had come unexpectedly. People could die. There was nothing he could do about that. All he could do was try to minimize the deaths.

"THIS BOAT, Bette. The children have done a wonderful job. Tell me more about it." Lisa walked around the barn. With the snow, they had come out to close it up. The winds had whipped up, and it was quickly approaching whiteout conditions.

She remembered seeing the craft when she was in the barn once before. The lines were beautiful, and it reminded her of the one Rocky had told her he and his father had never completed. The children from the Center were finishing it up, with help from one of the staff, and they were doing very well. However, whoever had started this originally had known what they were doing. Even Lisa could see that.

"That grandson of mine left it here. You know the one. With the storm windows. I'm sure you remember. This boat has aggravated the dickens out of me. He and his father started it. Then there was the heart attack. I've always prayed the man he might have hit was all right. My son made it to the hospital, but he died before he could tell what happened." Bette sat in exhaustion. "I think about it sometimes, but there was no way to find out."

Lisa thought of her father. It was something Rocky had said. *"He died a long time ago. A heart attack while driving his car."*

322

Lisa marveled at how similar people's lives could be, and often, no one knew. She'd seen that in the school's records over and over. Still, everyone thought their experiences were unique.

Hardly.

"The boat, Bette. What about the boat?" That had her interest.

Bette contemplated the nearly completed project. It had sat in the barn for fifteen years. To have it resurrected now was both a relief and something to grieve over. She hadn't always seen eye-to-eye with Royce, but he had given her Rocky. For that she would be forever grateful.

"My grandson was certain his father hated him. My son sent him to your school down there, and the boy always felt abandoned. The summer they built this boat, my grandson was convinced that if he did it well enough, worked hard enough, that his father would let him remain here. When summer ended and the boat wasn't complete, that boy was certain the boat was the reason he had to go back. He never touched it again."

Lisa looked at the boat, and when she turned to Bette, she felt her eyes burn. This was more than coincidence. It had to be. She stepped to sit at her side.

"Bette, three weeks ago, I was in the middle of that hurricane that hit the coast. When my boat sank, a man on an abandoned lighthouse pulled me from the sea." She paused and studied the boat sitting in the barn with them. She felt the tears pooling in her eyes, and she tried to blink them away. When she felt Bette take her hand, she looked down to see the gnarled fingers wrapped around her own.

"Go on, dear," Bette prompted. "I'm listening."

Lisa looked at the kind grandmother's face next to hers, and then she looked away again before continuing. "I haven't told anyone about this, but I think I fell in love with him." She smiled at the memory of that night under the yellow slicker. "He told me his father also died of a heart attack, and of a boat they'd started to build. He told me one other thing. He told me his father hated him and his handicaps, the autism he carried and his dyslexia."

It felt good to share this with someone who seemed to understand.

BETTE WAS smiling now. She had an idea just who this man might be. How he could be on Lisa's lighthouse during a hurricane, she didn't know, but that Tramwick seemed to get her grandson in more trouble than was good for him. It was certainly possible.

"This man, Lisa. If you fell in love, did he not love you back?"

"Oh, Bette. I thought so at first. Then, when the storm was over, my friends from the island came to rescue me. He called them idiots, and he said his friend was on the way for him. He told me to go, that I didn't owe him anything, and to just leave him there." She pulled her hand from Bette's and wiped her eyes. "I'm sorry. I know this has nothing to do with you. I should have kept it to myself. It's your story of your grandson. Something similar happened to the man I met, and I just couldn't help but think . . . but they couldn't be the same." She stood and turned to the door. "Thank you for listening, though. You are truly a wonderful person. That grandson of yours is a lucky man."

Bette looked at Lisa for a moment, and her eyes crinkled as she asked her if she knew one detail she hadn't revealed. "What was the friend's name, dear?"

"Friend?" Lisa paused, with a puzzled look on her face.

"Why, dear, the one who was coming for your young man?" Bette felt she would be prying if she asked for the name of the man who had rescued this sweet girl. However, surely Lisa wouldn't mind revealing his friend's name. If it was who Bette suspected, then she wouldn't need to ask the rest.

"Oh," she smiled. "Tram . . . Tramwell, maybe . . . no, Tramwick. That was it. And Fish. Fish, the dog. Why?"

Bette smiled, immensely pleased. "Dear, you really must meet that grandson of mine. Next time he's here, I won't let him get away so easily."

Lisa laughed, but it was short and humorless. "Thank you, Bette. Perhaps not. I appreciate your offer, however." She placed her hand on the door. "I'm heading back to the house. Do you need any extra help closing down?"

Bette shooed her out. Then she turned off the heat and reached to place her hand on the light switch. She was alone now, and she spoke her words to the walls, the boat, and whatever small creatures might be in hiding within the cracks and crevasses of the barn.

"No, Lisa. You need to meet my grandson. I think he's the man you're looking for. You just don't know it."

She flipped off the lights and headed out the door.

THE SNOW was wet, and it was heavy. If the trees had been bare, most of it would have drifted through to the ground, settling harmlessly to insulate the roots and seeds of the plants that would come up again the next year. However, the leaves hadn't all dropped. In fact, it had been a long, lingering fall, one often called an Indian Summer. The leaves had clung to the branches, and life had continued in the cells, transferring energy to the roots of the trees.

When the snow hit, it first coated the largest of the leaves, and it forced them to sag down to touch other leaves. That created a hundred pockets, where the snow piled even higher. As it did, the limbs began to feel the stress. As they bowed, weighted down by the ever-increasing mass of too-wet snow, cellular structures deep within the branches, ones that kept the limbs held high during the worst of winter's weather, finally began to weaken. At first one or two cells let go. The tree could have healed from that. However, the snow on the branches had only started to build. More and more cells would eventually start to go, and when enough had burst, the tree branches would come down.

Near one major transformer, an especially large tree was scheduled to be trimmed. The day of the trimming, a fuel line had clogged on the truck, and the crew had been delayed. Once a mechanic had looked at the truck and remedied the problem, it was early afternoon, too late to manage the massive amount of time that trimming the tree would entail. It was entered into the computer as rescheduled for the first week of November. The crew had taken the afternoon to trim smaller trees that were blocking sidewalks near the center of town. No one saw that as a problem. The old tree near the transformer hadn't been trimmed in years. What would one more week matter?

The power lines that ran directly underneath the tree were on poles that had been installed years before. The bases had been of the best type when they were put up, but years of micro cracks and the shifting of soil had weakened them. Road salts had infiltrated the concrete, and deep inside, the rebar had rusted through. The concrete looked strong, but it was ready to give way.

All day, the snow piled up. Being wet, it soon grew to the depth of a foot on the lines alone. It was deeper on the bunched leaves of the tree. As the wind whipped the limbs back and forth, a snap reverberated throughout the tree. The great mass of branches shivered once, and then with a great flailing of the air, they came crashing down.

The branches didn't hit the ground, though. The great expanse of the power lines that stretched from pole to pole was tested as never before. They sagged low to the ground, and the bases of their poles cried out in distress.

It was that night when the tragedy would happen. The concrete would give, slowly and imperceptibly at first, then in a great series of ever-expanding fissures. In one shattering scream, it would all come down, and the power lines would disengage from the transformers.

Frank had been right. People would die. It would be cold for a very long time, and there would be no power to much of the area.

In Bette's house, all the small lights that told of electrical consumption burned valiantly. In the interior of television cabinets, power diodes enabled small LED lights to indicate that cords were plugged in. Cell phone chargers pulled minute amounts of electricity to keep their circuits warm as well as to run small indicator lights. Clock faces glowed, and night lights kept everyone safe. The furnace thermostat shined a faint green, telling everyone who walked by that it was a cheerful sixty-eight degrees.

Long after everyone was asleep, all the small lights in Bette's house clicked off. No one knew, and they slept peacefully on. The house grew colder, and not even Rocky's storm windows could stop the temperature's slide down the thermometer towards freezing.

Outside, the blizzard raged on.

TRAMWICK GRABBED the edge of the quilt Rocky was sleeping on and yanked it hard. His friend flailed his arms and legs as he tumbled to the floor, finally awake. Fish yelped as he jumped out of the way, quickly running to the other room. Rocky lay there in his boxer shorts, with his eyes blinking in the morning light.

"What is it with you, Tram?" Rocky struggled to sit up. "Can't you just open the shades or something?"

"Don't give me that. For nearly a month you've moped and dragged around like a pond frog caught up by the short hairs. I've put up with you and worked on your boat shed for you, and still you won't tell me what's wrong. Well, I'm through listening, and I'm doing some talking. You get to listen to me now, whether you want to or not." He grabbed some roughly folded clothes from the top of a dresser and threw them at the man still on the floor.

"Hey! What's with the clothes?"

"Look at yourself. I got the new water heater in and got you in the bath last night for the first time in days. You haven't shaved in a week, and I only hope those are clean shorts you have on. I finally got the washer running again. Those clothes are clean. I even washed 'em myself." He turned to leave the room as he called back, "There's even clean boxers in there if you need them. I want to see you when you come out."

Tram closed the door. He was irritated at Rocky, but what he said about washing the clothes was funny. The machine was hooked up, but he hadn't washed anything. Not in the machine, anyway. He'd thrown them in the tub upstairs, the one with the shower nozzle he could hook up to the tub spigot. Then Tram had taken the longest shower he could, making sure to use lots of soap, stomping the clothes as he did so. Afterwards, he'd hauled them to the dryer. He'd had to fix that, too, and he'd run it three times to get all the water out of those clothes.

When Rocky came out, rumpled and still unshaven, Tram shoved his cell phone to the side and slammed a pan of scrambled eggs and sausage onto the table. He wanted Rocky to take him seriously, even if he wasn't as angry as he appeared.

"You need food, friend. Not just those crackers and that peanut butter you've lived on. You haven't been paying attention, and I've got to get some moxie into you. Milk or coffee?"

Rocky arched his eyebrows and looked askance at his friend. However, he did sit at the table. "Milk?"

"Good! I don't have any coffee made." Tram reached to the ice chest on the floor and pulled out a half gallon. "A month, and we still have no refrigerator."

"Nearly a month, Tram. Three Weeks. And it's me who

doesn't have one."

"We, Rocky. Where do you think I've been living while I've been working on this place? I'm upstairs, Rocky. I ain't ghosts. Pay attention."

ROCKY DUCKED his head and began to eat on the eggs. He reached directly into the pan with his fingers for the big chunks. He'd known Tram had been around a lot the past weeks, but he had no idea he'd been staying with him. His upstairs was a no-man's storage area, and Rocky never went up there. However, if Tram wanted it, he could live there all the time. Especially if he'd cook. Eating these eggs made Rocky realize he was starving.

"What's this all about, Tram? Everything's fine here. Insurance came. The check's there on the table in the other room. Furnace works again." He licked a finger and reached back into the pan.

Tramwick flipped a chair around and sat on it, resting his arms over the back. His eyes searched the man in front of him, as if unsure whether he'd find his friend inside or not.

"The news still comes on, too, Rocky. Do you ever watch *anything* anymore? Listen to the radio? *Anything?*"

Rocky chewed his food for a while, and then he swallowed. "What's the point? The only thing that matters is what happens here." He grabbed another chunk of egg from the pan and put it in his mouth. He saw Fish peering around the corner, and reaching to a jar on the table, he pulled out a fork. Spearing an especially large chunk of egg from the side of the pan, he flipped it to the dog with his fork.

Tram slapped the table, causing Rocky to jump and Fish to dodge behind the wall. "I've lost two hundred lobster pots, my boat is damaged, and I don't have a home, anymore. Did you know that, Rocky? The apartments where I lived were washed out nearly a month ago. That's why I'm living here. I'm not

329

moping around like I lost my best friend, and yet I feel like I have. There's a blizzard hitting up north, and your grandmother is right in the middle of it." He sat up and looked at Rocky, waiting for his response. He didn't like what he heard.

"She's a big girl. Besides, I've already put on her storm windows." He slid Tramwick's cell phone his direction. "You can call her if you want." He continued to eat, occasionally flipping something to Fish, who had decided it was safe to poke his nose back into the room.

Tramwick stood, and he flipped the chair back around. "Power outages, Rocky. No signal. Her house is right in the middle of one of the biggest storms ever to hit the White Mountains. She's got all those kids, the teachers there, too. Are you planning on sitting here, or are you going to get up and do something?"

Rocky listened to Tram's words, and he looked at the remains of the eggs in the pan. Tram hadn't said the magic words, yet. If he would say Lisa was there, Rocky would be tearing up the pavement in a minute. Rocky had rescued her from a hurricane. Did Tram not think he would do so from a blizzard? However, Tram didn't know about Lisa. Rocky had never told him.

He had no drive to face this, and yet he stood, anyway. Doing so was possibly more a test of the bonds of friendship, rather than his decision to do what was right. He stood more because Tram was right there, and when Tram insisted, then Rocky often went along. Besides, Rocky felt he couldn't fight Tram over this right now. Giving in was easier.

In resignation, Rocky spoke first. "What do you want to do?"

His friend's eyes sparkled as he laughed. "Go up there, of course. I've already got chains out in the back of the truck."

Rocky closed his eyes. "My truck, Tram?" Trucks weren't ideal for snow. They were too light in the rear end. Even four-wheel-drives like his.

"Yeah, Rocky." He reached to slap him on the shoulder. "I've already loaded the bed with gravel and sand. Got some other things, too, just in case. Water. Heater. Fuel. Let's go help the little ankle biters out."

With a groan, Rocky stepped into the living room to put on his shoes. He would need them. He'd like waterproof boots, better, but he bet they'd washed away in the storm. What he'd like would be to go back to bed, but he didn't guess he'd get that. Tram would just drag him out again, so he might as well make the best of this. After all, if Tram was living upstairs, he wasn't going away anytime soon.

Chapter 20

LISA WOKE with a start, and she was freezing. She heard the wind whistling outside, and it was nearly dark in the room. Her pulse pounded with the memory of three weeks ago, and without thinking, she reached for the warmth of Rocky at her side. When her hand felt emptiness, she remembered. He would never be there again. She felt a lurch in her heart, and she lay still a moment, feeling sorry for herself. She had moved on, she told herself, and she tried very hard to believe it.

Then she paid attention to her surroundings. She was at Bette's, and the house was *cold*. She wondered who was supposed to turn on the heat in the mornings. Throwing back the covers, she grabbed her robe and stepped to a window. Pulling the curtain aside, in the morning's dim light, she could see more snow than she thought she had ever seen at one time in her life. They'd be stranded for days, if this held up. She touched her new cell phone to get the weather to find there was no signal. At least she'd brought clean clothes.

Lisa stepped to Meagan's bed and tucked her covers in around her neck. When she stirred, she whispered, "Sweet girl. Stay asleep." Looking around the room, each of the sleeping girls was quiet in her bed.

"Oh, I do need to find the furnace controls," Lisa muttered. "I'm very chilled." Opening the door and prowling the hall, she finally located the thermostat. She flicked the levers, and she stood and waited. Nothing happened. Frustrated, she headed back to her bedroom. As quietly as possible, she slipped into her warmest clothes, even the long underwear her mother had insisted on. "Thank you, Mum," she whispered.

Stepping quietly down the stairs, she found Bette already in the kitchen. The doors were closed, and several candles were burning. It was warmer, at least.

"Dear, come in quickly," Bette said, jumping up from the table. "The power's out. I guess you noticed that. We've got gas for the stove, though. It'll give us a little heat for a while. When a couple of the teachers get up, we'll get a fire in the fireplace. That'll warm up the living room, anyway. Nothing'll get this entire place warm, but I guess we can huddle in together." She smiled.

"Nothing fazes you, does it, Bette? You just go on like tomorrow will be business as usual."

Bette laughed at that one. "It usually is, dear. Now, I've got a pot or two, and I've drawn up lots of water. Before long, the pressure in the well house will go down, and I wanted to have plenty to drink. If you want to wash up, now's the time, before any of the children get up."

Lisa shook her head. "Thanks. I'm fine. Coffee? Can you make some of that? It'll warm me up."

"Cinnamon roast? I love it, and if you'd like, I can put it on."

"That sounds good. Hurry, if you don't mind." Even in the

relative warmth of the kitchen, it wasn't all that warm.

Bette slid a small plate over to Lisa. "Try this while you wait. Jalapeno jelly. Some friends of mine from Fort Worth bring me a jar every year. They left a couple of weeks ago. Go easy on it. It's got a bite."

Lisa laughed as she reached for the plate. "I bet." She put a small amount on a cracker and bit into it. She continued to taste it for a very long time.

THE SNOW swirled around Rocky's truck. This wasn't a blizzard. It was a whiteout. There was no way to go on, and now that they were in New Hampshire, there was no way to go back. Tramwick ruffled Fish's coat as he reached once again to wipe the inside of the windows.

He looked at Rocky with a contrite look on his face. "I guess this wasn't such a good idea." Then he came back with a stronger response. "How was I to know you'd forget to bring your coat? Blizzard, Rocky. I said that. Blizzard."

Rocky reached to turn the wipers up, and he turned them off, instead. The windshield was instantly white. He fumbled and finally figured out the direction to shove the switch, making sure to push it to high.

"We need a place to stay, Tram. Can you see anything? I can follow the taillights in front of me, but I can only hope they know where they're going. They might be taking us to Vermont, or even Upstate New York. I don't think we'll find Bette there. I need to buy a coat, too."

Tramwick had been thinking about that. He was much quicker with sorting out new plans on the water, but he could think through things on land. He just needed a moment to figure out where they were in relation to what he remembered from all the drives he'd made up here in the past. The truck bounced, and it was one he recognized.

With a satisfied grin, he said, "I know there's a string of

motels along here somewhere. Remember that rough spot where the road drops off, the one where they're repaving the highway? It's about ten miles after that. We just drove over that, if I remember my roads."

"Maybe, Tram. I'm watching the taillights, not paying attention to the ride."

"Well, what's the odometer? Add ten to it. Then turn."

"That's a lobsterman speaking. It might work on water, but on land, we still need to find a road." He shook his head.

"No, Rocky. I'm thinking like my friend ought to be. No roads needed. We have four-wheel-drive." He hit his forehead like someone else in the truck wasn't quite all there.

"Oh, right," Rocky exclaimed. "That's right. I don't need roads. I can run over street signs, other cars, and even people because I have four-wheel-drive. That's just great. Now I'm not only autistic and dyslexic, I'm also a serial killer. Maybe even a mass murderer. Thanks, Tram."

Tramwick was quiet for a moment. "Did I hear you right, Rocky? You're autistic?" This was something he'd never heard his friend say.

THERE WAS a long silence. Rocky had hidden that information, certain that if it ever got out, the lobsterman would be gone in a flash. Who wanted to hang around an autistic invalid? Now, he'd blurted it out, and he couldn't take it back.

Panic roiled in his stomach, as the snow swirled outside.

"Rocky?"

"What?" He bit off the word.

"Talk to me. Don't just sit there."

"God! Asperger's, Tram. Are you happy? Now, let it drop, will you? I don't want to talk about it."

"At the lighthouse, Rocky, on the walk when we picked you up. You didn't fall. That was your autism, wasn't it?"

"Let it go." Rocky's words had taken an icy tone.

For a while they rode in silence. Then Tram ventured, "What triggered it?"

Rocky yanked the truck sideways and out of the lane of traffic, and he threw the transmission into neutral. He lashed out, "What do you want me to say? That a woman was drowning in the storm, and I saved her? That I spent the night in her arms, and that I made a fool of myself? That I told her to go away, because I hate what I am? That I feel like I died, because I can't have her? Is that what you want me to say?" Rocky's words blasted the inside of the truck, but his hand was on Fish, and in some bizarre way, he found comfort there. The dog was at least at his side and had never run from him because of his stupidity.

Quietly, Tram asked, "Is all that true? I saw the remains of the boat, but didn't think much of it. It really happened, didn't it? These past weeks, that's what's been wrong. I should have seen it." He leaned against his window to look out. "I'm sorry, Rocky. I should have seen it."

"I can deal with it." Looking straight ahead, Rocky continued, "We'll find someplace and get separate rooms. You can take my truck back, and I'll stay until I can find another ride."

Tram burst out, "God, Rocky! Why would we do that? Are you stupid?"

Rocky pushed his fingers into his hair, locking them there, and barked, "Look who's stupid, now, Tramwick. I've got autism. Why would you want to be seen with me? I'd like to keep Fish when you go." His hand was on the dog's neck, and he turned to watch the taillights crawling along past them. Every now and then, one would crawl off to the right just in front of where they were parked.

Tramwick reached and punched Rocky sharply on the shoulder. When Rocky looked at him, Tram grabbed his shoulder and squeezed it for a brief moment, then he dropped his hand to Fish's back. "You get the dog, but you have to take me with him."

Rocky sighed tiredly. "For how long?"

"Forever." Then Tram grinned. After a while, he pointed to the occasional taillights veering to the right. "I bet that's the motels. The snow seems brighter just there. Lighted signs, maybe? Let's give it a try."

Rocky looked at him a long minute, and his eyes were hard. "Are you sure?"

"About the motels? Pretty much."

With a long sigh, Rocky pressed him for what he really wanted to know. "About me, Tram. About Fish and, you know, the autism." He looked out the fogged window at his side, afraid of the answer he might hear.

Tram laughed and slapped Rocky hard on the shoulder with the back of his hand. "I'm as sure as I ever was, and I haven't had a drop to drink. You can attest to that. I've been living in your house. Besides, now that you've admitted it, it explains a lot from before. You were my friend then, and I thought you were just a nut. Now I know better. You're just a nut who's still my friend. It's all the difference in the world. By the way, if they have a king, I get it. First dibs on the spa tub, too. Wake me when we get there." He leaned his head back and closed his eyes.

Rocky growled and shifted the truck back into gear, using his blinker and waiting until he could pull ahead. He muttered to himself, "It would be easier with two headlights."

THE HOUSE had grown dark, and the adults were slowly realizing they might have to make a marathon of this. Several of them had tried their phones, but nothing was getting through. The living room had been sealed off with blankets hung from the doorways, and the fireplace was stoked to last through the night. Seventeen children were sleeping wherever they could squeeze in. The adults would work out what they could, but for now, they were gathered in the kitchen.

"How much wood did we burn today?" Bette asked. She kept a store in the basement, but what was outside was dangerous to go for. In a blizzard, getting lost was not an option. She also knew they could run the furnace, if only she'd had the generator repaired. She'd meant to tell Rocky about it, but with all the events of the past month, she just hadn't gotten around to it. Now they were reduced to wood and the gas stove in the kitchen.

"Too much, Bette," one of the teachers said. He looked at the others. "We should have closed up the living room sooner."

Another teacher soothed his words, "Who would have thought? Surely they'll get help out. Someone must know we're here. Bette?"

Bette was slow to speak, and it was because she didn't like what she had to say. Yes, help would come, and yes, they should have closed up the living room sooner. She should have also had the generator fixed, and that she hadn't done. There was fuel oil wasting in the basement, and it was doing no one any good.

"Nothing gets through until this clears. Maybe not for days afterwards. We're on our own. There's firewood the other end of the clothesline. It's there for a purpose. We hook a ring to the line, and we follow it out and back. I worry more about food."

"Water? I would hate to run out of that." One of the female counselors laughed nervously.

Bette smiled. "We have all that we need. We just melt the snow. Hot water might be harder. What about entertaining the children? This group's likely to get testy huddled in the living room. Not all of them have a heavy coat, not heavy enough to run around in an unheated house. Bathrooms? We have to organize the facilities, too."

The water woman asked, "Will we be able to flush?"

The man whispered to her, "Melt the snow and dump the water inside." Then he looked to Bette. "Right?"

"How much food do we actually have?" A timid voice

spoke, one they hadn't heard before. The question was one they all wanted to ask. The faces of everyone in the room turned to Bette.

"Today was grocery day. Twenty-four people take a lot. Lunch today, I think, will be fine. Dinner might be potluck. I can do breakfast in the morning. After that, I can only pray."

"I can skip one meal," the timid voice was stronger.

"So can I," said another.

"Me, too."

Soon they had all joined in, and Bette smiled across at Lisa. This was a good team, and the children came first. Bette was proud of that. So was Lisa. Together, they would prevail.

They moved out of the kitchen, and Bette left one burner on low. Looking out the window, she was glad the storm windows were up. Things would be even worse without them.

Before she left, she turned and watched the flame for a moment. It had been about time for the gas to be refilled, too. That worried her. This storm had come at the worst possible time. There was enough for the others to worry about, though. She would keep this to herself.

ROCKY JERKED awake, and he glanced over. The clock on the bedside table said it was morning, but the room was barely light. He'd been pleasantly pleased when the motel clerk had said they had their own backup generators and water system.

He glanced at the bigger bed next to him, and he froze in panic. It was empty. His friend hadn't stayed. Tram had lied to him. Rocky was engulfed in fourteen again, and it was the end of summer. The truth had come out. His father had sent him away again. All because of his autism.

Rocky closed his eyes. There was nothing he could do about Tramwick's abandonment. He swung his legs to the floor and stepped to the bathroom. He flipped on the light, and there was Tramwick, sprawled in the massive, jetted tub, snoring quietly

339

in the still water. It seemed the warmth must have put him to sleep, and the jets had cycled off sometime during the night.

"Tram!" Rocky grabbed the curtain and threw it across the offending scene. "At least pull the curtain!"

"What? What?" Tram's confused voice came from the tub, with the sound of splashing water as an accompaniment. Then, after a moment, it stilled. Rocky rolled his eyes, because Tram or no, he had to go. He did, too, flushing afterwards, then flipping off the light to leave his friend in the dark.

Walking to the window, he pulled back the curtain and looked outside. He could barely see the truck directly in front of the window. This was as bad as he'd ever seen. He bet his grandmother did need his help, and he didn't know what to do.

As he released the curtain, he glanced down to see Fish by the radiator. He hadn't moved. The dog had the right idea, to sleep as close to the warmth as possible. Rocky eyed his bed. It was nice and warm there. There was nothing to be done outside, so he might as well make the most of the comfort he had available.

"Thanks, Fish. Good idea," he said.

Then he crawled back into bed, and in its softness, he fell fast asleep.

BETH TURNED to the clock on the bedside table. It wasn't yet seven-thirty, and she could have sworn she heard the doorbell. She was about to lay her head back down when it went off again.

"Rand." She pushed on his shoulder. "Rand, I hear the doorbell. It needs to be checked."

He rolled over onto his back and let his head sink into the pillow. "What time is it?"

"Almost seven-thirty."

"Let Rosita get it. She's here by seven."

Beth groaned. "Not today. We gave her the morning off. Remember? I'll get up."

Rand put his hand out. "No, stay. No one would show up this early for you. It'll have to be for me, and there's no use in both of us getting up." He threw back the covers and stood. Reaching to grab his robe, he stumbled out the door.

Making his way through the living room, he glanced out to the pool. It was raining. He thought it was to be a blizzard weekend.

In the entry hall, he tightened up his robe, and through the glass in the door, he saw it was John. He sighed. If he had any real friends, John was one.

Rand reached to the side of the door and keyed in the security code, and he listened as the automatic door bolts withdrew into the ceiling and floor. Only then could the door be opened. Grabbing the handle, he pulled, and the massive door swung wide.

"Come in, John. I apologize for not being dressed. Seventhirty, you know. Beth and me last night. We were up late." He smiled.

John gave a distracted smile in reply and went straight to the point. "Your office. Can we get some privacy?"

"Sure. In here." He slid the paneled doors out of the walls. Once he had them in motion, he stepped away and faced John. The doors continued to close, coming to rest against each other with a soft click. "Now, what is it? Not Trish?"

John smiled at the thought of his wife. "No. Not Trish." His expression became serious again. "It's a boy at the Center. A Josh Reynolds."

Rand's eyes narrowed. "Not a lawsuit, John. Was he molested?" He motioned his friend into a chair and sat across from him, a worried look on his face.

"Stay with me. There are no lawsuits. This is convoluted, but once I wade through it, you'll understand why I'm here. This boy, Josh, is in his final year. Then there's one of the Center's nurses, a Lisa Bevier, and you don't know her, but in the past,

341

she's gone with Josh's family to their place in Maine, as a courtesy from the Center, to monitor the boy.

"Now, stay with me. You'll see there's a point to all this after I wade through it. That lighthouse contract on Goose Rocks? We gave it to that Royster guy. Rocky, I believe. You were at his grandmother's place in New Hampshire. That's how you get in the story."

Rand interrupted. "I'm already not following this very well. It's early. Coffee would help. Can I get us some?"

"Let me finish. I had to have it all explained to me, too. Anyway, this Royster guy went to the lighthouse the weekend of the hurricane."

"You're kidding me, right? He was in the lighthouse *during* the hurricane?"

"It gets better. That nurse was on North Haven with the Reynolds boy. She was leaving in a boat during the storm, and her boat sank at the base of Goose Rocks. You'll never believe this. Royster rescued her by pulling her into the lighthouse."

"He just reached into the water and pulled her out?"

"Apparently. Remember those children we sent to New Hampshire? That same nurse is there with them."

"The nurse. Lisa Bevier, from the Center. All right. I get it. So?"

John began to smile in anticipation, as he waited for Rand to catch on. "Rand, she hasn't been at the Center. She's been in New Hampshire with our group up there, and Josh Reynolds has been asking about her. He was finally told where she was, the part about being in New Hampshire, anyway. Now, his father has contacted us to let us know his son is very concerned. We have to rescue her."

"Rescue, John? I don't get it. I thought we had this place thoroughly vetted."

"Do you even follow the news? All central New Hampshire is in a blackout. The blizzard, Rand. They've had no power for over twenty-four hours. Our children, Rand."

"Fine, John. I get it. Rescue. I don't get the kid, though. Josh Reynolds. What part does he play in this?"

"Rand, you're not with me. It's not Josh. It's his father. You might know his name. Get this. Craig. Craig Reynolds." John sat back, with a very satisfied expression on his face. He watched Rand's face for the moment of understanding.

Rand's brow furrowed, and the connections began coming together. "You mean this is *Craig* Reynolds? National Aeronautics Craig Reynolds? Guggenheim Museum Craig Reynolds? New York Stock Exchange Craig Reynolds? Isn't he the First Lady's brother-in-law or something?"

John laughed. "Or something. Craig Reynolds wants his son's nurse rescued. He wants to know exactly where she is. I want you to go with the National Guard to New Hampshire. You just came back from there, so you should be very familiar with everything. You get to lead the way."

Rand took a deep breath to steady himself. This was big. This was very big.

TRAMWICK KICKED Rocky's bed. "Hey, you flatlander, you. Tub's yours." He tossed several clean towels on his friend's bed, and then he turned and flopped on his king-size one. It was still fully made.

Rocky tried to open sand-filled eyes, and they hurt. He blinked. Then he realized what it was. The curtains were open, and the sun was shining.

"How many days did I sleep?"

Tram began singing a rendition of an old song a drinking buddy had once given him on a CD. "In the year twenty-five, twenty-five . . ."

Rocky grabbed his pillow and put it over his head. His muffled voice called out, "Spare me. I don't care how long it's been."

343

The pillow was yanked away and dropped at his side. "The storm let up about noon. It's devil-may-care windy, but we can at least see. Do you want the tub?"

"No, I don't think so. I'll shower, thank you very much." He couldn't imagine climbing in after having seen Tram in there. A shower he might be able to manage, but to sit where that naked body had been? No way.

"Have your own way. The spa feature's great, though. I feel like a new person."

Rocky threw his pillow at him and climbed out of bed. "I don't even want to know. I'll be out in a minute, unlike eight-hour Tram."

As the water kicked on, Tram called, "Eight hours? It was ten, if anyone's counting." Then he began to throw what little they'd carried in into one of the plastic bags that lined the ice bucket. He yelled through the bathroom door, "I'm heading down to check out. Be ready when I get back. Fish has already been out."

Rocky emerged within minutes, dripping and taking hold of the towels that were on his bed. When Fish came up to him, he rubbed his head with one of the damp towels before hopping back into the bathroom to slip into his clothes. He grabbed his keys; and stepping outside of the motel room, he called to Fish. He held the door as the big animal followed him.

It was cold in the wind, and Rocky wasted no time getting the truck door open. He called to Fish to jump inside. He only had to attempt the key twice to get it in the ignition, and after he started the engine, he looked to the dog on the seat at his side.

"Cold in here, boy." Fish shook his body and looked around to find Tram.

Tramwick was pleased to see the truck drive up to greet him as he exited the office. Climbing inside, he produced a map the clerk had given him. On it was the shortest way to where they needed to be. It cut around several places the clerk had sug-

344

gested might be closed.

"Do you still think we can get there?" There was a good two feet of snow, and Rocky could see it was piled much higher in places.

"Is your grandmother still in New Hampshire?" Rocky looked at him as if the man asking the question was stupid. Tram grinned. "You get my point." Then he started singing one of Bette's favorite church songs. "Onward rescuing soldiers . . ." Of course, he butchered that one, too.

Rocky didn't notice. He was looking at the pristine snow with a grin plying his mouth, and he had something else in mind. He hit the gas and did a donut right there in the street. There was no one else on the road, and he did have four-wheel-drive.

Tram laughed, held on tight, and dug his fingers into Fish's fur.

THE FLAME under the pot of stew sputtered to a stop. Lisa looked at Bette. The kitchen would soon get cold, and it would happen very quickly.

"So, no more cooking in here, and we lose this room. Everything moves to the living room. At least the storm's stopped. It might be windy, but we can get to the firewood."

Lisa pulled her sweater around her a little tighter. "Bette, you are so practical. We're so lucky to be stranded here with you. You're going to get us through. Here. Let me carry this to the other room. We'll see if we can find a way to finish cooking this in the fireplace."

She picked up the pan with a towel and backed through the door. The dining room wasn't heated, and Lisa shivered. Backing through the blankets that closed in the living room, her senses were assaulted by the uproar of over twenty people involved in various stages of games and lessons. The teachers from the Center were handling this marvelously. However, now that the kitchen no longer had heat, this could get very claustrophobic. There would be no place for time-outs or a quiet conversation or just the much-needed meltdown. It would all happen here in this room.

Lisa whispered to the male teacher who had spoken first the other night, "Help me get this on the fire, somehow. The gas in the kitchen is gone. I also think we're about out of food."

He smiled at her, and he used a poker to shift the wood around. They got it on the grate, and they just hoped it didn't ruin the pan. On the other side of the blankets, they heard the front door open, and another well-wrapped teacher backed through the hanging cloth with an armload of wood.

"I've moved as much as there's room for onto the porch. We'll have heat, anyway, and it'll be convenient. Thank goodness Bette has plenty."

A subdued cheer spread among the staff, as the word spread.

BETTE HAD just stepped in, and she heard. It didn't make her feel good. She didn't feel like she had plenty. Instead, she felt like she had let everyone down. They were out of food to eat, out of gas for the stove, and the generator was broken. All they had was a fireplace that was just enough to heat one room. They needed help, and she was out of ideas. She wondered if Rocky knew she needed him. She was almost to the point of wondering if he cared.

Then a teenage boy came up to her with a grin and gave her a hug. "This is the best school year I've ever had." He released her and was gone. Bette took a deep breath. Rocky had better hurry. She wanted that boy's words to continue to ring true, and it could only happen if he were here.

LISA SAW the emotions running over the old woman's face, and she stepped to her. "Is everything all right?"

"It will be if my grandson gets here."

She laughed. "You know, I think I'm about ready to meet

346

him. I think we all are. We need a good strong grandson to rescue us about now."

Bette hugged her. "You're right about that. I hope he hurries."

"So do I." Then Lisa turned back to the fire. The last meal they had food for was almost ready, and she wanted everyone to enjoy it as much as possible. After all, if help didn't arrive soon, it might be their last one ever.

Chapter 21

UNDERNEATH THE *whup, whup* of the helicopter prop, Rand sat surrounded by men and women in full military gear. In front of him was a blank screen that would soon show a camera image of the ground as they flew over. It would also have a computer overlay mapping the area with roads and major points of interest, all determined by GPS. He looked up at the sound of the rotors as they increased in speed and pitch, and the scene around him began to move. Next to him, one of the women was talking into her headset.

"Yes, sir. He's sitting right next to me. Four, sir. We have our copter, and there are three more lifting off with us. We have room for them all. Trust me, sir, your people will be coming home today."

She turned to Rand, talking loudly over the noise of the machine, and she pointed to the display. "White out. When we're in the air, all you'll see is white." Then she tapped one section of the screen. A washed out, grainy image appeared, then names resolved alongside newly appearing highways and streets. "GPS. You won't be able to see it out the windows, but these streets are under the snow. Trust me. You're my guide once we get there. We can get you close, but this is New Hampshire White Mountain country. Your eyes will pick it out for us. We're told the house is a big, two-story affair. Something that large, it should be visible even in this. You've been there. You point it out when you see it." She paused and touched her earpiece. Then she spoke again. "That was Mr. Reynolds. He says good luck." She shot him a thumbs-up sign, and Rand returned it to her.

Rand smiled. Beth might have all the money, but he was the one sitting in a National Guard helicopter on a rescue mission for the ex-First Lady's brother-in-law. This was worth the loss of his boat, even if Royster's insurance had covered most of it. This was big, and that's where Rand had always wanted to be.

TRAMWICK HELD on as the truck engine roared. Clearing the ditch they'd drifted into, the big four-wheel-drive climbed back onto the road and began to move forward again. At least they could see, even if the driving wind continually picked up any snow they disturbed and flung it back at the truck.

"Nothing's even closed off. No roads blocked or anything. This blizzard came with too much snow too fast. You think we should be getting close?" Tram looked hard through the fogged windows. The overhead signs had snow on them, but occasionally something could be made out. The signs on the sides of the road were as likely as not to be completely obscured.

"Big drift coming," Rocky called, and he gunned the engine. The truck slammed into it and began to claw its way through. A section of the drift cascaded onto the hood of the truck, slipping back onto the windshield, and obscuring their view. Then, as the vehicle shifted up and over the drift, the snow against the warm windshield moistened and began to slide sideways, eventually dropping off the side.

"Wet snow. Doesn't move easily. That was a big one." Rocky looked at Tram, then back to the road. "The turnoff's gotta be here, somewhere."

Tram pointed to the side excitedly. "There. Three trees. There's a pond just behind, I think. That flat area. The turn's just ahead." He whooped. "We did it, Rocky. We're here."

However, Rocky wasn't quite ready to be ecstatic, yet. He knew they would be moving from well-marked to hardly-marked roads. Now would be the fun part. This was the White Mountains, and although it was only New Hampshire, falling off a 4,000-footer was as good as falling a mile.

Tram pointed to a sign they couldn't read, and Rocky slowed to veer off on a flat expanse that could be an exit. His eyes jumped to Tram as the truck jerked over something that didn't feel like road, and then it smoothed. The vehicle kept moving, and with a deep breath, he shifted into a higher gear.

Maybe Tram was right, Rocky thought. This was just like being out in a lobster boat. They had a four-wheel-drive truck, and they could go almost anywhere. Even as he smiled at the idea, he knew the optimal word was *almost*. They could go *almost* anywhere. He could only hope that *almost anywhere* was the exact same location as Bette's bed-and-breakfast. Otherwise, their trip was wasted. So was their help, and Rocky was certain now that Bette needed it, and soon.

LISA PULLED on her coat and slipped gloves on her hands. They'd had only two meltdowns by the children, and the teachers had quickly gotten those under control. However, everyone was growing hungry, and there was nothing else in the house.

During all this, people's attention had been diverted from the fire, and it had been allowed to burn low. It was cooling off in the room, and she needed to head out to the porch for more wood, out past the clothesline if there was no more on the porch. She saw Bette standing, and from the look on her face, it was clear her legs were hurting. Lisa hadn't thought of that. Bette seemed so strong and sure. Even so, she wasn't young. This must be very hard on her.

"Bette," Lisa started, motioning to the fireplace.

"We'll both go." The older woman motioned for Lisa to wait for her. When she got away from the press of bodies near the fire, she searched among a pile of outerwear to pull out her coat. She slipped it on and pulled her gloves from one pocket.

Working their way through the layers of cloth covering the doorway, they stepped into the front hall. They could immediately see their breath in front of their faces. Lisa laughed, and she reached with her hand to try to keep the sound down.

"It's cold in here, Bette." She looked at the sun she could see against several of the windows. At the same time, the wind could be heard outside whipping alongside the house.

Bette smiled. "All the pipes will be frozen solid, that's for certain. However, they're cast iron, and they might survive." Then, she murmured to herself, "Maybe." She brightened her expression and turned to Lisa. "Outside will be even colder. You can count on that."

Despite the old woman's attempt to keep it low, Lisa caught her remark about the pipes, and she knew this was a hard thing for Bette to have to face. However, she had kept the children safe and warm, and no one could have asked more. When Bette pulled the door open, the wind swirled through, and the two women hurried onto the porch. At first there was no wood to be seen, and they walked around to the side porch. Bette shook her head.

"This load and maybe one more. Then it's back to the woodpile." She smiled at Lisa. "Our turn next, dear."

Lisa smiled, although she wasn't looking forward to that

duty. Handing Bette several logs, she picked up three herself. At the front door, she stood back as Bette struggled with the latch. Glancing up, she saw something she hadn't seen before.

"Bette," she whispered.

"Just a minute, dear. This door hangs in the cold, but I'm about to get it."

Louder, Lisa called again. "Bette. That sign."

Bette turned. "What sign, dear?" She saw Lisa's eyes and followed them to the lintel above the door. "Oh," she said, pleased. "I see that grandson of mine got my sign repaired. My son made that, you know. How nice."

Lisa stood with her logs in her arms, and she hugged them tight. Her eyes burned. "Your grandson, Bette. The boat out back. The father. He's my rescuer from the lighthouse, isn't he?"

Bette pursed her lips before replying. Then, matter-of-factly, she said, "I suspect so, my dear. Did your young man have a name?"

Tears now flowed copiously down Lisa's cheeks. Her eyes were bright. "Of course, Bette. Rocky. Rockland, really, but he said he hated that name."

Bette smiled. "My grandson says the exact same thing. Now, girl, let's get this wood inside, or some of those poor children will soon freeze to death."

Lisa was dumbfounded, though, and she continued, "He was here. I saw him, his truck, and I didn't even know. Why didn't you tell me, Bette?"

She pushed open the door as she said, "I didn't know for certain, not until you told me your story in the barn. I thought so, then. He'll be back. You know, I told you I wanted you to meet my grandson."

"I do, Bette. Oh, you don't know just how much I do." There was only one thing. Would he want to meet her?

352

TRAM TURNED to look, and stretching in the distance past the items in the bed of the truck, he could see tire tracks that wound up and over the rise they had just topped. They were the only ones anywhere he could find. "I'm glad you know your way, Rocky. I'd have us in Canada by now."

"Or the Atlantic. At least I haven't gone left instead of right. We might yet make it."

"Left instead of right?"

"Dyslexia, Tram. I've got dyslexia, remember?" Rocky could smile at the question. He was over his pity-party from the day before. Tramwick had proved himself. Just then they topped the next rise, and a slender tendril of smoke ascended above a big, white mound of snow and white Victorian house. There was a flush of relief in Rocky's expression. "I think we're there."

Gearing the transmission down, Rocky worked the truck through the drifts until he finally reached the drive in front of the house. He could see a trail through the snow following along the old clothesline and out to the woodpile. The woodpile was still partially snow-covered, but he could tell much of it was gone. He should know, too. He had stacked every cord at the end of the previous winter. He also remembered how the generator had been acting up then. Bette had never asked him to work on it, and if no one else had, he suspected there wasn't any power in the house.

Driving around mounds that might be cars, his tires crunched to a stop. He instructed Tram, "You get the fuel. I'll bring the heater. That way they'll know we didn't just bring our warm bodies."

Tram chuckled. "You don't think our warm bodies will be enough?"

"No, I don't. Not by far."

At the same time, they grabbed the door handles and pulled. That got Fish's attention, and he scrambled over Tram to get outside. He'd sat a really long time, and he had to go.

353

As they say, never, never eat lemon snow.

RAND LOOKED out the windows of the helicopter. He was amazed. Even the trees were hard to distinguish. Glancing down at the display, the Realtime image showing the ground directly below the helicopter was all white with occasional shadowed areas indicating something underneath the snow. It was the computer-superimposed map that was guiding them. Finally, the woman in military dress next to him prodded him.

"Sir, this is Waterville Valley, and we're about as close as we can get. Do you see anything that you recognize? You're the only one who's been here, and if you can't find it, then our only option is to land and start a complete search of the area. If you can pinpoint a starting spot, it would make it easier on all of us." She did smile to let him know his help would indeed be appreciated.

There was nothing he could see until his eyes caught a tendril of smoke. Then he noticed a pair of tracks along the road. They seemed to lead to where the smoke was.

At the same time, the pilot of the aircraft pointed. "There's a truck that's not covered with snow. Someone's been out and around down there. Tracks. See? It looks like it parked after the storm cleared. Could that be a house?"

Rand searched, but looking for anything specific was comparing white against white. Then, studying the scene, he saw the garage and the greenhouse. He remembered the wood-pile, and he was certain. This was the place. He looked at the woman sitting next to him and nodded. She gave him a thumbs-up and spoke quietly into her headset.

"Tandog One to Team Bravo. This is it, team. We're setting down. Center on the old truck. Let's bring our people home. Tandog One out."

ROCKY STOMPED on the porch to clean his feet as he set the

heater down. He elbowed Tramwick to get him to stomp his, also. Tram complied, then, looking around, placed the fuel next to the heater.

To those inside the house, a whistle was heard as if someone was calling a dog. One of the children leaned over the back of the sofa and pulled the curtain aside.

"A doggie?" With that one word in a high-pitched child's voice, there was a scramble of feet as small and large bodies rushed to see.

Bette leaned to look and exclaimed, "Why, that must be Fish!" She also saw the old truck, and she knew. Several of the children looked at her with puzzled expressions.

"Fish?" A small face looked up at her in confusion.

Bette laughed and patted the child on the head, speaking to them all. "Fish, dears. It's the dog's name." She quickly stepped across the room to Lisa, ignoring the pain her knees shot through her legs. This was more important than pain. Her grandson was here.

"Lisa, dear, come with me. Quickly." She pulled at the younger woman's arm.

"Bette, if we're going out, let me get my coat. I don't want to freeze."

"Quickly, Lisa." Bette was already headed out of the living room. "He's here. My grandson!"

THOSE WERE words Lisa had thought she wanted to hear, but as soon as she heard them, she flashed back to Rocky's words on the lighthouse, the last ones he spoke to her. *"You owe me nothing. Your friends are waiting. Please go."* He didn't know she was here. He'd come for his grandmother. She would be intruding, just as she had during the storm. Her blood raced in her temples, and her heart jumped into her throat. In that moment, as she stood in the living room, she knew she couldn't face this man who had sent her away. He would tell her to go away once more. How could he not?

"Bette!" Lisa's voice took on a frantic tone, and she had no way to explain why she couldn't meet this grandson. Yet, at the mystified look on her host's face, she knew she had to try. "Bette, I can't meet him now. At the lighthouse, our last words . . . Oh, I can't face him. He sent me away, Bette." Tears began to stream down her face.

BETTE KNEW her grandson, all the behaviors and issues that made him what he was, and she saw what was happening to this woman. For her to be distressed by that grandson of hers was simply too much. At that moment, she did what she did best.

Bette took control.

"Lisa, my dear, you wait right here. I need to greet my grandson. You don't worry about a thing." Then, with steel in her manner, she was gone through the insulating curtain of blankets. As she did, she muttered to herself, "That boy needs my help, and I plan to speak my mind. He'd better be ready to listen, too."

It didn't take her more than a few steps to reach the front door, and when she did, she yanked it wide. There were the two men who had come to her rescue, and there was fire flashing in her eyes.

Bette stomped outside and slammed the door after her. "It's cold out here, Rockland Royster, and you'd better tell me the way it is. Did you tell that nice Lisa to go away and leave you alone?"

Rocky looked to Tramwick for help, who made a face and began to back away.

Bette was in control, though. "Stay, Tramwick!" Her eyes tore to the man, and they showed tenderness only when she found the dog. She snapped her fingers at the animal. Fish ran to her side. She reached to rub him between the ears. Her gaze riveted Rocky once again. "Rockland? I'm waiting."

Even without his answer, she saw what she needed to see. His eyes had turned red, and his breathing was shallow, ragged, and quick. She knew this boy, and he was in love with this woman. It was written all over that face she had loved for nearly thirty years. Her next words showed a greater level of tenderness.

"Tell me the truth, Rocky. Do you love her?"

THIS TRIP had been a trial for Rocky. His confession to Tram. The tiring drive. All of it was layered on the loss he'd been struggling with since that day on the lighthouse. His emotions were ripped open for those on the porch to see. Fish whined, and Tramwick stood frozen. However, they all heard his broken words.

"I tried to hold her, Bette. I couldn't. I let her get away."

Bette's words were brisk and sharp again. "That wasn't what I asked, Rockland. Tell me now, or get in that truck and go home." She crossed her arms in the cold air and waited on him, daring him not to confess. This time she saw tears begin to pour down his face. She did know her Rockland, and this was all the answer she would get at this point. His handicap wouldn't allow him more. For her, it was enough. She knew the truth, even if he couldn't say it.

She stepped to him and put her hand on his chest, and she could feel his warmth though his shirt. "If she gave you another chance, would you tell her that? Would you tell her you love her?"

Rocky nodded, and he brushed at his face as he looked away. His cheeks, however, remained damp with his overflowing emotions.

"Rockland!" Bette's words were instantly strong again. "Look at me. Say it. What would you tell her?"

His eyes locked on Bette's, and the words were whispered, but they were there. "I love her, Bette. From the moment I saw her, I loved her. I wasn't good enough. I couldn't keep her."

"Stop that, boy!" She slapped his chest, and he jumped at the sting of her hand on his skin. "You are the best grandson I've got, and any woman would be a fool not to see that. She's here, boy. You go in there and tell her that. Look her in the eye, and you tell her what you just told me. Now." She turned and pushed open the door. Standing aside, she grabbed his arm and forced him to start moving.

Once he was inside, she looked Tramwick's direction, all the while holding one hand on the dog at her side. "All right, boy. You may go." When Tramwick relaxed and started to follow Rocky inside, she barked, "I was speaking to the dog. Go inside, Fish. You, Tramwick, need a piece of my mind. You may not go." Bette reached to the door and pulled it shut. She had some venting to do, and Tramwick was going to catch his share of it right then.

LISA STOOD in the corner of the living room. She let the blankets that draped from the top of the wide doorways crowd against her. She had dreamed of this man, and she had wanted him. When Bette had told Lisa of her grandson, she had thought, she had hoped, and then she had let it go. This morning she'd seen the name above the door, and she had seen a new opportunity for that hope to be revived.

With Rocky's arrival, though, had come the memories. She had wanted him to love her, and for a while, she thought he might. Then he'd pulled away, telling her to go. How could she face this man that her heart cried out for? How could she go through that rejection again? Bette was wrong. She must be. Lisa didn't need to meet this man. Yet, she didn't see a way out. She couldn't run, and he was here.

As she heard the front door begin to open, she forced her way through the blankets, and with desperation in her feet, she fled up the stairs. She could not meet this man. She just could not.

Once in her room, a repeated *whup, whup* sound began to disturb the quiet. Looking out the window, she saw four helicopters quickly drawing near. She drew in a deep breath and released it, knowing someone somewhere would be rescued today.

Turning to her bed and sitting, Lisa realized she was doing what she had done on the lighthouse, refusing to take a chance on her heart. It had been her downfall there. She was having an opportunity handed to her, and she was afraid of it. She'd been hurt by Andrew, and now she was running away, because she was afraid of another rejection.

Irritated at the increasing noise outside, she stood and pulled the curtain back once again. She was surprised to see snow swirling and one helicopter already on the ground in the field across the road. She laughed at that. Military exercises in the winter? After a blizzard?

Then it occurred to her. The children were the ones they were here for. They had come to rescue Bette's children. She watched the helicopters as they landed around the house, relieved that help had come at last. A hubbub erupted as a mass of bodies of all sizes ran from the front porch and into the snow.

That she could smile at, the enthusiasm of her children. All it took was the unexpected landing of a few helicopters, and even hungry and tired, the enthusiasm of youth was instantly at full force. Following them were the teachers. Lisa could see Bette step from the porch, and even a strange man and a big, black dog.

Within minutes, though, a small woman in military dress stepped out of one of the helicopters with a corded microphone in her hand. A man in a tailored suit stepped out to stand at her side. As the woman spoke into the microphone, Lisa was surprised to hear her words:

"This is Lt. Col. Tina Littlejohn with the Air National

Guard. Lisa Bevier. We are here to retrieve Lisa Bevier. All other members of her party are welcome to join us as well. May we meet with Miss Lisa Bevier?"

Lisa's heart froze. Why would they name her specifically? She wouldn't be able to stay up here and hide from this. She searched to see if Rocky was outside with the others. If so, perhaps she could avoid meeting him. She could rush to talk to Lt. Col. Littlejohn, and they could be rescued in different aircraft. That would work. If she could get to Bette, maybe she would help her to hide from him. Surely Bette would understand.

Lisa pulled her coat tightly around her, and she flew down the stairs, her eyes on the treads as she skipped two at a time. To trip at this point would be a disaster! She laughed at that, knowing the past three weeks had been an even greater disaster.

When she got to the bottom and looked up, there in the emptiness of the house, standing right in front of her, with his eyes looking down, was the very man she was trying to avoid. As he raised his head, she could see his cheeks were wet. Her heart melted at his brooding face that was now so broken. This wasn't an angry man. He hadn't come here to call her out, to attack her for being in his grandmother's home.

"Rocky," she faltered and then stopped. She didn't know what else to say. In that moment, she envisioned a touching tenderness in this man, one she had seen in only one other place, Josh. That night at his bedside, Josh had shared a side of himself that revealed a little bit of what it must be like to walk the world feeling as if others' eyes were always looking down on him. Lisa had seen some of that in Rocky at the lighthouse. Then, when his handicaps had pulled him away, she hadn't moved to fill that gap with understanding. That could not be allowed to happen again.

"Rocky," she began again. "If you won't talk to me, then I'll talk to you. Afterwards, if you want me to leave, I will, and

I'll never return." She put her arms around herself, and then she dropped them to put them in her pockets. "I admired, perhaps more than admired you three years ago when I saw you for the first time." He frowned, confused. "You didn't see me. You were walking off the Vinalhaven ferry. We never spoke. However, I could never stop thinking of you. Then, when you walked into my office, I knew it was something more."

She closed her eyes. His broken look was taking her confidence from her. She couldn't stop, now, though.

"I fell in love with you on that lighthouse. You saved me in every way I could be saved. You were charming and giving. You held me and let me warm myself in your clothes. I should have kissed you then. If I had . . ." She couldn't force herself to go on.

As she stood silently, the tears running down her face, she felt the pressure of his arms around her. It was his spoken words whispered in her ear that told her what she needed to hear.

"No, you're wrong. I should have kissed you. I fell in love with you then, and I love you now. From the day I met you, I've been able to think of nothing else." He pressed his face into her hair, and his arms held her tight. "I won't ever let you get away again. I love you, Lisa."

She knew it was true. He'd come for her, and he had rescued her. He was her hero, and he was more than that. He was the perfect love she had looked for and finally found.

Epilogue

LISA WALKED around the lighthouse and found a place to stand in the sun. The water of the Thorofare brushed the sides of the sturdy sparkplug structure with gentle fingers, unlike the first time she'd been here. Rocky was headed down the ladder to run an errand and would be back shortly. She leaned over to watch, and as he climbed down the vertical rungs, she marveled at the connections they had never known between their families. The school, Boston, and even Bette at the end.

Then there was the other thing Bette had shared with Lisa. Together they had worked it out, and it had given Lisa's mother, Terese, a sense of closure she'd never known. It had been Lisa's father that Royce had hit when he had his heart attack, an unavoidable accident, and no malice had been intended. No one had ever known. Nor could they have. Royce had died before he could tell.

Bette had been horrified, but Lisa had assured her that all

had been forgiven long ago. Lisa had made Bette promise that Rocky would never know. She hoped one day to repair the fractured relationship between the man she loved and the father he'd always thought hated him, even if only for Rocky's sake. Then and only then did Lisa want him to know.

This morning, however, was perfect. The sea sparkled in the brilliance of the Maine sunshine, and birds flew through the air, announcing that spring was their own. From somewhere across the verdantly green islands, she could hear the distant horn on the ferry, announcing it was coming into the landing. As she smiled, she knew there was one thing about all this that she could never deny. The end of May was a much better month to be here than the end of September had been.

Rocky waved to her from the water below. He was headed over in the lighthouse's small skiff to pick up Josh. He was finishing up his freshman year at his new college in Boston, and he had driven his car up for the weekend. Later, they would all ride over to the Reynolds' in the skiff for dinner. Josh had his El Camino on the island, and he wanted to show it off.

As Lisa moved away from the rail, her wedding ring shimmered in the sun. The Preservation Society had given them this weekend as a gift. It was their first anniversary. It had been a sweet thought and very enjoyable. Rocky had done such a nice job finishing out the renovation. However, she liked better the gift that no one else could see. Rocky had given it to her, and not another soul had been told. She absently rubbed her stomach. It didn't even show much, she thought.

Then she heard loud music coming from somewhere off the water. She turned and covered her face as she laughed aloud. No! It couldn't be! They had left Tramwick in Massachusetts, dogsitting with Fish. Surely that man hadn't followed them to Maine!

When the music grew louder, she knew without a doubt it was headed her direction. Finally, she turned to look. Flying by with his party lights flashing and the music up full was that man who was her husband's good friend. She waved and smiled.

In the end, he was her friend, too. That's the way it should be. When she'd married this man of hers, this Rocky Royster, she'd married everything that went along with him, and she hadn't regretted it one day.

Did you enjoy this book?

Find more by this author at:

 THREE SKILLET

www.ThreeSkilletPublishing.com

www.ingramcontent.com/pod-product-compliance
Lightning Source LLC
Chambersburg PA
CBHW072322280626
47159CB00027B/257